THE HOUSE *in the* HIGH WOOD

Also in the Western Lights series

VOLUME TWO OF THE WESTERN LIGHTS SERIES

THE HOUSE

in the

HIGH WOOD

A Story of Old Talbotshire

JEFFREY E. BARLOUGH

ACE BOOKS, NEW YORK

F

THE HOUSE IN THE HIGH WOOD

An Ace Book / published by arrangement with
the author

PRINTING HISTORY
Ace trade paperback edition / August 2001

All rights reserved.

Copyright © 2001 by Jeffrey E. Barlough.
Cover art by Aleta Jenks.

Visit our website at
www.penguinputnam.com

Check out the ACE Science Fiction & Fantasy newsletter
and much more on the Internet at Club PPI!

Library of Congress Cataloging-in-Publication Data

Barlough, Jeffrey E.
  The house in the high wood : a story of Old Talbotshire / Jeffrey E. Barlough.
    p. cm.
  ISBN 0-441-00841-0 (alk. paper)
   I. Title.

PS3552.A67246 H68 2001
813'.54—dc21   00-048494

ACE®
Ace Books are published by The Berkley Publishing Group,
a division of Penguin Putnam Inc., 375 Hudson Street,
New York, New York 10014.
ACE and the "A" design are trademarks
belonging to Penguin Putnam Inc.

Printed in the United States of America

10 9 8 7 6 5 4 3 2 1

To my Father and Mother

ERNEST AND IRENE BARLOUGH

CONTENTS

CONTENTS

CHARACTERS

MR. TONY ARKWRIGHT, *a veterinary surgeon and breeder of horses.*

MR. NICODEMUS BINKS ("Coddy"), *a hunting chemist.*

MR. SHANK BOTTOM, *a stone-cutter by trade, and the parish sexton.*

MISS BETTY BREAKWINDOW, *a pretty chambermaid at the Village Arms.*

MISS VIOLET CRIMP, *the proprietor of a waffle-house.*

DELILAH, *a speedy mare belonging to Miss Margaret Mowbray.*

MR. THOMAS DOGGER, *a self-important attorney, very respectable; lord and master of Prospect Cottage.*

MRS. DOGGER, *his wife.*

MRS. JANE FIELDING, *the widowed aunt of Miss Mowbray.*

DR. WILLIAM HALL, *a pale, placid-faced physician.*

CAPTAIN HOEY, *an eccentric freeholder residing at the Peaks.*

MISS CHERRY IVES, *the daughter of Mr. Nim Ives; a picture of efficiency.*

MR. NIM IVES, *the good-humored landlord of the Village Arms.*

MR. JARVEY, *a mastodon man.*

MR. JOHN JINKINS, *drawer at the Village Arms.*

JOLLY-BOY, *a lively shorthaired terrier belonging to Mr. Mark Trench.*

MR. OLIVER LANGLEY, *friend and confidant of Mr. Trench; a city man from Crow's-end, on holiday.*

LARCOM, *foppish servant to the Doggers.*

MR. LASH, *a schoolmaster.*

MR. HUGH LINCOTE, *a sugar-baker.*

MISS MARGARET MOWBRAY ("Mags"), *the young cousin of Mr. Trench.*

MRS. DINAH SCATTERGOOD, *wife of the Rev. Mr. Scattergood.*

THE REV. MR. HORACE SCATTERGOOD, *the vicar of Shilston Upcot.*

MR. SHAKES, *a gentleman rover of the celestial sphere, otherwise a teratorn.*

MRS. SIMPKINS, *Mr. Dogger's cook at Prospect Cottage.*

SLACK, *servant to Captain Hoey; an amateur philosopher.*

CHARACTERS

MR. SMITHERS, *butler in the service of Mr. Trench.*

MR. ALFRED SNOREM, *the boots at the Village Arms.*

SPLAYFOOT, *a short-faced bear inhabiting Skylingden Wood.*

MISS ELIZA STROUGHILL, *a chambermaid at the Village Arms.*

TINKER, *a bay gelding owned by Mr. Trench.*

MR. MARK TRENCH, *the squire of Dalroyd; a moody and skeptical man.*

MR. THOMAS TUDWAY, *the village chandler.*

DR. TWEED, *a medical practitioner from Crow's-end.*

WESLEY, *a joiner's lad.*

MR. BEDE WINTERMARCH, *the mysterious tenant of Skylingden.*

MISS ROWENA WINTERMARCH, *his daughter.*

MRS. SEPULCHRA WINTERMARCH, *his wife.*

THE HOUSE *in the* HIGH WOOD

THE HOUSE *in the* HIGH WOOD

ANTE SCRIPTUM

NOT long ago, the occasion of my receiving a substantial legacy from an uncle I had never met necessitated a journey by traveling-coach to the distant town of Hoole, where my late kinsman had resided. Having spent the better part of my life in the seaside environs of Crow's-end, Chiddock, and Cargo, without having once ventured east into the mountains — Hoole lying in a wild, rugged district far back of those mountains, in the county of Ayleshire — the news was received with a blend of enthusiasm and apprehension, in perhaps equal measure. There was of course all the anticipation of visiting an unknown place, a remote corner of the landscape very different from anything I had seen or known. But such a journey was not to be undertaken lightly, particularly by one of such regular habits as myself; moreover there had been trouble on the roads of a sort I had a mind to avoid. Nonetheless it rapidly became clear that journey I must, to inspect the properties my uncle had left me. And so, having put my own affairs in the capable hands of my solicitor and my few servants, and having bid my friends *adieu* for what I trusted would not be the last time, I boarded a Cattermole coach with my portmanteau, one dark cold morning, and was on my way.

The carriage traffic at such an hour being negligible, we rattled along at a considerable pace and in no short order had left the limits of the city behind. In our wake lay Crow's-end, before us the open road! The coach was not a full one, inside or out, and as a result I had been able to procure a window seat. There was a gentleman in the corresponding place opposite, a fellow somewhere beyond middle age, though I discovered afterwards he was rather younger than he appeared; for in addition to his traveling-clothes he wore a pale, disquieted expression, which he exchanged frequently for a look of gloomy rumination, all of which added imaginary weight to his years. The gentleman said nothing at all for an extended interval, responding to my pleasantries with little more than a nod or the flicker of a smile, all I suspect for courtesy's sake. He was preoccupied with staring out at the coach-window, though from my vantage-point it seemed he was not much interested in the scenery passing by, for his eyes followed it not. I attributed his introspective mood to the earliness of the hour, or perhaps to some unpleasant errand that

had called him from town; and so were it not for me I believe I would have had
very little in the way of conversation for most of the morning (the large bundle
of a person on my left, and the other, smaller bundle across, having gone
instantly to sleep once the coach had drawn out from the yard.) After some
coaxing, however, the introspective gentleman managed to get up a few
indifferent remarks concerning the weather, which at this season of the year
was liable to change swiftly and without regard for human endeavor. The mist
of daybreak had given way now to a sort of dreamy sunshine, and it was
cheering, as we commenced our climb into the foothills, to escape at last from
those coastal fogs which lie so thickly about Crow's-end, a city perched on a
mighty headland overhanging the sea and so ever prey to nature's whims.

By late afternoon we had traveled a fair distance into the mountains. Before
us I saw looming a bold line of cliffs of a mottled, bluish-purple appearance,
a characteristic which marked them out for the Talbot Peaks. This long, ragged
curtain of stone with its topping of snow, like the powdered heads of so many
lumpish footmen, lies just at the boundary of Talbotshire, the county
intervening between Crow's-end and that of my destination. Among its cool
and shadowy ravines we encountered all manner of precipitous slope and
yawning chasm; several times I thought for certain there would be an upset of
the coach, as we negotiated some particularly harrowing twist in the road. But
our coachman had a sure hand, and our horses sure hooves, and we survived
each episode unscathed. On a few occasions, however, we were obliged to quit
our vehicle and trudge along on foot to allow the horses some relief, owing to
the extreme steepness of the grade.

It was drawing on towards evening of the second day — the slanting amber
sunlight was about to be lost below the Talbot Peaks, which were now behind
us — when our pace slackened, and the coach rolled to a stop at the outskirts
of a drowsy village on the shores of a large lake. I thought at first we had
come to the conclusion of the stage but quickly found this was not so. The
coach had developed an irregularity in one of the wheel-rims, it seemed, and
so the coachman found it necessary to make an inspection. Most of the
passengers took advantage of the delay to step from the coach and exercise their
limbs. The introspective gentleman declined the opportunity at first; the pale,
disquieted look was in his face, as he sat looking out at the door with all the
eagerness of a man going to execution. I prevailed upon him to reconsider,
however, and in the end succeeded in extracting him from the conveyance. As
he set foot to ground he threw a host of anxious glances round the area, as
though he half-expected something to come flying at him from the underwood.
Thoughts of saber-cat encounters lately reported on the roads flashed

unpleasantly through my head; but as I was to learn that evening, the gentleman's unease was related to quite another thing entirely.

We were standing at a little height above the village, the main body of which trailed down below us to the dark waters of the lake. The cottages were built largely of that bluish-purple stone of Talbotshire, with some black-and-white cage-work in wood and plaster, and russet-colored roof-tiles. It looked to have been once a very picturesque little market-town, but had fallen into decay. Signs of neglect and disuse were everywhere evident, in the general disrepair of the houses, in the tattered casement-windows and tottering chimneys, the disarticulated doors, the extensive overgrowth in the churchyard and gardens and village green. We saw no trace of any villagers, either human or animal; over everything lay a ghostly pall of silence. All about us, on the farther side of the coach-road and the flanking hills above the village, stretched a vast forest domain of pine, cedar, fir, and oak. A wild and lonely scene it was that day, in that high mountain valley, among the fast-gathering shadows of the trees and the dusky beams of the fading sun.

A gentleman spoke at my side, and it took me a moment to realize it was my introspective fellow-passenger. He had offered so few words to anyone the day before, or during our night's sojourn at the staging-inn, or all of the present day, that his voice struck me as oddly unfamiliar. Now, with his hat pushed back a little and some of his unruly curls shot through with gray flowing from beneath it, he seemed less burdened by fear than by regret — as though he had for a moment conquered whatever it was had been troubling him — and was viewing all he saw around him with a melancholy eye.

"Eleven years," were the words he had uttered.

"Yes?" I returned, after a startled pause.

"Eleven years now have sped their way into the past."

"I see. You're certain of this?"

"Yes."

"Indeed. And eleven years it is, since — ?"

"Since I last was in this place. I've stood in mortal dread of returning to it ever since; and yet — and yet — "

Here the gentleman lapsed into another episode of gloomy self-absorption. He sighed, and as he did not appear keen to reveal anything more very soon, I looked about me again. I found my eyes drawn to the large mansion-house on the promontory off to our right, across a sweeping inlet of the lake. There was a beautiful hanging wood adorning the promontory, the house itself lying deep amongst the timber and so only imperfectly visible. It looked to be a great rambling estate of that same local bluish-purple stone, with glimpses through the trees of gable-ends and chimney-stacks and a lichen-spotted roof. A round window of sizable diameter peered out from among the tall firs; I took it for a rose window, though I couldn't be sure owing to the distance. It was then I noticed that a blue curl of smoke was rising from one of the chimneys.

"It would seem there is life here after all," I said, hoping for a response from my companion. He glanced round again with his melancholy eye, and still some appearance of anxiety, but said nothing.

"Driver," I called out, "what is this place? This hamlet below us?"

"Shilston Upcot," replied the coachman, turning from the wheel; then added, slowly and enigmatically — "or more rightly *was*."

"Ah! This lake then I take to be Lonewater, of which I believe I've heard something or other in the way of gossip. But as to the town itself — Shilston Upcot — who lives there?"

"None what has a decent brain, sir," answered the guard, who was assisting the coachman with his inspection. "Though there be some — some folk as yet at the great hall, up there in the wood. But none takes to the village now, sir, unlessen they be off the latch."

"Off the latch?"

"Aye. Crackers I mean, sir. Daft."

"I see. And why is that?"

Strangely, neither the guard nor the coachman seemed eager to reply.

"Do you know what house it is? The great hall there, standing atop the point that juts out into the lake?" I asked.

"It is called Skylingden," spoke up my gloomy fellow-passenger at last. "And that is Skylingden Wood that invests it."

"Aye, that be it," grumbled the coachman with a scowl, and evident hostility in his voice, having intended the remark more for himself perhaps than for my acquaintance or me.

"And who is it who lives there?" I asked, indicating the blue curl of smoke.

The coachman and the guard traded glances and shook their heads. Either they didn't know the answer or they chose not to divulge it, I couldn't tell which.

"Naught but dust and cobwebs, if we're fortunate," murmured my introspective companion. "If we were fortunate…"

"What happened here?" Even to my own ears I had begun to sound like a busybody, from the asking of so many questions. "I'm very much deceived if this was not once a thriving community, despite its present lorn appearance. The situation is rather pleasant and romantic, if isolated, and there is ample space for agriculture and of course no shortage of timber. Shilston Upcot. Lonewater. Where is it I've heard of them before? Some *contretemps* there was, no doubt of that, but I can't recollect it."

I repeated the names several times more, hoping to jar something loose from the cluttered shelves of my memory.

"There's deviltry here," said the guard. "The village, the mansion-house, the woods, the black waters — mischief — devil's work — "

"Aye," nodded the coachman, grimly. "The kind as don't bear thinking of!"

Puzzled, I again addressed the gloomy gentleman beside me. "It seems that such a place as this, on the coach-road and in such a spot, would provide an ideal staging-place for Crow's-end coaches. Why, an inn here ought to do a comfortable parcel of business."

"So it did," he replied. "It was known as the Village Arms, and can be found at the end of town, farther along this very road. We shall pass it directly. There — you can see the span-roof of it, just there, rising from the trees."

"Ah, so that was a coaching-inn?"

"One of the finest. Mr. Nim Ives was landlord in those years — 'Ives of the Arms' they called him — and there were as well his daughter, and long Jinkins, and Snorem the boots, and the rest."

"So you have stayed there?"

"No. But I lived in Shilston Upcot for a brief time, and was a regular visitor at the inn."

"Then you must know what it was that reduced the town to its present sorry condition."

"I was here at the very moment of it, sir. It was high midsummer, eleven years since. I saw and heard all. As I've told you, the dread of passing this way again has never left me. Since finding myself lately called into Talbotshire, to Wycombe, it has been preying all the more on my mind. Sir, there is no way else to Wycombe but by the coach-road, no way else."

The coachman and the guard turned round again from the wheel, with looks of mingled curiosity and suspicion towards my fellow-passenger. The men seemed torn between their work and giving ear to whatever more my new acquaintance might have to relate.

"What was it, then? Why have the villagers departed, and where have they gone? Who lives now in the mansion-house?"

Lost once more in his reflections, my companion seemed hesitant to provide anything more on the subject. I believe he must have been regretting his disclosure, and wishing perhaps he could return to his introspective ways. His glance strayed to the mansion-house, his eyes growing by degrees harder and darker, and his fingers balling themselves into fists, as though he had half a mind to smite the offensive structure.

"I'll tell you," he declared, drawing himself up, "this evening at the Waterman. That is the inn we shall likely have resort to, in the village on the farther lakeshore. Yes, I *shall* tell you, and if I don't I'll — I'll — I'll eat this coat, sir!"

Fortunately the inspection of the wheel-rim revealed that the coach was not irretrievably *hors de combat* and should be able to carry us to the end of the stage, though the affected wheel would require attention before the start of the next day's journey.

"We'll be off, gen'l'men," announced the coachman, ascending hurriedly to the box. It was plain he could not be away from Shilston Upcot too soon.

We made all appropriate haste, and shortly thereafter found ourselves ensconced at the Waterman, a well-fortified mountain retreat in the pretty town of Jay. Our evening's meal consumed, my fellow-traveler and I, well fortified now ourselves, retired to a private chamber off the tap-room, and there settled down to our pipes before a comfortable hearth-fire.

This then is the tale substantially as I had it from my companion that night, from what he himself had witnessed directly or learned from others or surmised. It was no wonder such a deep troubling of the spirit had taken hold of him. All thought of Hoole and Ayleshire and the estate of an uncle I had never met fled my consciousness as I listened; while through the lattice windows a glowing patch of moon like a human face climbed up and up, its reflected image eerily afloat in the stillish dark waters of the lake.

Part One

DARKNESS

A Stranger here
Strange Things doth meet.

THOMAS TRAHERNE

CHAPTER I

IN THE LODGE-ROOM

THERE were tenants again at Skylingden.

For a host of years the mansion-house on the point overlooking Lonewater and the village had lain vacant; no tenants, evidently, could be found. It was a mystery who held title to the great hall now. Even the village attorney, Mr. Thomas Dogger, inquisitive gentleman that he was, with a lawyerly finger in every pie in town, had no notion who the owner of Skylingden might be. Such knowledge was but one of many closely kept secrets in the records office at Malbury, the county town of Talbotshire. Some in Shilston Upcot conjectured that the new tenants were themselves the owners, come to take charge of the house; but no one actually knew. A huge, ungainly, ungovernable thing it was, this house, unkempt and disordered, with a long, lazy roof-line, glimpses of which could be seen roaming about the high wood. Infested with lichen and sprouting its own architectural forest of finials and gables and chimney-stacks, the house lay hid like a Cyclops amid the trees, far above lake and village, with its great round window — the "eye of Skylingden," as it was popularly known — staring down on all.

As expected, there was a good deal of interest in who these new tenants were and what they were like; their backgrounds, their interests, what their intentions were, how much money they had. Ripples of speculation washed over the village like waves upon Lonewater's pebbly beach. Were they country people or did they come from the city? From the county town, or from Crow's-end perhaps? Were they respectable folk? Did they intend to involve themselves in local matters, or remain aloof as people from the city often did? Above all, what was their income? How much per annum? Were they fabulously well-to-do, or merely wealthy?

The first reports, from the tradesmen who had been called on to effect improvements about the house and grounds, were of mixed consequence. They were a respectful, retiring, sober-minded family who inhabited the great hall. The patriarch was a mature gentleman of austere appearance, with a handsome, hawkish face, prominent side-whiskers, and mustaches. His hair was solidly black without any traces of age, and so it was immediately suspected that he dyed it. He was partial to dark evening coats with velvet collars, snuff-colored waistcoats, and odd, spotted neckties, this latter affectation perhaps in deference to his new country neighbors (which of itself pointed to his coming from the city, as smart country people never wear such things.) By name the gentleman was Bede Wintermarch, history and connections unknown. There was as well a plain-looking wife, rather meek and somber, and a pretty little daughter with a subdued expression very like her mother's; such qualities were taken to be the fruit of a domineering husband and father. The wife was considerably younger than her partner, the child perhaps no more than ten. As for servants, there were not nearly so many of them as ought to be found in such a household; which, together with other evidence, led Mr. Ives of the Arms to conclude that the family Wintermarch was less than prosperous.

"The gentleman's not laying out coin as you might expect," was the landlord's assessment, which he was propounding to some of the regulars gathered in the lodge-room of the Village Arms, on a summer night. "He's telling it down in pence, which makes it clear to me he's tight with his money. Now, some would argue that signifies a wise man; but in this case I say, hardly. Why should a gentleman from the city move house, deliver his family into Talbotshire where they're less than strangers, and settle on such a monster as Skylingden, only to pinch pence when it comes to his domestic arrangements? Simple parsimony, gentlemen? No, sirs; no, say I. He pinches his pence because he's very few pence left to pinch, not least from the sizable rent payment as must be owing on the quarter-day."

Such was the opinion of Mr. Nim Ives, and such the opinion of certain others in his circle in the lodge-room that evening. This lodge-room of the Arms was an interesting place. Opening from the entrance-hall, it was conspicuous first for an enormous, free-standing chimney-piece of cobbled stonework, which occupied the very center of the room. A spacious place the room was too, square as to sides and vaulted as to ceiling, and rather snugly appointed, with sofas of rustic but comfortable design, ottomans and easy chairs, dim soft lamps, tables and writing-desks, and flowered carpets over a boarded floor. There was a badly tuned pianoforte, for the questionable pleasure of guests; a tall chime-clock (out of tune as well); a pile of county newspapers, most of them hopelessly obsolete but still in fine shape to be read; a cupboard of musty books; and in the other half of the room beyond the chimney-piece, a billiard-table flanked by a lengthy row of French windows. Many were the hours idled away round that table by devotees of the sacred rite, with the click and chuck of billiard-play and the voices of the company often heard well into the night; for it was a sport as popular with regulars from the village as with travelers stopping at the inn.

The most remarkable thing about this lodge-room, however, was its rather more silent inhabitants — mounted trophy-heads of deer, elk, short-faced bear, bison, tapir, peccary, moropus, megathere, and not least saber-cat; which made the room something like a temple of taxidermy, with the heads starting out of the walls as if the living creatures themselves were in the midst of bursting through from outside. The cat with its fearsome sabers was an exception, being affixed instead to the chimney-piece and giving rise to the uncomfortable notion that flames from the hearth-fire might at any time come shooting from its mouth. City visitors unaccustomed to such novelties found them appalling; but to Mr. Ives and his circle the menagerie was rather more prosaic, though touched with something of that grim humor so common to mountain people who every day must confront nature at her most elemental.

One such mountain person and member of the Ives circle was Dr. William Hall, long the village physician. He was a spare, slight, elderly man, with a smooth, featureless face like pale calfskin, a face of unyielding composure, such that one could hardly tell if he approved or disapproved of the verdict of Mr. Ives regarding the Wintermarches. The doctor was not a man to wear his heart on his sleeve; indeed, even the sleeve was rarely glimpsed. He was a circumspect man, a characteristic well befitting one of his position and vocation, and so responded to Mr. Ives and his verdict with little more than a raised eyebrow. There was much the doctor knew about Shilston Upcot, about its inhabitants and its history, which the constraints of his office prevented him from revealing. To some in the village he was a sphinx — seeing much, hearing much, saying little. He was discreet, he was diplomatic; above all he kept his own counsel.

His entire opposite in these regards happening at that moment to put her head in at the door, a more timely contrast could not have been offered. She was a pretty young woman of about twenty, with ringlets of soft dark hair framing an open, undesigning face. Her forehead was a bold one, her gaze bright and unflinchingly direct. She moved with that kind of quick, purposeful stride that bespeaks earnestness and efficiency. Her friends called her affable, generous, plain-spoken; she was incapable of dissimulation and unafraid to challenge received wisdom. She was, in brief, an unusual young woman. She had come now, she said, in search of her father — who it should be no surprise was that same Mr. Ives we already have met.

"What is it, Cherry, m'dear?" inquired the landlord, glancing round from the table where he and the regulars were assembled. The likeness to his daughter was at once perceptible in the lively gray eyes and forthright expression with which he regarded her.

"Coach in the yard!" she announced, with a toss of her head.

Mr. Ives at once clapped hands to apron and rose from his chair.

"Hallo! There she is at last," said he. "The 'Flying Blue Maid,' I'll warrant, from Malbury. She's hours past due. You'll pardon me, gentlemen."

And so he hurried off, calling for his assistant and drawer, Mr. John Jinkins, which long, tall, and very dour fellow joined him and Cherry in the yard to meet the coach-party. Already the voice of the ostler could be heard on the night air, giving instruction to the stable-hands for racking up the horses.

"It's my view he's a sly one, and brainy too," said a youngish, thickish gentleman among the landlord's circle at the table. He wore a helmet of short dark hair on his head, the fullness of this hair making his face seem small by comparison. His eyebrows were extravagantly overgrown and fused into a single long brush, like a bristly caterpillar. The eyes beneath the brush were agile and alert, and constantly roving. He had large yellow teeth, which he held in a tiny prison of a mouth; each time he spoke it required every effort of his lips to keep his incisors from escaping.

"Who is a sly one?" asked another of the regulars, one Mr. Thomas Tudway, the village chandler.

"The gent up at Skylingden. The new tenant. It's my view that fellow's keeping a close rein on his fortune so as not to give out to all and sundry how rich he is. It's to deter the local spongers, o' course. That's sly and brainy, it is, in my view."

The person tendering this opinion was Mr. Tony Arkwright, veterinary surgeon and sporting man; a hard-riding man and a smoking man, and a gaming man and a drinking man. This last qualification he demonstrated now by causing half his drink to vanish in one swallow.

"And so, gents," said he, looking significantly round at his companions, "there you have my interpretation of it. In my view it's obvious to anything with eyes, and so I've no intention to sift the matter further."

"I'm inclined, I fear, more to the landlord's view," said the reverend gentleman beside him. Unlike Mr. Arkwright, the youthful vicar of Shilston Upcot was neither a sporting man nor a smoking man, and certainly not a gaming man; though he was known to like his spirits. "Although we've not yet had the pleasure of meeting the Wintermarches, we have managed to obtain one or two snippets of information from Wesley, the joiner's lad, who has been several times to the manor. As he informed my dear wife, the family looks to be a plain and proper one, reserved, studious perhaps and not given to unnecessary chatter, and without the physical adornments one often associates with wealth. The house itself is, he reports, but sparsely furnished."

"Aye, we've heard the same," affirmed several of the others.

"All of which could be a bad thing, or a good thing," said the veterinary.

"How so, Mr. Arkwright?" asked the vicar, pushing back his plated spectacles.

"Consider this. When a gent is given much to palaver, it's often the case as only a particle of that talk can be relied on; the rest is sheer humbug. Now, that's a bad thing, in my view. It's like a young trotting-horse with a mind to jib. You'll not know from one moment to the next what the meaning of it is, what part is substance and what part folly."

"That is unfortunately, Mr. Arkwright, sometimes true."

"And as is often the case as well, a gent who's very proper and given to reserve in his externals, may be underneath it all a deep one with motives and strategies he'd not care to advertise, as they offer no good to anybody concerned. That, too, is a bad thing."

"Yes, I agree, very bad. And too common."

"On the other hand, a gent who's very proper and given to reserve may simply be an honest, straightforward soldier, and just as he appears, nothing more, nothing less. A straightforward gent, a reliable gent, like our Ives. Now that's a good thing, in my view."

"That too is true. All you say is true, Mr. Arkwright."

"Which leaves us exactly where?" inquired Dr. Hall, speaking for the first time that evening.

The vicar shook his head; the other regulars shook theirs; the veterinary hunched up his shoulders and asked, rhetorically —

"I wonder, then, what Mark thinks of it all?"

"The squire of Dalroyd will, I fear, be little interested in these new people," sighed the vicar. "For you see how he neglects matters in the parish, and affairs in Shilston Upcot generally. There's no need to remind you of the last vestry meeting, so I shan't mention it. It's Mr. Trench's prerogative, of course, though if he can't be bothered with important matters involving the church and the vicarage, which are on the whole his own province, why should he have concern for newcomers to Skylingden?"

"You're being a trifle unjust, aren't you, vicar?" returned the doctor, composedly. "Young Mark is, after all, reigning master of Dalroyd and as such the sole patron of the benefice. Although it may be traditional for the squire to be involved in daily matters in the parish, it's far from obligatory. He is but one of many in the village with an interest in parochial business."

"Pray do not mistake me, doctor. Mr. Trench is an excellent man, a worthy man, an honest man, and I commend him for it. However, it has been my experience," sighed the Reverend Mr. Scattergood again, "in the brief two years my darling Dinah and I have been settled at the vicarage, that he has shown but scant interest in matters *vis-à-vis* the church and her flock, to say nothing of her poor shepherd. The living of Shilston Upcot is already heavily mortgaged; I'm sure if I don't take care I'll next be surrendering the surplice-fees. But it's all in the life of a country clergyman, I suppose. Unstable as water are we in our posts, and must be satisfied with the lonely usefulness of our lot."

"You'll not get anywhere, vicar, in my view, with levying a rate for repairs to the church steeple," said Mr. Arkwright. "It was that as rankled Mark at the vestry meeting. And I ask you, who here can blame him? In my view the church wardens and yourself would be wise to raise a subscription for the purpose."

"I suppose we shall be forced to consider it."

"No one will stand for a rate — no one substantial, that is, and o' course the poor have few resources. It may be custom but it simply isn't on, in my view, not with the state of feeling in the parish. And you'll not levy a rate against the will of the majority — no, no, I'll not sift *that* matter further tonight."

Several of the listeners were seen nodding in agreement with Mr. Arkwright. The vicar and Mr. Trench were not always on the nicest of terms, and often it was indeed the fault of the testy young squire, but neither was Mr. Mark Trench quite so neglectful of his duties as the vicar sometimes made out. Nor was the Reverend Mr. Horace Scattergood so dreadfully short of funds, for he had in addition to the living a small private income, as well as the interest from his wife's dowry, which, even allowing for his parochial expenses out-of-pocket, must have eased the burden of his lonely, useful existence considerably.

So went the conversation that evening, and such were the relayed accounts of Mr. Bede Wintermarch and his *ménage* newly established at the mansion-house. There was no want of discourse on the topic of Skylingden elsewhere in the town as well: at Gray Lodge, at the grocer's, at the waffle-house of Miss Crimp, or at Prospect Cottage; at Prospect Cottage in particular — it being the abode of Mr. Thomas Dogger — for there was little doubt among villagers that the inquisitive attorney would soon be on the case.

At about this same time, very soon after the arrival of the new inmates, there arose late one night a disturbance in the town. Dustbins were overthrown, panes of glass shattered, horses and dogs unnerved. The parish sexton, roused from sleep in his hut behind the church of St. Lucy of the Lake, looked out from his window to see a shadowy form prowling about the church-garden. As it lumbered forth into the moonlight he recognized it, from its immense size and rolling gait, from the shape of its head and the unusually long reach of its limbs — a short-faced bear. He recognized it too as the venerable, arthritic specimen known as Splayfoot, a grizzled male that had for some years haunted the dense thickets round Skylingden Wood and the point. Annoyed perhaps at the reoccupation of the mansion-house, at the daily activities of the household and the comings and goings of the tradesmen, the old veteran had come down from the wood to seek his bread elsewhere this night.

But there was more to the incident than that, or so it would appear, for the sexton was greatly troubled by it. Just why he should be so troubled, and filled with gloomy forebodings, is a matter that cannot be disclosed at present. Suffice it that the appearance of this creature in the church-garden gave him much cause for concern, nearly as much as his first glimpse of the family Wintermarch had on the Monday last.

CHAPTER II

THE SQUIRE OF DALROYD

THE village of Shilston Upcot, unlike Caesar's Gaul, is divided into but two parts, a lower part and an upper part. The lower part or village proper is the larger by far and that part rising from the lakeshore. Its chief thoroughfare is termed, predictably, the Low Street, and originates as a branch of the coach-road at its emergence from Grim Forest, that vast domain of evergreen and oak lying between the Talbot Peaks and Lonewater. Along this street are situated the commercial establishments of the town, the church and churchyard, the almshouses, the village green and market cross, the grammar school, and many of the residential cottages. At its farther extreme, at Town End, the street runs out at the flanking hillside, down which a line of stone steps descends from the Village Arms. By means of these steps access to the lower village can be conveniently gained from the inn, which sits on the high-road above.

This high-road is a continuation of the coach-road from Crow's-end and serves the upper village, which lies scattered about the hillside. Here can be found the houses of the more substantial citizens of the community. The bolder of these dwelling-places stand free of the timber, and readily present themselves to view; others, more modest and retiring, lie deep within the woods. A short distance along this road, past the gates and gravel drive leading to the Arms, at the end of another drive a little farther beyond, on a summer's day, the mellow walls of Dalroyd lay glowing in the sun.

The manor-house of Dalroyd, like Skylingden Hall and the residential cottages of the lower village, was built largely of good Talbotshire stone. Sturdy, square-eyed windows peeped from among the shrubberies cushioning the house; overhead a high-pitched roof of russet-colored tiles, graceful gables, and delicately molded chimneys rose to the sky. A spandreled entrance beneath gently drooping eaves, an ivy-laden porch, a chuckle of birds in the hedges, a lengthy terrace-walk, a smiling stretch of garden and trelliswork with a rosy sea of flowers, all gave joy to the passer-by. Here in splendor lived the sole direct representative of the ancient Talbotshire line of Trench, the squire of Dalroyd, who you shall find has a not inconsequential role to play in this history.

The present squire was a gentleman somewhere in his fourth decade, and possessed of what might best be termed a lounging disposition; which is to say that he never seemed at any time to be in any particular hurry about any particular thing whatsoever. No matter the occasion, no matter the circumstance, no matter how pressing the issue, his response was the same: a carefully crafted indolence, a deliberate and careless ease, often couched in cynicism — an attitude which was as much a part of his being as his mustaches and long side-whiskers were of his face.

As regards that face, the mustaches and side-whiskers he held in common with Mr. Bede Wintermarch, but there all resemblance ended, for the face of Mr. Mark Trench was a singular face indeed. There was nothing the slightest bit handsome or hawkish about it; it was more like a wasteland. It was a gray, drab, lumpish thing, rather haphazardly put together, as though the Almighty had been sorely pressed for time while fashioning it, tossing an eye here and a nose there, all in a rush and without laying out the plan of it before leaping in. As a result the eyes of Mr. Trench were somewhat too small, somewhat too narrow, and somewhat too closely planted, with one slightly above the other, and a craggy brow overhanging them both. His nose was short, squat, and globular at the tip, with prominent nostrils. His mustaches were of common size, true, but the lips beneath them were too full. The side-whiskers ran up to his ears and there abruptly disappeared, the hair above them having fled the field somewhere about his twenty-first birthday. As a consequence the squire was almost never seen without his sportish turf hat, whether taking the air in the woods or taking his ease at Dalroyd, or a black beaver when riding. A dark cutaway coat and white waistcoat, black neckcloth, gold watch and seals, pepper-and-salt trousers and lacquered half-boots, and a cigar held loosely in his fingers, completed the usual picture of his lounging self.

In point of fact Mr. Trench was quite conscious of his shortcomings and on occasion even offered comment upon them. He was casual, nonchalant, even at ease with them, as befitted one of his disposition; he was resigned to what nature had provided — or so he said, for it was nonetheless clear that a deeply rooted contempt for these failings underlay his words. So it was he cut a rather fashionable figure in local society, as to clothes and pedigree; too bad, was the common plaint, that he had not the physiognomy to match.

On the summer day described — it was a day not long after the discussion in the lodge-room of the Arms recounted in the previous chapter — the squire of Dalroyd was giving utterance to just such opinions as the worthy vicar had predicted as regards the tenants of Skylingden, to a guest who had only recently entered his household.

"I'll tell you again, Noll," said Mr. Trench, as he and his guest strolled upon the terrace-walk, "it matters little to me who has taken up residence there or why. Tenants will come and tenants will go, though to be sure the place has been empty for a jolly long while now. To all effects it's little more than a tithe cottage, despite its size, and equally dilapidated. I'm shocked anybody would volunteer for it. Why should anyone sensible want to come here? I can assure you, they'll quickly recognize their error and be off home. They'll not stay long. And so I tell you again, what's it to me who they are?"

"But there's the very point, Mark," returned his guest, a gentleman like Mr. Trench in his thirties but rather more agreeable as to countenance, with regular features, a wide luminous gaze, and abundant curling hair. "Why are they here? Surely it must stir the fires of interest in you. I can't believe it doesn't; it's inconceivable. As for anyone *sensible* wanting to come here, you'll recollect perhaps that I myself have come here from Crow's-end, and am not a person generally accounted to be lacking in sense. Though I arrived but a few days ago, already I'm wild to know who these new people are and why they've chosen such a remote spot to set up house."

"And jolly welcome you are to it," said Mr. Trench, drawing lazily on his cigar. "But you are a sensible sort, truly you are, Noll, and so I'll except you from my broad swath of condemnation, at least for the present. Besides which you're a different species altogether, a guest for the summer season at Dalroyd. As your host I've no hold upon you; how you occupy your time is your own affair. You're jolly welcome to pay these new people a call, and free as well to provide me with a report of your visit, should you choose to trot up to Skylingden and offer your card."

"Good God! At times I don't know how to take you, Mark. It seems to me you were a cheerier fellow at college. I recall your having a quite varied assemblage of interests at old Antrobus, and not all of them related to tutorials. Cricket, for example. You were rather a sharp bowler, as I recollect, and not without admirers in the field. And of course there were the theater and the opera-house — half-price for a private box, owing to your influence — and the spouting club, and skating, and billiard bagatelle and piquet and casino and other like games of chance at the Flying Horse, to fill in the hours. I carry with me many fine memories of those days. You were a clever and quick-witted fellow to knock about with, Mark, but I fear the years have hardened you terribly. I should be sorry now for anyone who got into your bad books."

"Mr. Langley," said Mark, turning to his guest, "I invited you to pass the summer here so you might pursue your translation of the works of an obscure and largely worthless poet of old Rome, not to make an analysis of some morbid condition you suspect in your host. You're wholly unqualified for the latter task, I can assure you. I suppose next you'll be diagnosing brain fever and prescribing laudanum. How much more simply can I put it to you? I am not a man of many friends. I'm not the sort for it. I'm the sort who's jolly better off without them, leastways those of the human variety."

His guest discharged a laugh. "Dear old Mark, I see it still isn't hard to get your goat. And it's early days yet! Of course I was most pleased to receive your kind offer, which was all unlooked for and which I accepted at once. It's astonishing to consider that this is my first visit ever to Dalroyd and your delightful village at the lakeshore. All those years together in Salthead and never once did an invitation come my way, though you yourself made several calls on us at Crow's-end, as I'm sure you'll remember. I admit it's a mystery now what has triggered this sudden burst of magnanimity."

"It's all rather simple, as you very well know, sir. I received some badgering correspondence in the post from one Mr. Oliver Langley of Bucket's Court, Highmarket, Crow's-end. This gentleman wrote me a series of lengthy, tiresome letters describing his current literary endeavor, relating how disagreeable it was to peg away at it in that busy city of his on the cliff, in the fogs one day and the rains the next, and with the coach-traffic outside making it wellnigh impossible for him to summon his muse. Naturally I felt compassion for the poor drudge, and offered him the balm and solace of Dalroyd. There is nothing more mysterious than that, I can assure you."

"No, no. I say there is more than that and it is not so very mysterious. I suspect you've grown into a lonely soul up here in your mountains, in this isolated spot — this *insulated* spot — with only a handful of rustic villagers for company and blessed little in the way of culture apart from billiards and horseflesh. So tell me now — what of Miss Mowbray?"

"Who?"

"Oh, stuff and nonsense, Mark," returned Mr. Langley, setting hands to hips. He broke into a smile that well became his sunny outfit, which was nearly all checks — a light checked country jacket, yellow, with checked waistcoat to match, a checked scarf neckcloth, and yellow checked trousers. "Miss Margaret Mowbray, just along the road there at Gray Lodge, that fine-looking villa, very prettily situated, with the tall thatched roof. Your cousin Mags, of course."

"My exceedingly distant cousin Mags, who might just as well come from the opposite end of the earth, if such still exists. We're very nearly not related at all, in point of fact; it's the most tenuous of connections. Yes, perhaps there really is no relation. Perhaps it's a hoax, perhaps I've been gammoned; I suppose I should look into it. It would be a jolly sight better for her, you know, for then she'd not be hindered socially by being known as Trench's cousin."

"And what of her aunt with whom she lives there at Gray Lodge, and provides with companionship?"

"Be advised I am even less akin to Mrs. Jane Fielding than I am to Miss Mowbray, for she's an aunt by marriage only and mature in years."

They stood in silence for a time, each immersed in his own reflections while admiring the view from the terrace-walk. They could see the plump, pleasant face of the Village Arms with its air of snug concealment, a little down the road, and beyond it the dark sheet of water that was the lake, and beyond that a distant line of hills. The roof-tops of the village proper, beneath the inn, were visible in patchy glimpses through the forest, which was pierced at one point by the broad spire of the church rearing up from below.

And across the inlet, looking out at them from the shaggy expanse of the high wood, the skulking Cyclops of Skylingden.

"Magnificent perspective," murmured Oliver. "A splendid place it is, your Talbotshire, this valley, these mountains, sacred to hawks and solitude. Surpassingly beautiful."

Mr. Trench nodded and smoked.

"Soothing. Restful. Reviving."

The squire nodded again.

"Such a marked change from city bustle. I'm still adjusting to the air, but it shan't take long. This is very much like a heaven come to earth for me. Yes, yes, I *can* work here."

"Jolly glad to hear it. You'll not mind explaining, then, your comment as regards our billiards and our horseflesh?"

"You're so very critical at times, Mark, and cynical too. You've grown so much darker than I recollect from our Salthead days."

"I should think it were you who were being critical of me. Darker, did you say? Perhaps my chin requires shaving."

"Stuff and nonsense again. So tell me — pray be serious now — why is it you haven't married your cousin? Frankly I'm surprised."

"Marry Mags? Whatever in the world should impel one to such a rash action? I'm jolly comfortable as I am, a reigning bachelor. And she's jolly comfortable as she is, down the path there with her aunt. We're two jolly comfortable people. (Three people, in point of fact, as I'm sure her aunt is jolly comfortable as well.) Why should comfortable people seek to ruin their lives with something like a marriage?"

Another pause. Mr. Trench smoked his cigar, while Mr. Langley listened to the soft rush of wind in the pine needles.

"You're not still going on about your father?" asked Oliver at length.

"What is there to go on about, as you call it?"

"He left Dalroyd to you, after all."

"He left Dalroyd to my mother and me, sir, after he very conveniently left the both of us," replied the squire, with a vengeful bite of his cigar. His eyes drifted away to roam about the stately files of timber, rather than light on his friend. "He abandoned his wife and small child without so much as a 'by-your-leave.' Well, thank you very much! No, I never can forgive him, Noll, for what he did to my mother. Never, never. The light went out of her spirit when he left her, and I am convinced it hastened her bodily end. She never was the same woman in after-years. Before his going, always so gay and happy; after it — "

His voice trailed off, not from sentiment but from displeasure.

"I must admit, to my mind it's a colossus of a puzzle," said Oliver. "I've simply never understood it. I couldn't have imagined my poor father even contemplating such a thing. And to what purpose? Why should the master of Dalroyd forsake his family, his title, his holdings, his position in the community? How could he possibly gain by it? It confounds me no end. Ah, well, they've the both of them passed on now, mine for a certainty and yours more likely than not. But I do wish I could have known your father, or at the very least had the opportunity of meeting him."

"You're jolly lucky you didn't. A fine lot of male forbears we've had in the family Trench," grumbled Mark. He made a move to go, having evidently wearied of the conversation.

"But to speak again of your cousin," said Oliver, detaining him for the moment. "There is good news to report, for Miss Mowbray and Mrs. Fielding are to join us tonight for dinner."

"As I have been duly informed. It appears my cousin and her aunt have gotten it into their heads that you require a sort of formal welcome to your holiday home. Naturally they called upon our forces here at Dalroyd to take the trouble of it, rather than impose upon their own household at Gray Lodge. Jolly gracious of them."

"Oh, come, come, Mark! You're exaggerating terribly. To my mind they are a most amiable pair. True, I've had the pleasure of their company but twice before — once on their visit to Crow's-end a few years back, when I entertained them at my humble lodgings in Highmarket, and then again this very day on my morning's ramble through the village. I assure you there's no design on their part, none whatever. It was I, not they, who proposed Dalroyd, after the ladies had conveyed to me their idea for a welcoming dinner. I thought Dalroyd an altogether suitable choice, as it is the squire who is the patron of my visit. I trust he'll not take offense?"

"Ha!" was all that Mr. Trench could muster in reply.

"What is more they're but two people and no added burden for your kitchen staff. Mark, Miss Mowbray and Mrs. Fielding are your last living relations in all the world. Consider my case — I've no one left now, absolutely no one. I would gladly surrender what little I possess to see my poor mother and father walk in again at the door. You're very fortunate, you know, and you should not forget that; though I expect you'll now be putting me sharply to rights on the matter."

"Ha!" said Mark again, who was finding something to decry in almost everything his friend had to offer.

Oliver smiled; in truth he knew the ways of his old college fellow — though indeed they were harder ways now — and had known them for above fifteen years, since he and Mark had first shared rooms at Antrobus. His friend had always been moody, obstinate, perverse; blind to opinion, and always in a bit of a temper; a rank radical who was without question his own man. These qualities had nothing if not intensified through the years, in concert with that lounging personality of his, that attitude of negligent ease which Oliver found so paradoxical.

"Well, we've jolly little left to contest here, I warrant," said Mark. "We all must rub through life as best we can. I've a flood of accounts awaiting me at my escritoire. You and your dusty Roman friend may freely commune with one another in the interval, until Smithers announces the dreaded hour of dining."

The squire turned and strode into the house, leaving Oliver to admire again the sea of flowers in the garden, the hedges and shrubberies, the venerable mansion itself in its framework of pine and fir woodland, its tranquil and sylvan solitudes; and to wonder how it was such a charming place as Dalroyd had come to have such an irascible master.

CHAPTER III

MISS MOWBRAY AND MR. TRENCH

As Oliver walked in at the door he was met not by Mr. Smithers, the butler, but by a lively shorthaired terrier-dog, a small white bundle of energy sprinkled over with liver-colored spots, among them a patch just above one eye, which gave to his face something like a quizzical or a doubting expression — an expression that served the dog marvelous well, I think, in his capacity as companion and confidant to Mr. Mark Trench.

"Jolly-boy is very keen on you, I see," called Mark from a corner of the drawing-room, where he had gone to prepare himself a fresh cigar. "Well, he is a sensible sort."

"He's a most agreeable little fellow, to be sure," laughed Oliver, kneeling to pat the terrier about the head and ears. The dog responded eagerly to such attention with a dripping tongue and frenzied oscillations of his tail.

"He's a great comfort to me," intoned Mark, drolly.

"Yes, I suppose he must be. It makes for an affecting tableau, the master of Dalroyd dwelling here in manorial splendor with only his loyal canine to bear him company."

"You're forgetting Smithers," said Mark, nodding as that equally loyal attendant now made his appearance. He was a dignified, self-assured serving-man, with a florid complexion, gray hair thinly swept over his cranium but curling at the back of it, frosty whiskers, and a smooth upper lip. He stood looking on in his dark suit, linen shirt, and splendid waistcoat, the shining ideal of a country gentleman's manservant. He had been a member of the household since long before the present squire had slipped into the world. His every feature and action marked him out as belonging to Dalroyd; indeed, he was by now almost a physical part of it, as indispensable as any of the building stones, bricks, or beams of timbers that composed it.

"Your ledgers, rent-rolls, and related materials are laid upon your desk in the study, sir," said he. "It is as you requested, that you might powder away at them in the afternoon while awaiting the arrival of Miss Mowbray and Mrs. Fielding."

"You see, Noll?" said Mark, with an approving glance at his servant. "However should I manage without him? 'Show me your butler and I'll tell you what you are,' or something or other. Well, he's a treasure to me, absolutely matchless, that much I can say. Thank you, Smithers. I believe our sunny visitor here, Mr. Langley, has some affairs of his own to occupy him.

And so we shall each be employed at our respective tasks for the next few hours, I suppose, until my cousin and her aunt come trotting up the lane. Pray inform us when they're within spotting distance, will you, Smithers?"

"Very good, sir."

"And so far as Tinker is concerned, Mr. Langley — I expect in his proud horsy heart he'll see his way clear to forgive you, for slighting him as regards Jolly-boy and myself."

"I apologize for neglecting to mention the loyal equine," returned Oliver, "but as he is at present cropping grass in the paddock he cannot be at your side here in the drawing-room, *en tableau*, as your dog is. I must assume moreover that he can neither overhear nor comprehend our words, being so engaged, and thus cannot know of the slight."

"Ha! Never assume, Noll, never assume. Tinker is, after all, a horse, a sixteen-hands bay hunter," said Mark, smilingly, "and with a horse, well, one just never quite knows."

He doffed his hat, and with Jolly-boy scampering at his heels disappeared — hat, bald head, terrier and all — behind the door of his study.

The remainder of the afternoon was passed in mental exercise, Mark at his accounts and correspondence (though in rather desultory fashion, it must be confessed, and with much recourse to his cigars), and Oliver at his Latin, endeavoring to translate in an intelligible manner the ideas, images, and rhythmic forms of a long-dead poet, who in his wildest fancy could never have conceived of anything so haphazard as the English language, nor known how much of his own precise tongue would survive in it.

Towards seven o'clock it was announced that the ladies of Gray Lodge were approaching in a chaise, at which news the gentlemen promptly extricated themselves from their labors — with no little relief, I suspect — and returned to the drawing-room.

There they soon were joined by a young woman of sprightly countenance, with a ready smile and a profusion of rich, creamy hair. A playful, grinning countenance it was, full of laughing eyes and glowing cheeks, planted on a frame something shorter than the norm but altogether firm, graceful, and athletic, with not an ounce of spare flesh; all of it set off by a colorful summer dress with large pockets into which the young woman was wont at times to rest her hands, in the country manner. Her demeanor was so wholly invigorating, so charged with spirit, in sharp contrast to that of the lounging Mr. Trench, that the very room seemed to brighten for her presence in it. The countenance and demeanor belonged to no other than Miss Mowbray — otherwise Mags — who as the squire had confessed was distantly related to him, but rather so distantly he'd forgotten just how.

With her was Mrs. Fielding, the mature aunt by marriage — a kindly and pleasant if somewhat diffident lady, a widow of long standing, with a set of features that had once been quite beautiful. Remnants of that beauty still could be seen about her lips, her eyes, her brow; but on the whole it was sad how time had dealt with her. Beauty, which lies dying even as it lives! At all events she was blessed with a fine good humor, though much given to allowing her niece the larger share of their conversation. She was, like the tenants of Skylingden, a little reserved by nature; but unlike them, altogether approachable and unmysterious.

"And here is our friend Mr. Langley, of Crow's-end," said Miss Mowbray, flashing a smile at the visitor. "Welcome again, Mr. Langley, to our little corner of Talbotshire."

"Thank you, Miss Mowbray," returned Oliver, gallantly. "I am delighted to see you again so soon, and you as well, dear Mrs. Fielding. It was most opportune, don't you think, our encountering one another this morning in the Low Street?"

"Ha! There it is then, it *will* persist in eluding me, the fact that you're all three acquainted," said Mark, snapping his fingers at the recollection. "So tell me again, cousin, just what was the purpose for this hastily arranged *soirée?* I'm simply the host here, you remember, the fellow charged with settling the accounts, and it's jolly bad form to keep me so thoroughly in the dark about it."

"You know the purpose very well, cousin, as I have just divulged it in welcoming Mr. Langley," said Miss Mowbray. "It is to offer him our kindest regards and to wish him joy for the duration of his visit, so that in future he will recall his summer among us with fondness. And so you'll not be keeping him all to yourself, will you, Mark? You may delight in playing the grumpy squire all the day long and locking yourself away in your gloomy rooms, but surely your guest should not suffer the same fate."

"To which I ardently protest, madam. Firstly, there are no gloomy rooms at Dalroyd. Absolutely none. Secondly, I am *not* grumpy, nor have I ever in my life been grumpy, and I most certainly do not keep myself locked away. Ha! You know yourself that Tinker and Jolly-boy and I have passed more hours together than I ever have spent with Noll here. They're excellent company."

"Agreed," said Oliver. "Since my arrival it has become clear to me that Mark is quite devoted to his two companions, with whom he spends much time roaming about Cranberry Chase and the surrounding woodland. I myself have ridden with them on several occasions now."

"And so you yourself are *not* excellent company, Mr. Langley?" inquired Miss Mowbray. "Don't you think it an impertinence, this comparison of my cousin's?"

"I assure you, I think it nothing more than dear old Mark and his ways," replied Oliver, laughing.

"Please tell us something of your work, Mr. Langley," spoke up Mrs. Fielding. "Mark has made mention of a literary project you have in hand — your 'dusty brain-basher,' as he terms it. You must tell us of it."

"Silla," interposed the squire.

"How is that?"

"Silla."

"I'm afraid I don't understand — "

"Silla," echoed Oliver, dashing to the good lady's assistance. "Gaius Pomponius Silla, to be correct. An obscure Roman philosopher and poet, an army man and native of Spain like his emperor, Trajan. He flourished in the first half of the second Christian century and was the author of five books of epigrams, none of which has ever before been rendered into English or any other language."

"A *very* obscure sort," nodded Mark. "I'd never in my life heard of the fellow myself, I can assure you, before receiving letters from Noll outlining his endeavor."

"My dusty brain-basher, you mean?"

"Absolutely."

"I've not heard the name either," said Miss Mowbray. "Have you, Aunt?"

The widow shook her head, to indicate her total unfamiliarity with any person or thing calling itself Silla.

"And so I have set myself the task of remedying the deficiency," said Oliver. "I'll admit, it's been tough slogging but I've made headway. Thanks to Mark I expect to make even greater progress over the course of the summer."

"I'd like to hear something more about this man Silla himself. I'm sure he must have come to some frightful end, as so many of those old Romans did," said Miss Mowbray. "Did he fall on his sword or take poison, like a good fellow, or was he by chance assassinated?"

"Nothing so gruesome as that. He retired from soldiering to a small rural estate in the north of Italy, where he lived to a considerable age. He directed most of his efforts toward the writing and revising of a relatively small body of work, some bits of philosophy but epigrams mostly, which he modeled after those of his late idol, Martial, another native of Spain. Because he had no influential patron and was far from Rome, living as a gentleman farmer amid his vineyards and olive groves, his works never received wide circulation. Eventually they lapsed into perfect obscurity. In the Middle Ages the epigrams were preserved by Saracen scholars, who made fresh copies, one of which happened to fall into my hands this past winter. An acquaintance of mine in Crow's-end, an antiquarian bookseller named Flyford, brought it to my notice. And that is how I have come to be translating the *epigrammata* of a long-deceased and little-known Roman author into English."

"Didn't you say he was a Spaniard?" asked Mark, beetling his brow.

"Perhaps Mr. Langley will read a few of his translations for us this evening," suggested Mrs. Fielding. "I'm sure he is as facile with his rhythm and meter as Margaret is with our flower-beds at the Lodge."

"Ah," exclaimed Oliver, delving into a coat-pocket, "I have here just the thing, a very recent effort. Frankly I was in hopes someone would ask."

"Oh, jolly good Lord, Noll!" sighed Mark. "Forgive me, Auntie, for employing such language, but *I* was in hopes that Mr. Langley would hold off — *hold off, sir!* — at the very least until we'd digested our food, before trotting out his dusty Spanish friend."

"Mark, you will be quiet," commanded Miss Mowbray. "By all means proceed, Mr. Langley. Let's have the brunt of it. Not to worry, we are most of us here your friends." She threw herself back in her chair and folded her arms, prepared to enjoy whatever was coming. "Are you ready, Aunt?"

"Oh, yes, indeed," replied Mrs. Fielding.

"This particular epigram was written in imitation of another by Martial," Oliver began.

"By which you mean he pinched it," said Mark, lazily inspecting the tuck of a new cigar. "Theft. Plunder. Plagiarism. *Ha!*"

"I prefer to think of it as homage to the master," returned Oliver, unruffled. Whereupon he cleared his voice and delivered up the following —

> "When Marcus sends round that he's 'ill,'
> His *GUESTS* suffer more than their host.
> It's all a sham, the prankster's well,
> While *THEY* die for want of a roast."

"Well, thank you very much, sir," said Mark, with polite applause. "That is most revealing. You see now, ladies, what our visitor from town thinks of *this* host, I warrant!"

"I chose something along the general lines of food and refection, as I considered it apropros," Oliver explained.

"It was apropros, Mr. Langley, and very clever, too," replied Miss Mowbray, to counter her cousin's rather less enthusiastic response. "Wasn't it, Aunt?"

Apropos it was indeed, for at just that moment the dinner was announced; and so they all sat down to it. Unlike the unfortunate guests in Silla's epigram they did not want for a thing, for it all was there — turtle soup, some biscuits, and some good Talbotshire cheese; hot jowl of lake trout, a plate of summer venison, mince pies, and sundry dishes of vegetables; kidneys and potatoes, garnished with caper sauce and wild celery; bread and butter; sweetmeats and olives, dried cherries, larchberry pudding, apricot marmalade, a sponge-cake, and blancmange; all of it washed down with liberal quantities of sherry, lemonade, and peppermint tea. Oliver found himself repeatedly complimenting the squire on the quality of the viands, as he had indeed at every meal since his arrival; and though Mark always received such praise with cynical affectation, he was, his visitor knew, secretly pleased. Oliver recognized that beneath that difficult exterior beat the heart of a Talbotshire Trench, proud of his household. No matter what Mark may have thought of his vanished father, he certainly thought much of his father's house.

The conversation round the board revolved about a pair of topics — reminiscences of college life in Salthead, and the new tenants of Skylingden. The chilly Salthead fogs, the winds on Whistle Hill, rambles about Snowfields and the Exchange, the chain bridge, nights of jollity in chambers and at the Flying Horse in Tower Street: such comprised the mental meat and potatoes of the gentlemen's recollections. It was above a dozen years since Mark and Oliver last had traversed the steep narrow streets and byways of Salthead town, had viewed its headlands and high places, its lofty crags and wild soaring pinnacles; for neither gentleman had been back since obtaining his degree. They wondered now what changes had taken place in the interval, and what had transpired at Antrobus, their old college, and how some of their companions of those former times were faring.

"Have you heard anything from Timmons?" asked Oliver. "He was always a decent chap."

"Nothing," said Mark.

"Or from Massingberd? You'll recollect he was going to the bar."

"Nothing."

"Or Howells, the organist? Or Marston?"

"Not a line."

"Nor have I. Strange. It's as if they'd taken a plunge straight off the side of the earth."

"If it were Marston I shouldn't care a fig. He cut me once — gave me the go-by. Didn't you know? I should welcome a plunge by Marston. Though I'm in agreement with you as regards Timmons — a jolly decent sort."

"Yes. Of course, I must admit I've never written to Timmons myself, so perhaps he's had no motive or inclination to correspond. Perhaps that explains why I've not heard from him. Nor have I written to any of the others. Have you yourself ever written to Timmons, by chance?"

"Never in my life!"

"Or to Howells? Or Massingberd?"

The squire answered again in the negative. The former collegians exchanged glances.

"Hmmm," murmured Oliver. "No cause then for any of our fellows to be posting correspondence to Dalroyd, I shouldn't think."

"Nor to Bucket's Court, I shouldn't think."

"Hmmm."

There followed a thoughtful pause.

"We *are* rather isolated here, Mr. Langley, despite the coach-road," said Miss Mowbray, restraining her amusement at the gentlemen's discovery. "Shilston Upcot is a very small place in a very large county. Not many people pass this way who haven't their business elsewhere. But I have a notion my cousin likes it so; it suits his reclusive nature. He likes to think of himself as stranded here, you see — marooned in the provinces."

"And what of you, cousin?" retorted Mark. "I warrant you're stranded here as well. All of us are who live in this village. As for me I'm jolly comfortable in my stranded state, and not above telling you so. I ask you, where else should I live but at Dalroyd?"

"It is Mr. Langley, perhaps, who has the proper outlook. He finds the high mountain country restorative, if a trifle daunting at times, after the trials of city life. It is a pleasure for him to be here among our scenic hills and valleys and our pine forests. Crow's-end — such a vast concourse of people! Such traffic! Such noise and bustle! And Salthead has not the monopoly on fog, as it can be as thick or thicker at Crow's-end. Is that not so, Mr. Langley? There are many material advantages to a place like Shilston Upcot — advantages which often are better perceived by those outside looking in."

"Just today Mark inquired of me why anyone sensible should come here. Which brings us," said Oliver, "to the subject of your new neighbors."

"Oh, yes, they're rather a puzzle," smiled Miss Mowbray. "The mansion-house as you know, Mr. Langley, has been to let for some time. Really, it's been years since anyone lived there. The last family to inhabit it — the Davagers, wasn't it, Aunt? — did not remain long."

"I suppose it must be in a dismal state at present," said Mrs. Fielding. "Skylingden. Such a wild and lonely name, I've always thought."

"On the contrary, Aunt, I think it a rather fashionable name. It calls to mind the *sky-line*, you see, and that is just where Skylingden is — perched there in the sky, on top of the point, with the high wood swirling round it like a cloud."

"What is its history?" asked Oliver, his large luminous eyes fired with interest. "A house like Skylingden has always a history of some note behind it. It cannot help but have."

"Rather a troublesome one, throughout the several hundred years of its existence," replied Miss Mowbray. "A history of ill fortune and unexplained loss, of tragedies hushed and secrets jealously guarded. If ever a place on earth should be termed ill-starred, I believe it is Skylingden. But that is what makes it all so very intriguing, don't you think? For the true romance of history lies in all those many things we never can know for certain, and so must endlessly speculate upon. And with such things Skylingden is replete, from what little I've managed to learn. Be aware, Mr. Langley, that Skylingden past is a topic of scant popularity among the inhabitants of Shilston Upcot. Oh, they're all very keen to gossip about these new tenants, of course, it's quite natural; but as regards events that may have transpired at the great hall in years gone by, they're little inclined to unburden themselves. They'll close up tighter than oysters once they see what you're angling at, most of them. I know little else than this, really, as I've not passed my entire life hereabouts. I'm sure Mark can tell you more than I."

"I believe you've summarized it nicely," said the squire.

"Everyone is so very tight-lipped. Why do you suppose that is, Aunt?"

Mrs. Fielding turned several shades of pale, and dropped her eyes to her plate.

"It is just as you have stated, dear," she answered, after a few strengthening sips of her tea. "A train of unfortunate circumstances — accidents, I suppose one should call them — and so the mansion-house has acquired a certain reputation."

"Like Mark," said Miss Mowbray, with an eye to her cousin.

"That morsel of wit, my girl, will cost you dearly!" exclaimed the squire, looking suitably piqued.

After this the current of conversation drifted into shallower waters, until at length the party broke up and the gentlemen retired to the billiard-room for a leisurely match. Pulling off their coats and rolling up their sleeves they pitched in for an hour or two, to the accompaniment of some trifling jests and a remark now and again on the relative skill (or absence of it) of the striker; until Oliver, having just made a losing hazard after pocketing his own ball, happened to broach the subject of short-faced bears.

"We've nothing to compare with them at Crow's-end," said he, "aside, of course, from the few bears at Strangeways — that's the zoological gardens on the cliff. But *our* bears are not dashing round loose in the city, as yours are in these mountains! This late incident, when one of your fellows kicked up a row in the vicar's garden — I must admit as a city man it concerns me. Surely you haven't saber-cats prowling about these streets as well?"

"From time to time," replied Mark, in all candor — "but normally the bears draw them off."

This answer did not go far toward reassuring Mr. Langley, who had heard much of short-faced bears and their ways, and had no desire to confirm in the flesh what he had been told over his spirits.

"By the by," Mark went on, applying some chalk to the tip of his cue, "we shall have occasion to explore the matter tomorrow."

"Explore the matter?"

"The matter of our short-faced bear — old Splayfoot. No, no, do not wonder at it. And you'll get no more out of me tonight. You will simply have to trust me, Noll."

Oliver appealed repeatedly to his host, without success. "So I must wait until morning for an explanation?" he asked.

"Just so. Look here, now — the red ball into the lower corner pocket."

There was a tap and a click; the red ball promptly jumped off the table, bounced once on the cushion, and fell with a thud at Oliver's feet.

"Ha!" cried a very surprised Mark, crushing his cigar in his teeth. "What think you of *that*, Noll?"

"I trust it is not a foretokening of tomorrow's adventure," Oliver answered.

CHAPTER IV

"HAVE YOU SEEN OUR GIRL?"

THE morning was a pale and a dreary thing to awaken to. As Oliver rose he saw through the casement-windows that the trees were cloaked in a misty gloom, their limbs trembling now and again in response to a breath of wind. Looking off in the direction of Lonewater and the village, he could see neither; nothing but thin clouds of vapor drifting through the garden and over the coach-road. The air was sharp for a summer morning, though perhaps no more so than one ought to expect in such altitudes. *In such altitudes!* So the drowsy Oliver found himself reminded again that such conditions would not stand; that he was no longer on the fog-bound coast but high in the mountains, at the back of the Talbot Peaks, where the white mists of morning frequently gave way to sunshine and so did not plague the inhabitants from cock-crow to cock-shut time.

After a prudent breakfast of wheaten griddle-cakes, new-laid eggs, brown toast and larchberry jam, the squire of Dalroyd and his city visitor, with a basket of provisions in hand and an exuberant Jolly-boy at their feet, set off along the terrace-walk, past the garden and down the drive to the coach-road. Over the way a line of stepping-stones trailed down to the shore, to a pier of planks that ran out onto the lake. At the end of the pier a fine small sloop lay quietly at her moorings, her sails bagged and her stern sheets covered with tarpauling.

As they went along little Jolly-boy found much to delight in, scampering through the brush beside the steps, yelping and barking, rejoicing in his freedom and the crispness of the morning air. Several times Mark himself — looking remarkably skipper-like in a blue jacket with mother-of-pearl buttons, canvas trousers, cotton neckerchief, and oil-skin cap — leaped from the path and into the brush and there briefly gave chase, the terrier crying out for joy while describing rapid circles round his master. Then the dog would veer short and heave to, panting, and brace himself on his haunches, his tongue hanging from his mouth, and beg with his eyes to be pursued again. There was laughter in the faces of both dog and squire; surely Mark enjoyed the romp as much as or more than Jolly-boy. All of this Oliver saw and duly noted — for there, in such eager, childlike sport, he recognized something of the best of Mr. Mark Trench as he remembered him from university. The intervening years had wrought a strain on his friend, of that there could be no question; though how much of it was extrinsic to his person and how much self-inflicted, Oliver could not begin to reckon.

"Look here, Noll — roll up that tarpauling and stow it below, will you, while I secure the rudder," the squire directed. "There is a light breeze running down the lake this morning. It should serve us well for a time."

"Where are we off to?" asked Oliver, quite reasonably, as he busied himself with his assigned task.

"Lonewater."

"That's rather clear, it seems to me. But what's it to do with old Splayfoot? Surely your bear has not taken to bathing in these dark waters?"

"You're jolly impatient with me this morning, Noll," replied Mark, with a lazy laugh. "Not such an unforeseen result, I suppose. You'll recollect, however, that I asked you to trust me. I can assure you, I know what I'm about."

"We both may be terribly sorry if you don't. Very well, then. I'll admit, I've been far too sedentary of late, what with the dusty Silla and all, and despite our few pleasure-rides through Cranberry Chase. It will do me good to be out there on the water; though quite frankly I'd prefer a shell boat with a crew of collegians about me, all of us bending to our oars and the coxswain calling for the strokes — the catch, the pull-through, the finish! To feel again a fine walnut pole in my hands! How swiftly the memories come flooding back — our rowing-matches on the Salt River — the heats at the finish of Easter term — "

"We may have our chance at the sculls yet, should we find ourselves becalmed in the midst of the voyage. Oh, it could very well happen; these mountain draughts can be jolly perverse. They'll run out on you at the slightest provocation. That is why we must grasp the opportunity while we may. Here, Noll — insert the battens into the mainsail like a stout fellow, while I break out the jib."

As they labored to ready the sloop they found the inquisitive muzzle of Jolly-boy intruding itself into their activities, poking about as if to inspect the quality of the work (this accomplished by the rub of a cold nose), and to determine if any material assistance was needed (this by the lick of a slimy tongue.) To Oliver, however, a more likely translation involved a demand to be chased round and round again, and an inquiry into the availability of certain foodstuffs. The gentlemen had with them in the wicker hand-basket some jugs of hot tea and coffee, some sandwiches, a corner of cheese, a goose-pie, and a few *et ceteras*, to fortify themselves during the excursion; this Oliver knew for a certainty, for he himself had aided Mr. Smithers and the cook in assembling the provisions. Thus his surprise at the item that now appeared in the squire's hand

— a cold chop, magically extracted from a hidden corner of the basket. Alerted, Jolly-boy caught the treasure eagerly in his mouth, and bounding to the foredeck settled down with it in his paws; being thereafter content to observe from a distance, rather than supervise directly, the ongoing preparations of the crew.

It was not long after the discovery of the chop, as Mark and his new first officer were preparing to raise the sails, that a queer little growl came stealing from the throat of the terrier. Mark and Oliver both turned at the same instant, to behold two figures making their way along the water's edge. Somber, elderly figures they were, a gentleman and a lady, both in black, the gentleman wearing as well a white collar which marked him out for a clergyman. Their eyes were much engaged in roaming about the lakeshore, about the pebbled slopes and clumps of verdure; now watching the black water, now the shingle beach, as though in search of something. They spoke not a word to one another, trudging along in silence until they were no more than a few steps from the foot of the pier.

"Morning!" Oliver called out, touching a forefinger to the brim of his wide-awake. He signed to Mark for an explanation or at the very least an introduction, but the squire had nothing to offer apart from a look of imperious curiosity directed at the newcomers. From this Oliver concluded that the two must be strangers to him.

As no response to his salutation was forthcoming, Oliver supposed that the pair must not have heard him, for being aged they could very well be hard of hearing; so he jumped nimbly from the boat and strode to shore, to greet them at closer quarters and inquire if he and Mark might be in a position to help them in some way.

At his approach the old couple turned their faces to him — limp, weary, wintry faces, full of anxious concern.

"Have you seen our Edith? Have you seen our girl?" asked the clergyman, in a thin voice.

A mystified glance from Oliver, suspicion from Mr. Trench watching from the sloop. Jolly-boy on the foredeck uttered another growl, which on this occasion ended with something like a disguised bark.

"Your girl?" said Oliver. "Who is your girl?"

No reply; the faces of the old people returned his gaze, their strange sad eyes fully as uncomprehending as his.

Girl? They were too advanced in years to have a small child. Oliver looked to Mark again for guidance; as he did so his eyes fell upon Jolly-boy, and so he thought he understood.

"Your girl?" he asked, turning back to the old couple. "It's your dog, is that it? She's gone missing?"

Again they made no answer; instead they looked towards the boat, the clergyman inquiring in the same thin voice if *he* (meaning Mark) had seen their Edith, had seen their girl? The squire shook his head, at which point the pair abruptly walked off to resume their slow, steady trudge round the lakeshore.

"That was most certainly not the vicar, your Mr. Scattergood," said Oliver, rejoining his friend.

"No, it was not."

"Who can they be? Guests, perhaps, at the Arms?"

"Possibly."

"I believe it is their dog they're searching for. She's gone missing."

"Jolly odd," murmured the squire, fixing his eyes on the spot where the old couple were receding into the gloom; which sentiment was promptly endorsed by another growl from Jolly-boy.

The gentlemen pressed ahead and in due course hoisted the sails, cast off the mooring, and pushed away. Mark leaped to the foredeck to grasp the jib, sending Jolly-boy scampering into the stern sheets with Oliver, who had command of the tiller. The jib caught the wind and swung the bow away from shore; as the sails filled the boat seemed to draw a breath and come alive. Mark released the jib and hauled in the sheets. The sails rattled, quivered briefly, then filled again as they swallowed more air, driving the sloop forward onto the broad dark surface of the lake.

It took the skipper and his first officer some little time to gain their rhythm, while steering a straight course and adjusting the trim. The water was generally smooth with occasional ruffled patches and small waves. To starboard they could discern the outlines of Shilston Upcot, the shops and cottages along the Low Street and the spire of St. Lucy, gliding by. On the hillside above, the Arms and parts of the upper village were visible through the misty woods.

The sloop ran to the southwest, past the town and across the inlet, then heeled to larboard and skirted the majestic curve of the promontory, on the top of which lay Skylingden Wood and the mansion-house. The water hissing and snorting, the boat stooping to the breeze and beating up the spray in little clouds from her bow — all was joyous, all was cheering to Oliver in position at the tiller with Jolly-boy at his feet. The atmosphere was cool and bracing, the roll and play of the waves reviving.

Looking down into the water, Oliver observed how pitchy dark and syrupy it was, and made mention of this fact to the skipper.

"That is because there is no bottom," said Mark.

"What!"

"At the very least none that anyone has been able to identify. Attempts have been made to sound the deeper parts, but always the length of line has been insufficient to touch ground. Jolly comforting, is it not, Noll, to know that untold fathoms of cold dark water — a vast inky void, black as Erebus — are lying just beneath our feet, intervening between ourselves and whatever may be lurking in these grim depths. *Ha!*"

"It's very much like the sea in that respect," replied Oliver. "But surely nothing more ominous lurks here than that delicious lake trout served at dinner yesternight."

"Hoey claims Lonewater is so very deep because it sits in the throat of an ancient volcano, and that these mountains you see round about, the Talbots, are the remains of the volcanic cone itself. He seems very sure of himself on that point."

"Hoey? Who is Hoey?"

"A jolly irregular sort whom you must get to know. His place is called the Peaks, and is quite as irregular as he. It lies just off the coach-road, in Grim Forest, westward a few miles of the village. His proper title, by the by, is *Captain* Hoey, though just what or whom it was he may have captained in his career no one has any knowledge of. I'll lay you fifty guineas it was not in the merchant nautical line, for he's petrified of water. He is, however, a fine horseman and our local MFH. It's settled, then; we must go to him before the week is out. He has always a deal of amusing information on offer."

"Perhaps this Captain Hoey can tell us something more about your new neighbors."

"It should not surprise me, though for myself I don't care a fig so far as Skylingden is concerned. Ha! Look there, Noll!"

The sloop had come about and was standing before the south face of the promontory, that part which could not be seen from Shilston Upcot. It was largely free of mist now, and on its densely wooded slopes Oliver could at first identify nothing of particular interest. But gradually, as his eyes grew accustomed to the ragged undulations of the trees, he spotted a number of dark clefts or notches of varying size, here and there amidst the timber.

"Caves?"

The squire nodded. "This side of the point is filled with them throughout. And what do you suppose, sir, can be found loitering about such things?"

The luminous eyes of Oliver went wide as an explanation for the day's voyage on a sudden presented itself.

"Short-faced bears?"

"Spot-on. Look *there*, now!"

A bulky form could be seen emerging from one of the caves. It was a bear, and of the short-faced variety too, as evidenced by its long and sinewy limbs, arching back, and ferociously flat muzzle. Its coat of fur, which had once been dark and brown, was now almost entirely gray. It ambled out onto a broad ledge before the cave, dropped onto its hindquarters, stretched, yawned, and began to chew at one of its paws.

"Is that the same creature that rambled through the village the other evening?"

"Old Splayfoot," said Mark. "He's lived in and about the caves and thickets of the point for years. Like most bears he's a solitary sort, very nearly a hermit; a connoisseur of fish, berries, acorns, and the honey-making bee; your roots and your fruits, and your occasional stray swine or mountain sheep; in the main a self-reliant fellow who cherishes his privacy, though I'll admit for your common short-face our Splayfoot is not an overly aggressive specimen. He's never actually harmed anyone human, I don't believe, though there have been more than a few threatening displays after an unintended encounter. So long as Skylingden has lain vacant he's had the run of the grounds and outbuildings, but now that the property has been attached, as it were, it's likely causing him no end of aggravation. Probably it accounts for his straying into the Low Street, to escape for a time the sights and sounds of Mr. Bede Wintermarch and his household."

"He looks deceptively tame from such a distance, though I've no doubt as to his fierceness if challenged. I should not care to happen upon one under any circumstance, no more than I should like to confront a saber-cat in Cranberry Chase."

"When Splayfoot was in the prime of his bearhood he was, I'll warrant, quite formidable, but he's rather played out now and has not the same vitality of spirit remaining in him. In some sense I feel for him, for he represents the passing of an era. As the saying is, 'he may be a short-face, but he's our short-face.' In all likelihood his continued presence in the vicinity has kept some of the jolly awful sorts from venturing near."

"Are there many of these bears in and about the town?"

"Yes, a number of them, though generally your short-face prefers loftier ground. He'll wander down if he has particular need to, as for example to fish the streams round Lonewater; otherwise the game in the higher forests serves him quite nicely. Many bears are omnivorous eaters, but it seems our short-faced chaps require more in the way of meat than other of their cousins — or so Hoey surmises."

"Is this Captain Hoey of yours a student of natural history? Someone perhaps of the same tastes as our old tutor, Professor Humphreys, at Antrobus?"

"He is a student of the world, or what remains of it," said Mark, hauling in the mainsheet, "and as I understand it attended no university."

"What other forms of wildlife have you here in this valley?" asked Oliver, gazing round in admiration of the vast expanse of upland rising from the lakeshore.

"Bears and cats are the principal characters we must guard against. Saber-cats tend to stay clear of the village this time of year, being more of a concern in the colder months. Nonetheless one can never be too cautious. (You've noticed of course the bars and shutters on the windows of most of the cottages — I can assure you, they're not to discourage bandits of any human sort.) And we have our megatheres — our ground sloths, slow-witted creatures that can be found in and about the shallower ravines. Then there are the wolves — those eerie wails you may have heard in the thick of night. And every now and again one wakes to find the odd family of mastodons grazing in a dew-drenched meadow. There are as well a few of the old mastodon trains still running in these mountains; one of them passed this way shortly before you arrived. I tell you, a caravan of fully laden thunder-beasts marching along the coach-road makes for an impressive spectacle."

"And what of birds?" asked Oliver. "For I had a most troubling dream last night. My sleep for some reason was fitful at best, and broken by wild imaginings. At some point, well past midnight, the feeling stole upon me that someone was looking in at my casement-window. I didn't at first realize it was a dream; in it, I rose from my bed to find a thing like a huge bird squatting on the window-ledge. In the darkness I could discern little of its appearance aside from two round shiny eyes, like owls' eyes. I thought then that the creature touched me — not in a physical sense, however, for the casement was shut; rather, I felt as though its consciousness had somehow reached into mine. Immediately I awoke, gasping for air and in a monstrous sweat. For a dream it made the strongest impression on me."

"Perhaps it was not entirely a dream," Mark suggested. "Perhaps it was a teratorn there at your window."

"You have them here?" asked Oliver, a little uncomfortably.

"Of course."

In cities like Crow's-end, teratorns were regarded by a suspicious populace as harbingers of ill-fortune, the most evil of portents. They were vicious predators with a fearsome reputation. There were those who claimed to have seen fully grown saber-cats brought to ground by three or four such birds leagued together. Fortunately teratorns were but rarely glimpsed in coastal skies, eschewing the fogs for the lighter air of the mountain meadows.

"Not my notion of pleasant animals," Oliver confessed. "I admit my preference runs more to robins and bobolinks."

"I'll lay you another fifty guineas teratorns prefer them as well," said Mark, with a crooked smile.

Oliver found his thoughts momentarily filled by the image of a teratorn he once had seen at Strangeways — the huge black body like a vulture's, the crimson head and neck, the flaring wings, the wicked sharp beak and talons, the soulless stare from the eyes.

"Ill-looking creature," he muttered.

"Were you speaking of me?" asked Mark, his attention in part diverted by his skipperly duties.

"Rather not!"

"Well, you could have been, you know, for there's another thing bequeathed to me by my dear vanished father — his jolly good looks!"

"Aren't you being a trifle excessive?"

"My dear Noll, I am simply being forthright. You'll admit I'm not the handsomest of specimens in this part of the world — or in this part of Talbotshire — or in Shilston Upcot even, by God!"

At which point the squire turned round and began to attack the trim in silent earnest. Oliver, thinking it best to leave off conversation for a time, quietly resumed his management of the tiller.

The short-face on the ledge above them had wandered off. The mansion-house of Skylingden was nowhere in evidence, as it lay on the opposite side of the point; but there was visible, Oliver saw now, on the verge of the summit, some fragments of masonry and a scattering of gray stone blocks, strewn about in haphazard array. He had not noticed these features before and wondered what they signified. Nonetheless he was obliged to bottle up his curiosity and cork it down, at least for the present. Feeling now the keen edge of appetite, he began to loft yearning glances toward the wicker hand-basket.

"An odd business, that clergyman," said Mark, carelessly, as he watched the sails fill with a fresh breeze.

"Yes. A disheartened pair, it seemed to me, rather too much in the dumps for being on holiday. Well, don't you suppose they must be on holiday?"

Mark was weighing this and other possibilities in hand, when he observed the stray glances of Oliver towards the basket. He relented; and so they drove the sloop in close to shore, dropped anchor, and broke out the provisions.

"We're fortunate it wasn't our reverend vicar. He's rather sensitive when the subject comes round to me," said Mark. He swallowed some of his coffee, but before diving into his sandwich removed fully half the contents and tossed them to little Jolly-boy.

"How is that?"

"He claims I neglect him. Oh, not the reverend *him* personally, you understand, but the parish. Not only am I master of Dalroyd but patron of the living of Shilston Upcot, and a vestryman, and a benefactor of the parochial coffers, just as my honored forbears have been for eons. Yes, Noll, we *do* look after our parsons here. And for what? For the very particular privilege of being called to account on a Sunday morning and scolded for our grave criminality of spirit, and then instructed how to grovel for the mercy of a so-styled loving God. Well, let me tell you, the entire lot of it is so much rubbish. Devil take all preaching and doctrine! If credulous sorts round this parish choose to set store by such gammon, they're jolly welcome to it — but they should then take responsibility for their own clergyman and his needs, and leave those of us with greater soundness of mind out of it."

"You seem rather confirmed in your view."

"It is a rational view, the merest common sense to any clear-thinking individual. I'm surprised you don't agree."

Oliver frowned. He had been conscious since their days in Salthead of his friend's nonconformist tendencies, but this was rather much!

"As patron it must be you who recommended Mr. Scattergood for the benefice. Your good opinion of him has something changed, I gather."

"As has his opinion of me. And he constantly into my pockets for this expense or that! Why doesn't that sanctimonious Tom Dogger step in?" said Mark, with a languid defiance. "He's forever prying into vestry matters. And he's rich enough, I'll warrant, though he cries poverty at every turn. Show me an attorney who claims to be poor and I'll show you a lying humbug — *ipso facto!*"

"Tell me more of this Mr. Dogger of yours," said Oliver.

CHAPTER V

GREEN TEA

MR. Thomas Dogger was the village attorney, and as such he had the ear of the village. Or perhaps it was that he had the village by the ear; it was a point open to debate. Suffice it that as village attorney and sole legal light for many darksome miles around, the law was his business, and in Shilston Upcot the business of the law was his. As in any society in town or country, citizens will have their squabbles, their covenants and freeholds, their testaments and codicils. In Shilston Upcot all such matters found their way to Mr. Dogger, in the small set of chambers he maintained there at his spacious abode, Prospect Cottage, a place which, in accordance with its title, afforded a lovely view of lake and forest from its mullioned windows.

Mr. Thomas Dogger had his professional finger in nearly every pie in town, and had for some while, having succeeded his predecessor and former partner, Mr. Parker Pring, upon the demise of that worthy gentleman. Mr. Dogger, a native son of the village, having shown promise while still a clerk articled to Mr. Pring, had gone on to achieve great distinction at Clive's Inn, that most celebrated of the Inns of Court at Fishmouth. Upon the conclusion of his terms he was called to the Bar, and being entered upon the honorable roll of solicitors of the Court of Chancery and attorneys at Common Law, was reunited with his benefactor Mr. Pring in the capacity of junior partner, before ultimately supplanting him in the practice.

A humble and respectable man by nature, Mr. Dogger was not one to trumpet his merits or his exclusive education; nonetheless, one way or other, whenever the subject arose (as it for some reason often did), Mr. Dogger was at pains to place his hearers at their ease, assuring them with a tolerant smile it was no very great accomplishment, that rising of his from the ranks at the celebrated Clive's Inn at Fishmouth; no, no, it was nothing, do not wonder at it, for if plain country Tom Dogger could manage it, anyone could. Never let it be said that Tom Dogger (he was fond of referencing himself in the third person) was above anybody else, or smarter than anybody else, or better than anybody else, for he was the same plain country fellow he always had been, the very same, with no city airs, and so let us speak no more of it — not, at least, till some few more minutes hence.

Mr. Thomas Dogger, as I have mentioned, had a set of lawyerly chambers there in his lovely cottage with its pleasant prospect of lake and forest ("As nice a house," as he was known to say, "as any gentleman could wish to hang up his hat in.") He had there too a pleasant and a very silent wife, known to everyone simply as Mrs. Dogger — a little squab figure, very drab as to face and dress, and by her husband's own admission without so much as a particle of personality to recommend her. She favored plain holland frocks, old-fashioned bonnets and gray cotton shawls, all very dowdy. She acceded to her husband's every wish without complaint, bowing before his acknowledged expertise in all matters domestic, financial, and philosophical. Hardly anybody in the village knew her well, for apart from Sunday service she was rarely glimpsed beyond the pale of Prospect Cottage and its gardens, owing to her many responsibilities there. While Mr. Dogger practiced the law in chambers on one side of the house, Mrs. Dogger practiced her housekeeping on the other. But while Mr. Dogger was free to wander from chambers at any time of the day or night (which he often did), Mrs. Dogger had little opportunity to be from home.

Mr. Dogger had as well a manservant, a kind of steward who assisted him and his wife in the management of the household, a tall, spare, sober fellow called Larcom. He had coarse yellow hair, parted in the middle and hanging down the sides of his head, like yarn from the head of a mop; a high, dry brow, solemn eyes, rather more nose than one should like, and a pinched mouth. In manner he was as pinched and solemn as his countenance. He discharged his duties at Prospect Cottage with grim efficiency, though his devotion to Mr. Dogger was rather less enthusiastic than might be supposed, owing to certain disparities of temperament that existed between them. As a consequence Larcom had found ways and means to place himself chiefly in the employ of Mrs. Dogger, with whom he shared not only a russet-colored roof, but common domination by the lord and master thereof.

By dint of constant association this same Larcom had acquired, albeit unconsciously, something of the propriety and sense of plain dealing of his employer. Seeing for example the high esteem in which the attorney was held by most of the villagers, it was natural for Larcom to expect, as the retainer of so consequential a person, that he himself ought to be accorded the same esteem by the servants of these same villagers. Which fantasy of course existed solely within his own brain, for his reputation in Shilston Upcot was unenvied at best, and the topic of much sly humor round hearth and oaken bar. He was by all accounts a prim, prideful, self-complacent grouch, a spoil-sport and a wet blanket, bursting with conceit. He was short in his temper as well as his knee-breeches, and rather too impressed with his own appearance, particularly his cocked hat with the feather in it (he thought this fashionable), and the turn of his long bony legs (set off to supposed good advantage by bright cotton stockings), and other like oddities, all of which only contributed to the villagers' mirth.

Mr. Thomas Dogger himself was a familiar sight in Shilston Upcot. Often, to relieve his mind of the accumulated clutter of the law, of its writs and true bills and contingent remainders, he would go for a stroll through the town, lubricating his lawyer's golden voice by stoppages at the Village Arms and other places where such things as cider, brandy, and spruce-beer were not unknown. In his mingling with the villagers, many of whom were clients at one time or other and so a valuable source of costs, Mr. Dogger was a marked egalitarian. He was just to a fault, often persuading his fellows that they were in the right and that plain country Tom Dogger must have it wrong, while in the same breath conveying an impression to everyone else that the very opposite was true. He was a sturdy defender of the Church, fancying himself a confidant of the young vicar and the young vicar's young wife, and scarcely ever reminding them of the few trifling gifts he had made to the parish (though he made quite sure that everybody in the parish knew of them.) He never saw a child in the Low Street without stopping to compliment the parents upon the very promising attributes discernible in the hatchling, at the same time managing to implant in their minds certain doubts as to this or that quality in the youngster that might or should or must be improved. For Mr. Dogger was after all a professional man and very respectable, a product of the celebrated Clive's Inn at Fishmouth, and so knew whereof he spoke; and if he, plain country Tom Dogger, and Mrs. Dogger had had the good fortune to be blessed by Providence with a child themselves, Mr. Dogger would "go bail" it should never have been nearly so promising as the offspring in question. Then he would utter a sigh and incline his head in a retrospective manner, while the parents offered their ready sympathy, for it was the will of the Almighty that the union of Mr. Dogger and Mrs. Dogger had been unfruitful. After this the attorney would walk on, leaving Mamma and Papa to reflect upon the deficiencies of a child who only moments before had been perfection personified.

As to the form and figure of Mr. Dogger, it was above middling height, very straight in the back, and strong. There was an almost military perpendicularity to his carriage, though he had never been a soldier. It was, he humbly let on, a thing he had been blessed with as a youth, and had cultivated while keeping his terms in Fishmouth; for Fishmouth was the center of politics and the law, and a straight, strong, soldierly bearing was an asset in both. So would Mr. Dogger sprinkle before his hearers such little secrets of his, relating how he had continually fought to improve himself, and fought to improve himself, and how his hearers too might improve themselves if they truly wished to, just as plain country Tom Dogger had done.

No less remarkable a component of Mr. Dogger was his face. It was on the whole roundish as to forehead, with a substantial chin and a long, sharp nose, and neither mustache, beard, nor side-whisker to obstruct anybody's view of it. His eyes, from lengthy legal polishing, were shiny and sleek, and had a way of noting things without appearing to see them. His hair was still thick but largely gray, and full of great curling waves that rolled and splashed their way round the shores of his neck and collar.

Besides his servant-cum-steward Mr. Dogger had in his employ a cook, a woman by the name of Simpkins, whom Mr. Dogger had taken in from kindness and offered the prize of feeding his household; in return for which he paid her no money, not a ducat, and as well refrained from prosecuting a suit against her for larceny at the county assizes. This equitable arrangement Mrs. Simpkins had agreed to with dispatch; though a closer examination of the details found that Mrs. Dogger was required by her lord and master to taste all of the food concocted by this Mrs. Simpkins — from her buttered eggs and her venison pasties to her plum porridge and syllabubs — prior to its devourment by Mr. Dogger. A sound precaution, the attorney was quick to declare, considering the low state of morality in the county, a condition standing in sharpest contrast to that of the revered days of his youth. It was partly the fault of a wayward clergy for sinking into sloth and abandoning their duties in favor of material gain, which had become all too common practice — an opinion Mr. Dogger was not shy of propounding to the Reverend Scattergood, which he felt of course was his obligation as a benefactor of the parish, and which he expected the vicar to receive in the spirit in which it was offered.

Despite the presence of Mrs. Simpkins in the kitchen of Prospect Cottage, there was one staple of the attorney's diet which Mrs. Dogger herself alone prepared, twice each day, from long habit. This was the brewing of a particular variety of green tea which Mr. Dogger relished highly, the composition of which only Mrs. Dogger was privy to. It was purportedly excellent for the eyes (the better to spot an easy mark), for the circulation (the better to pursue said mark), and for mental acuity (to keep track of costs) — all recognizable points of advantage for attorneys everywhere.

There were some few wags in the village who suspected that plain country Tom Dogger was not all he appeared, that in reality he was a cunning rascal full of clever dodges and long-headed maneuvers, that he mingled only to acquire bits of intelligence or to troll for clients, or to parade his own worth before lesser folk. So these few said, not to Mr. Dogger's face, of course, but rather to his coat-tails; even so, their suspicions were voiced in careful tones, for with the attorney one had always another suspicion that there were eyes and ears in those coat-tails as well as in his head.

Thus Mr. Thomas Dogger, a respectable gentleman and humble practitioner of the law, an upright husband, a magnanimous employer, and a faithful adherent of the Church and her virtues.

One night, not long after the arrival of the new tenants at Skylingden, Mr. Dogger, like Mr. Oliver Langley in the preceding chapter, had himself a little dream. He was lying quietly there in his bed, trying to sleep, when there came to his attention a noise like a feathery rustling. Lifting his head — it was a heavy object, what with the load of knowledge it contained — he turned it towards the noise and saw at his open casement, silhouetted against the moonlight, the outline of a dark form. He could not at first make out what manner of form it was. It looked to be about the size of a small person, and was crouching on the window-stone outside, with its face pressed forward between the iron bars of the window.

A burglar? And at Prospect Cottage! But how could a burglar hope to squirm his way in through those bars?

Alarmed, Mr. Dogger sat up in his bed and felt for his slippers. It was then he heard the dark form utter what sounded like a chuckle, after which it spoke to him. In Mr. Dogger's dreaming mind what a rush of sinister thoughts began to flow! Such thoughts as had not flowed for years upon years, but like buried detritus had lain dormant in the winding river-bottom of his memory. Upon waking from his dream, however, although he remembered the dark form at the window, he could not recollect what had been said to him or why his thoughts had been so troubled; but a cold shiver, like a presentiment of doom, had pierced him through and through. His final glimpse of the dark form had shown it to be not a person but a kind of bird like a large owl, of which he could recall little else apart from two green eyes shining in the darkness.

And so once awake he had started up, and felt himself a-tremble; then just as quickly recovered, reminding himself of the humble dignity of his calling, and feeling again the weight of his lawyerly responsibilities, and deeming it unprofessional to have been agitated by anything so incompetent, irrelevant, and immaterial as a dream.

That morning as he sat down to his breakfast, he saw before him on the table, side by side, two cups of green tea, the one for him and the other for Mrs. Dogger, exactly as he found them on every morning. But as he peered down now at these particular cups, on this particular morning, they seemed to him not so much like two cups of tea as a pair of green glowing eyes in the night.

At which point Mr. Dogger abruptly quitted the room for his lawyerly chambers, leaving his breakfast all untouched behind.

CHAPTER VI

An Encounter in the High Wood

"LARCOM," said Mr. Dogger as he rose from his chair, later that same day.

"Sir," nodded his servant and steward, entering the lawyerly chambers from the passage upon hearing his master's call.

"I'm for Skylingden this afternoon. It is high time I paid a visit to the people there at the great hall, high time. This Mr. Bede Wintermarch, you know, *et uxor*, *et filia*. To be frank I am a little surprised the gentleman has not as yet sought my professional advice, or requested that I do him some service. Certainly there are affairs of a legal complexion with which Tom Dogger can be of assistance to him. Perhaps he has his own solicitor, some man in the city. Oh, I'm quite convinced he's from the city, from Crow's-end no doubt. He simply must be. Well, little good city counsel will do him here! He'll require someone surely, a professional adviser, to attend to his interests in Talbotshire. The interests of clients are never to be neglected, Larcom. How can a Crow's-end solicitor attend to his client's interests here, in this county, so many long miles from town? Likely the family are not to be blamed, however, Mr. Bede Wintermarch *et uxor*, *et filia*, for what do the laity know of such delicate points? I must look into the situation, and gauge the mettle of these new people for myself. For you know I have heard things, Larcom, I have heard things."

"Sir," said Larcom again, with a bob of his yellow head.

"In my absence I ask that you take the opportunity to reflect upon your shortcomings, and resolve to cast aside your lethargic habits — which have become rather too perceptible of late — and strive towards greater punctuality and dispatch. Put a little more steam on, man! Far be it from Tom Dogger to find fault with another human being on this earth, particularly a subordinate, but certainly you can be more assiduous in your exertions, within the metes and bounds of your responsibilities as per Mrs. Dogger. The silver tea-service, for example, is in a disgraceful state, or so it looks to me. See that something is done about it. There is crockery to be mended, brass-mounting to be polished. There is the wainscot in the parlor. The chime-clock, which persists in striking at intervals of its own manufacture. The bell-handle at my bedside. There is my silver standish here, and the lock on that door behind you; the key will hardly turn in the wards. And there is the broken step in the back-passage that has been creaking for a month of Sundays, and is liable at any time to fail.

Don't tell me you haven't noticed the creaking. If Tom Dogger has noticed the creaking, everyone has noticed the creaking."

"Sir," said Larcom, outwardly pinched and solemn as usual, but inwardly affronted by these aspersions which he knew to be wholly and utterly unjust. They jarred upon his ear and stung his heart. Sadly, it was not the first time he had been so maligned. So much for the grim efficiency he brought each day to the performance of his labors!

"All these items require attention, diligent attention, and have for some time. There are as well above a hundred other things that must be looked to, and which I am sure Mrs. Dogger can point out. See, however, that funds are not squandered unnecessarily upon tradesmen in the process. Remember, Larcom, we all of us here must be frugal. Country law is a poor provider, and Prospect Cottage is not made of gold, nor even gingerbread. Prodigality, extravagance, they are strangers to us. It's a sad selfish dog who burns the house to frighten the mice.

"And do try to comport yourself with greater pride of purpose. Yours is a dignified situation, and like a mirror your habiliments should reflect it. You have oft heard the phrase, no doubt, how the clothes make the man. We absolutely must insist upon your conforming at all times to certain guiding principles of fashion. Tom Dogger cannot have a serving-man roaming about the village in feathered caps and garish stockings like any common lout. For you know I have heard stories, Larcom, I have heard stories, and I have seen you as well, in after-hours, parading yourself through the Low Street and Town End. I must tell you, it reflects very badly upon this office and these chambers."

"Sir." (Larcom externally calm, but internally seething at these fresh slights to his person.)

"And do endeavor to get yourself some vocabulary while you're about it. For a solicitor's man your conversation is rather meagerly furnished. We may be poor as to chattels here, Larcom, but not as to education. Far be it from Tom Dogger as a gentleman to find fault with another's upbringing, particularly a lesser man's, but as an appendage of this office and these chambers you represent me by extension in your personal and professional transactions. You really must learn to be more articulate."

"At once, sir," said Larcom, demonstrating thereby a significant expansion of his lexicon.

The attorney threw on his hat and his good nut-brown coat and stepped from the door, to where his horse and trap were waiting to convey him up the road to the mansion-house. From this same door his lean servant and steward watched him go. As the wheels of the trap went whirling fast away, were there not perhaps wheels of another sort even then whirling round inside the head of Larcom? Apart from the fact that his solemn eyes were sharper than usual, and his mouth more pinched than usual, there was little outward show of it (though if his yellow hair could have curled itself up with indignation, I imagine it would have done so.) Afterward he turned on his heel and very calmly resumed his activities as if nothing whatever had occurred. An inspection of the back of his mind, however, would have revealed the imprint of this latest humiliation suffered at the hands of Mr. Thomas Dogger, and which likely would remain emblazoned there for some time to follow.

From Prospect Cottage the attorney directed his horse into the Skylingden road, really little more than a narrow track diverging from the crossroads just west of the village. As he began the winding ascent to Skylingden, Mr. Dogger's own mind turned itself round to the odd dream of yesternight, which had troubled him mightily. All the morning he had worked — it had distracted him from the usual zealous and active discharge of his lawyerly duties, ashamed as he was to acknowledge it — all the morning he had worked to recall the words the creature at the window had spoken to him. Why had they disturbed him so, those words, causing him such unease that he'd been shaken to wakefulness in the dead of night, a thing that scarcely ever happened to plain country Tom Dogger? Now it was afternoon, and still the solution eluded him — though there was in the voice that had uttered the words something familiar, something of the past, which he could not for the life of him explain. He was exhausted from thinking on it; and as there seemed little else to be done to restore his failed memory, he shrugged the matter off for now and channeled his thoughts instead towards the object of his afternoon's excursion.

Skylingden inhabited again! It had been years since the last tenants had departed, returning into Ayleshire whence they had come. It piqued the inquisitive attorney that his efforts at investigation had come to naught, his attempts to discover the present owner of the house baffled by the municipal authorities; for the records were kept in the county town, and as elsewhere in Talbotshire and every place else such records were sealed, until such time as a legitimate transfer of property was set in motion. Even the considerable legal armamentarium of Mr. Thomas Dogger had been unable to break that seal. This precaution was taken in respect of privacy, and protected by counsel; though ownership of most real property was a matter of common knowledge, without cause for concealment, those who wished to disguise their interests it was felt had every right to do so.

As regards Skylingden Hall, it was all indeed something of a puzzle. The family of Campleman had owned Skylingden, of course, and resided there until some twenty or more years ago. But Mr. Dogger was pretty sure that line had died out — it seemed unimaginable to him that it had not, considering what had transpired — and it was an issue of some personal and professional curiosity to know who owned Skylingden now. To whom could the property have devolved? To what heir? Mr. Dogger didn't think one existed. Had there been creditors with claims upon the estate? Or an escheat? The conclusion seemed inescapable — someone unconnected to the Camplemans had purchased the house. But if so, why had the new freeholder not occupied it sooner? Perhaps there was a suit in the High Court of Chancery. Perhaps Mr. Bede Wintermarch was indeed the owner of Skylingden, despite all intelligence to the contrary. Mr. Dogger this afternoon was of a mind to fish for clues, and perhaps put the question to Mr. Wintermarch rather more directly, should their conversation happen to come round to it. Whether Mr. Wintermarch should choose to answer, and if answering answer truthfully, was of course another matter.

The narrow track climbed higher and higher, the black waters of the lake dropping away on the attorney's left hand as the tall firs, pines, and cedars of Skylingden Wood crowded in around him. Close and still was the air in the forest. The grade was measurably steeper now, with a sharp turn in the road looming just ahead. As Mr. Dogger was negotiating this difficult stretch, going up, he found himself unexpectedly nose to nose with another horse and trap coming down.

When he saw who was driving the other cart, the attorney's personal face darkened a shade, though his professional face, like his servant Larcom's, registered scarcely an iota of change. He brought his vehicle to a stop and touched a finger to his hat; the gentleman coming down the hill did likewise.

"You have been to the new people of Skylingden," said the attorney, more as a declaration of fact than an assumption.

The other gentleman nodded stiffly. He had a smooth, featureless face like pale calfskin, with soft blue eyes and a placid expression. Thin wisps of white hair covered the head beneath his hat; a suit of navy-colored cloth covered the rest of him.

"I have made my compliments to Mr. Wintermarch and his family, yes," said Dr. Hall — for it was he — "and have extended to them a cordial welcome on behalf of all those in the village."

"And what sort of reception did you receive?" asked Mr. Dogger, sitting very straight in his seat with his arms folded.

"A most gracious one, to all effects. They seem to me on the whole an excellent family, if a bit reserved."

"Settling in, are they?"

"Apparently."

"There is a wife and a young daughter, I am told, Wintermarch *uxor et filia.*"

"Yes. The wife is rather a youthful figure herself, for a gentleman of Mr. Wintermarch's years, and the daughter not above nine or ten. A pretty child, she quite resembles her mother. An altogether respectable household. You are embarked upon a similar errand, I expect?"

"You are all perception," smiled the attorney, with just the smallest hint of irony. "But of course it harmonizes well with your calling. A physician must be an attentive and a vigilant ally of his patients, or so I'm informed."

There was a polite but very tangible coolness between these two gentlemen, the cause of which was not immediately evident, but which appeared to be of such long duration that their forced manner towards one another had become a habit neither took notice of any more.

"I wish you joy upon your office," said Dr. Hall, preparing to maneuver his horse and trap around those of the attorney. He had his medical rounds to attend to and already was behind in his schedule.

"What kind of fellow is this Wintermarch?" asked Mr. Dogger, abruptly. "Your professional opinion, if you please, sir. Not to worry, I shan't detain you long."

The doctor paused to digest this unexpected inquiry. His cautious nature urged him to say nothing more, though his common sense saw little harm in disclosing such details as had come his way at the mansion-house. At length his common sense won out.

"Mature, dignified, intelligent; a handsome profile, mustache, side-whiskers. Unexceptionable manners. Neither too stern nor too familiar, and not in the least standoffish towards a stranger calling in the middle of the afternoon."

"He is a city man? From Crow's-end, perhaps?"

"Yes, he is from the city, I believe."

"As I have suspected," said Mr. Dogger.

"But whether from Crow's-end, or Foghampton, or Salthead, or some other place I cannot tell you, as he did not tell me."

"That is disappointing, very disappointing. Though I should think Crow's-end the most likely."

"Yes, I should expect so."

"You could not gather more than this from his conversation?"

"No. I did not remain long. We spoke largely of Skylingden, and of his efforts at improving its present dilapidated condition."

The doctor hesitated again, his eyes full of thought. There was a trifling little something, half shadow, half vapor, stuck fast in his consciousness. It had planted itself there during his interview in the drawing-room of Skylingden, and would not leave. It was nothing of sufficient substance to be spoken of, oh, no; it was in point of fact an illusion, imagination carried to excess, complete bosh and nonsense. It was a product of his own fancy and nothing more. And yet —

Should he or should he not broach the matter? More particularly, should he broach it here, now, and to Mr. Thomas Dogger? His composure wavered for an instant. It was enough; the sleek, shiny gaze of the attorney fastened itself upon the doctor's irresolution, and held there.

"You have something more to add?" he asked.

A further pause, as the doctor weighed his alternatives. They were dismally few in number. Try as he might he could not prize the trifling little something from his mind.

"I have a notion," he answered — slowly, carefully — "I have a notion I have somewhere encountered that family before."

"Where?"

"I can't say. It is little more than an impression, arising from the briefest of audiences. It mystifies me more, and confuses me more, the longer I consider it. Though perhaps I am wrong in charging it to the *family*, for surely it is an impression relating to Mr. Bede Wintermarch alone. I am quite at a loss to understand how I should know either his wife or his daughter."

"Perhaps you had the pleasure of the gentleman's acquaintance when he was a younger man," suggested the attorney. "And he has of course changed much since that time."

"Yes, perhaps that is it."

Crossing the retina of the doctor's memory was an image of the tenants of Skylingden as they had appeared in the drawing-room, and of Mr. Bede Wintermarch in particular. Where before had he seen that austere gentleman of the handsome, hawkish face? *When* before? Beneath the abundance of mustache and side-whisker, the dye-drenched hair, beneath the wrinkles laying siege to the aging countenance, beneath the accumulated alluvium of the years, was there not a telling resemblance to —

The doctor started at the recognition of it. *Gracious God, could it be possible?*

"What is it?" asked Mr. Dogger, working hard to restrain his curiosity. "Do you know him?"

"I can't say. Almost certainly I am mistaken."

"An admirable caution, sir. A false accusation may have material consequences," sniffed the attorney, vexed by the other's indecisiveness.

"I've made no accusation, sir," returned Dr. Hall, sharply. He consulted his watch, frowned, and taking up the reins again guided his horse round the lawyer's trap and away down the hill. Neither parting word nor glance did he leave behind for the attorney's benefit.

"Off you go then, Aesculapius," chuckled Mr. Dogger to himself, as from the corners of his eyes he observed the doctor's retreat. He remained where he was for some little time, inhaling deep thoughts and forest air till long after the rattle of the trap-wheels had faded. He then took whip in hand and resumed his journey, to see for himself what there was to be seen in the drawing-room of Skylingden; while far below the doctor's trap bounced along the coach-road and into the Low Street, the doctor himself having discarded the mystery for now in favor of his patients, who likely were wondering what had become of him.

CHAPTER VII

LORE OF THE LAKE FRIARS

THAT evening as the summer darkness drew lazily on, until nothing of the sun was left but a faint glow behind the ragged dark curtain of the Talbot Peaks, Dr. William Hall, having completed his rounds and his solitary supper, and finding himself thoughtfully a-stroll in the Low Street, in the vicinity of Town End, ascended the file of stone steps that led to the Village Arms. A very pleasant evening it was, with the stars blinking and staring overhead, and a very pleasant hostel too, the Arms — a plump and genial harborage for dusty travelers, a good house with clean rooms, clean beds, and flower-boxes in the windows; a place where the linen was soft and white and smelled of lavender, the food more than exemplary, and the landlord and his staff welcoming and respectful. And not only travelers but others too found refreshment at the Village Arms, for its great oak bar and its entertainments were as valued by the citizens of Shilston Upcot as by those passing through in the coach-road.

The doctor made his way through the yard to the house-door — a very heavy, old-fashioned door, with a tiny pane of glass stuck in the middle of it, head-high and as round as the eye of Skylingden though not nearly so ominous. Walking in he deposited his hat and coat in the entrance-hall, where the boots of the establishment was seated in high chat with a group of idlers and hangers-on, at his station opposite the booking-desk.

"A fine night, doctor, sir!" was the loud salutation of that burly, wild-eyed gentleman of the iron jowls and untidy haircut, grand vizier of boot-blacking and the clothes-brush, and luggage-porter nonpareil, in his close-fitting waistcoat and black calamanco sleeves. Born into this world one Alfred Snorem in the town of Jay, on the farther lakeshore, he was known equally well by his professional name, the Boots of the Village Arms. "A e-normous fine night it is, doctor, sir — for the soomertime's coome on, and as I've heard the soomertime's like to be e-normous fine this yar!" Mr. Snorem spoke always thus, in thunderous exclamations, even when whispering, for he was three parts and a fraction deaf and never sure if he had been heard aright. He had at one time been under-gardener at one of the great houses in the upper village, but had been given the chop, as he was wont to express it, on account of his voice having frightened the cats.

The doctor nodded in acknowledgment of Mr. Snorem and his fellows and walked on through the entrance-hall, having detected the rather less vociferous tones of the landlord in the card-room just ahead. A host of contests were in progress there, he saw, all of them necessitating a good deal in the way of liquid refreshment for the players, which in turn was keeping Mr. John Jinkins, the tall drawer, on the hop at the beer-engine behind the great oak bar. Numbers of people were lounging in chairs along the gallery of windows, holding conversation with one another or watching the players at piquet and ombre and *vingt-et-un*.

In the adjoining lodge-room, to the doctor's right, a clattering game of backgammon was proceeding apace, while the billiard-table beyond the chimney was receiving from its votaries no less than the full measure of their attention. A few weary travelers were draped about the sofas and easy chairs round the hearth, idly perusing the antique newspapers or smoking in tranquil silence, or simply imbibing the atmosphere of a mountain inn (and perhaps recovering their breath owing to the unaccustomed rarity of mountain air.) At the pianoforte a young lady was running through her finger exercises, though not to general acclaim, owing as much to a want of talent as to the odd tuning of the instrument. Over all the company there in the lodge-room hovered the fearsome menagerie of mounted trophy-heads — the frozen images of bison and bear, tapir and peccary, deer and elk, starting out from the oak-paneled walls, and the saber-cat from the chimney-piece — their glassy eyes taking silent stock of the human menagerie below, their shriveled brains contriving perhaps a due measure of revenge for their predicament.

Notable among the staff of the inn was Miss Cherry Ives, the daughter of the landlord. Her earnest, obliging voice, quick, purposeful stride, and industrious activity were everywhere evident, whether hurrying off one or more of the servants on this or that mission, or attending to the requests of patrons, or providing needed assistance to her father. For his part Mr. Nim Ives spent the evening roving about the premises, stopping now in this quarter, now in that, in the lodge-room, in the card-room, in the stable-yard, at the booking-desk, inquiring into this matter or that which might require attention, in the midst of it all joking with the regulars from the village and making merry with his guests, some of whom had only just arrived by the late coach. This, then, was his chief purpose in life, his *raison d'être*: to supply his customers and his friends with humor and good cheer (of which he had much), while leaving to his daughter the supervision of the household staff and the preparation of the comestibles.

The Reverend Mr. Scattergood and his plated spectacles were in evidence in the card-room, absorbed in a game of piquet with Mr. Lash, the village schoolmaster. Mr. Mark Trench and his visitor from afar, Mr. Langley, were present as well, and kitted out with a store of beer and cigars were doing their utmost, by means of sundry clever remarks and dry flashes of wit, to fluster the vicar and his opponent, who were struggling mightily to keep track of their scores amid the distraction.

Observing the well-charged glasses in the hands of so many of the company, the doctor bethought himself again of his solitary supper, and of the meagerness of his cupboard *vis-à-vis* the stronger waters; whereupon he stepped to the bar for a pint of sixpenny spruce from the busy Mr. Jinkins, before gradually immersing himself in the ebb and flow of conversation in the room.

As darkness had fallen little was visible now from the row of gallery windows, which were composed of old diamond-paned lattices, and where during the day a very pleasing view of Lonewater through the trees could be obtained. Several of the casements were standing open to the night, to admit fresh air. Posted beside one such casement while observing a foursome at whist, the doctor heard a sudden rush of wind and feathers outside. Moments later came an eerie cry, followed by something like an owl's shrill laugh. The doctor's face of calfskin paled to an even fainter hue, if such were possible. His eyes narrowed as he peered through the iron bars in the window. He repressed a shudder at the eerie cry, which he knew to be that of a teratorn on the hunt. As a precaution he gingerly shut the casement, and lifting his glass found that it was nearly empty; which discovery sent him off again in the direction of Mr. Jinkins and the beer-engine.

After a time the squire of Dalroyd and his guest, having exhausted their store of banter on the piquet-players — it appeared that as usual the cagey Mr. Lash was winning and the vicar was not, an arrangement with which the reverend gentleman was rather too familiar, and which he attributed to the designs of an inscrutable Providence — after a time the squire and Oliver wandered across to the oaken bar where Mr. Tony Arkwright, the veterinary, and Mr. Ives had been joined by Dr. Hall and his fresh pint.

"Jolly pleased to see you, landlord," said the lounging Mark. "There is something my friend Mr. Langley here is rather keen to inquire of you. I have put him off it for a day at least, as I'm pretty sure there's little to it, but here we are, and here you are, and so there's no getting round it, I suppose — besides which he'll plague me no end till he's had his answer."

"And what might that something be, sir?" asked Mr. Ives, turning his lively countenance to the visitor from Crow's-end.

"Have you an elderly clergyman lodging here at the Arms?" Oliver asked. "I inquire only because Mark and I had occasion to encounter such a person yesterday morning at Dalroyd dock. He was walking along the shore with his wife, or a woman we took to be his wife. The both of them were looking rather poorly, with much anxiety and concern in their faces."

"An el-der-ly cler-gy-man," Mr. Ives repeated slowly, with a frown and a thoughtful rub of his chin. "Surely not the vicar there, sir? Our Mr. Scattergood? He's the most likely clergyman to happen on roundabout, and the *only* one, to speak truth, though he's not elderly as I make out."

"Rather not. This clergyman proceeded to approach us with a few of questions, and when we could provide no satisfactory answers he and his companion walked off without an exchange of introductions. As a result neither Mark nor I has the slightest notion who they were, but it seemed reasonable to suppose they were guests here at the Arms."

Mr. Ives shook his head. "To my knowledge, sirs, there's no aged clergyman with us now, nor has been at any time recent. But if you'll pardon me a moment I'll consult the final authority." Looking round he hallo'd for his daughter, who arrived at the bar in short order, a picture of bustle and efficiency in shiny dark hair and ringlets.

"Cherry, m'dear," said her father, "have we a clergyman lodged in the house? An ancient sort, and with a wife perhaps?"

The reply of Miss Ives was in the negative.

"Have we had such a person, and with a wife perhaps, lodged in the house this week past?"

No, Father, they had not.

"Have any of you seen a clergyman and his wife — aside from our Mr. and Mrs. Scattergood, of course — walking in the village of late?" pursued Oliver. "A couple passing through by coach perhaps, and who might have found time for a ramble during the change of horses."

No, no one had seen such a pair.

"At what time precisely was it you met these people, sir?" inquired the landlord.

"At about half-past eight in the morning."

"Ah, well, then it wouldn't be a *public* coach, sir, as there's no conveyance from either direction arriving before eleven o' the clock. You're welcome to examine the road book at the desk to substantiate the fact. As to private carriages, now, I couldn't swear; no, sir, I could not. What say you to private carriages, Cherry, m'dear?"

"No clergyman as I've noted, Father, on any of the private drags," replied the capable Cherry.

"If this clergyman and his wife were at Dalroyd dock t'other day, at the time you report, sir, then perhaps they've lodged with a private party in the village. Cherry, m'dear?"

"No one, Father. I've heard of no clergyman about."

"Well, sir, if my Cherry says there's no clergyman in the village, then it's so," said Mr. Ives, clapping hands to hips and smiling, "as she knows all that goes on for miles roundabout, what with her women friends, the vicar's wife, and Miss Violet of the waffle-house, and Miss Mowbray there at Gray Lodge — your cousin, Mr. Trench — and her aunt, Mrs. Fielding. There's little that escapes *their* attention! If the women have seen no clergyman, sir, then there's no clergyman to be seen."

"That's the case truly, in my view," agreed Mr. Arkwright, with a nod of his helmet of short dark hair.

A rather confused silence followed on the part of Oliver, after which he continued —

"Is it possible they could have lodged at another inn? At the Waterman in Jay, perhaps?"

The landlord admitted it was possible, but not likely, as the distance from Shilston Upcot to the village of Jay was deemed excessive, particularly for an aged couple in apparent poor health.

"Might you specify further as to the externals and the manners of these people?" asked Mr. Arkwright, knitting his long bushy brow.

Oliver responded as best he could, with some desultory assistance from Mark; though both gentlemen were obliged to admit that the old couple were rather plain and unremarkable, apart from the strange, sad looks in their faces — so careworn, as though their last light had gone out.

"What was it the clergyman asked you, Mr. Langley?" inquired Cherry. "The questions you had no satisfactory answers for?"

"They concerned a child, or so we thought at the outset. He asked us, first myself, then Mark, in each instance using precisely the same words, whether we had seen their girl. In the end we concluded that this 'girl' was not a child at all but a dog, which had gone missing somewhere about the lake."

"Did they have a name for their dog?"

"Yes. They called her Edith."

At these words the landlord's forthright and jovial expression underwent a profound change. A cloud settled over his features; his gray eyes darkened; his smile vanished, erased by a little shuffling motion of the fingers of one hand upon his lips. It was clear that the name meant something to him, but just what it was the landlord appeared unwilling to share with them; nor did he respond favorably to Oliver's subsequent queries.

"This dog, it's a mystery, I'll warrant," said Mr. Ives, by way of terminating his part in the discussion. He cleared his voice, and recollecting that his attendance was required in the lodge-room, hastily propelled himself thereward.

"Jolly odd of him," murmured the squire, showing genuine interest in the topic for the first time.

"Whatever can be wrong?" asked Cherry, mystified by her father's behavior.

"I believe that hearing the name Edith has disturbed your father in some way," said Oliver.

"I don't know why that should be, sir, for I know of no one by the name of Edith — either dog or person — and neither, I think, does my father."

"It seems to me that clergyman must have friends in the village," said Oliver in a little while, after Cherry had departed on an errand of her own. "She simply hasn't spotted him, that's all. What say you, Mark?"

The squire answered with a grunt, and swallowed some of his beer; which response told Oliver that his friend had no firm opinion on the matter.

Throughout most of the discussion Dr. Hall had remained largely his placid self, but now, as Oliver and Mark turned to him for his counsel, they instead found him seeking yet another glass from long Jinkins. The doctor was not by nature a toper; a single pint of an evening normally sufficed, as the physician subscribed more to the benefits of hot tea and coffee than of alcohol. Mark understood this, though Oliver, being a stranger, did not. By the time the doctor returned — his expression subtly altered, as though he were recovering from some private discomfort of mind — the stream of conversation had flowed on to the subject of Skylingden, and the excursion the previous morning of Mark and Oliver in the sloop, and the sighting of the short-face at the mouth of the cave. Mention by Oliver of certain of the architectural features of Skylingden, as viewed from the boat, and what appeared to be scattered ruins lying on the verge of the summit, brought a response not from the doctor but from Mr. Arkwright.

"O' course, Mr. Langley, there hasn't been always a Skylingden Hall there in the high wood. The mansion-house was, in point of fact, thrown up hard by the remains of quite another edifice entirely."

"What edifice was that?" asked Oliver, his antiquarian interests suddenly a-stir. "Tell me, the ruined structures there — the gray stone blocks, the fragments of masonry walls — they once were part of it?"

"They were."

"And what was it that stood there?"

"It was an abbey," replied Mr. Arkwright. "The home of a religious order calling themselves the Lake Friars. They were hermits, and very deep ones, too. The abbey was their mountain sanctuary, where the friars and their brethren gents could meditate and keep near the Lord, for being hermits they were given much to the contemplative life."

"The name is wholly unknown to me."

"As it is to many, o' course. It was years upon years ago the friars built their abbey, from bricks and mortar and good Talbotshire stone. They were by all accounts the devoutest o' gents, tending to their own business and mixing little with village folk. What is more they refused to accept alms, which was either a good thing or a bad thing; and in that, they differed much from certain of your modern orthodoxical clergy."

"Modern orthodoxical clergy," smiled Mark, sourly, as he lighted a fresh cigar.

"I am aware of certain of the squire's unconventional attitudes towards religion, churches, and churchmen in particular," said Oliver. "No need to point up the contrast further, Mr. Arkwright."

"As I have said," the veterinary went on, warming now to his subject, "these friars o' the lake lived mostly in seclusion, in their cells there and their cloisters within the abbey, and all in all seemed to conduct themselves like proper monastic gents. Over time, though, this seclusion o' theirs gave rise to suspicion on the part of the villagers. It was rumored about that the Lake Friars were not all as they seemed in their externals; that in fact they'd renounced their vows of obedience to the Almighty, and what was worse, had resorted to the practice of black and secret arts. It was said at the time they'd been corrupted by devils, which, taking the long view of history, would be my view as well."

"But what should be the cause of it? However should the townsfolk have acquired such a notion?"

Mr. Arkwright laughed, his large yellow teeth bulging from his tiny prison of a mouth. "Friars — papists! Weren't that enough? Though there's little more to go on but stories, o' course, and as to how much truth they may hold, the stories as were told to me by my father and his brother, is in my view a moot question. My father and his brother, unlike myself, were gents not much given to palaver, particularly in matters o' such kind, and so the stories are few. But consider this example. It seems that every now and again one of these friars, in his black habit, his cowl and his sandals, would escape from the abbey, or perhaps be shut out of it, and so find his way to the village. A great stir always would be caused by it, what with the friar's having about him every appearance of madness — wild of eye and raving, and drooling from the lips like a hound struck with the rabies, and cursing all and sundry with a foul tongue. From stories such as this, which were repeated more than a few times, on more than a few occasions, it's plain how those in the village might have sifted the matter, and formed the opinion that black and secret arts were behind it all.

"One summer round Bartholomewtide, after yet another of these episodes, and after enough emotion had been aroused, the townsfolk, afraid for their souls and their salvation, confronted the abbot. There was a hard tussle, but all to no purpose, o' course. An assault on the abbey itself was next devised, but when the people were arrived there they found no friars, none at all — the sly monastic gents had cut their lucky before any harm could come to 'em. The villagers of Shilston Upcot, in fear and rage, burned the abbey and all its contents, its church and cloisters and dormitories, and razed them to the ground."

"Stout fellows!" exclaimed Mark, with an approving rap of his hand upon the bar. "Jolly sensible, brave-hearted citizens we had in years gone by, Noll, as far from our weak-as-water species of today as can be imagined. But naturally, I am out of joint with the times."

"I must admit, I can't see that sort of thing happening here and now," said Oliver. "It must have been a frightening spectacle."

"The bricks and mortar as you've spied at the summit," said Mr. Arkwright, "are the remains of the abbey foundations. I've picked my way through them myself while riding round the high wood. When the mansion-house was built there beside the ruins, the family that put it up, the Camplemans, used surviving building-stones from the abbey in the constructing of it."

"So you see, Noll, how Skylingden Hall was fashioned from the rubble of a house of hobgoblins," smiled the squire, smoking ferociously, "and why it is there should be so much gossip concerning the tenants of such an unholy habitation. *Ha!*"

"Yes, a word now about this Mr. Wintermarch and his family," said Oliver. "I have learned this evening, Dr. Hall, that you yourself paid a call on them just today."

The doctor, lifting himself from the reverie into which he had fallen, could not deny the fact, and so was obliged to offer a brief narration of his visit. Although he tried very hard, he could not avoid relating how he had found something unaccountably familiar in the family there, how Mr. Thomas Dogger, whom he had met in the Skylingden road, had been intrigued and puzzled by the doctor's suspicion; and how in the end it all was due, more than likely, to the doctor's fanciful imagination — though of this conclusion he seemed not nearly so convinced as before.

Which remarks but served to fire Oliver's own imagination, and rouse the curiosity of Mark as well, for anything that intrigued and puzzled the sanctimonious Tom Dogger was of interest to the squire. Mark knew there was an antipathy of long standing between Dr. Hall and the inquisitive attorney, which he had ascribed to their widely divergent personalities, or perhaps to some professional disagreement; though in truth he had never known the root cause of it for certain, nor known anyone else who knew it.

By the time they departed the inn later that night, and under a breathless canopy of stars gained the road and so made the ascent to Dalroyd, both the squire and his visitor — that very same squire, who earlier hadn't cared a fig so far as Skylingden was concerned — were determined they should inspect the tenants of Skylingden for themselves the very next day.

CHAPTER VIII

THE TENANTS OF SKYLINGDEN

"TINKER, my lad, you are beyond doubt the most unsightly specimen at Dalroyd — apart from your master, of course," said Mr. Mark Trench, as he leaped into the stirrups. His horse, a sixteen-hands bay gelding with a head as large as a fiddle-case, a barrel chest, coarse, sturdy legs, and a hint of a sway in his back, pawed the ground and whinnied with delight as his master stepped aboard.

"He's not so ill-looking a beast, Mark," said Oliver, springing atop the handsome chestnut mare provided him by the Dalroyd groom. "Frankly, you could do worse — a farmer's crop-eared cob, for example, or a broken-down cart-horse, or a dun pony with a Shire-sized temper. To my mind, you know, Tinker seems rather an agreeable old fellow. Reliable. Steady. Devoted."

"Hush!" the squire admonished him. "You'll not want to feed his vanity, Noll. Didn't you see his ears just then, hearkening to you? He'll be getting some jolly high-handed notions now, and thinking the world of himself, rather like our village solicitor. Soon I'll not be allowed to approach the lad without a fistful of grain, after which he'll promptly buck me off the moment I've landed in the saddle."

"There are occasions when I feel these animals do hear what we say, by which I mean they understand our words. Horses, hounds — they can be remarkably intuitive at times. Do you recollect that spaniel of Professor Humphreys's, at old Antrobus? He appeared always to know when our good tutor was about to slip off to the wine-vaults, and would post himself at the door with the professor's walking-stick in his jaws."

"Tinker is pining for Jolly-boy. I know it, I can feel it. You see how he peers round with those soulful eyes of his? He's so very accustomed to having his tiny companion with him on these rides. Well, Tinker, my lad, we're calling at Skylingden today, and it's not the sort of errand for a fellow like Jolly-boy. Calling on polite society with one's horse is *de rigueur*, you understand, but carting along one's dog is simply not on. I'll lay you fifty guineas he'd not be welcome there. Nor should I wish to have him from my sight during our visit, particularly not with Splayfoot roaming the wood."

"Certainly the groom there at the mansion-house would look after him," said Oliver.

But the squire was adamant, he would sooner trust his terrier to a butcher's boy or a drunken peddler. Which remark might have caused his own stableman to scowl, had he heard it; but fortunately that amiable gentleman was now occupied about his other duties. It was plain the welfare of Jolly-boy was of utmost concern to the master of Dalroyd.

Oliver looked up and about at the dull morning, disappointing heir to the brilliant starlit sky of yesternight. A drab, gray, lumpish morning it was, very much like the drab, gray, lumpish countenance of his friend the squire beside him, who himself was taking stock of the day through his uneven pair of eyes, too small, too narrow, too closely placed. Beyond the trees the motionless surface of Lonewater lay spread before them like the skin of an enormous black-pudding. The squire sniffed the air, delighting in the dewy fresh aroma of the trees. It was, apart from the overcast, not an altogether unhealthful morning, not too cold, and without a whisper of wind; nearly ideal, in point of fact, for a leisurely trot up the Skylingden road.

"How long have you had him?" asked Oliver, in reference to Tinker, as the gentlemen swung their horses into the coach-road.

"Twelve years. He was foaled here," said Mark, with more than a little pride. "Truly, he's a gentle sort for such an ungainly monster. He's a good goer and has a tender mouth, though he steps a bit short at the off side — Arkwright tells me there's no help for it now — and is perfectly pleased with his lot. What more should I ask? Never another horse like him shall I find, never in my life. I've no idea what Jolly-boy and I would do without him. Yes, it's so, Tinker, my lad!" As he spoke he patted the horse briskly upon the neck and shoulders, to reassure him that his place at Dalroyd was secure. The bond between master and monster was strong indeed.

"Tinker and Jolly-boy," murmured Oliver. "And so your household is complete, or very nearly."

"And jolly sufficient a household it is for a man such as I, thank you very much. But again you're forgetting Smithers the Indispensable, who keeps me organized and on my toes. Good Lord, he virtually runs Dalroyd for me! Look here, what else could a gentleman want? A life of hounds and horses, cider and spruce, billiards and tobacco, country sport and country duties. I tell you, Noll, I'm in a jolly comfortable position."

He eased back in the saddle, very satisfied with himself apparently, and looked the country round with a proprietorial air — which was only natural, as so much of that country belonged to him.

"But it's been my impression you were 'marooned' here in Talbotshire," said Oliver, with feigned puzzlement. "Stranded in the provinces, as it were."

"I tell you again, you'll pay no heed to what my young cousin Mowbray has to say," retorted Mark, his eyes roving about the files of gigantic timber rising from the hillside. "She hasn't the depth of experience to know whereof she speaks. She prattles on about a great many things, it's true, but her breadth of knowledge of any *one* thing is negligible. As for yourself, sir, I should invite you to ponder the adage, 'Guest ever, welcome never.' Perhaps, Mr. Langley, if you were to confine your 'impressions' to your studies of your dusty Roman Spaniard friend and his *epigrammata*, you'll find you'll get along much better here in Talbotshire — in the provinces, as you call them."

"Ah, but was it *sensible* for me to come into Talbotshire, to Shilston Upcot?" countered a slyly grinning Oliver. "After all, why should anyone sensible want to come here?"

"*Ha!*" growled Mark, and giving a firm tug at his black beaver-hat, poured forth a stream of mutterings as regards city folk in general, and Crow's-end sorts in particular.

Oliver suppressed a laugh at the many contradictions in the character of his old Salthead companion. Dear old Mark! *He* needn't fear anyone's getting too close to him — too close to the quick, as it were — for his defenses against self-disclosure were reflexive and unerringly sure.

Passing by on their right was Gray Lodge, the home of the young lady with the shallow depth of experience. It was a picturesque, stone-built cottage of two floors, neither too large nor too small in scope, with a high, sloping roof of gray thatch — a wondrously thick and furry sort of thatch, with rounded meandering ridges, and gentle curves that embraced the upper windows like brows over latticed eyes. Oliver was about to offer something witty concerning a particular inmate of the lodge, but a glance from Mark warned him off it. The squire had fallen into one of his moods, and so the two gentlemen ambled on in silence at an easy, steady pace. On their left was the steeple of St. Lucy of the Lake, rearing up from below, and in the timbered hollow formed by the side of the church and the hillside supporting the road, the tombstones and other memorials of the parish churchyard. The squire gazed upon that lonely spot, as he always did when he rode past it, with a solemn expression, and a gravity otherwise unknown to him in his everyday existence. He said nothing about it to Oliver, however, and before long both church and churchyard were left behind.

Arrived at the crossroads, which spot was marked by a grimy milestone, the riders turned their mounts into the narrow track leading to the high wood. Their ascent of the Skylingden road was a quiet one, apart from the clink of their horses' shoes and the jingling of bridle-bits, and the chatter of jays in the forest, very pleasant music conducive to introspection. As they rode along their minds were filled with thoughts of what lay before them. What manner of people might these Wintermarches be? Why had they chosen Skylingden Hall of all places to inhabit? What of the gossip that had been circulating through the village? What of the vague familiarity Dr. Hall had sensed while among them? Could it be these new neighbors were not who they represented themselves to be? Was there a deeper mystery here — or was it simply country people's common mistrust of strangers?

Oliver, a stranger to Shilston Upcot himself, but one fired with interest in the mythology of Skylingden, was today determined to observe and record in his mental notebook every detail of his visit to the fabled mansion-house. His luminous eyes eagerly scanned the road as it wound upward. As the way grew steeper the forest grew thicker and wilder. The birdsong faded, as though perhaps even the jays found Skylingden Wood a disagreeable place. The limbs of the taller pines met and mingled overhead, blotting out the drabness of the sky. Silence and shadow plunged in all around. Throughout the whole of the journey the squire maintained a cautious watch, mindful of the antics of Splayfoot and not wishing to stumble upon him unawares. Moreover there was, summer or no, ever the threat of saber-cats in a darksome wood such as this. But neither bear nor cat did he detect, nor did the horses, the both of them remaining calm and untroubled as they trotted on.

At length the summit drew near. As the horsemen gained the final rise they came upon a length of discolored, ivy-grown wall — the perimeter wall of Skylingden estate. It was composed of an assortment of bricks of uneven dimension, with an entrance framed by two gate-piers, square and plain, each surmounted by a heavy stone ball. The gates themselves were of molded iron in the form of arabesques of leaves, spikes, and stars, very fancifully wrought, and very rusted; what was more, they were unlocked. The gentlemen dismounted and led their horses through, shutting the gates behind them. What appeared to be a keeper's lodge stood just inside. No one came forth to greet them, however, and after a brief inspection they concluded the lodge was a derelict. In consequence they regained their saddles and proceeded on towards the mansion-house.

Through the avenue of trees directly ahead Skylingden Hall began to take shape, growing ever larger as they approached. It was a very large structure indeed, with several wings, all of them in a state of sorry disrepair, as was evident at once to Oliver. The shrubbery had grown up round the house to considerable proportions, in places obscuring whole tiers of windows; everywhere, moss and ivy competed for possession of its dreary frontage. The old bluish-purple stone was pitted and worn, the dressings cracked and crumbling. Gables and walls alike were streaked and crossed with oak timbers, dingy chocolate-colored planks badly in need of painting. The tiled roof was heavily stained with lichen. There were bricks missing from some of the chimneys, as though a giant had been gnawing at the stacks. On the whole it was not the prettiest of architectural pictures.

They rode round towards the stable-yard, behind what appeared to be a servants' hall, now abandoned, and heard from the barns a whinny to which Tinker immediately responded. Steps had been taken at least in this regard, as the stables looked to be in better trim by far than the house itself. A chaise could be seen in the coach-house, and from a distance looked to be in credible shape.

"I incline towards their being not so well off, which accords with the view of landlord Ives. Nor have they been well off for some time," said Mark, lazily wringing suppositions from all he saw about him like water from a sponge. "There's but a single carriage and a pair of nags, it seems. The shrubberies are sorely in need of trimming, everywhere you look. The vinery is wholly overrun. Look there at the condition of the terrace-walk, the barge-boards on that line of gables, those intricate moldings there — "

"But the new family have been in residence for only a short time," Oliver pointed out. "You can't expect them to have all in apple-pie order straight away. What is more they are simply tenants, or so we have been led to believe. Is it not the freeholder who is responsible for maintenance of the property?"

"Certainly, Noll, but there are things a gentleman notices. For instance — *where is everyone?* Have you spotted any servants?"

"Not a living leg."

"Why is there no bustle, no to-ing and fro-ing? Where is the groundskeeper? Where the laborers? Do you see any evidence of their activity? Where is the groom? I'll tell you where he is — *no*-where, because there jolly isn't one. And where is that groundskeeper? Same place — there isn't one. Why was there no man at the gates or along the avenue to meet us and inquire into our business here? Don't you think it odd? And consider again the equipage — but a single chaise and two horses. Rather a paltry turn-out, I'd call it, for a gentleman of means."

"Perhaps the family are taking the air in another vehicle," suggested Oliver. "Perhaps they have a brace of them."

The squire tipped back his beaver and shook his head, with a tolerant smile playing about his lips. "There's jolly little to puzzle out here, Noll; it is just as we've heard in town. Oh, indeed, they've had some of the tradesmen out to putter away in the stables, that's clear, and perhaps inside the house as well. Apart from that there's little to please the eye. Hardly anything has changed since I last visited, when the house lay empty. I am convinced what we have here in this Mr. Wintermarch is a reasonably successful city man, but certainly not a rich one, who has retired into the country and for whatever cause has chosen Shilston Upcot and Skylingden to make his home. The family are tenants here, of that I'm certain. As I've heard landlord Nim express it, virtually the whole of their income must be applied to the rent on quarter-days."

"Surely you won't hold it against them. It isn't everyone who is fortunate enough to be squire of Dalroyd."

"How sadly you mistake me, Noll, for I assure you I've no such prejudice," returned Mark, with a wrinkling of his craggy brow. "In point of fact I am heartened by the arrangement, for as tenants these new people are unlikely to be as insufferable as certain freeholders now resident in this village."

"Ah, to be sure, I understand you now. You think you'll be able to converse with this Mr. Wintermarch as though he were any agreeable fellow in the street, to discuss with him matters of common interest, without his excess of pride coming between you," ventured Oliver.

"Just so. *Excess* is indeed the key factor. Consider my situation, now, consider Dalroyd. It's a modest estate, tidy, practical, profitable, having nothing more than is needed for the running of it, and so I manage it quite easily, without excessive show. All is balanced, all is in due proportion. Excess, the overstepping of proper bounds, leads to pride in the accomplishment, and pride leads to insufferability. All in all I prefer a simpler, humbler existence. One should strive always for simplicity in one's life, Noll. It makes for jolly easy sleeping at night."

"I shall endeavor to remember all you say. By the by, did you not just tell me it was Mr. Smithers the Indispensable who ran Dalroyd for you?"

"*Virtually* runs it, I believe, were the exact words, Mr. Langley," the squire replied, "though you comprehend my meaning. Come along, then, my lad" — these latter words to Tinker, a gentleman less inclined to captious arguments — "there's little more to interest us round here, I warrant."

As no one had yet emerged from the stables to take charge of Tinker and the chestnut — confirming Mark in his opinion in this regard — the gentlemen returned to the grounds fronting the mansion-house and there dismounted. They picketed the horses on a little plat of grass beside a cluster of fir trees, and from there made their way to the entrance.

The house soared above them to a height of three stories, with a great top-hamper of decoration in its sloping tiled roof, saw-edge gables, and brooding nests of chimney-stacks. Two large wings, dismal and weather-beaten, extended to either side of the main hall and entrance; the remainder of the house roamed here and there about the hinder grounds, with other wings, just as dismal and weather-beaten, protruding at odd and often unexpected angles. Gloom, decay, and an eerie quiet pervaded the scene.

The entrance was framed by a heavy stone porch, reached by a short flight of steps leading up from the gravel drive. The porch was an elaborate affair rising the entire height of the house. At the foot of it was the doorway, arched and pedimented, the door itself being recessed and in shadow. A coat-of-arms, with mantlings, crest, and supporters, lay just above; above that was a three-light window framed by octagonal angle turrets, and above that a high gable topped by crow-steps. In the flat of the gable-wall was an ornate round window of some size, an architectural curiosity that immediately drew Oliver's interest. It was a rose or Catherine window, he saw, very elegantly fashioned, with intricate, carved mullions converging towards a circular hub, like spokes in a wheel. Tracery marking out the letters *S* and *C*, elaborately intertwined, occupied the center of the hub. The porch and window were so placed as to be visible through a wide break in the trees, which extended to the verge of the promontory, allowing the window to be seen from far and wide. Here then, Oliver observed, in this glowing work of impressive artistic achievement, was the sinister eye of Skylingden.

"What a magnificent piece!" he exclaimed, standing before the towering facade in admiration of its most outstanding feature. "Wondrously executed, and very nearly perfect. And so large! It's quite as fine a work of its kind as any I ever have seen. Whose idea do you suppose it was?"

"The original builder, I should suspect," returned Mark. "One of the species of Campleman. Belike he spotted it in a textbook of architectural design and had it copied for his own purposes. It's not an uncommon practice."

"Its chief purpose would seem to be the illumination of that room up there, whatever it is, for you can see how the trees round it give way, permitting the light to filter through. All the more important as the house faces due north. Hmmm. The letters *S* and *C* as inscribed there represent Skylingden and Campleman, I should imagine."

They mounted the steps and approached the shadowy door, the squire announcing their arrival by means of a few sharp raps at the knocker. It was some time before the knock was answered, by a sober, snowy-pated footman who took their cards and promptly returned to that obscurity from which he had emerged. After the lapse of another few minutes he reappeared to escort the visitors into a dark foyer, and so through a low archway, along a dim passage, up a broad staircase of oak with richly carved newels, down a dark and silent gallery, and at last into a high-ceilinged chamber that was rather brighter than might be expected, considering the shadowy path they had taken to get there.

Most of the light in the room, the gentlemen noted at once, came from the round window, which was looking down on them from above, and through which the drab cloudy day was shining.

"The master — will be along — directly," said the footman, with a painful stutter. "Pleased — to find yourself — seats there." And so he withdrew again into obscurity.

"It seems to me we've answered the question," said Oliver.

"Question?"

"As to the particular chamber harboring the dreaded eye of Skylingden. It's the drawing-room, to be sure. Not so very mysterious."

"I should think it a natural choice for such an architectural singularity," returned the squire, his glance straying curiously about the apartment.

"It is a comfortable chamber," Oliver remarked. "And reasonably well maintained, considering the woeful state of the exterior."

If not the most cheerful of drawing-rooms, it was at the very least not an uncheerful one. A carved stone hearth with a fire burning in it, ornamental cornices, worsted tapestry-work, a floor-cloth with a trefoil pattern, and lustrous oak wainscoting — all these the gentlemen saw there. Portrait paintings and bookcases, a looking-glass and *étagère*, a sofa or two, a rosewood table, high-backed chairs and easy dittos, these were there as well. The furnishings were neither elaborate nor showy, but serviceable and of decent workmanship. Everything in the apartment appeared to be in good order and neatly arranged.

"I can't disagree with you, Noll," admitted Mark with a frown, upon completing his examination. He seemed disappointed to have found so little fault with the place. "It's in jolly fair shape — though gloomy for all that, despite yonder great staring eye. There certainly are no gloomy rooms at Dalroyd, I can tell you."

"You forget it is a gloomy morning. I don't believe they can be occupying the whole of the house, as it's far too large. Most likely they've opened up selected apartments for use, here in the hall and in the adjoining wings."

Before the squire could respond the door from the gallery opened, and a gentleman of respectable appearance stepped into their presence. He was attired in a brown day coat and dark trousers, a snuff-colored waistcoat, spotted necktie, and half-boots. His was a mature figure, with a face that had been handsome and hawkish in its youth, and still was handsome and hawkish today, if a degree faded. His hair was full and long but rather too black, with a wilderness of side-whisker that met beneath his chin. He had as well a pair of thick dark mustaches, penetrating eyes much wrinkled at the edges, a blade-like nose, and a heavy mouth. The gentleman introduced himself as Mr. Bede

Wintermarch, and welcomed the visitors to his home. His voice was strong for a man of his years, though a bit on the dry side. When he spoke it was in an austere monotone with little in the way of inflection. He informed the gentlemen that his wife and daughter would be along shortly to join them. The family had, he said, received visitors several times during the week, and were looking forward to meeting the squire of Dalroyd and his guest, about whom they had heard. He thanked them for presenting themselves at Skylingden, but stopped short of expressing a desire that they become more closely acquainted in future.

"Are you by chance from Crow's-end, Mr. Wintermarch?" asked Oliver, boldly, after they had seated themselves and a maidservant had delivered the tea and sundries. "I inquire only because I am from Crow's-end myself, and am here visiting for the season."

The question elicited what Oliver interpreted as some unease in their host, which the gentleman attempted to conceal by a prolonged clearing of his vocal cords.

"Yes, Mr. Langley. I was in the commercial line — finance — for a host of years there, and am now retired," was the eventual reply. "My wife desired a more tranquil, less hurried existence, and so prevailed upon me to abandon the fatigues of the city for country air. She had heard good reports of your little community of Shilston Upcot here in Talbotshire — and so here we are arrived, and settled."

Additions to the party now made their appearance in the shape of a woman of about thirty years, rather plain and somber, and a pretty little girl aged about ten. The gentlemen rose.

"My wife Sepulchra," said Mr. Wintermarch, "and our daughter Rowena."

The daughter bore an evident likeness to both her parents, though her features seemed to derive chiefly from her father. She said almost nothing during the whole of the interview, her mother little more. Both were politely attentive, sitting composedly by but claiming little share in the conversation. When Mrs. Wintermarch did speak it was on matters relating to the mansion-house and her husband's plans for its renewal. She was much younger than he, and evidently of a submissive temperament.

"And so you too are from Crow's-end, Mrs. Wintermarch? Originally, that is?" pursued Oliver the bold.

"Yes," the woman answered, hesitantly, after a look of caution from her marriage-partner. "My father and mother were close friends of the Wintermarch family. That is how my husband and I became acquainted."

"And he informs us that it was you who suggested Talbotshire for his retirement."

"Yes."

"Had you visited here before?"

"No, never. I must confess to you, Mr. Langley, I don't quite know why I chose it — a kind of feeling, I suppose, which told me we belonged here. A quiet home in these mountains, far from city life, is what we sought. We looked out for a comfortable house, and discovered that Skylingden Hall was to let."

Mark directed a faintly triumphant smile towards Oliver, in confirmation of his assertions respecting these *tenants* of Skylingden. He then volunteered a compliment as regards the condition of the stables, which seemed to unleash Mr. Wintermarch a little, who it turned out had a certain fondness for horses. *Why then had he only a pair of them?* was the question that came immediately to the minds of both the squire and Oliver.

"Now you must tell us something of yourselves, and of your fine estate of Dalroyd, Mr. Trench," said Mr. Wintermarch, getting up a little smile of his own, which seemed to derive more from pleasure at a change of subject than from any genuine interest in his visitors.

The remainder of their half-hour together was made over to table-talk, the squire chatting of Dalroyd and Tinker and cigars, and Oliver of epigrams by a dusty Roman Spaniard, and the both of them of this and that, and concluded with an invitation to the Wintermarches to call at Dalroyd, so soon as it was convenient for them. This elicited a response that dangled somewhere between a yes and a no, like a stray note endeavoring to find its proper key, and so was not nearly so enthusiastic as might have been hoped. Mr. Wintermarch having consulted his watch three times in the past minute, the visitors recollected that they must go; and offering their *adieus* to the host and his family, were shown from the apartment by the same snowy-pated footman who had led them there.

As they were traversing the dark and silent gallery towards the staircase, they happened by a room whose door stood slightly ajar. A servant within was that moment arranging the curtains at an open window. The curtains being momentarily parted, a gray flood of daylight streamed into the room. From the corners of their eyes the gentlemen glimpsed there a heavy, feathered creature of some kind, in full silhouette, roosting on a perch. They thought it at first a product of the taxidermist's art; but at the last moment the head of the creature swiveled on its body, as if following their brief journey past the doorway.

The gentlemen spoke not a word to one another until they had retrieved their horses, cleared the iron gates, and were trotting down the Skylingden road.

"Did you see that, Noll?" asked the squire, looking straight before him as he guided Tinker along the narrow track.

"I did," replied Oliver, upon the chestnut.

"What do you think it was we saw there?"

"A bird of some type."

"A parrot?"

"No. Far too large and heavy, and the wrong shape."

"A hawk?"

"No."

"A crow?"

"Rather not!"

"A blue jay, then?"

"Hardly, Mark!"

"What say you to an owl?"

Oliver nodded slowly. "A monstrous large owl indeed."

"Cod or genuine?" asked Mark.

"Genuine. It watched us as we strode past. I tell you, Mark, it sent a shiver through me."

This exchange gave birth to a period of quiet rumination, so that it was some little time before the gentlemen spoke again. When they did it was the squire who broke the silence, by bending forward over the neck of Tinker and addressing his horse on a different matter entirely.

"Your opinion, Tinker, my lad," said he. "I give you *Sepulchra*. Jolly odd name for a woman, don't you agree?"

CHAPTER IX

THE CAPTAIN IS INDISPOSED

HAVING made his point as regards one jolly odd thing, the thought came now to Mark that today was as decent a day as any for him to introduce Oliver to Captain Hoey — a jolly odd sort of thing himself, the Captain, though the term "irregular" had perhaps gained greater currency roundabout. A call at the Captain's residence being thereby proposed, it was eagerly seconded by the visitor from Crow's-end. As the two horsemen came to the foot of the hill, and were directing their mounts westward into the coach-road, towards Grim Forest, a rider from the village came flitting by on a long gray steed. They identified the rider at once as Miss Margaret Mowbray, who, after tossing them a sprightly wave, drew rein and wheeled round to join them. The noses of Tinker, the chestnut, and the gray met in the middle of the road, sniffing inquisitively at one another, as horses and riders came together. Oliver thought it appropriate, a gray horse from Gray Lodge; though as for Miss Mowbray she was anything but gray, looking her usual spirited self in a brightly colored riding-habit, her smile shining from beneath her hat like the sun that had gone missing all the drab, gray, lumpish morning.

"Hallo!" Oliver called out, gallantly lifting his wide-awake. "You've a beautiful mare, Miss Mowbray."

"A gray horse for a gray day," said Mags, with a glance at the dull clouds sailing overhead. "I was spurring Delilah into a hard gallop, getting her thoroughly warmed for her morning's exercise, when I happened to spy two gentlemen turning out of the Skylingden road. One I of course recognized as yourself, Mr. Langley, and the other as Tinker of Dalroyd, with my grumpy cousin aboard. I've an idea you've come from the mansion-house."

"Indeed we have," Oliver volunteered, when the grumpy cousin appeared disinclined to respond.

"You have engaged the Wintermarches? By all means you must tell me what you think of them. Be they tranquil or warlike?"

"We have met them, and I am happy to relate found them sounding the pipes of peace."

"Of what sort is the gentleman himself — Mr. Bede Wintermarch, as he is called?" asked Miss Mowbray.

"Genteel, respectable, and rather reserved, on the whole, as are his wife and daughter. It is just as has been reported in town, to be sure. The accounts circulating have been remarkably accurate."

"Did he disclose anything of importance about himself? His background? Where he hails from? Anything of his wider family, his history, his connections?"

"Of these matters he told us little, aside from his having been a financier in the city — Crow's-end it was, just as we supposed — and having moved house in search of a less harried existence, apparently at the urging of Mrs. Wintermarch."

"It's a quiet life he seeks, which means he shan't want *you* plaguing him, my girl," broke in the squire, rather smartly he thought.

"Do you think it can be true, what they are saying in the village this morning?" inquired Miss Mowbray.

"Can what be true?" asked Oliver.

"Who are 'they,' and what is it they're saying?" demanded her grumpy cousin, looking perturbed at the mere suggestion of gossip.

"We have not been to the village today, having ridden to Skylingden directly from breakfast," Oliver explained. "Pray tell us, Miss Mowbray, you have news?"

"What they are saying is that this Mr. Wintermarch has very much the look of Charles Campleman about him," answered Mags.

"One of the Camplemans, of Skylingden Hall?" Oliver glanced curiously at Mark, for confirmation if this could possibly be so.

"The young heir to Skylingden, in point of fact," continued Miss Mowbray. "Though to be truthful he'll not be so young any more. His family departed the mansion-house almost thirty years ago in favor of Crow's-end. Why they left is rather a puzzle; a disagreeable incident, some illness or other on the part of the young Charles, is all I've managed to winkle out. Certainly his parents must be deceased now; he may very well be the last of the Camplemans. Likely he has returned for the purpose of claiming his birthright."

"But if he is this Charles Campleman, this heir, why call himself Bede Wintermarch?" asked Oliver, looking from Mark to Mags, and so back to Mark again.

The squire met his gaze with an irritated frown, and turned to Miss Mowbray. "Who is it has been sending round this tattle?"

"I had it at Miss Violet's early today from Cherry Ives, who overheard Mr. Dogger expatiating upon it in the Low Street," his cousin replied. "He contends the notion originated with Dr. Hall. Both evidently have looked in at Skylingden — on separate occasions, of course."

Mark threw up a hand in sign of his displeasure. "Tom Dogger — oh, jolly good Lord! Well, there it is, then, Noll. Shall I confess I am not in the least surprised?"

"You'll recollect the account given us by Dr. Hall at the Arms — how he had sensed something familiar in the people there at Skylingden, which he could not explain, and which intrigued and puzzled your meddling solicitor," said Oliver.

"So you knew of this already!" exclaimed Mags.

"Not in its entirety, Miss Mowbray, for the doctor made no mention to us of this Charles Campleman."

"Which suspicion like as not is solely an invention of the mind of Mr. Thomas Dogger," declared the squire. "And there's an end to it."

"This Mr. Wintermarch is wellnigh the proper age to be Charles Campleman, or so it appears, and there is a faint physical resemblance as well — though naturally, time alters people's memories as well as their features, in a host of ways," said Miss Mowbray. "From Cherry's observation, however, it would seem our village attorney is mightily convinced."

"And it's jolly well no concern of ours," said Mark, with a forceful nod. "In all likelihood Charles Campleman is dead, the line of Camplemans extinct, the estate much encumbered. Why else should Skylingden have been left to rot these many years? Why else should it have been let out to a string of tenants? Even were we to allow that Mr. Bede Wintermarch *is* this Campleman, what then is it to us? Let him claim his birthright and devil care how he styles himself. *I* certainly shouldn't care a fig if he were Bede Wintermarch or Romeo Butterhead. As to why he is here, I'll be only too happy to tell you. I'll lay you fifty guineas that creditors in the city have been hounding him on account of some peevish debts, so he has chosen to cut his lucky and go to ground for a time. That would explain why he has but two nags and a single carriage, and few servants, and is jolly shy as regards his family connections. *Ha!*"

"But why earth himself at the family seat? Terribly obvious, is it not, if he is looking to retain his incognito?" objected Oliver, hardly convinced of his friend's argument.

"Perhaps it is because Skylingden Hall is no longer the family seat — particularly as he is dead, key-cold dead, chapfallen, and all the Camplemans with him," was the squire's rejoinder. "And *that*, Mr. Langley, I have little doubt is jolly far closer to the truth."

"No one knows who is master of Skylingden now, not even Mr. Dogger," said Miss Mowbray.

"Just so — and as I have told you, there's an end to it. Now, then, Noll, before we were ambushed by my galloping cousin here, we were — "

"Preparing to call on Captain Hoey," said his cousin, not galloping at present, but having noted the direction the gentlemen's horses were pursuing when she and the gray had come upon them. "Is that not so, Mr. Langley?"

"There is some other party in Grim Forest we would be riding out to see?" returned Mark, as he and Oliver spurred their mounts into a trot.

"And as you are going that way now, I shall accompany you. It will be fine employment for Delilah," said Mags, falling in beside them. "I understand, Mr. Langley, you have yet to make the Captain's acquaintance. You shall not be disappointed. Whenever I crave some new diversion, something startling to challenge my wits, the Captain has rarely failed to supply it — though I admit I've neglected him shamefully these past weeks."

"Jolly lucky fellow these past weeks," remarked her cousin, dryly.

Proceeding westward along the coach-road, in the direction of Cedar Crag and the passes through the Talbot Peaks, they were quickly absorbed into the dim cool shadows of Grim Forest, that wild domain of evergreen and oak lying twixt the Talbots and Lonewater. At once the squire's senses were on the alert. He fingered the handle of the gleaming cutlass that hung always about Tinker's saddle, for one never knew what dangers might threaten in these rich sylvan fastnesses a distance from town. As it happened, however, no danger was to threaten today. Arriving safely at an unmarked bypath, a private lane fringed by cedars and shaggy firs, the riders turned into it. Soon the ground began to rise, and rise some more, the trees thinned and fell back on either side, and a vast upland meadow, lush and green, opened up before them. In the heart of the meadow was a gently sloping hill with a few clumber pines growing on it. Among the pines stood the dwelling-house of Captain Hoey — the place known as the Peaks.

This abode of the Captain's provided a notable contrast to the architecture of Skylingden, in both its compactness of scale and its air of tidy arrangement. Where the great mansion-house was long and rambling, the Peaks was tall and straight, and rather oddly proportioned, its narrow frame shooting up towards the clouds like an obelisk. Beyond it, above the line of forest, stood the ragged curtain of the Talbot Peaks, still dusted with the remains of the winter snows even at high midsummer. Viewing the house from square in front, one could hardly help but see there, in its towering façade and high arching gables, an echo of the Talbots rising behind; and so it became clear to Oliver how this house of the Captain's had gotten its name.

After settling their horses in the meadow — with the aid of a superannuated stable-hand, who came out of nowhere and accosted them with a toothless grin

— the visitors climbed the steps up the hill to the entrance doorway, and so made their presence known to the inmates of the house.

"Oh, it's you, Squire Mark," said the little dreamy-eyed servant who ushered them in. "And Miss Margaret, too. Good day to you both. And you, sir? Oh, I suppose you're that Mr. Oliver, that city man of Squire Mark's at Dalroyd. Good day to you as well. I'm pleased you've come, all of you, you too, Mr. Oliver. *He* is in a parlous condition today, and sorely vexed, and I fear it's all on account of me. I must admit the mischief was my doing. I am the guilty dog."

"What has happened, Slack?" demanded Mark, brusquely. "Where is Captain Hoey?"

"I'm here, Markham, I'm here," came a resounding voice like a bass viol, from somewhere beyond the passage. "And in a damned embarrassing predicament, too!"

Servant and voice led the visitors to a kind of study at the corner of the house — nearly every room in this largely vertical structure being at one corner of it — where they found Captain Hoey lying extended on a sofa, with an octavo volume open in his hands. The first thing they saw upon entering was his long, bald head propped against a pillow, facing them, the sofa being so arranged as to allow the drab daylight full play upon the leaves of his book. Immediately the Captain glanced up, shut the octavo with a smash, and waved his guests to the elbow-chairs near by, as the voice like a bass viol enjoined his servant to get up some coffee.

The Captain was a raw-boned giant of a man, tall like his house (when he was not reclining), with a pair of horn spectacles framing tiny eyes like buttons, a red nose like a strawberry, and waxed mustaches. He wore a flannel dressing-gown of which only the upper reaches were visible, the majority of his anatomy lying hidden beneath a blanket. Oliver thought the sofa upon which that anatomy reclined altogether too light and fragile for the supporting of it, and imagined he could hear the sofa's own anatomy groaning beneath the weight of the Captain's.

"Ah, Markham! Welcome. And Miss Mowbray — I am becharmed, my dear young madam, as ever, by your presence. And you, sir? I don't believe I know you, but welcome, whoever you are. You'll forgive me for not being upstanding, the three of you, as you may observe the predicament I am in."

"What is the matter here?" asked Mark.

"Agh, the churl scullioned me," replied the Captain, motioning towards the door through which his man Slack had disappeared. Apparently this was meant to be explanation enough; but as his visitors looked wholly at a loss, the

Captain very gingerly lifted a corner of the blanket to reveal his immobilized foot, enveloped in bandages and smelling of a poultice.

"It's plain enough," said he, pointing to the foot and glaring daggers at it, as though he held it partly responsible for his situation.

"Jolly plain, I warrant," the squire agreed. "And the cause?"

"The wretched thing strayed within the trajectory of an earthward-tending receptacle, said receptacle being fully charged at the time, and steaming hot."

"Within the trajectory — ?"

"Precisely. That path through space described by an object moving under the influence of gravitation and momentum. You see, here I am striding through my own kitchen of an evening, on course to rendezvous with a tumbler of hot gin-and-water, so to assuage a thirst, and having only just exchanged top-boots for the comfort of list slippers — when the churl roundly scullions me!"

"You are telling us that Slack dropped a glass of hot gin-and-water on your foot?" asked Miss Mowbray.

"No, no, no, my dear young madam, not gin, only water; matters had not progressed so far as the mixing of liquids. I tell you that I was standing at the side-cupboard, hunting up the gin-bottle, when my vassal there" — the dreamy-eyed Slack having returned now with the coffee — "when my vassal there comes rushing in from the scullery on some errand or other, his arms loaded up with pewter, and so collides with me. Round I spin — the pewter goes flying and crashing — my leg contacts the chimney-crane standing on the hearth, wrenching it forward — the kettle of hot water suspended from the hanger comes rattling off — the lid is displaced, the kettle upturned, and so *this* thing" — here he shook his bandaged foot a little, wincing — "chooses that moment to wedge itself between the kettle and the hearthstones. Kettle then crashing clean upon slippered foot, the water spills out, blazing hot. You see? Scullioned! And it pains me damnably."

"The Captain is given to accidents of such a nature," the squire confided to Oliver. "He is drawn to them. It's rare he is seen without evidence of recent mischief of some sort or other."

"Patently false," protested the voice like a bass viol. "False, utterly. And you know it, Markham."

"You may deny it all you wish, but you jolly well know it to be true."

"False, false," reiterated the Captain, shaking his bald head and smiling, with his arms crossed and his button-eyes fixed on Mark. "Utterly."

Mark in his turn looked to Slack, who responded with a weary sigh.

"Ah, it's ever the same in this quarter, Squire Mark," said he. "One has no fear of that. What *I* fear is the trouble I have now in distinguishing the passage of the days. Life's an odd sort of play, you know, with a measure of comedy, a dash of melodrama, a sprinkling of tragedy. Always, every day, the larger mysteries of existence return to pummel me, leaving me restless and uneasy. And so what is the point of it all, I ask?"

"The point, chuff, is to drink our coffee," grumbled the Captain, and suiting the action to the word promptly drained half the contents of his cup. The guests drank of their coffee too, at which point it struck the squire that his visitor from the city had yet to be presented to their host.

"By the by, I've brought my guest Mr. Langley round to make your acquaintance," he said. "Jolly bad form not to have introduced him. We've been intending to undertake the journey since his arrival in town from Crow's-end."

"Ah, yes, quite, so that's who you are," said the Captain, with a nod at once friendly and fierce. "I've heard tell of you, Langley, good to see you. Come to visit the Peaks and view the master, eh? You are new to these shores — tell me, then, have ever you seen the like of *that* before?" he inquired, with a flourish of his hand towards the dreamy-eyed servant.

"The master is too kind," smiled the philosophical Slack.

"He really is quite remarkable, and can do wonderful sums in his head, particularly when they concern his own wages. Very chatty he can be, too, chiefly about himself."

"He seems most efficient," was Oliver's politic reply.

"Your servant, sir," said Slack, bowing his head.

"Now, as I understand it, Langley, you are pursuing something literary, some translation or other," the Captain went blithely on, smoothing and smoothing his waxed mustaches. "Pray tell — of what, precisely?"

"Gaius Pomponius Silla."

"What say?"

"Silla. A Latin epigrammatist, second century. It's not so surprising you've not heard the name, as most haven't; he's very obscure. He composed five books of epigrams, none of which has ever before been rendered into English, so far as I can discover."

The Captain paused for a moment in thought. His hand ceased smoothing his mustaches; his brow darkened; his button-eyes shot Oliver a glance of significance.

"There's likely a damned good reason for that," he said.

"Spot-on," exclaimed Mark, in a bantering manner. "As I myself have been obliged to endure the recitation of no fewer than a dozen of these effusions. You're a jolly sensible sort, Captain Hoey, truly you are."

"Agh, Markham, I'm merely sporting with him. One can see clearly he's a baw-cock — a true-penny, and a fellow scholar to boot. No harm intended,

Langley. Bolts and shackles, man, it's this damned foot of mine, it's left me all in a muddle. A man of my kidney, a gentleman of consequence and property, a pupil of the natural sciences, and the boldest rider in Talbotshire, reduced to a state of the most wretched enfeeblement. Scullioned by a churl! It's put me quite out of countenance. Agh, I could go on — but have a care, the lot of you, lest I grow weary and tiresome on the subject."

"An impossibility, as my friend's dusty Roman Spaniard is holder of the current records for weariness and tiresomeness. We ourselves have become quite immune to him. Is that not so, cousin?"

"There is nothing so wearying or tiresome about it," returned Miss Mowbray, coming to Oliver's defense. "Granted the underlying *œuvre* is not of the first water, it does not necessarily imply that Mr. Langley's translations are without merit. Now then, sir, surely you've one or two examples of the dusty Silla about your person today, for the entertainment of the Captain?"

"Oh, jolly good Lord, coz!" cried the squire, making a face.

"No, no, quite, Markham — let us hear one of these effusions, as you call them," said the Captain, raising himself a little on his pillow. "Elsewise any assertions concerning their merit are no more than rank hearsay. And a pox of all hearsay!"

Oliver reached into the pocket of his country jacket and withdrew a folded half-sheet of bluish foolscap. He cleared his voice, a little nervously, for he was unsure how his efforts might be received in the house of the Captain.

"Yes, indeed it is the case, I have a sample with me — one I have been working at all too fitfully, I must admit, and was unprepared to deliver so soon into the world. It's early days yet for this piece, and I fear there are some imperfections remaining, though the topic will perhaps be of amusement."

And so, despite the squire's protestations, another jewel from the literary crown of Gaius Pomponius Silla was laid before an inquiring audience —

> "My estate has a fine *château*,
> Stables, and a most charming view.
> But the view I'd find best,
> My *PESTIFEROUS* guest,
> Is a view of the *BACK* of you."

Applause and general approbation followed, relieving Oliver of certain of his doubts, as with wry humor he noted the unexpected and rather too enthusiastic response of his host from Dalroyd.

"Slack," said Captain Hoey, hitting suddenly upon a new thought, "in what condition did you find the pluviometer? You know I meant to inspect it today but for this damned foot. And my weather-glass? The atmospheric pressure, the nature and temper of the air, its density or rarity, its content of moisture, all require looking after, and I mean to look after them, too, scullioned or no."

"The pluviometer is in good order, as are both the hygrometer and the windvane," replied Slack. "As for the weather-glass, it stands against the wall there beside the farther bookcases, in its customary position."

"A pluviometer?" said Oliver. "From the Latin *pluvia*, meaning rain — hence an instrument for the measurement of rainfall?"

"A rain-gauge, yes, sir."

"But we have had no rain."

"Ah, but we *shall* have precipitation, it is inevitable," said the Captain, with a wag of a scholarly forefinger, "and it is only wise to have all in readiness. Here at the Peaks we maintain a diligent accounting of all meteorological phenomena in the vicinity. Information concerning the state, content, and alteration of the weather is vital for those living in such altitudes. Slack, what says the weather-glass now? I cannot read it from such a distance. Be it rising or falling?"

"Falling," answered Slack, after a very businesslike examination of the instrument.

"As I suspected. I have noted a change in the condition of the atmosphere, and such devices allow me to verify the fact. It is true, then — the pressure of the air about us has fallen."

"Not on his foot, I trust," murmured Slack, in an aside to the master of Dalroyd. "Ah, it is ever the same here, Squire Mark. The winds and the pressures may vary, the rains come and go, summer pass to autumn and so on to winter, but circumstances at the Peaks never change; they are as immutable as granite. But there is so little point to granite, all in all."

"Captain Hoey," said Mags, leaning forward in her chair, "I have an idea Mr. Langley might find your celebrated cottage in the tree-trops of particular interest."

"His celebrated what?" asked Oliver.

"His *chalet en l'arbre*," explained Mark, less than satisfactorily perhaps.

"The sky-house," said the dreamy-eyed Slack.

"*Spy*-house, more like," countered the squire.

"The Captain's villa in the pines," said Miss Mowbray.

"His toft aloft," smiled Mark.

"Yes, yes, precisely, but I fear you'll need to return another day, Langley, as there's little chance of my scaling a world of stairs with this damned foot — it's a stopper!" said the Captain, wincing (for purposes of demonstration he had made a movement to lift the injured appendage, with painful results).

"Not to worry," said Miss Mowbray, confidently, "as I'm sure that your man here — "

"Ever at your service, Miss Margaret," said Slack, with a deferential nod. The philosopher looked inquiringly at Captain Hoey, which gaze the Captain sternly returned through his horn spectacles, as he debated whether or not to trust the churl with an office of such importance.

"It is plain I have little choice," he grudgingly replied, after a few moments passed in contemplating the ceiling. "Very well. My vassal the scullioner shall take you up, while I'm left to my prisonment here with my book and this damned foot and the ruination of my day. Off you go, then; it would play Old Harry with my conscience if I denied you. Bodikins! It's so damned humiliating. A man of my kidney, a gentleman, a polymath, and the boldest rider in the county — and it has come to this. A pox of all scullioners, I say!"

"His toft aloft?" inquired a bewildered Oliver of his companions, as they filed into the passage.

"This way, if you please," said Slack, with a sign to the others to follow. At the last moment the squire excused himself, explaining how it was jolly bad form to abandon the Captain to his melancholy mood; and so he returned to the study. That left but three of them — Slack, Miss Mowbray, and Oliver — to pursue the expedition, the dreamy-eyed philosopher first snatching up a parcel from the kitchen before mounting the staircase.

The stairs went up, and up, and up some more — for in a place like the Peaks *up* was very nearly the only way to go, when one wasn't going *down*. Six floors already had come and gone when they arrived at a landing, a kind of blind end with nothing but a pair of French windows leading to the outside. The servant drew open the windows; immediately beyond lay a parapet or balcony, rather like a captain's walk — most appropriate for the house of the Captain — and open to the air, though it was overshadowed to some extent by the eaves of the roof. Oliver craned out a little, peering towards the ground. At once he decided this was a bad idea, as the ground was so very far away, with little supportive between it and the captain's walk. Consequently he retired a pace or two behind the others.

From a break in the parapet stretched a series of three-foot planks, woven together by thick cords and forming a kind of suspension bridge to the nearest clumber pine. Ropes and cross-ties running along both sides of the planks served for handrails and balusters. The plank-bridge swayed a little with the breeze and the gentle movement of the tree, within whose furry branches, perhaps twenty feet away, Oliver could discern a maze of planking of a different sort, very cunningly hid.

"This way, if you please," said Slack, and with parcel in hand sprinted nimbly across the bridge. He was followed by the more tentative Mags, her fingers gripping the corded handrails as she went. Oliver, swallowing his fear and trying very hard *not* to look down — or almost anywhere else, for that matter — drew a long breath and flung himself out over the dizzying chasm. With quick, light steps he scampered over the planks, and at the end of them found a thing of most particular interest indeed.

CHAPTER X

SPIES AND SPYGLASS

THE clumber pine to which the plank-bridge was secured was a noble one, at once rugged and serene, with dense, coppery bark, shaggy clumps of branches, and a graceful crown rising to an almost unthinkable height above the arching gables of the Peaks. The point at which the bridge was anchored lay eighty feet or more above the floor of the meadow; and nestled in that spot, with the spreading limbs of the tree for support, was an irregularly shaped cabin or cottage, itself crafted of the same sturdy planking that formed the bridge, and with the bole of the clumber pine rising through the middle of it. The cottage was possessed of four tall windows, the foliage adjacent having been so sculpted that the line of sight from each window was largely unimpeded, while allowing the better part of the cottage to remain hidden among the branches. The general effect was to render the Captain's chalet and its planking nearly invisible from a distance, the windows appearing as natural breaks in the greenery. The cottage being lodged high in the clumber pine, the clumber pine in its turn rising from the hill, the windows naturally commanded long views of the surrounding district — Lonewater and the village to the east, the Talbots to the west; to the north, beyond the Peaks, a lengthy tract of Grim Forest; to the south Skylingden Wood and the mansion-house.

"What a magnificent perspective!" exclaimed Oliver, his eyes brimming with admiration. He took off his hat and rubbed his forehead, glancing round him in a dozen directions at once. "Hallo! This cottage — what ingenious construction! And you have furnished it so — so very naturally, so like a sitting-room — why, there are comfortable easy-chairs here, and a settee, a table and escritoire, a chest of drawers for books and such, a chime-clock, a small brazier for warmth — "

"The sky-house having been built by the master's tenants and crofters, and by the master himself, and by this humble servant, to the master's own particular specifications. Here you are, Mr. Oliver, sir," said Slack, touching the astonished visitor upon the arm, "this will improve the perspective further."

From the chest of drawers he retrieved a spyglass, very elegantly wrought, which he fastened to the head of a tripod riding on spidery legs of fir-wood. The assembled instrument he placed before the window with the eastern look-out.

"It is the master's own glass," smiled the little servant. "With it he surveys the countryside round about, like the lord of the manor."

"I was under the impression he was the lord of the manor."

"That's partly true, sir; lord of the Peaks to be precise, but not of the entire mountain valley. Did you know it was volcanic, sir?"

"The valley or the manor?"

"The valley, sir. Did you know that Lonewater itself occupies the mouth of a primeval volcano? Or so claims the master, from his extensive researches into the geological formations in the vicinity. Did you know that the bottom of the lake at its deepest point has yet to be sounded?"

"Ah, I see. Yes, I must admit I was aware of these things, Slack. The Captain feels it is definitely so, as regards the volcano?"

"He does. He is a stout Plutonist, sir, an adherent of the theory of the volcanic origin of basalts. Have a peer through the glass, Mr. Oliver," invited the servant, with a deferential nod towards the instrument.

Oliver peered, and found the perspective tremendously improved indeed. With singular clarity he inspected the line of hills rising from the farther lakeshore, and lo! peeping from behind them now were the snowy tops of some very high and very distant mountains, most likely in far-off Ayleshire. Where had *those* enormous forms been hiding? Oliver wondered how even much better might be the view were the meridian sun standing overhead. He moved the glass a little to one side, and the outlines of the neighboring village of Jay floated into its circle of vision. Upon Lonewater a sprinkling of tiny skiffs and fishing smacks was out and about, plying the dark waters of the lake. Nearer at hand the glass swept the face of a second village, that of Shilston Upcot itself. There Oliver could easily discern, in some detail, the stone-built cottages with their russet-colored roof-tiles, the market cross and village green, the lone spire of St. Lucy of the Lake, the Village Arms embowered amongst her trees, even a curl of smoke rising from one of the chimneys at Dalroyd. In the Low Street people could be seen strolling to and fro, as an occasional trap or farmer's cart rambled past, and horses and their riders trotted noiselessly by. At one point Oliver brought the glass to a halt, after spotting the Reverend Mr. Scattergood and his red-headed wife, in conversation with none other than Mr. Thomas Dogger — a gentleman whose substantial chin, curling gray hair, and perpendicular carriage were distinguishable from most any distance.

"Marvelous!" Oliver exclaimed, stepping aside to allow Miss Mowbray a turn at the instrument.

After a time they removed the apparatus to the south-facing window, for the purpose of examining Skylingden Hall. And there it was, the mansion-house, looking as gloomy and weather-beaten as ever, with its long, lazy roof-line

roaming about the high wood. They could make out some of its many windows
— those the shrubberies had not yet occluded — and the architectural forest of
finials and gables and brooding chimney-stacks; above all the imposing porch,
with its huge round eye looking out upon the good citizens of Shilston Upcot.
And just beyond the mansion-house, at the verge of the summit, some scattered
fragments of masonry and gray stone blocks, the remains of the ill-fated abbey
of the Lake Friars.

"Marvelous!" Oliver exclaimed again.

"Ah, yes, that I suppose it may be, Mr. Oliver, sir — but what, after all, is
the purpose?" mused the dreamy-eyed Slack, standing composedly by with his
arms folded, while Oliver and Mags shared the glass between them.

"How do you mean?" asked Oliver, looking round.

"In general, sir. In the grand posture of affairs. In the *larger* perspective.
In the chronicles of this sorry, sundered world — what is the point of it all?"
He waved a hand to indicate the cottage and its contents. "Are we the better
for it, in the long term?"

"Frankly, Slack, I don't follow you."

"What is the significance of our little lives here, in comparison with the
greater panorama of existence? What is the significance of this sky-house, this
clock, that spyglass? Does everything round us not serve to point up how very
small, how very inconsequential, how very insectiform we are, and how
transient is our essence? The breadth and enormity of this natural world that
imprisons us, simply must dwarf whatever may transpire at any given moment
here at the Peaks, or in the village, or in Malbury town, or at Crow's-end for
that matter. And what indeed is any given moment, as compared to the endless
breadth of eternity? Ah, such mysteries, such mysteries! When one considers
how abruptly, and how thoroughly, our little lives may be extinguished through
the agency of a shooting star — if indeed a shooting star it was that brought
about the sundering, as the master holds — does it not give one serious pause?
Think, think, Mr. Oliver, how very parlous is our situation here!"

"You are philosophizing again, Slack — most mightily, too, and altogether
too gloomily for my taste," said Miss Mowbray. "There seems to be more than
a dash of melodrama seasoning your own little life these days. It would appear
the mysteries of existence have been pummeling you something fierce."

"Oh, a tremendous beating I have taken of late, Miss Margaret, you would
not believe it. But I am sorry — it is an all-too-familiar frailty which on
occasion I am subject to. I have surrendered myself too often to morbid
contemplation of late; I fear you find me grown rather hippish. But standing
here in the sky-house just now, so high above the world — well, it obliges one
to consider such things, you know."

"I suppose there is some justification for it then. But really, Slack — you do it all the time!"

"Ah, yes," sighed the philosopher, clasping his hands behind his back and nodding gravely, as though he fully intended to reform himself. "Yes, Miss Margaret, all you say is true. You have caught me at it, you and Mr. Oliver. I am the guilty dog. It is an unfortunate habit, a sorry habit, a most persistent habit, and one which, like any guilty dog, must be roundly curbed."

"Hallo! There's no need for penitence," smiled Oliver, fearing that the little servant might be taking matters too close to heart. "It seems to me there is blessed little for you to be — "

A harsh, eerie cry burst upon their ears, followed at once by a rapid rush of air at the east window. The entire cottage quivered and shook. Miss Mowbray voiced a little cry herself and staggered forward, while Oliver clutched at the nearest chair, thinking that the "ingenious construction" was about to give way. The daylight in the east window had been expunged by an immense dark form, with a great swash of crimson about its head and neck, sharp cold eyes, a fearsome beak strong and hooked, and pitchy black wings. Before Oliver could utter a warning the huge bird, something along the lines of a vulture, launched itself into the room; then on a sudden it reared back, prompting another storm of air from its flight-feathers. Talons like razors gripped the window-ledge to steady the intruder, as its cold eyes scrutinized the human captives within.

"Good gracious God!" Oliver cried out in alarm. "If that is not a — not a *teratorn* — then as a Christian man I shall eat this jacket of mine!"

"It is a teratorn," said Miss Mowbray, recovering a little, having been taken aback herself by the manner of the creature's arrival. "Though you've no need to dish up your garments just yet, Mr. Langley."

"Oh, no, not to worry, sir, not to worry, it's simply Mr. Shakes," exclaimed the little dreamy-eyed servant, rushing forward to offer up a stream of kindly words to the intruder, whose ugly head was thrusting itself in and around him for a look at Oliver, its huge body taking up nearly all of the space in the window-frame. Remarkably, the teratorn appeared to respond to the servant's calming speech; it very delicately folded its wings and settled down upon the ledge, seeming more at ease than before — though with its attention still diverted by the human stranger, whom it was eyeing fiercely all over.

"How comes a teratorn — *here?*" asked Oliver, very pale as to countenance.

"Mr. Shakes is the Captain's pet," answered Miss Mowbray.

"Pardon for making so free, Miss Margaret, but Mr. Shakes is most assuredly no one's pet," said Slack. "He is an aerial wanderer, a gentleman rover of the celestial sphere, whose pleasure it is to come to us each day, at about this hour, and grace us with his presence; to pass time with the master —

when the master is not indisposed — wholly as an equal, and might I say with his humble servant as well."

"You're being philosophical again, Slack."

"Begging pardon, Miss Margaret, but it is difficult not to be philosophical when confronted with such a creature," replied Slack.

Oliver found himself in complete agreement with the little servant, despite having as yet only a partial understanding of matters. *A teratorn!* That most odious and loathsome of aerial predators, whose sky-hugging image — black outstretched wings and crimson head — was to most people in the city a foretokening of evil to come, was here, at the Peaks in Talbotshire, to all appearances a welcome guest. Still, Oliver could not rein in his fear at sight of the ill-looking bird — it made his skin creep, and set his heart a-racing — and confided as much to Slack and Miss Mowbray.

"Ah, not to worry, Mr. Oliver," the little servant assured him, undoing now the parcel he had snatched up in the kitchen. "It was near the hour for his calling, you know, and so I took care to bring something for him — in the event he happened upon us during our turn round the sky-house."

From the parcel he removed a half-jowl of lake trout, a baby perch, and a brace of pork saveloys. Its sharp cold eyes and keen sense of smell alerted the teratorn to these dainties at once; but rather than lunging for them greedily, as one might have expected, the bird suffered Slack to place the items, one by one, in its great jaws. A single hindward jerk of the bird's head, and the trout was gone, vanished down its long gullet; another jerk, and the baby perch was gone; two jerks more, and the saveloys followed ditto, ditto. Slack then murmuring some few further words of comfort to the gentleman rover, the teratorn stared once around him — as if to bestow a parting glance on Oliver — before leaning from the window, extending its mighty pinions, and heaving its body into the air. The cottage rattled and shook as the bird flung itself away; the wash of drab daylight returned to the window, and the evil apparition was no more.

"That was the most extraordinary thing I have ever witnessed," declared Oliver, as some of the color began returning to his features. "The spectacle of a teratorn — *tamed!*"

"Mr. Shakes is in no way tamed, sir," Slack made haste to point out. "He is simply being agreeable, from long habit."

"But how is that possible?"

"It is the Captain's doing," explained Mags. "He found the creature, you see, when it was little more than a fluffy chick; evidently it had been abandoned by its mother. It was injured — I have a suspicion the Captain identified with its plight, as he seems always to be doing his own self some mischief — and so he took to the feeding of it and the nursing of it, until its health recovered. In the fullness of time the bird grew into its wings, and made a life for itself in the sky; yet still it returns daily to the cottage for morsels of food and something like companionship. It is a remarkably intelligent animal, is it not, Slack? I must confess, I sense a kind of guiding consciousness there, some spark in Mr. Shakes, however primal, with the capacity to understand. Why else would such a creature consort with human beings? Why else run the hazard of vulnerability?"

"Wondrous," was the most Oliver could reply.

"Yes, is he not?" smiled Captain Hoey, upon hearing this same summation of Oliver's a brief while later, after the cottage-goers had returned to the sick-room. "So our celestial wanderer has looked in upon you. A real stopper, is he not? What say, Langley — you'll understand of course why we address the gentleman as Mr. Shakes?"

"To be sure. When he thundered down upon us, it set the entire cottage shivering!"

"Precisely, though it has not always been the case. At first I called him Tiny Osbert — for I had discovered him on St. Osbert's day — but as he ripened into young birdhood it became clear the name no longer served. It was then my vassal the scullioner there rechristened him, one year round peasecod-time, after one of those shivering fits in the villa. Ah, but have no concerns as to the sturdiness of the timbers; the villa is as solidly wedged there among the boughs as if it had sprung from the tree itself. It supports me quite handily, and as you may notice I am not a small man. By the by, Langley — what say you to the spyglass?"

"Incomparable lenses. The lake, the pine-clad shores, a range of distant snowy mountains — all are brought readily to view for close inspection. One may peer into every corner of the village, and make out the individual physiognomies of the people there. I suppose one might even spy upon the mansion-house," replied Oliver.

"Indeed, one might," said Slack.

"Which puts me in mind how your Mr. Shakes is the second curious species of avian Mark and I have encountered today."

"The second? How do you mean?" asked the Captain.

Oliver responded with a concise account of his and the squire's call at Skylingden that morning, describing something of the nature of the family there, and of the mysterious round window, and — most significantly — of what they had glimpsed in the curtained room off the dark and silent gallery. Captain Hoey displayed great interest in the report, as evidenced by various dark contractions of his brow, and thoughtful strokes of his mustaches, and indecipherable viol-like mutterings.

"That's most provocative, most provocative," he was heard to say, as the narrative reached its conclusion. "For I'll be sworn my scullioner there has been telling me, for a week at least, how he feels there is something troubling Mr. Shakes. What say you, chuff?"

"There is little I can point to with certainty," replied Slack, "though I have a sense the gentleman's concentration has been disturbed of late. As for what the cause may be, who can tell? He has been spending far less time round the Peaks than is usual for him, however — as though something of uncommon interest has been occupying his hours."

"Is there perhaps a Mrs. Shakes, and a clutch of hatchlings?" inquired Oliver.

"There could be," said Captain Hoey. "In point of fact there may be several, though the male of the teratorn species is not a party to the care of offspring. That responsibility is left wholly to the female — in truth to groups of females, as I have observed, who assist each other in the tending of the young."

"A tidy arrangement," noted the squire.

"But about this Skylingden owl," pursued the Captain, who had left off smoothing his mustaches in favor of smoothing his long bald head. "It is more than possible it may be released at night."

Oliver was reminded of the bodeful dream that had wound its way into his sleep, the dream of the large bird squatting at his casement-window, and its two owl-like eyes glowing in the darkness. Although he said nothing of it to the others, his own eyes happened now to catch those of the squire; and so the gentlemen traded looks. Perhaps it had not been a dream at all, as Mark had suggested; though if Oliver recollected aright the explanation had involved a teratorn rather than an owl.

"I suppose it would have to be freed from time to time," said the squire, frowning. "It would jolly well need to hunt, for an owl is a bird of prey. During the hours of daylight it naturally would prefer the atmosphere of the curtained room, as owls are for the most part nocturnal sorts."

"The hawks of the night air!" proclaimed the Captain majestically, in his voice like a bass viol.

"Perhaps then it is this owl that has been troubling Mr. Shakes," suggested Miss Mowbray.

"Jolly likely. And so there it is, then," said the squire, with a lazy throw of his shoulders. "You've solved it, cousin."

"By my soul, Markham, it's a damned ferocious owl that can disquiet a teratorn," said Captain Hoey.

"*That's* true," nodded Slack.

"It is a very large and heavy bird, from the glimpse we had of it," said Oliver.

"Exactly," said Mags. "I have an idea there is some fresh competition in the valley, and Mr. Shakes is struggling to adjust."

"Hmmm. That may be. On the other hand I should think an owl, regardless of size, would prove no match for a teratorn, as Captain Hoey suggests. But of course I speak here as a Crow's-end man, with little experience of country matters. Thankfully we have no teratorns in city skies!"

The Captain was staring straight before him — which direction was towards the farther arm of the sofa, and his injured foot there beneath the blanket — and looking very profound, with his arms crossed and his lips working soundlessly behind his waxed mustaches.

"Beshrew me, there is something about these people, these Wintermarches, whoever they are," he said, at length.

"And what is that, sir?" asked Miss Mowbray. She was unsure if the Captain had heard the news regarding Charles Campleman, but was unwilling to bring the subject up herself, knowing her cousin the squire's dislike of tattle.

"It concerns the spyglass, my dear young madam. Not two days past — just prior to my scullioning, when my foot was sound and I was yet the boldest rider in Talbotshire — I was taking a stroll round the villa, completing a survey with the glass, when I observed one of these Wintermarches, a woman by sex, standing at one of the high windows of the mansion-house. The sash was up, the curtains drawn aside, the woman peering out. The day was pretty far gone, and the remainder of it going fast, the bright Phoebus having by then slipped behind the Talbots. I thought at first the woman was contemplating the prospect from her window, but it was not so, as her eyes instead were fixed upon a creature hovering in the air nearby. I strove for a closer look, and at precisely that instant the creature dipped into view — a large horned owl, with upperparts a light golden brown, mottled and barred, and underparts and face a ghostly white."

"Ha!" exclaimed the squire, snapping his fingers. "So you knew already of this bird, did you, sir?"

"It would be a stopper indeed if it were not the very same owl you and Langley glimpsed in the curtained room, and if indeed the window there were not the very same window, and the curtains not the very same curtains."

"If it were this same owl, this pet, then likely the woman had only just freed it for the night," said Miss Mowbray.

"I wish you had beheld the expression upon this woman's countenance, my dear young madam," returned Captain Hoey, "for I saw it all too plainly in my glass. A look composed of equal parts resentment, resignation, and *fear* — an odd jumble of emotions to be trotted out while observing one's favored pet, I'll be sworn!"

"But you were so very far off here at the Peaks, at dusk, gazing through the spyglass to Skylingden. Granted the instrument is very powerful — still you observed all this?"

"Ah, quite, yes, my dear Miss Mowbray, for you know I have been observing through the glass for a very long time now, and so am something accomplished at it."

"The boldest spy in Talbotshire, is the master," nodded Slack.

"The woman may have been a servant, and obliged to perform this duty," suggested Mags.

"True, Mark and I noted a servant arranging the curtains in the room where the owl was pent up," said Oliver.

"It was clear from her manner of dress and carriage she was no servant," intoned the bass viol. "And with a countenance full of doom!"

"Then surely it was the wife — Mrs. Sepulchra Wintermarch," Oliver concluded. "She did impress us as having rather a compliant nature. I must admit, though, it remains something of a puzzle. An owl is not *so* odd an animal for a pet — for I've heard of the like before at Crow's-end — but certainly, a pet is a thing one ought not be frightened of."

CHAPTER XI

THE RUMINATIONS OF SHANK

HAVING departed the Peaks the three riders made direct for Gray Lodge, where Miss Mowbray bade her companions stop a while and look in on Mrs. Fielding. Her aunt had passed a busy day about the flower-beds, garden gauntlets on and trowel in hand — an avocation she shared with her niece — and so was looking even more than usually pleasant and amiable, as she always did after a fine spell of gardening. She inquired of her new friend Mr. Langley how he liked the Captain, and the Captain's household, and what he thought of them. Oliver responded with a generally favorable report, conveying his admiration for the Captain's unusual obelisk of a house and his cottage in the clumber pine, with rather less enthusiasm for his ill-omened visitor from the skies. Mrs. Fielding for her part assured him that the Captain was a monstrous fine man, uncommonly amusing in conversation, learned but not pedantic, and very well thought of in the village, if a trifle irregular. Oliver heartily agreed, adding that the Captain's man Slack was of interest as well, especially as regards his skill in governing the mighty teratorn.

It was getting on for dark before the gentlemen quitted the Lodge, having accepted Mrs. Fielding's kind offer to stay to dinner. I needn't relate that the dinner was an excellent meal, for excellent meals were synonymous with Aunt Jane and the staff of Gray Lodge. This particular dinner featured such choice country items as gravy soup, black rabbit pie, stewed eels, some sets of pettitoes and some toasted cheese, goose tarts, and of course larchberry pudding, accompanied by a quantity of local cider. It will come as no surprise then to find that the gentlemen were rather comfortably disposed, by the time they retrieved their mounts and turned them into the coach-road towards Dalroyd and home.

Hardly a minute had elapsed before their ears caught the sound of a person singing, somewhere below and to their right, in the hollow beyond the roadside trees. A coarse, gravelly voice it was, belonging plainly to a gentleman who had seen many winters. Although the words were not distinguishable, the melody was to the squire a familiar one, one of those maudlin, melancholy plaints of grief and loss so favored by people of the mountains. Oliver having expressed both surprise and curiosity at the phenomenon, the squire suggested they investigate — full well knowing himself who the singer was, and thinking that here was another inhabitant of the village whose acquaintance might enliven Mr. Langley's holiday.

They guided the horses down a covert bridle-path, down, down into the darksome hollow and towards the churchyard, with the spire of St. Lucy of the Lake rising before them like a white fir against the sky. As they skirted the burying-grounds where the vanished company of faithful lay in blessed repose, Oliver noted again how pensive his companion became while gazing upon those melancholy precincts; and noted too that the singing, which was rather louder now, appeared to emanate from a small hut or workshop behind the church, its windows aglow with the ruddy flush of firelight.

"It's our sexton," said Mark, extracting himself from his thoughts, to inform Oliver of the identity of the mysterious warbler. They picketed their horses beside the quaint old lych-gate with its overspreading gable roof. "Mr. Shank Bottom by name, a veteran of the parish. Old Bottom has served five vicars in his time, as he'll soon tell you himself, I'm jolly well sure."

They strode towards the hut, under the close overhanging trees, and knocked at the door. The singer left off his singing at once; a chair creaked, and a gruff voice called out to demand who it was that meant to disturb him. The answer given by the squire was evidently a satisfactory one, for the door was opened and the gentlemen beheld there the figure of Mr. Shank Bottom, leaning with his fist upon the jamb.

His was a short figure and a thick one, attired in rusty black sable, very much patched, with a wing-collar that once was white and a worn scratch-wig that once was kempt. His face presented the hard features of a man of sixty-five or thereabouts, with a shabby mustache, and a restless sea of stubble roving about his double chins; a broad forehead, creased and knotted; a nose swart and tuberous; and close, suspicious eyes that glistened in the light. This ill-conditioned appearance of Mr. Bottom was to prove deceptive, however, for once the squire and Oliver had entered the hut, which smelled of mold, pipe-smoke, and *aqua vitae*, their host grew rather more sociable, and it became evident that his manner was largely a bluff designed to ward off those he didn't much care for. The gray smudges on his hands and cheeks, the two-foot rule, mason's hammer, and untoothed iron blade standing against the wall, the sack of sand, the litter of stone chips about the floor, all hinted that Mr. Bottom had this day been toiling at his profession, which was the cutting and dressing of stone. It was in his capacity as sexton, however, that the bulk of his hours each day were spent, for as sexton he shouldered many responsibilities, including the preparation of the graves, the sweeping and airing of the church, the ringing of the bells, the provision of water for baptisms, the lighting of candles, and the opening of the pews and the keeping-out of dogs and disorderly persons during services. As his reverend employer with the plated spectacles might have phrased it, Mr. Bottom was an excellent man, a worthy man, a man of incalculable value to the parish. By virtue of his occupational activities, Mr. Bottom naturally spent much time in his own company; though this did not preclude him from knowing most everyone in the village and most everything that happened there, for he had passed his entire life in Shilston Upcot and had served five vicars, as he proceeded now to inform his gentlemen guests.

"It's a lonely occupation, anyrood, is what it is, sirs," said Shank, taking a whiff of his pipe. He had returned to his chair by his pleasant bit of fire, after first retrieving two chairs more from the depths of the workshop for the comfort of Mark and Oliver. "Abiding here in the loom of those trees there, of that church-house there, of those cold stones there, in summer and in winter too — why, it does give a man time to think on certain things. And the cutting of stone, sirs, is likewise a lonely occupation, and teaches a man things as well, I tell thee true."

"What kinds of things?" asked Oliver, brightly.

"As for example, sir — a thing such as the impermanence of things."

"It seems to me that stone should remind one of something quite different, of the *permanence* of things. One need only consider one of your well-built houses of Talbotshire stone."

Mr. Bottom shook his head gently. "Not in the least, sir. For what is the true and sacred calling of stone, I ask thee? It is to serve as a remembrance, sir — a memorial to those of old what have lived and loved afore us, and so have gone off the hooks. Stone it is, sir, what marks that spot where the earthly husk has been coffined up, once the glowing spirit has moved on to wakefulness in the other world. It's a short life at the longest, sirs, and comes the dread exit too soon, and to all of us, one day. That is what stone teaches a man. All fear the grave as the child does the dark — this I tell thee true."

"Good Lord, listen to this humbug — the rankest spiritism!" exclaimed Mark, only half in jest, for he recognized that Mr. Bottom as an employee of the parish was in some sense obliged to advance the articles of faith; whereas the squire was a man who was known on more than one occasion to have called upon the devil to take all preaching and doctrine. Then he recollected that old Bottom was in a manner of speaking an employee of his as well, as his own fortune of Dalroyd contributed a not inconsiderable sum towards the living of Shilston Upcot, and the maintenance of the church and vicarage.

"Thou canst not help but see things, sir, and know things, in an occupation such as mine. For sirs, I tell thee true — there is spirit all about thee!"

With this remark Mr. Bottom glanced uneasily round the hut — at its walls of plaster full of moving shadows cast by the turf-fire, at the fire itself mirrored in the window-glass, at the farther dim recesses of the workshop lying beyond reach of the light — round the hut he glanced, expecting to see he knew not what, and hoping not to see it at all.

"What I mean, sir, is there's a kind of spirit what grows in those trees there. There's a spirit in the wind as howls through the night, and a spirit in the creatures of the pine wood. A lesser kind of spirit, too, there is, in this good Talbotshire stone. But stone is an imperfect vessel, sir, and given time will crumble to powder just as the stiff-uns do. Examine those most ancient of the monuments in the bone-yard there, sir, and thou'llst see how that same Time has worked his changes, scraping away at the 'scriptions there with his cruel hand till nowt is left for human eye to read. The stiff-uns screwed up under those ancient stones are forever nameless now, in this world at least, as the unseen lodger, the spirit what has fled from the world, is all that survives; for anything smelling of matter, sir, even this good Talbotshire stone, is liable to dissolution."

"Look here, Noll," said Mark, slowly relaxing into a crooked smile, "how well our parish sexton has absorbed the teachings of his five great and good benefactors. It's something affecting, is it not, how blind faith rules the mind of man? So very like the child, who comes to believe all its father tells it — a child taking all its father says *on faith*, as it were, as though the father were the supreme authority in all matters on this earth; indeed, as though the father had himself set up the earth and made it run. One would do well to recollect, however, that the father was once a child himself, and so knows it all for a humbug."

"Thou'rt unlike thy father in many a diverse way, sir," said Mr. Bottom, looking on Mark and smoking. "Thy father, Mr. Ralph Trench — there, *there*, sirs, was as fine, as honorable, as upstanding a gentleman as ever was birthed in this parish. An open-handed, just-minded man was he, one what saw his obligations and rightly stood by 'em, and was ever a great and good friend of the clergy. Nowt there was that Mr. Ralph Trench would not do to aid his friend the vicar."

"Look again, Noll, how jolly fond Mr. Bottom is of comparing me to my father, and rather unfavorably, too. By implication I suppose I am not the fine, honorable, upstanding gentleman of the parish my father was — though as Mr. Bottom has had the acquaintance of the both of us, perhaps he's better qualified to render judgment. I'll confess I haven't the energy or the inclination to trouble myself with these touching articles of faith, which it's clear to me are so much gammon, but which are swallowed whole by credulous sorts all round this parish. Though you must admit, Mr. Bottom, that as the unlikely patron of the benefice I have fulfilled my obligations so far as money is concerned.

Our fine vicar has received his vicar's wages every quarter-day since his arrival, and though he may complain bitterly as to the amount that is no fault of mine. This is a small parish and tithes will go only so far. Without the added funds provided by Dalroyd and the few other estates we should have no parish at all. As for our Mr. Bottom, he has done jolly well for himself these many years, in first procuring his situation and then clinging to it like a burr on the parochial trouser-leg."

"True, I've nowt to complain of in my life, Mr. Trench, sir," returned the sexton, hardly offended by what he heard — he'd heard it all often enough before — and reaching aside for an old wicker-bottle, offered the gentlemen each a measure of his favorite intoxicant. They at first declined; Mr. Bottom was an ardent disciple of Bacchus, the *Fufluns* of old Etruria, and Mark, knowing both the quality and potency of the sexton's grog, made light of the fact in his refusal. But their resolution gradually faded — the mild cider from Gray Lodge having already exhausted its effects — and so at length they succumbed, taking in hand a couple of tumblers of Mr. Shank Bottom's hospitality. At once their throats were awash in a hot burning flood, which went surging through their limbs and rushing into their brains, and welled up behind their eyeballs, until a vast ocean of hospitality seemed to fill the entire hut; though luckily the small volume consumed was insufficient to wash them completely away.

"This is — a remarkable decoction," was Oliver's sole comment, made with some difficulty between bouts of coughing and gaping.

"Ain't it! And but a small portion o' the whole, I'll tell thee true," chuckled Mr. Bottom, with a knowing wink, and a toss of his thumb over one shoulder.

"Our sexton maintains a trove of this nectar where even the vicar can't find it," said Mark. "For as you know our Mr. Scattergood, whatever his other failings, like a stout fellow does enjoy a glass now and again. I'm jolly glad for him in that, and jolly glad as well for a species of spirit one *can* have faith in. *Ha!*"

"He does relish his potables, just as thy father did, sir, as I recollect," smiled Mr. Bottom, with a sort of retrospective serenity.

"So you knew Mr. Ralph Trench quite well, did you?" asked Oliver, dreadfully afraid he might swoon at any moment.

"That I did, sir, and proud to relate it. Mr. Trench was very kind to me. Mr. Trench was very kind to all of us as served Mr. Marchant."

"Mr. Marchant?"

"Our vicar at the time, sir. He followed after old Mr. Scroop, as was the first vicar I served while still articled to Mr. Hardcastle, he what was stone-cutter in the parish afore me. Have I mentioned, sir, as I've served five vicars now, the best I recollect it, our present Mr. Horace Scattergood being that fifth man?"

"Tell us, Mr. Bottom," said Oliver, hitting upon a subject that promised to lift him from the tide of hospitality, "have you by chance seen a strange clergyman about the village of late? An elderly gentleman with a sad face, and a sad wife?"

"A clergyman? Not as I know of, sir," replied the sexton. He swallowed some more of his grog, without its creating the least appreciable effect upon his person. "None but Mr. Scattergood have I seen, and Mrs. Scattergood, o' course. There were Mr. Pound, as is vicar at Tarnley, and Miss Pound, his daughter, were here a month past for his niece's nuptials. But none else than this, sir, as has come to my attention."

Here Oliver described for him, as best he could under the circumstances, the encounter with the mournful couple at Dalroyd dock. While he spoke a shadow came over the face of the sexton, and then another, and another, each darker than the one before, as the details were set forth. Mr. Bottom drew a hand across his mouth, his chin, his grimy cheeks; his brow visibly paled, his eyes swiveled in their sockets with restless calculation.

"Edith?" whispered the sexton, hoarsely. "Thou'rt dead sure, Mr. Langley, it were — it were *Edith* — as the old clergyman asked for? Asked for very particularly, and by name?"

"Yes."

"Thou couldst not have misheard, then?"

"I don't believe so. He made the very same inquiry twice over, once of myself and once of the squire."

"Surely, sir, thou wouldst not gammon one such as I?"

"Rather not, Mr. Bottom! Does the name mean something to you? Might this Edith have been the clergyman's dog — a retriever perhaps, or a terrier?"

The sexton responded with something between a retch and a laugh. He clapped hands to the sides of his chair to steady himself, his eyes roving wildly about the interior of the hut. He shook his head with the scratch-wig on it, and muttered under his breath the words *Damn and blast*, before declaring with the most forceful certainty —

"No, sir, I don't know nowt about no dog."

"What of the short-faced bear, then?" Oliver pursued. "The bear that wandered into the village late one night and upset the dustbins. The bear from Skylingden Wood. What do you know of him?"

"A short-face, sir?"

"Yes. Splayfoot he's called, I believe."

"Well, now — I suppose I may have seen him, true, Mr. Langley, from my window there," replied Mr. Bottom, licking his lips. Talk of the short-face appeared only to intensify his discomfort. "He may have come down to root about the church-garden. Yes, it were Splayfoot, sir, of that I'm sure now, come down from — from the caves."

"We suspect he'd been disturbed by the recent activity up there, now that Skylingden Hall is occupied again, that perhaps he had been driven from his customary foraging sites and was obliged to seek his food in the village. The squire maintains it was most unusual for him, as the creature prefers to avoid contact with humanfolk, so long as he has food enough."

"That's likely, sir, it could well be, sir," replied the sexton, paying only scant attention to Oliver, so distracted was he by a crush of uneasy thoughts. He looked about him in what amounted to a silent panic. More than once his eyes strayed to the window-glass, as he mumbled something unintelligible about persons walking who should not be walking.

"Did you know the family keep an owl there at Skylingden? It is pent up inside the mansion-house during the day, but may be freed at night to hunt. The squire and I have had a glimpse of it, and Captain Hoey has observed it through his spyglass. Have you any knowledge of this owl, Mr. Bottom?"

"*An owl!*" cried the sexton, with a little gasp of horror. Evidently this latest revelation was the most discomforting to him of all. He took a ferocious swallow of his grog, poured another dram from the wicker-bottle and quaffed it off, without troubling to offer anything more to his visitors. Indeed, he had by now grown almost insensible of their presence. "An owl!" he said again, in an awful whisper, as if fearing the very sound of the words as they rolled from his lips. "And what — what *manner* of owl might that be, then?" he asked, looking neither at Oliver nor at Mark, but fixing his gaze instead on the darkness beyond the window-glass.

"A very large owl, with golden brown feathers, horns, and a white face," answered the gentleman from Crow's-end. "Oh, I must admit it's not so very unusual, for I have heard of people's keeping owls for pets — very curious pets, though, to be sure."

"And what then of our ancient clergyman and his lady companion?" put in Mark, returning to the original subject of interest. "You're jolly well convinced you've not spotted them about?"

"Convinced I am!" replied Mr. Bottom, staring at the window-glass. "I don't know nowt about 'em, sir, and don't care to know nowt about 'em — and neither should thee!"

The squire and Mark exchanged glances. They pressed him no further, however, as Mr. Bottom seemed little disposed to pursue a discussion of the topic, or of any other topic for that matter, what with the imbibing of his nectar and the staring at the window-glass. The fire had burned low and consequently it was very dark now in the hut. As their host's attitude seemed expressive of a desire to be left to himself, the two gentlemen rose, thanked him for his hospitality, and took their leave. Mr. Bottom chose not to see them to the door, but like a barnacle remained fastened to his chair, in a state of mind considerably altered since their arrival. The gentlemen therefore let themselves out, and jogging their horses round to the front of the church and into the Low Street, returned by that way to the coach-road.

Despite the lingering influence of the sexton's hospitality, both horsemen were vigilant and alert as they rode, for night in the mountains is a dangerous thing. The squire's cutlass was at his right hand, a knife and small-sword within Oliver's easy reach. But call there was for none, as nothing of an untoward character transpired; and so they gained the security of Dalroyd unmolested. After racking up the horses the two friends made for the warmth and comfort of the library, and there flung themselves down into the cushioned chairs upon the hearth-rug. A log-fire was flickering in the grate, having been kept in readiness for them by the indispensable Mr. Smithers.

"Is there anything you require, gentlemen?" asked that loyal attendant, he of the frosty beard and whiskers.

"Nothing now, Smithers, thank you," returned the squire, settling into a chair with a long, lazy stretch of his limbs. "I warrant we both shall be retiring directly."

"Very good, sir."

"We have had on the whole a lengthy and profitable day, have we not, Mark?" smiled Oliver. "First to Skylingden and the family Wintermarch, then on to Captain Hoey and the Peaks, and his fabulous villa, and Mr. Shakes, and so to a fine supper at Gray Lodge, rounded out by a rather interesting call upon the sexton."

"You have been to Mr. Bottom at his workshop, sir?" inquired the butler with a dignified but friendly curiosity, as he was preparing to withdraw.

"Indeed," nodded Mark. He slipped his hands behind his head and extended his legs very comfortably before him, with his boots resting on the fender. "And a jolly odd call as it turned out, too."

"Mr. Shank Bottom has occupied the office of sexton in this parish for many a year now," remarked Mr. Smithers. "He was sexton even in your father's time, sir."

"Yes," said Mark, gazing listlessly on the flames. "In my father's time, Smithers."

Here ensued a pause, while the butler waited to see if the conversation was over; evidently it was.

"If there is nothing more then, sir, I shall bid you a good night. And a good night as well to you, Mr. Langley." Saying which he respectfully departed the room.

"That fellow," said Mark, still eyeing the fire, "knows more than he's told us tonight, Noll."

"Mr. Smithers?" returned Oliver, with a puzzled frown.

"Hardly! I refer to old Bottom."

"Ah! I see. Yes, there now I would agree with you. From my brief observation of him, Mr. Bottom would seem to share at least one thing in common with Slack — his philosphical bent."

"He's a wary sort. There is a world of secrets lurking behind that grimy countenance of his. He's very like our village physician, in that respect — though of course the doctor has not the grimy countenance. Nonetheless they have something in common."

"As you and the Captain have something in common?" smiled Oliver.

The squire had tossed aside his hat, thereby exposing the baldness of his head to plain view. Although he guessed the tenor of his guest's observation, he was too much absorbed in his musings now to offer the usual crisp rejoinder.

"I must admit, I've the distinct impression myself that Mr. Bottom knows who that old clergyman is, and where he's earthed himself," said Oliver, his fingers drumming a devil's tattoo upon the arm of his chair.

The squire offered no immediate comment, but remained gazing at the fire with his hands behind his head, in an attitude of lounging. He had sunk into one of his moods.

"We must learn, Noll," he murmured softly, after a time. "We must learn what the secrets are."

"Hallo! I had the equally distinct impression you weren't interested in secrets, or in gossip," returned Oliver, in some surprise.

"I am not. I care not a fig for gossip; truly, I don't. But look here — I'll be hanged if old Bottom will be applauding my revered father's virtues to my face, without my hatching up something in response."

CHAPTER XII

A DASH OF VILLAGE CHAT

MISS Violet Crimp was a cheerful, amiable, good-natured woman in the ripe full blossom of middle age, as plump as a partridge and nearly as gregarious. Her head of dark hair was sprouting lacy veins of silver like a spider's web, and framed a visage that most any observer would have termed *delicate*. Delicate, in that it had always such a quantity of artifice applied to it — so much cream rouge here, so much white rice powder there, so much everything everywhere — as to invite resemblance to a fubsy little china doll, whose dainty features may be liable to crack at a moment's provocation. But as that same observer might not unreasonably have supposed, the resemblance went deeper than this.

Miss Crimp was the proprietor of a waffle-house, a drowsy establishment situated near the foot of the Low Street, in Town End. She had passed almost all her years in the service of her parents, both of whom had been invalided early in life. The waffle-house had been the property of her father and had devolved to her care upon his death, as her mother was by that time too ill to manage her own affairs let alone a commercial enterprise, however drowsy. Though that was many winters ago her mother still lived, clinging to existence in a comfortable bedchamber above the public room of the waffle-house. She left her apartment but seldom, on account of the weakness in her legs and hips, and only when aided by Miss Violet or Molly, her maidservant and nurse, to inhale a few breaths of air or for a brief turn in the village road. Mostly she preferred sitting before the open casement of her room, where she enjoyed a very pleasant view of the dark lake and the green, shaggy mountains. She was unable to read now, due to a growing confusion of mind, and so this avenue of recreation was closed to her. As well she had trouble with her speech, being capable only of grunts, titters, and occasional wild shouts; in consequence of which she made frequent resort to a crutch-handled cane, to pound the floor at her bedside as a signal that help was required. This drumbeat being transmitted all too perceptibly to the public room below, either Molly or Miss Violet herself, so summoned, would obediently climb the staircase to address the old woman's needs.

Miss Crimp had for many years harbored a secret desire to flee the confines of her drowsy establishment — indeed, to flee the confines of Shilston Upcot itself, and of Talbotshire altogether — and travel at least once beyond the mountains; in fact, if the truth be told, she would have preferred to have moved house entirely and gone to live in one of those magical places called cities, the most magical of which was Crow's-end. *Crow's-end!* What wondrous, exotic vistas of beauty and fashion it conjured up in her imagination, the mere sound of it. Crow's-end, a roiling metropolis filled with people, and so the very opposite to Shilston Upcot; a place where one might meet and mingle with all manner of new and fascinating society, and where a host of new and fascinating diversions would be thrust upon her, at all hours of the clock, to the amazement of her mind. Thus far, however, this dream of hers had yet to be realized. She had been to the county town of Malbury once, years ago, with her father; but in this she felt cheated now, for the journey had been *so* long ago she barely recollected what kind of place Malbury was, or what she had seen there; felt doubly cheated, in point of fact, in that it was this same father and his infirmities that had prevented her from returning. And now it was her frail old mother who kept her from her dream.

Ofttimes it seemed to Miss Crimp that she must burst, must crack, must shatter inside, to know that in all likelihood this dream of hers would never be. She had grown so used to her life as it was, to its rhythms and its reassuring regularities, so much like the seasons of the year; she was feeling too old now for change. Did she blame her parents for that, or her own self? So much desire, so much struggle hidden behind that mask of delicate china! So much unperceived by an unperceiving world. Yet one must be careful, however, not to misinterpret the nature and character of Miss Crimp's inmost heart; she had violently loved her parents, and it was this extreme attachment to them that had held her fast to Shilston Upcot and the waffle-house. It was this very love for them that had made of her a prisoner.

Miss Crimp had had a beau, once, and he very nearly managed to lure her away. He was a young gentleman with dreams and desires of his own, and his sights were set on the great roiling metropolis; but then her father intervened and so that had been that. Her father had been that species of man who gravely mistrusts all fellow members of his gender, believing there was no need for *that* sort of thing tainting his daughter's life and depriving him of her. After his demise, and with the host of added duties and obligations accruing to her, Miss Crimp fell gradually into the habit of thinking no more of her young beau, or of any other beau, or of beaux in general; so that now there was no such gentleman in her life and had not been for a very long time. Miss Crimp was through setting her cap at anyone, particularly as there were so few eligibles left to set it at. Now and then, when a free moment was accorded her, her plump figure might be glimpsed at the shingle beach, a little distance from her drowsy establishment, leaning with her head against a tree and her hands clasping its bole, as she looked off towards the mountains, or into the sky at a soaring jay, and imagined what it would be like to possess such a thing as freedom. On such occasions one might have seen moisture glimmering under her lashes, and the delicate china face tremble as though it would crack, as if the phantoms of murdered time and lost opportunity were passing there before her eyes.

Early one morning, as Lonewater lay steaming in the mist, beneath a damp sun, Miss Crimp emerged from the kitchen of the waffle-house to find Miss Margaret Mowbray and Mrs. Fielding arrived in the public room. Soon after they were joined by young Cherry Ives of the Arms, and Mrs. Dinah Scattergood, the red-haired wife of the vicar. Once each week these ladies assembled at the drowsy establishment for a breakfast of waffle-cakes and eggs, hot honeyed toast and larchberry muffins, and thick black coffee, to retail the latest items of news in the village, and to talk over those sorts of things that country ladies everywhere are fond of talking over.

They settled in at their customary table, Miss Violet for the duration turning over her duties to one of the serving-girls so that she might be free to mix with her friends. The table stood in a corner near the broad stone fireplace, and offered both privacy and snugness. Indeed, this waffle-house of Miss Crimp's was, like Miss Violet herself, as snug, precise, and well-ordered as could be imagined, if drowsy, its faults existing in far fewer number than its virtues. The walls, exclusive of the dark oak beams and wainscoting, were papered in a cheery pattern of flowers, and hung with idyllic portraits of woodland scenery. There was a large old-fashioned cupboard here, and a tall cabinet there, and a chiffonier, all of rosewood, and all much prized by Miss Crimp and before her by her mother, when her mind had been clear. On a high, narrow shelf running along one wall, just under the cornice, stood a line of ceramic dinner plates, a decorative collection that had been amassed by her paternal grandfather, a crockery merchant. In a subtle way these plates, ranged along the high shelf like so many observing faces, served as reminders to Miss Crimp of her confined situation in life; for the plates had been brought to Shilston Upcot from all over the realm — from Saxbridge and Salthead in the north, to Richford and Candlebury in the east, to Crow's-end and Fishmouth, and far-away Nantle in the south — and so had themselves been to all those magical places beyond the mountains that Miss Crimp herself would never see.

Mrs. Dinah Scattergood, she of the fiery red hair and sharp blue eyes, was in some respects rather the converse of Miss Crimp. Unlike Violet, Mrs. Scattergood had traveled a good deal in her young life, and after meeting and marrying her husband had traveled even more, to three parishes in three very different counties, where the Reverend Mr. Horace Scattergood had received successive preferments as curate and vicar, before settling two years ago at Shilston Upcot. Mrs. Scattergood was a pretty, resilient, resourceful young woman with experience of the outer world, qualities that Miss Crimp privately envied and admired. But of course, this was a thing Miss Violet never would have revealed to any of her companions, least of all to Dinah, for she loved her dearly and would not have burdened her or anyone else with her disappointments. What she would not have given, though, to have had Dinah's share of life's experience, to have viewed through her own soft eyes all that Dinah's sharp blue ones had seen of the world beyond the mountains — even if it meant being yoked to a stiff and stuffy clergyman!

"No, he is not *stuffy*," Dinah was saying at just that instant, as regards her reverend helpmate with the plated spectacles, the shepherd of his flock, just as this same adjective happened to be drifting through Miss Violet's head. Miss Crimp was startled; she turned her delicate china face to the others at table, to ask if there was anything more they required in the way of food or drink, now that the waffle-cakes and eggs and toast and muffins and coffee had been laid on; whereupon she directed one of the serving-girls to the kitchen to fetch some butter and clotted cream.

"No, not stuffy," Mrs. Scattergood resumed, puckering her brow, "but the vicar can be frightfully dogmatic at home. Once he's convinced of something, of some particular course of action, for example, no matter how wrongheaded it may be — and it often is *most* wrongheaded — he'll stubbornly resist being dissuaded from it. Oh, yes. He cannot tolerate that sort of correction, you see, on personal matters. We have discussions every day at the vicarage, he and I, on just this very subject."

"But, my dear, surely it is a useful quality in clergymen to be dogmatic," said Miss Crimp. "Otherwise they should all be off founding their own religions, and preaching whatever doctrine might come into their heads at any given moment."

"Perhaps that would be a good thing," suggested Cherry Ives, she of the bold, bright gaze, "for at times I think there is only so much tedious dogma and preaching one can bear in one's life. So much monotony to it — so much humdrum — so much of a drearisome *sameness!*"

"Oh, Miss Cherry!" exclaimed Mrs. Fielding, a little frightened by such heresy from the mouth of a landlord's daughter; this despite the fact that her own niece sat snickering beside her.

If nothing else these weekly gatherings at the waffle-house were celebrated for their frankness!

"Yes," murmured Miss Crimp, in a sudden rush of thought. "Yes, it is indeed so, after a fashion. Such a sameness to it! Though to be sure, 'dogmatic' does not much describe the kindly Mr. Scattergood I am acquainted with."

The voluble Dinah appeared not to note what was said in reference to her clergyman husband, but went blithely on. "I suppose I should be hopeful of some change on his part, or some readiness to change, and certainly would welcome it, but thus far I have been disappointed on that score. For the knot of the problem is, you see, that the vicar has always reserved his most dogmatic views for his wife. He may have the sturdiest of opinions on some fine point of doctrine, or philosophy, or parochial business, but once he is out and among his flock he cannot follow through; he finds himself yielding, relenting, subordinating his opinions to those of others, like a tree bending to the wind. In his defense he claims that being so 'forward' respecting his own attitudes and beliefs with those he must shepherd is somehow presumptuous and uncharitable. But of what use is a shepherd who does not lead? He must learn to stand faster by his rights, and not give ground. Indeed, he can be quite bewildering at times, if not maddening; I know, for I am witness to it every day. It is only in his household affairs that he chooses to assert himself — in his dealings with *me*. It is plain the hardiness of his backbone varies according to the company he keeps. He is never quite the same man to all people. I must say, what a dichotomy a husband is! How I have endured it I shall never understand."

"And what of you, Mags?" said Cherry, turning the conversation in a related direction. "You have no dichotomy as of yet. Do you consider yourself lucky or unlucky in that regard? How goes it with you and the squire?"

"There is nothing *going*, as you term it," replied Miss Mowbray, coloring a little.

"He's quite the obvious match for you. He is a *very* distant relation, many times removed, and so there should be no impediment in that regard. He is eminently suited to you. Why then haven't you married him?"

"I have not married him for the simple fact he has not asked me to marry him."

"Whatever can be wrong?"

"There is nothing wrong."

"How many years has it been, dear?" inquired a sympathetic Miss Crimp, who always warmed to any conversation having marriage as its topic.

"In point of fact," said Mags, growing a little self-conscious now as regards that topic — "in point of fact my cousin has been settled for too long in his comfortable life there at Dalroyd, with his bay horse and his terrier, his tenants and timber, and has simply neither the time nor the desire for anything so troublesome as a wife. I admit, there may once have been a moment in history when this was not so, but the moment has passed."

"You have no expectation, then?"

"None, Miss Violet. And what is more, what care should I have of it? What is it to me? I have my dear Aunt Jane, after all, and speedy Delilah, and the charms of Gray Lodge and our flower-garden. I certainly don't want for money or anything else of consequence. And I have all of you and our weekly talks here to challenge my wits! And too, there are these great natural wonders that surround us — these wild and somber forests, these glades and hollows, these soaring mountains, these mysterious waters. What more could one ask from life?"

"What more, indeed?" asked Miss Crimp of her own self, roaming for a moment through her mind's attic where her secret desires lay hid, all the while knowing very well the answer.

By and large the company seemed fairly divided with respect to the merits of Miss Mowbray's case.

"Well, I for one am in complete agreement with you," said Cherry, with a lively nod and a bounce of her shiny dark curls. "There is no earthly cause for fretting because you have no dichotomy."

"And so you have been simply testing me with your questions," said Mags.

"Just so. I myself too have no dichotomy, as everyone well knows, and am perfectly glad of it. You'll not catch me fretting; I haven't the time for it. There's certainly no sense making a ruin of one's life on account of such a thing, as did that poor girl who drowned herself in the lake."

"What poor girl?" inquired Dinah, with a mystified countenance. "The vicar and I have heard nothing of this. Has something happened?"

"Not to worry — it was many years ago, a matter I heard my father and some of his fellows whispering over at the Arms yesternight," replied Cherry. "Some few scraps of conversation — they had not the least idea I was near, and listening. It was the first I ever had heard of the incident. It occurred some thirty years back, apparently, when they all were young lads fresh from school. To think of my father, Nim Ives, as a young lad! It bears not the thinking on, *I* think."

"Never mind your father," said Miss Mowbray, eagerly. "What of this girl who drowned? Who was she?"

"A village girl who had sorely pined for a young gentleman, and when she couldn't have him, or was rebuffed by him, or some such thing, ran a boat out upon the lake and leaped into the water, thereby putting a most final period to her existence. Shameful! You may be sure, you'll never hear the name of

Cherry Ives in such a connection. And so you should take heed, Mags Mowbray, of so unfortunate an example of womanhood. So should we all."

"Is this true?" asked Dinah, looking round to the others for confirmation. "Did this sorry event happen? Mrs. Fielding — I judge from your expression you know something of the matter. Is it true, what Cherry has told us?"

All eyes turned to Aunt Jane. Her face that had once been beautiful looked to be grappling now with indecision, guilt, distress, perhaps even fear. Reserved by nature, though in an altogether kindly and pleasant way, the widow hesitated before replying. She spread some butter on her waffle-cake, and bathed it in a quantity of dark syrup, and sliced it neatly into several portions, to gain time while a crowd of memories pressed for her attention. At length she drew herself up a little, and drank some of her coffee, in preparation for her response.

"Yes, it is a true account — or at the very least I can attest to it in part, for I have never been privy to the whole of it," said she, choosing her words with care.

"Aunt Jane!" exclaimed Mags, in a prolonged tone of surprise. "You've told me nothing of this. All this time, such a thing has been lurking there beneath my own nose — at Gray Lodge!"

"I did not mean to conceal it from you, dear," replied her aunt, fidgeting with her spoon. "It is a subject that simply never arose. The young woman should be allowed the privacy of rest, after the suffering that must have impelled her to so rash an act. So irremediable an act, and so contrary to the precepts of our faith."

"Who was she?" asked Dinah, sensible naturally of this latter point. "And what impelled her?"

"She was, as I understood it, very deeply in love with the heir of Skylingden Hall. Young Mr. Campleman."

"Mr. *Charles* Campleman?" said Mags, glancing at Cherry.

"Yes. But really, dear, I'm afraid I recall so few of the particulars. It's not the sort of thing one cares to speak of, you know, from respect for the poor young woman's departed soul. I suppose Mr. Campleman must have been cool to her attentions, and on account of this she sacrificed herself in the lake, which as you know is terribly treacherous in spots. Her body was never recovered."

"The lake in places is immeasurably deep," said Miss Crimp. "So I have been told by Captain Hoey."

"She rowed herself out into the very middle of it, into the very deepest part, and there slipped over the side. They looked for her for a long time after, without success. The sexton, Mr. Bottom, placed a loaf of bread weighted with quicksilver on the water, near the spot where he had found her boat adrift. It is held by some that such an object will come to rest over the place where the body of a drowned person lies. But nothing came of it; and as a suicide she had forfeited her right to burial in hallowed ground. Her death was a terrible blow to her parents, who were advanced in age and had no other children. They did not long survive the shock of it. Sadly, her father was our vicar at the time."

"And who was that?" asked Dinah.

"Mr. Edwin Marchant. Oh, he was long before that quaint Mr. Mallard, who preceded your husband at the vicarage."

"So the daughter of the vicar was head and ears in love with young Mr. Charles Campleman, of Skylingden Hall," said Mags. "And now it is said that Mr. Bede Wintermarch of Skylingden bears more than a passing resemblance to Charles Campleman."

"That is so, for the vicar and I have heard it from Mr. Thomas Dogger's own lips," nodded Dinah.

"As regards the subject of vicars, and clergymen in general," said Cherry, "is anyone by chance acquainted with the old parson and wife whom the squire and Mr. Langley encountered, some days ago, at Dalroyd dock?" She provided them with a brief description of the incident, as she recollected it from Oliver's account, the very same incident that had so inexplicably troubled her father that night at the Arms. No one at table admitted to having seen such a couple at any time in recent weeks.

"We should have inquired of Captain Hoey, if perhaps he has observed this clergyman with his glass," thought Miss Mowbray. Not lost on her, however, nor on Dinah, nor Cherry, nor Miss Crimp, was the odd expression that had settled on the face of Aunt Jane — eyes looking askance through the far window, a hand raised to her mouth, her brow ruffled, as though the good lady were trying to make sense of something she found perfectly nonsensical. Visibly ill at ease, she lowered her gaze and resumed operations upon her waffle-cake.

"What was her name, this girl who drowned herself, this Miss Marchant?" asked Dinah.

Aunt Jane's face betrayed her again, as she chewed at a morsel of her breakfast.

"You know her name, do you, Aunt?" said her niece.

Mrs. Fielding nodded reluctantly. She swallowed, and patted her lips with her table-napkin.

"Edith it was," she replied. "Miss Edith Marchant. Such an unfortunate young woman!"

There followed a pause.

"*Gosh!*" exclaimed Mags, drawing a long breath. Again her eyes sought out Cherry's bright, unflinching glance.

"This then is what my father found so disturbing in the report," said Cherry. "But certainly it's the merest coincidence — that, or the squire and his visitor have fashioned the tale from the cloth of their imagination, for some unknown purpose. Indeed, I felt it might be so that very night."

"Impossible," declared Miss Mowbray. "My cousin has no interest in manufacturing falsehoods. On the contrary, you all know how offensive such things are to his nature. And what of Mr. Langley? Does he seem a likely partner in such an enterprise? Thoughtful, generous, learned Mr. Langley? Surely not he, for he is as honest and courteous a city man as I've ever met."

Here, indeed, was a puzzle; and one, it seemed, with no easy explanation on offer.

Abruptly Dinah rose to her feet and announced that she must return to the vicarage, to inform her husband of this intriguing turn of events concerning the parish and one of its former shepherds. At the same moment came a loud pounding overhead, transmitted from the room above; and so Miss Crimp too started up, and wheeled her plump form round towards the staircase, in response to the call from her aged parent — leaving Mags, and Cherry Ives, and Aunt Jane to fend for themselves amongst the waffle-cakes, pitchers of sweet dark syrup, and gleaming butter-boats.

CHAPTER XIII

LARGELY DOMESTIC

AS she hurried along the street in the direction of St. Lucy's and the vicarage, a great many thoughts went flying through the pretty head of Dinah. There were thoughts of Miss Crimp, whom Dinah admired for her careful industry and her devotion to her mother; thoughts of Mags Mowbray and her quiet life there at the Lodge with Mrs. Fielding; thoughts of the bold young Cherry, who knew her own mind and did not shrink from expressing what was in it; thoughts of her husband the vicar, not a stiff or stuffy man to be sure but a man nonetheless, and so prey to a host of manly foibles; and lastly, thoughts of a matter that for wellnigh thirty years had lain as thoroughly submerged as the remains of poor Miss Marchant.

Why had her husband not known of it, not heard of this drowned girl who had been the daughter of one of his predecessors at the vicarage? Not known that the drowned girl herself had lived there — *there*, in the very house wherein Dinah and her reverend yoke-fellow had made their nest? What of the mysterious incident at Dalroyd dock, the chance encounter between the squire and Mr. Langley and the sad old couple? How much store to set by it? Was there the slimmest chance the incident had been a prank, executed perhaps at the urging of Mr. Trench to goad her husband, whom the squire found it pleasant to mock, to deride, to challenge? For was not the squire of Dalroyd a professed skeptic in all things religious — if not indeed something worse? Did this not give color to the notion of a hoax? How it irked her that the vicar and the parish needs must accept money from such a man as Mark Trench, one who attached so little importance to his parochial duties, to say nothing of his faith, and who never let pass an opportunity to advertise his disregard.

As she drew near the church there reached her ears the sound of her husband's violoncello, from an upper window of the vicarage, the violoncello being one of the Reverend Mr. Scattergood's passions quite apart from his sacred calling. The vicar, she told herself as she quickened her steps, if not stiff or stuffy was most certainly a faint-heart — though as a 'cellist he had something to commend him — and as well a weathercock, a man who never stood his public ground with any constancy, however much he might hold forth in private with his life's partner. Never did he present anything but his kindest vicar's face to Mr. Mark Trench, irrespective of any personal or parochial affairs concerning which he and the squire might be at variance. It was uncharitable, reasoned her oddity of a husband, to be so outspoken, so partisan, with a member of the flock; uncharitable to express one's disapproval so openly and frankly. What! Uncharitable to be vertebrate, to have a backbone? Was chine of clergyman so unfashionable an item in the clerical market-place? How perfectly ridiculous, thought Dinah, and not a little hypocritical too. Mrs. Scattergood herself had no such fine scruples, no such anxious niceties, none whatsoever; she would have taken on Mr. Mark Trench eyeball to eyeball at a moment's notice, in the defense of her husband or her faith, and quickly sorted him out — though of course, as the wife of the vicar it was hardly her place to do so. And regardless how keenly it might vex her, the parish still must have the revenue from Dalroyd's coffers to survive.

As if her helpmate had not already failings aplenty, no children from their blessed union had yet put in an appearance, to brighten the rooms at the vicarage — no children, not one, not so much as a hint of one; and as a result Mrs. Dinah Scattergood, particularly when she was in such a frame of mind, did not hesitate to assume that this too must be the fault of her husband.

She found the reverend gentleman bent over his 'cello in the sitting-room, his bow momentarily at rest while he squinted through his spectacles at the music on the little stand before him. His brow was clenched, his lips working slightly, as he examined with rising alarm the thick cloud of notes obscuring the staves. He was about to start in again, about to draw his bow again like a musical top-sawyer, about to plunge fingers-foremost into a singularly daunting passage with which to try his skill, when he caught sight of his red-haired wife in the doorway. Immediately all thought of plunging and top-sawyering was laid aside for the moment, and the violoncello too, so that he might deploy the full orchestra of his attentions upon Dinah.

"Yes, my love?" he said, a little hesitantly perhaps, for Mrs. Scattergood had now that particular look in her face that signaled an impending inquisition. "You'll forgive me, I have been at my bowing-exercises as you may see. These here by Raviola are quite the most challenging I have yet attempted, quite difficult for a player of my limited gifts."

"Do you know something of this old clergyman and his wife who were seen at Dalroyd dock?" asked Dinah.

"Which old clergyman would that be, my love? And which wife?"

Whereupon the good lady found it necessary to inform her husband of what she had learned at the waffle-house of Miss Crimp. The vicar's immediate reaction to it was difficult to gauge; though he appeared to be considering all he heard with the utmost solemnity, and a slow, steady rub of his chin with his bowing-hand.

"Well?" said Dinah, at length.

"It does look to be something of a coincidence," her husband replied. "But I must confess I know nothing of either incident."

"I thought not."

"My love?"

"What do you know of this Mr. Marchant?"

"Very little. Oh, there are the gravestones there in the yard, of course, both Mr. Marchant and his wife Elizabeth. He was several vicars past, you know. I suppose there will be some information in the churchwardens' accounts of the parish. And of course there is our Mr. Bottom, who served him."

"*Your* Mr. Bottom," said his wife, pettishly, "is an addled tosspot who sees and hears things that aren't there, and who knows things that never were, and I shouldn't believe one-half of anything he might tell me though I had seen and heard it for myself. Your Mr. Bottom would as soon dream up a thing in his cups as report the truth."

"My love, that's most uncharitable. You must remember that Mr. Bottom has flourished in this village for many a twelvemonth, since long before we arrived — since long before we both were born, in fact — and has accumulated a store of knowledge in a great many areas. He has served the parish since he was a young man, I'm told, and despite occasional lapses his memory is to all effects quite solid."

"The personal history of Mr. Shank Bottom is of no concern to me," returned Dinah. "But although I shan't believe a word your Mr. Bottom might have to say, I *shall* believe words I see in writing — in a particular vicar's handwriting — in the very Mr. Edwin Marchant's own hand."

"How do you mean?"

"The letters. What has become of the letters?"

"Ah! I see. You refer of course to the little bundle of correspondence, tied up with string, which we discovered in the locked press not long ago. The bundle of old letters I had been meaning to give over to Mr. Trench."

"Yes, yes. You have not given them over, then?" said his wife, her eyes of blue sharpening themselves upon him.

Her husband smiled and pushed up his spectacles. "Oh, but my love, I have."

"Why?"

"Well, my love, you *have* been reminding me how I must do something with them, must give them to Mr. Trench, perhaps, as they appeared to concern his father, and the late vicar, and certain parties residing at Crow's-end. Surely you'll recall your injunction to me, my love — either the letters should be thrown out or given over to the squire, to be disposed of at his own discretion, as you wished not so much as a particle of scribbling-paper with the name of Trench on it to be lodged in this house."

"Yes, yes, I recollect it, you needn't reacquaint me with every detail of it. And do *you* recall the name of the vicar we saw written there, on the direction of certain of those letters?"

"The name of Marchant, yes, my love."

"Why then did you have to give them over so readily?" asked Dinah. "Whatever were you thinking?"

The poor clergyman was quite bewildered by his wife's response, a not uncommon happenstance at the vicarage. Face to face with woman's logic he was reduced to a state of reverent acquiescence, a condition that by now seemed woven into the very warp and woof of his domestic bliss. So much for the vicar's supposed assertiveness in household affairs!

"I'm very sorry, my love," said he, delivering up his customary surrender.

"What was in those letters?"

The vicar peered at her in astonishment. "Oh, my love — I pray you did not expect I should *read* them? They had every appearance of private correspondence, bound up together as though they belonged together, or touched upon some common issue. It was only proper that the squire should receive them into his care, relating as they evidently did to private matters in which his late father had an interest."

Bravo, vicar! Stand fast by your rights and don't give ground.

"You didn't read them," said Dinah, crossing her arms in a flush of disappointment.

"Of course not, my love. It would not be charitable."

So Mrs. Scattergood was left to wonder again how a person such as her husband, a gentleman of the cloth and a learned man, had survived for so long in this world without a backbone, and how it was a just God in heaven should have ordained such a thing; but she did not dare say as much, for she quickly recognized how shifting was the ground she herself stood upon. There was no getting to the mystery now, and so she folded and folded her arms, and tossed up her chin a little, and looked out of the window, rather than bestow the favor of her gaze upon the beneficed clergyman and amateur 'cellist with no backbone.

Backbone her husband might have not, but violoncello he did. In no little time the instrument was again between his knees, his bow was in his hand and his eyes once more upon Raviola. So the mystery of the Trench letters, or the Marchant letters, or whosever letters they were, was put aside for the moment, in her husband's mind if not in the mind of the inquisitive Dinah. As she descended the staircase she heard again the sound of the vicar's bow on the strings, and in some surprise recognized the melody not as an exercise of the maestro Raviola's, but as a jaunty little air known by various names roundabout, the most common being *Silver Billy*; the words to which ran, in the prevailing version, something as follows —

> Silver Billy the bailiff's man,
> Had a wife, a fair enslaver;
> > Handsome and fine,
> > She kept him in line —
> A bossy-boots, to bicker,
> Needle, and nag.
> Welladay! sigh'd Billy,
> > Cry you mercy, madam,
> In the name of charity!

CHAPTER XIV

POINTS AT PIQUET

THE night promised to be another chilly one, after a pleasantly fine day. The air at times can be rather dry in the mountain valleys, particularly in summer, and holds no warmth once the source of that warmth has gone. Even on such chilly nights it was not uncommon to find the Village Arms packed out, with both guests and regulars alike, and this night was no exception. Conviviality and good fellowship were everywhere in evidence. A steady flow of conversation, a river of voices, splashed its way about the lodge-room, the participants laughing and chuckling round the central hearth-fire, some disputing this point or that, some smoking, some drinking, some playing at billiards, some at backgammon or draughts, all under the grim, glassy stare of the trophy-heads hanging from the walls.

Discussions of equal import, and other, quieter games of chance, were in progress as well in the card-room, overseen there not by trophy-heads but by tall and dour Mr. Jinkins, the drawer, from behind the oak bar at the farther end of the room. Mr. Tony Arkwright, the veterinary, was there, expatiating upon the merits of his new foal, which had been born only that afternoon and which he promised to show off at the very next opportunity. Mr. Thomas Dogger and his long sharp nose were there, inhaling the atmosphere of the place while taking great pains to be humble, and subtly pointing out the fact to all who listened. The village physician, Dr. Hall, was there, smoking his pipe in a comfortable arm-chair beside the row of gallery-windows. There too that night was Mr. Mark Trench, sitting at piquet with none other than the vicar, the play of the cards being observed by Oliver Langley and the good-humored landlord of the establishment. It was, however, not so much the skill exhibited by the players as the nature of the discourse between the squire and the Reverend Mr. Scattergood, that most intrigued these two students of the game.

"And so I'd be obliged, vicar, if you'd see your way clear to explain how it is that what I have read in the county paper, as regards an event of some notoriety at Crow's-end, about a month back — a shocking event, really — may accord with your holy rhetoric," said Mark, lazily discarding three of his cards to draw replacements from the stock. The players had begun a fresh round and were exchanging cards in order to improve their hands.

"What event would that be, Mr. Trench?" smiled the vicar, adjusting his spectacles.

"You've heard something I suppose of the late coach upset, which occurred on a particularly hazardous stretch of the cliff road? A Cattermole coach it was that overturned, as I recollect. A number of passengers were thrown to their deaths from the precipice into the frigid waters of the harbor, this number including a pair of lovely children, a brother and sister, not yet five years of age." Here the squire paused to look at his cards, while awaiting with interest the vicar's reply.

"Yes, I have read of it. A most grievous loss, Mr. Trench. Shocking, as you yourself have said."

"And these two lovely children, this brother and sister not yet five years of age — do you suppose they were deserving of such a fate? They had it jolly well coming to them, did they? Is such now the punishment for incivility to one's governess?"

"The upset was a regrettable accident, Mr. Trench — the result of an affrighting of the coach-horses."

"Ha! An accident, most regrettable, that surely will go far to clarify it. It follows then that this so-styled loving God of ours must have been slumbering at His watch, to have permitted so grievous a loss, so shocking an accident. Or was it perhaps instead a conscious act of this same drowsy deity? Is that not the common term for it, an *act of God?* Death by misadventure, death by the visitation of God, as our esteemed law-courts have defined it? Well, it jolly well affronts me, vicar, as it should any thinking individual, to offer Sunday homage to a being so grotesque as that. I'm surprised you don't agree; but I suppose I am out of joint with the times. Score for point, vicar?"

Noticeably flustered, the vicar declared his cards.

"Four spades, forty, Mr. Trench."

"Not good. I have here four clubs, for forty-*one*. Bad luck, vicar. Your best sequence, then?"

"Three diamonds, thirty."

"Again, not good. Look here — here are three clubs for thirty-*one*. Top card ace trounces you, naturally. Your best set?"

"Four jacks, forty."

"We're equal there, a pair of quartets. Four tens are as good as four court cards. That's seven for dealer, nothing for you — *nihil*, as the dusty Silla might term it. And so it's your deal this next turn, vicar, you are younger hand."

"I fear it is not for me, a poor country clergyman, to justify the actions or inactions of the Almighty, Mr. Trench," said the vicar, returning now to the squire's argument, as he shuffled the cards and dealt the requisite twelve each to Mark and himself. The remaining eight cards he spread face-down between them to form the stock. "There are certain questions to which Providence affords us no satisfactory answer in this life."

"There you are, attempting again to wriggle out from under. You clergymen, country or otherwise, are all of a piece. You cling to doctrine like so many wrens to birdlime, but the moment there's matter you jolly well can't explain away by means of platitudes you resort to sanctimonious blather, saying how it's all too vast and unwieldy for ignorant mortals to comprehend. Should it not at the very least make some *sense*, even to mortals? Is that not logical?" This speech the squire pursued in a rambling sort of way, while preoccupied with his new cards in hand. He drew three replacements from the stock.

"What would you have me say, Mr. Trench?" returned the vicar, exchanging some cards of his own. "Do you expect me to have special knowledge as to the intentions of the Lord? Snippets of information from the throne of grace?"

"What I expect is for you clergymen simply to admit it when you haven't the least notion what you're talking about. Proclaim *that* from your pulpit at service some fine sabbath morn, and I'll lay fifty guineas you'll garner more plaudits from your flock — from those with soundness of mind, at any rate — than any shepherd of St. Lucy's has, or has deserved to have, in living memory."

The vicar was at a loss how to respond — he never knew how to respond to Mr. Mark Trench, face to face certainly, in anything less than a charitable fashion — and in desperation grabbed hold of that creaking maxim, which instructs us to say nothing if we have nothing useful to say. Moreover Mr. Trench was his benefactor, and his darling wife's benefactor, and the parish's benefactor; it wouldn't do to upset him. Unfortunately, thought of upsetting the squire reminded the vicar of the coach upset at Crow's-end, and the horrid fate of the little children and the other passengers. Despite his outward show the questions raised by the squire troubled him deeply; such ticklish points of belief, so apparently contrary to common decency and common sense, never failed to trouble him, though he rarely spoke of it. So he calmly turned his other cheek and counted up his cards. A smile crept into his face at the sudden prospect of a winning hand.

"Point, Mr. Trench?"

"Six diamonds, fifty-eight."

The smile lost a fraction of its luster. "Ah, yes, well, that's rather to be expected, I suppose. I've only five spades for forty-seven, as you may see. Your best sequence?"

"Five *diamonds*, forty-seven."

"Ah! I see. Well, that's quite good, I'm sure. I've only three clubs, twenty-four."

"Bad luck, vicar," lamented the squire, drawing stiffly on his cigar.

But the reverend gentleman and his smile were not to be routed so easily. "Set, Mr. Trench?"

"Three jacks, thirty."

In triumph the vicar spread his cards on the table. "Not good enough, I fear. Four kings, forty. A quartet — *quatorze* — fourteen points, Mr. Trench!"

"Jolly good, vicar — how lucky for you! So there it is, then. Nonetheless that leaves me still with twice your game score. But not to worry, it's early days yet."

This mismatched pair played on in relative silence for a time — silence only so far as they themselves were concerned, for their ears remained filled with the voices of the larger company populating the inn, with the occasional teasing jest from Mr. Ives or droll remark from Oliver — until the squire started in again with his lazy but insistent questioning of matters metaphysical.

"Have you never observed, vicar, how it is that so many of our inventive geniuses in the history of the world — our great figures in art, music, literature, natural philosophy, mathematics, and the like — have been something like monsters in private life?"

"A few, certainly, I've found, from my reading of such subjects. Yes, I might agree with you to a small extent," said the vicar, rubbing his chin.

"It is a thing that has often puzzled me. Such giants of creative endeavor, possessed of such intelligence, and yet such monsters, driven to no end of mischief by self-absorption and self-indulgence. I wonder, vicar, if this may not by inference tell us something of the *supreme* Creator? Do you suppose the Almighty too is a monster in private life? A deity, true, but at heart a demon — a lurking fiend. It would go jolly far towards explaining the coach upset at Crow's-end."

The vicar could only shudder in disbelief. How to answer *this* challenge from the squire of Dalroyd, this newest gauntlet hurled at his clerical feet?

"Gracious, Mark, you're embarrassing Mr. Scattergood," said Oliver. He knew his friend enjoyed ruffling the good clergyman in these little intellectual combats of theirs, but really — this was too much! "Might I offer you, Mark, in rebuttal of your thesis, the example of our own gentle Shakespeare? Hardly a monster, either private or public, if any of his contemporaries are to be believed."

"The passengers thrown from the precipice, from the cliff road, and drowned in the sea," continued the squire, undaunted. "Not the most pleasant way to meet one's fate, though a jolly direct one."

"And what of the girl drowned in Lonewater?" asked Cherry Ives, happening upon them at this juncture. "The village girl who drowned herself for love of a young gentleman, one Mr. Charles Campleman?"

"How's that?" said Oliver, perking up his ears. "Mr. Charles Campleman — of Skylingden Hall?"

Eyes darted quickly from side to side in the head of Mr. Nim Ives, and in the heads of several others hard by who had heard Cherry's remark. There was an exchange of uneasy glances among these older men, these veterans of the village, but particularly as regards the landlord, who had had no idea his daughter was privy to the business. He clapped hands to his apron and smoothed it down, frowning.

"I'd jolly forgotten about her," said the squire, lazily. "It happened when I was little more than a boy, Noll — I recollect hardly anything of it, apart from the fact that it was scandalous. You refer no doubt to the suicide whose body was never found?"

"The same," said Cherry.

"I'm surprised you know of this matter, Cherry, m'dear," said Mr. Ives, with an uncharacteristic note of caution in his voice. "To speak truth, it's no happy remembrance for the public of this village. It was not a happy time. No, sirs, it was not, and I believe I am unopposed in this. Little has been said of it, or made of it, since a score of years and more."

"And the littler made of it the better, Nim Ives," declared one of the more grizzled of the regulars.

"A suicide in Shilston Upcot?" said Oliver, glancing round with his wide luminous gaze. "Who would have supposed it?"

"What then befell Mr. Charles Campleman — afterwards?" asked Cherry. Since first learning of it by chance that night at the Arms, she had found herself increasingly drawn to the mystery of the village girl who had taken her own life for love; had found herself drawn to it despite herself, and despite whatever contrary views she may have expressed at Miss Crimp's as to the womanhood of the victim.

In response to her inquiry that eminent limb of the law, Mr. Thomas Dogger, approached the group — his shoulders square, his carriage perpendicular, his nose long and sharp, his eyes shiny and sleek from much polishing — and gathering himself up with lawyerly authority, and an acknowledgment of that deference generally accorded him by lay folk, favored them with a pronouncement.

"Mr. Charles Campleman," said the attorney, gravely, "amidst a shame and disgrace of which he was wholly undeserving, was driven from this village by the weight of public sentiment; whereupon his remaining family, who numbered among them an ailing father, then master of Skylingden, relinquished their domicile, their emblements, and their chattels real to the care of God and nature, *sine die*, and have not returned. Such indeed has been the state of the case — until very recently."

"How do you mean, sir?" asked Oliver, who knew full well what he meant, as did Mark, but who had a desire to hear it at first hand from Mr. Dogger himself.

"I mean," said the attorney, looking askance at Dr. Hall in his arm-chair by the gallery-windows, "that it is my firm suspicion — mind, it remains a suspicion only and not established fact, for I make no accusation — it is my firm suspicion that the gentleman presently calling himself Mr. Bede Wintermarch, our neighbor there at Skylingden Hall, is in truth Mr. Charles Campleman, returned to this village."

A dead hush ran round the immediate company. Most already had heard this rumor, and promptly discounted it; but hearing it now from the upright and eminently respectable Mr. Dogger — a professional man, a product of the celebrated Clive's Inn at Fishmouth, an honorable solicitor of the Court of Chancery and attorney at Common Law — they knew there must be truth in it, or at the very least what the law took for truth. But mind, Mr. Dogger made no accusation!

For a long moment Dr. Hall regarded the attorney with the faintest of odd looks upon his face of pale calfskin. His gaze being briefly captured by Mr. Dogger, it appeared some shared intelligence passed between them; the doctor then turned away without comment.

"Do not wonder at it, my good friends, for I have seen things," said Mr. Dogger, hooking his thumbs in the pockets of his waistcoat. "True, it has for some time been my professional opinion that the line of Campleman had been extinguished, that the freehold of Skylingden had been conveyed to another party, and that these new people were but the latest in an erratic string of tenants. But in this, plain country Tom Dogger must acknowledge his *mea culpa* — must humbly confess that he has been in error. It is evident to me now that the freehold of the great hall remains firmly in the possession of the Camplemans."

"What does he want here?" Oliver asked. "If indeed it is this Mr. Campleman who has returned, *why* has he returned, and after so long an absence? And why under a different identity?"

"What indeed, sir? Who can say? A matter for speculation, certainly, and an issue of some personal and professional curiosity. But country law affords one little time for speculation, either personal or professional. Though if pressed — and only if pressed, mind — I should 'go bail' he means to avenge himself."

"Avenge himself for what, sir?"

"For the unjust treatment he received at the hands of not a few people in this village. Mr. Charles Campleman was a young gentleman of discerning, if unorthodox, tastes — as more than some of you here will recollect — and I believe felt himself misapprehended and greatly maligned by popular opinion; there was even some talk of an action in the courts. I imagine it all must have affected his mind. It was no fault of his that a silly chit of a girl lost her head over him and flung herself into the lake, dissolving her existence, in contravention of our most sacred moral and religious principles. There was no engagement; Mr. Campleman had no obligation, no liability under law. If that silly girl was unwilling to respect the wishes of a gentleman of property, so far above her station, it was by her own choice; if anyone is to be blamed let it be she. A bad lot she was, wholly bad."

"My word — the poor dear child," murmured the vicar. He pushed up his spectacles in dismay, having all but forgotten his cards, his points, his intellectual contest with the squire. Of the drowned girl he had of course already heard; so perhaps it was more Mr. Dogger's uncharitable characterization of her, and the fierce short way it was delivered, that moved him now.

"I submit, this gentleman should like nothing so much as to make some in this village ill at ease by his presence, particularly those who so ungenerously served him in those days," the attorney went on, with a smile and a sweep of his shiny eyes round the assembled group. He touched a hand to his breast in sign of his own humility. "Far be it from Tom Dogger to find fault with any person on this earth, or to dwell upon the transgressions, real or imagined, of any person, living or defunct. What I have told you with respect to past deeds I know of my own certain knowledge, *ipso facto*. Of my suspicion as regards the identity of the gentleman at Skylingden, it remains just so, a suspicion, following my late interview with the family there at the mansion-house, Mr. Bede Wintermarch *et uxor*, *et filia*."

A pause ensued, during which the listeners took occasion to digest what they had heard.

"Frankly, it troubles me a little," said Oliver. "There must be more to the matter, sir, than what you have related. This Mr. Campleman has now a family of his own, and has been living far from Talbotshire, out of sight and out of mind, these many years. What should impel him to return and exact his price after so long a time? Why has he waited? Why did he not return sooner? It seems to me that at his time of life he should be content to enjoy all he has been blessed with, a dutiful wife and a loving daughter. If he has returned to Skylingden it is to make it once more his home, as it was in his youth. The family there seem to me most content to be about their own affairs, unheralded and undisturbed."

"One never should underrate the power of vengeance, sir," returned Mr. Dogger, a little sternly. "Driven from his ancestral seat by scandal and unwarranted imputations, he and his father — a most griping injustice. Imagine the injury, sir! Such a wound as that may become progressively morbid, may ripen and fester there within the brain, until the resentment flowing from it all but overwhelms the will. Moreover I put to you now your own interrogatory — if Mr. Charles Campleman has no design for mischief, why then has he chosen to disguise himself and assume another's name?"

To this Oliver had to confess he had no answer.

"And what of the Marchants?" said Cherry Ives. "What of Miss Edith Marchant's father and mother, who roamed the lakeshore for months after, searching for her body and never finding it, and perished of broken hearts? And her father the vicar, too!"

Such words quickly gained the attention of Mark and Oliver, which of course may have been Cherry's intent, to gauge their effect upon the suspected pranksters. The squire for his part never had heard these details of the story before. The incident had been kept so very dark for so very long, he realized now he had never known the drowned girl's name; though he had received shadowy hints of the matter now and again over the years, and vaguely recollected some involvement of a clergyman in it. But the squire of Dalroyd had never been one for tattle, for rumor, and so had paid little heed. He glanced at Oliver, and Oliver glanced at him; before their eyes floated the images of the old clergyman and his wife, with faces so strange and sad — limp, weary, wintry faces, full of anxious concern. The clergyman's thin voice came drifting back —

"*Have you seen our Edith? Have you seen our girl?*"

The squire looked across his cards to the vicar, then round to the landlord and the other veterans of the village. What more was there to be learned of this tragedy, he wondered, how much still stubbornly kept from view? Was this the entire story now, the lot of it, or was there more yet to be told? And how could what he and Oliver had been witness to at Dalroyd dock possibly be?

"Will you deal, Mr. Trench?" inquired the vicar.

The squire dealt, his eyes upon the cards but his mind upon Dalroyd dock; and so the contest proceeded without him.

Later that evening a leisurely game of billiards was undertaken at Dalroyd, with cigars and brandy in attendance, and Jolly-boy too — who, once his initial excitement at the return of his master had passed, settled himself in his rush-basket by the billiard-room fire, and with heavy lids was there content to meditate upon the many joys of his life. At the long table the two champions of the cue played on in relative quiet, with the sounds of the game and the crisp, cool night breathing through the half-open windows to bear them company. It was chilly, true, but the squire preferred a chill; and as the noon of night made its approach, the ghostly shadows from the log-fire, the uneven glow of the wax-lights, the clouds of smoke from the cigars, the cold shaft of moonlight pouring through the casement, the repeated tap and click of the balls, under the influence of the brandy all combined to produce an eerie effect.

"Well, then?" said Mark, breaking the silence after a time.

"Well?" returned Oliver.

"What do you suppose we saw there at Dalroyd dock? Who was it approached us?"

"I haven't resolved it yet in my mind. Surely not what you suppose?"

"What do you suppose it is, Noll, that I suppose?"

Oliver brushed a hand through his curling hair. "I must admit, the entire business confounds me no end. I'm familiar to a degree with your peculiar beliefs, Mark — or perhaps *want* of belief might be more appropriate — and they hardly seem given to the acknowledgment of a life beyond that we know here. So I fear I must disappoint, as I can offer no satisfactory answer."

The squire struck with his cue, and the red ball was holed.

"Revenants," said Mark, blowing smoke. He shifted the cigar from his mouth for a quick swallow of brandy.

"Apparitions?"

"Apparitions. Specters. Phantoms. Spirits, as old Bottom tried to tell us — persons walking who should not be walking. Revenants. Ghosts. Call them what you like."

"Perhaps this is one of those secrets of Mr. Bottom's you have vowed to uncover. Though it seems to me rather a puzzle, Mark, how you may accept the existence of spirits if you are unwilling to accept an existence beyond the grave."

"A bit of a rub, is it not? *Ha!*" exclaimed his host, after a carom of considerable beauty that resulted in another score. Oliver was suitably impressed. There followed another tap, another click, and again the red ball was holed.

"Do you believe your father is dead?" Oliver inquired abruptly. He was watching the squire's play from a spot in front of the fire, silhouetted there with a hand to his hip and his cue planted on the ground.

"Absolutely," replied Mark, following through with his stroke — a winning hazard, worth two points — before turning to his friend. "Old Noll, whatever made you ask that?"

"I've not the least idea, though it is something I have rather wondered about. What age would your father be now?"

"I haven't troubled myself to calculate it."

Another few minutes of methodical play passed into history.

"When did all of this occur? This drowning of the vicar's daughter?" asked Oliver the curious.

"About eight-and-twenty years ago. Round the same time my revered father took fright and cut his lucky, over the hills and far away."

"Perhaps he is alive, somewhere. Perhaps like Mr. Charles Campleman he has taken on another identity. Perhaps at Malbury — perhaps at Fishmouth — perhaps at Crow's-end! Perhaps I have passed him there in the street, in Highmarket, a thousand times and not known it."

"Unlikely. I jolly well hope it isn't so."

"I've never understood it. What could have induced him to abandon his heritage, his estate, his family? What could he have stood to gain by it?"

The squire paused for a scratch at his side-whiskers. "Really, Noll," he answered, making a face, "you have plagued me no end with this same theme, already so well ventilated, innumerable times before. Never in my life have I been so bedeviled! Look here, you're in danger of becoming tiresome."

"I suppose I have. I suppose I am," Oliver admitted with a sigh. "Point taken."

"Why should I care so much as a pin what happened to my father? What was he to me?" said Mark, champing upon his cigar as though he meant to crush it out of existence.

"I know *I* should care, if he had been my father — my poor old father, heaven rest his soul! Though I do suppose my views on the matter are of little consequence to you. Nonetheless, despite your unfavorable opinion of him Ralph Trench *was* your father, Mark, you cannot deny that. How true are your childhood recollections of him — of his temperament, his character, his principles — and how much has been manufactured by your own imagination, from much brooding and supposing, in the interval?"

The squire made no reply, preferring instead to concentrate upon the game. His eyes — too small, too narrow, too closely planted, with his craggy brow overhanging them both — marked out the shot. Tap. Click. Red ball disappears into the lower corner pocket.

"Regardless how much his leaving may have harmed your mother — "

The squire looked up sharply. "We'll not speak of her," he warned his guest, in tones as chilly as the night air. It was clear that Oliver had plucked a tender string. "There's no necessity for that, none at all. She was a woman who endured much in her life, and there's an end to it."

The gentlemen pursued their breaks quietly for a space. The play went forward rather more quickly now, with the squire making some good runs and scoring several consecutive cannons.

"I talked briefly with your friend the vicar, before leaving the inn tonight," said Oliver, by and by. "He inquired rather obliquely after some letters he gave over to you, about a week or more ago — letters he'd found concealed in an old press at the vicarage. A share of them concerned your father."

"I seem to recall he gave me letters of some kind; but truly — I've had neither the inclination nor the spare moment to peruse them. It was just prior to your arrival here, if memory serves, but I'll be hanged if I can remember where I've put them. I jolly well should have burned them. Perhaps I did burn them; I really couldn't say."

"Dear old Mark, at times I don't know how to take you. I believe you should have had more faith in him."

"Faith in whom? The vicar, or my father?"

"Stuff and nonsense! You know the answer very well."

"Again you return to that tired subject. You're indefatigable, Noll, like Jolly-boy there, once you've got your jaws into something," grumbled the squire, laying aside his cue. He had long since lost count of the score, and seemed bored now with the play. "*Faith!*" he exclaimed, with a bitter stress upon the word. "Another of those humbugs over which the fine vicar and I have had a tussle or three. Faith? It doesn't signify straw. I ask you, Noll, what is so jolly commendable about it? Where is the virtue in blind allegiance to a thing that cannot be proved? I ask you further — what do you call a fellow who accepts a stranger's assurances on some issue of vital interest, without a whit of evidence to support them? I'll tell you what you should call that fellow. A gull. A flat. An easy mark. A Simple Simon. Fair game. The barest sort of dupe. A jolly fool. That, Noll, is what you should call that fellow. *Ha!*"

With a fresh cigar in hand he marched out upon the balcony, a pensive Oliver trailing behind. There the gentlemen spent some time examining the night, gazing across the back lawn towards Cranberry Chase, and the somber dark mass of Grim Forest beyond, and beyond that the curtain of the Talbot Peaks, under a silvery glow of moonlight. It was dead quiet on the balcony.

The moon was standing far above the ragged line of the Talbots, the better to lavish her virgin beams upon the countryside. The gentlemen smoked their cigars for some minutes, in calm reflection, until the squire touched a hand to Oliver and whispered —

"Did you hear that, Noll?"

Oliver froze at once, listening. He craned out a little over the balustrade.

"No, I heard nothing. What did you hear?"

"A cry of some kind, there at the edge of the lawn. From that grove of trees."

"It seems peaceful now."

"The night has more eyes than Argus," said Mark. "There is something in that fir-tree there. Do you see it? That blue fir, just over there. Look how the topmost limbs will tremble now and again, ever so gently. And there is not a breath of wind."

"Yes — yes — I see!" Oliver replied, excitedly.

"There is something lodged there, in and among the branches, and it is watching us."

Just as he spoke the limbs of the tree recoiled, and a heavy form lifted itself into the air. It had a roundish, faintly humanish head, painted a ghostly white, with green glowing eyes and paired tufts of feathers like horns. Moth-like wings bore the creature noiselessly upward towards the moon.

"The Skylingden owl?" whispered Oliver.

"And I'll warrant it is not alone. Look there!"

What the squire had guessed was true. Another bird, larger even than the first, but of a sinister, vulture-like appearance, rose out of a neighboring tree in pursuit. It climbed smoothly into the sky, making rapid gains on its quarry. At the very last moment the owl swung about, and so the combatants engaged. At once the air was alive with furious screeches and weird, evil cries. In the stream of moonlight the creatures circled and dove, dodged and plummeted, pivoted round one another in tight, angular circles, flashing their wings and striking out with their talons. Several times they vanished behind a screen of trees, only to reappear quickly and resume their attacks, with no slackening of purpose — vanished, appeared — vanished, appeared — then came shooting over the heads of the two onlookers, before being lost to view over the roof-line of Dalroyd. As the sounds of the conflict receded into the distance, quiet returned to the balcony, to the back lawn, to Cranberry Chase, to all indeed but the billiard-room, where Jolly-boy had set to growling.

"The second creature was a teratorn, beyond doubt," said Mark, after calling to the little terrier, to soothe him. "The general form and appearance of it. And the cry is jolly distinctive."

"I'll not bet against you," said Oliver, shivering from the cold, as much as from the unearthly disturbance he and Mark had witnessed. "Could it have been our Mr. Shakes perhaps, out upon one of his nocturnal rambles?"

"A reasonable conjecture. If true, it would seem he has indeed made the acquaintance of his fellow rover of the celestial sphere — and found it not to his liking, not by a long chalk."

"Perhaps this owl presents some unwanted competition for Mr. Shakes, as your cousin suggested. Perhaps this is what has been keeping him from the Peaks recently. You recall what Slack told us of it."

"I do."

"It appears to me this Skylingden owl acquitted itself rather well under the circumstances. What were Captain Hoey's words? 'It's a damned ferocious owl that can disquiet a teratorn.'"

So said a troubled Oliver, so agreed the squire his host; and together they smoked their cigars out in the moonlight.

CHAPTER XV

LAST OF A SHORT-FACE

IN the morning, after a late breakfast of tea, fried ham and eggs, and brown bread, topped off by another epigram of the dusty Silla's, Oliver and his host came to the decision that a brisk outing in the sloop might be just the thing to help them sort out their thoughts. Accordingly they left word with the indispensable Smithers as to their objective, and after a change of clothing struck out for the lakeshore, Oliver in his sunny outfit of yellow checks and Mark in his skipper's garb, with an enthusiastic Jolly-boy scampering beside them.

The thin, transparent mist off the lake had earlier given signs of lifting, and so it was, the gentlemen now saw, as they made their way to Dalroyd dock. More than a few times, as they worked to prepare the sloop, they found themselves glancing round, in expectation that the sad clergyman and his wife might put in an appearance. But no one came; evidently the old couple were otherwise engaged this morning. Soon all was in readiness, the preparations having been overseen by that most assiduous of first mates, Mr. Jolly-boy, rendering his usual capable assistance. The mooring was cast off, the pier shoved away; the sloop drifted out upon the dark water. The squire, having been disturbed by a host of unintelligible dreams in the night, amidst a fitful, restless sleep, and having declared at breakfast how he was inclining towards one of his moods, set course for the very middle of the lake — that part where, presumably, the depths were at their deepest.

"Where the bottom cannot be sounded," he announced from the mainsail, "and where it is, most likely, that vicar's girl drowned herself. Fell from the side of her boat, and so drifted down, and down, and further down still — lost to sight forever in the inky void, in a chasm as black as Grecian Erebus — here in the very mouth of the volcano!"

"Aren't you being excessive?" Oliver asked, growing a little uncomfortable. Gazing into that void so pitchy dark and syrupy put him in mind of their earlier excursion upon Lonewater, not so long ago; put him in mind of it, and showed him too how something changed he was, for every fishy form glimpsed there beneath the waves seemed today indistinguishable from the body of poor Miss Marchant.

"Am I? Well, I expect I am, Noll. It's this foul humor that plagues me. I warrant seeing a pair of corpses out for a trot at the lakeshore will have its effect upon a person."

"We've not yet established just what they were, Mark, or who; though of one thing we can be certain — they were *not* corpses. That would be an impossibility."

"Revenants, then — spirit forms, without substance. Bear in mind, no one has seen these two people apart from you, and myself, and Jolly-boy there. Shilston Upcot is a jolly unsuitable place in which to hide; there's always someone round who knows what is what, I can assure you. And yet no one claims any knowledge of them."

Oliver had no answer for him, and so turned his attention to the passing scenery. To starboard rose the grand, majestic slopes of the point, and atop it Skylingden Hall and the family Wintermarch — or was it Campleman? As they swung round, Oliver descried several of those dark clefts or notches sprinkled about its southern face — like eye-holes in the skull of Argus, as the squire in his present mood might have phrased it — marking out where the caves were.

"Hallo!" he exclaimed.

"What say?" returned the squire, straining to hear.

"I believe your short-face is with us again."

"Splayfoot? Where?"

"On that lofty ledge, near another of the cave-entrances. Care to look?"

He offered Mark the small field-glass which he had borrowed from the library at the suggestion of Mr. Smithers. A distant cry from the wondrous instrument in the Captain's villa at the Peaks, true, but it would serve. The squire accepted the piece and trained his eyes upon the indicated spot, while maintaining a firm hold upon the mainsheet. With the swaying of the boat it took him some moments to be sure of what he saw.

"Spot-on, Noll!" he called aloud. "Though from here he looks to be sleeping. That's odd — not the sort of thing the old fellow ought to be doing there, surely, in plain view. Jolly bad form, at the very least. Normally he's an altogether private bear."

"Perhaps he's had a short night, as we did. Perhaps he'll be up and about in a trice."

Mark did not immediately reply. He was peering very hard through the lenses, so hard that he was obliged to remove his hand from the mainsheet to help steady the glass.

"I fear old Splayfoot will be neither upping nor abouting again, Noll."

"How do you mean?"

"I'll lay you fifty guineas he's dead."

"What! Dead?"

The squire nodded. "As a coffin-nail. Look closely," he said, returning the instrument to Oliver. "You see how he's positioned there, with his head drooping from the ledge? Jolly unnatural. No bear sleeps in such a manner."

"How can we be certain he's dead?"

"There is but one reliable method — we'll ride to Skylingden directly and make sure of it ourselves. Poor old Splayfoot!"

"To Skylingden? Today?" said Oliver, rising in his seat.

"At once, as soon as we've put to shore."

"So you're not nearly so keen then on the inky void, the realm of Erebus — the Greeks' mythical corridor to hell?"

The squire answered with one of his crooked smiles. "There is another corridor of interest, a lone bridle-path through Skylingden Wood, leading round the mansion-house and outbuildings to the verge of the summit. Like Erebus it has been there for years upon years; I've explored it myself many times, and Tinker knows it well. From there we may gain access to the ledge and Splayfoot by means of one of many natural trails crossing the south face."

Oliver lowered the glass from his eyes, his expression grim, as he contemplated the bold promontory standing before them. "Rather steepish, is it not?"

"Not to worry. Likely we'll be able to diagnose the old fellow's condition from the summit itself, by spying on him from above. Look here, Noll — we must grasp the opportunity while we may. Prepare to come about!"

Oliver obediently pushed the tiller while the squire attended to the rigging. When the sails began to luff the gentlemen shifted sides; the jib was released, the tiller straightened. The boom swung to larboard. Round went the sloop, beating up the spray as she heeled on the new tack. The village hove in sight, the sweeping curve of the point fell astern. The crew made quickly for the pierhead and there secured the boat, then retraced their steps to Dalroyd. At the stables they relieved the groom of Tinker and the chestnut mare, after first informing Mr. Smithers of their change of plans. To Oliver's surprise the squire voiced his intention that Jolly-boy should accompany them to Skylingden. Oliver recollected his host's prior reluctance on this point, upon their first ride to the mansion-house, and said as much.

"Ah, but we need not allow him from our sight, on this occasion, as we've no Wintermarches to visit," the squire pointed out.

Once the girths had been tightened and the horsemen were in the stirrups, the groom held up the excited terrier to Mark, who placed the dog into a leather pouch attached to his saddle. With his head and ears poking out of this compartment and his tongue excitedly a-wag, Jolly-boy appeared more than happy with his lot, in a position now to observe everything about him from a safe elevation. Clearly he was not unaccustomed to this method of traveling.

"Most ingenious!" Oliver exclaimed.

"Isn't he?" smiled the squire, with a little conscious pride; at which remark both friends laughed very heartily.

Away they went, past Gray Lodge and the spire of St. Lucy's, through the crossroads and up the road to Skylingden. They skirted the ivy-laden perimeter wall at a little distance, making use of the aforementioned bridle-path through the high wood. Glimpses of the lazy roof-line, sinister gables and chimney-stacks, and topmost tier of windows of the mansion-house could be seen through the trees, which as usual were devoid of bird-chatter. Silence and shadow engulfed the horsemen as they rode. Oliver had the disquieting impression that their passage was being observed from one or more of those upper windows, that eyes even at that moment were engaged in tracing their movements. Of course it was nothing but fancy; likely the inmates of the house, if indeed any were watching, were rather more amused than agitated by the sight of two such interesting riders, the one in a sunny checked suit, the other in a blue skipper's jacket, canvas trousers, and oil-skin cap.

The gentlemen pursued their lonely way through the wood, following the path round to the more southerly precincts of the estate. Gradually the trees melted away and they found themselves in the midst of a glade littered with scattered fragments of masonry, much of it half-buried, like the submerged remains of some ancient, earth-going vessel. Beyond lay the verge of the summit, with its broken line of firs and bits of underwood standing against the horizon. Oliver gazed about him at the ruins of the abbey foundations, at the gray stone blocks, shivered crockets and ashlar, bricks and mortar, and found his curiosity set ablaze; at which point the squire slyly advised caution, lest a frothing madman in black cowl and sandals should come bouncing from behind a shrub and annihilate them.

They picketed their horses in a grove of young trees beyond the ruins, where Mark extracted Jolly-boy from his traveling-compartment and set him to ground.

"You're not afraid for him here?" Oliver asked. "I certainly should be. What of the Skylingden owl? What of Mr. Shakes or some other creature of prey? We have our weapons to defend ourselves, but Jolly-boy has none."

"The owl is nocturnal and so we'll see nothing of him. As for the teratorn, I warrant he'll be roaming now round the Peaks or Grim Forest. At any rate there is sufficient cover here. Should you, however, observe a bird with black wings and head of crimson gliding overhead, give a shout and I'll collect Jolly-boy double-quick."

Oliver agreed, and followed his two companions to the brink of the summit. It was a dizzying prospect there at the junction of land and sky, with a soft breeze blowing from the north and the far-spreading sheet of water laid out below. The squire noted his friend's unease at once.

"I had no idea you'd be affected by the height," said he.

Oliver admitted as much.

"Living as you do at Crow's-end, on that blasted headland overhanging the sea — and yet fearful of the height?"

Oliver admitted as much again, and more. "Rather like the plank-bridge at the Peaks," he remarked, looking down, "only far worse."

"Well, I for one am jolly comfortable with it. Look here, Noll — it's just such a view as this that gives one a true sense of proportion in life, an appreciation of one's place in the hierarchy of existence. Here before us lie the many vast constituent elements of that existence; here are the respective divinities of earth and air, wind and water, presiding over their temple which is the world. Such a view concentrates the faculties; it simplifies the mystery of purpose no end. And all in all it is the simpler life I prefer, the uncomplicated, unencumbered life. One must ever strive for simplicity, Noll, if one is to be content."

"There you are again, Mark, speechifying like a regular pagan."

The squire grinned — with no little satisfaction, Oliver guessed — and dropping to one knee began his hunt for the ledge, the one with the bear on it. He soon found it some distance to the left. It was a lengthy, irregular shelf of dark stone, some hundred feet or so below them; upon it lay the body of the short-face, on its side with the head drooping over the edge.

"Dead," muttered the squire, with sad finality. "Deceased. Stout old fellow!"

"Can we be sure?" said Oliver. "He could simply be ill."

For answer Mark gathered up a handful of stones and let them fall, one by one. A few landed squarely on the short-face. They bounced from it and soared off into space, without any response from the bear.

"Convinced, Noll?"

Oliver was, nearly. He took up the field-glass and trained it on the body. What he saw bore out the squire's contention. "The left eye at the very least is gone," he reported. "And there looks to be blood upon the head, what I can see of it — quite a lot of blood, actually — and blood elsewhere upon the body as well. And upon the ledge itself."

"Yes, I would agree with you. Poor old Splayfoot! We must make an inspection."

He glanced about him, right and left, and shortly found what he sought — the beginnings of a trail running down and across the slant face of the promontory, skirting the trees. It was littered with pine needles, and not more than a few yards wide at most, and crumbly at the margin — perhaps the very route by which the agile short-face had made his way to the rocky shelf, there to meet his death.

"Come along, Noll," urged Mark, already starting his descent. "Look here at Jolly-boy. He's not in the least affected by the altitude. He knows nothing of it."

It was true; the terrier was trotting along at the heels of his master, as nimble it seemed as any mountain goat. In a trice both dog and squire dropped from sight. Screwing up his courage in the form of a bold lip and a manful brow, Oliver reluctantly joined in, with his left hand upon the reassuring solidity of the rock-face and a close eye to the placement of his steps. It was a sometimes awkward, sometimes harrowing endeavor. After a time, however, he realized that the trail was simpler to negotiate than it appeared, so long as one did not look off towards the right, into that vertiginous gulf between the flanking pines. He resolved not to allow his glance to stray any farther afield than his boots, and merely follow the trail where it led, ceding to his friend the squire the myriad joys of the prospect. He found this did the trick rather well, and before long he was reunited with Mark and Jolly-boy upon the rocky shelf.

Before them lay the huge carcass of the bear. It was Oliver's closest look ever at one of the creatures, closer even than that he'd had at Strangeways. He found his interest gripped — metaphorically, of course — by the animal's queer long limbs, by the blunt, cat-like head, by the sheer enormity of hair and claw and muscle of which the beast was composed. Its stupendous bulk made for an impressive spectacle, even in death. The muzzle and indeed much of the coat were stippled with guard-hairs of gray and white, reflecting the creature's advanced age. Oliver shuddered to imagine what the mighty long arms and fearsome claws of even so ancient a bear might do; which in turn set him to thinking — most unreasonably, yet most uncomfortably — how old Splayfoot might just be a bluffer, might simply be toying with them, waiting for the proper moment to rise up and attack. But the quantities of dark blood spilled about the body and on the ledge rightly convinced him otherwise.

"Note the face, Noll," said Mark.

They saw that Oliver had been correct, that the eyes of the bear had been plucked out by marauding birds. They observed too the abundance of frightful wounds about the drooping head and throat, and across the shoulders, spine, and haunches. It was clear this bear would do no rising and attacking today. This view was seconded by Jolly-boy, who, after sniffing suspiciously at the carcass and growling, raised his little liver-colored patch that served for an eyebrow in quizzical fashion.

"Was it a — *saber-cat*, do you think, that did this?" Oliver asked, alarmed by the very sound of the name of that most feared of mountain devils.

"Hardly. He was most grievously ill-used by something, true; but from the nature and position of the injuries I should guess it came upon him from the air," said Mark, with a kind of lazy fascination.

"The birds of yesternight?"

The squire shrugged. "Perhaps one of them took advantage of the old fellow's time of life — though it is jolly difficult to picture any but Mr. Shakes in that role."

"In Crow's-end one hears stories of how teratorns may league together to bring down a fully-grown saber-cat," said Oliver, uneasily. "Can this be true?"

"Perhaps, though I myself have never seen it. But I expect it could happen."

"It's a quelling thought."

"Look here, Noll. It's plain he's not been dead for long, having likely met his end in the night. Those injuries appear to me to be talon marks. What other conclusion can we draw? I'll lay you fifty guineas our Mr. Shakes and perhaps one or more of his fellow rovers may lay claim to this. There is no other species dwelling in these skies that could produce so furious an onslaught. Though I'll confess I remain mystified on a single point, and that is this: why is it the assailant failed to consume much of the prey? Ha! I see you share my puzzlement. Apart from the eyes there's not the least evidence the carcass has been feasted upon."

The squire turned thoughtfully on his heel. Almost at once his gaze fell upon the dark cleft in the rock, farther along the ledge, and something like cheer brightened his drab gray features. "Well, come along then," said he. "Let us see what awaits us in this cavern."

"You propose to go in there — *now?*" asked Oliver.

"Naturally. Have you never been in a cavern before?"

"Never."

"Well, hardly a cavern, I admit, for these fissures are not so large. I can recollect scrambling about in one of them as a child. My revered father must have brought me when I was rather young, though I admit my memories of the episode are imperfect. I have explored a number of these caves myself since that time, some of them uninhabited, some of them not. They are made use of on occasion by bears and certain other denizens of the wood as a retreat, for a few hours at a time. Likely that was Splayfoot's custom."

Standing in the twilight just inside the entrance, they could see that the passage extended forward for a considerable distance. It was generally oval in outline, much broader than it was tall, with dimensions sufficient for one to walk upright without colliding with the roof. The walls were composed of bare black earth, with here and there a thin deposit of clay or sheet of flowstone. The floor was smooth but undulating, with fragments of fallen rock and occasional small bones and mats of hair lying about. Patches of ice glistened in the corners. There was little appreciable circulation of air within the cave, suggesting that no other avenue to the surface existed.

"Are you not concerned this cave might be occupied?" asked Oliver, attempting to pierce the darkness of its farther reaches. "At the very least there may be bats here, or some of those very substantial cave crickets I've seen displayed at Strangeways. I must admit I am not fond of such things; but of course I am a city man."

"There look to be bats, though not to excess, as there is little odor and the accumulation of their refuse is trivial. They are not so common in these altitudes. In truth I see no evidence of any other recent inhabitant apart from Splayfoot, whose sleeping apartment this likely was. He was ever a solitary sort, much like myself, Noll; I have not known him to consort with anything more substantial than the watches of the night. If he had himself a companion these last years there's been jolly little trace of her round here."

The squire removed from his jacket a number of wax tapers, half of which he gave to his friend.

"Hallo! You must have pocketed these upon our return to Dalroyd. You had it in mind all along to explore this cave," said Oliver.

"Just so. As I've so often told you, Noll, we must grasp our opportunities while we may. We could not have you pass the season in Shilston Upcot without having toured one of our more singular geological curiosities. Hoey for one never would have forgiven me."

The squire struck a light; a pair of tapers flared, throwing a ghostly radiance upon the walls of the cave, upon its dark arches and frowning buttresses of rock, its shimmering deposits of ice and flowstone. With their tapers aloft the gentlemen advanced slowly, cautiously, peering into this crevice and that as they went, their senses very much on the alert. It was cool and damp in the cave, and utterly still, apart from the noise of their breathing and the crunch of earth under their boots.

"Where's Jolly-boy gotten to?" asked Oliver. "He's gone very quiet. I can neither see nor hear him."

The squire whistled softly. For reply a queer little growl was heard in the passage just ahead. Instinctively Oliver placed a hand upon his knife.

"There is another chamber forward of us there," said Mark, who was in the advance. The next moment he stumbled a little, and discovered at his feet some pieces of masonry not unlike those seen among the ruins of the abbey foundations.

"Ha! What's this, then? Jolly-boy!" he called. At once, echoes of his voice came charging back towards him from every direction.

They crept through a narrowing of the passage and gained entry to the farther chamber, where a thing at once commonplace and mysterious met their eyes. It appeared to be a rubble pile, a midden of sorts, built of waste fragments of ashlar and flint and brick and mortar, rising to a man's height from the floor of the cave. Beside it they found Jolly-boy, crouching there with his ears raised and a worried look in his terrier's face.

"What is it?" asked the squire, as if the dog were as human as Oliver and wholly as capable of responding. "What have you got there, fellow?"

As the gentlemen examined the pile of debris they came to the realization that a structure of some kind lay hidden within it — a generally cylindrical structure perhaps three feet high, built of thin, tile-like stones, and over which the waste masonry had been deposited, either to conceal its presence or to hinder access to it.

The squire reached again into his jacket and provided a set of small brass candlesticks. Into two of them he placed the wax-lights. Two tapers more were then quickly prepared and mounted.

"Hallo!" cried Oliver, in admiration. "Most sensible of you."

"Jolly difficult to have at it, otherwise," said Mark. "One never knows what one may find in these caves; it is wise to come prepared. Now our hands are at liberty for exploration."

They doffed their hats and jackets and pitched in. It was the work of some half-hour or more to remove the overlying debris. It was no easy task; many of the fragments were weightier than they appeared, and rather sharply edged — for this their riding-gloves proved of invaluable service — and though in reasonable trim the gentlemen found themselves put to it. In due course the level surface of the cylinder was brought to light. At the top of it was a heavy capstone like a lid, fastened down by means of cords running through iron rings in the walls of the understructure.

Wiping his brow, Oliver stepped back to survey the excavation.

"It's a well, don't you think?" he concluded. "Yes, that's what it is. It's a well, and that flat sheet of stone upon it, lashed down with ropes, is its cover."

"Jolly fascinating," said the squire, rubbing the dust from his gloves. "I'm inclined to agree. I can't recollect having seen the like of it before."

"Evidently you've not visited this particular cave."

"Never in my life."

The squire walked round and round the well in one direction, then in the other, chin in hand, peering at it from every angle, tapping at it, testing the strength of the bindings that held the cover in place. Jolly-boy, who had respectfully stepped aside while the gentlemen went about their labors, now resumed his crouching posture, ears erect, eyes staring fixedly at the well. He voiced a queer little growl, followed by a snort, then a whine; then he stood up and uttered a short, unearthly, broken cry, sniffing the air as he had the carcass of Splayfoot.

"What is it?" Oliver asked. "What does he smell?"

The squire knelt and placed an ear to the side of the well. He listened for what seemed a very long time, every now and again urging Jolly-boy to silence with a brisk "*Hush!*" On a sudden he rose and darted a swift glance towards his human companion.

"I'll be hanged, Noll, if I don't believe there is someone in there."

"Gracious, Mark, you cannot be serious!" returned Oliver, in an awful whisper.

"I assure you I am. Though I cannot make it out exactly, there is beyond doubt an activity of some kind there within the stone — vague, featureless sounds, indicative of movement."

"The plashing of water from below. The well must descend to the level of the lake surface and beneath. Surely what you hear are the transmitted sounds of Lonewater, the breakers against the shore, magnified through the hollow length of the shaft."

"Perhaps. But do you imagine we should be able to detect such distant sounds — that they should be of such magnitude as to penetrate the stone?"

"Perhaps there are defects in the mortar and the rats have gotten in. Oh, I admit it does confound me," said Oliver, shaking his head. "Why on earth put a well here, in this place, in a cave? Why go to the trouble of digging it out and yet not extend the shaft to the summit above? It's rather an inconvenient means of drawing water, don't you think?"

The squire was inclined to agree.

"And what of this debris heaped upon it? It would appear that someone has tried to conceal the very fact of the well's existence. Splayfoot himself looks to have been picking through it, and thereby exposed some of the underlying stonework. You'll note how certain of the fragments already had been pushed aside before we arrived. You stumbled upon them yourself."

The squire admitted he had no respectable alternative.

"It seems to me, Mark," said Oliver — with a look to the wax-lights, and a less-than-subtle inspection of his pocket-watch — "it seems to me we'd best be returning to Dalroyd."

The squire glanced at Jolly-boy, and as he bent to scratch the dog's head he noticed something lying amid the undisturbed masonry nearby, something that was neither rock nor stone nor mortar. He extended a hand and drew the object from the pile. It was made of lacquered wood, and was cloaked in the accumulated dust of ages. He looked at it in his palm for a moment, brushed some of the years from it, and passed it to Oliver.

"Here you are, then, Noll — have a peep at this."

It was an antique crucifix, much worn and partly disfigured, joined to a fragile string of rosary beads. Oliver looked up inquiringly.

"Lake Friars," nodded the squire.

CHAPTER XVI

AT THE BRINK

A lantern, some few more candles and sulfur matches, Mark's tinder-box, a short coil of line from the sloop, some wire, some various tools and other implements — chisels and hammer, a crowbar, handsaw, and the like — having been collected into two canvas bags, were transported by Oliver and the squire from the summit to the rocky shelf a hundred feet below. The gentlemen had returned to Dalroyd, deposited Jolly-boy there and retrieved these needful items, and ridden back again — Oliver with that same unpleasant sense of being spied upon in the high wood — to pursue their exploration of the cave, as Mr. Mark Trench for one was impatient to know what lay beneath the capstone of the well.

The cords binding the stone in place were far too gnarled and knotted for untying, and so the handsaw was employed to sever them. Even as he worked a degree of doubt arose within the breast of Oliver as to the wisdom of the endeavor. His antiquarian's curiosity was one thing, but danger was quite another. What could possibly be alive and stirring there beneath the capstone? Cave crickets? Some species of forest creature? A brother short-face, perhaps, or even a saber-cat? Or simply rats? Despite his misgivings he labored on, at Mark's urging, for he was as intrigued by the secret of the well as he was by the uncommon energy exhibited by the squire in uncovering it.

Once the last of the cords had been stripped away, some remaining bits of waste masonry that lay piled up round the base of the well were pushed aside, to create sufficient space to maneuver while removing the capstone. The discovery of the ancient crucifix suggested that this place and this well — if well it was — bore some connection to the Lake Friars, the reclusive order dwelling within the great abbey that once had stood upon the summit above, the great abbey that was no more, as the friars themselves were no more. What could have induced them, Oliver wondered again, to sink a well in so inconvenient a spot?

It required some effort, by means of the chisels and crowbar and the coil of line, not to say main force, to prize the capstone from the well. The stone was very heavy, and as they worked to ease it to the ground it slipped from the line, went sliding through their gloved hands, and crashed headlong. The result was an immense echoing blast of sound that Oliver fancied must have been heard clear to kingdom-come and back; unfortunately, something like a quarter of the capstone was broken off in the process. The gentlemen exchanged glances of mutual dismay, but there was little to be done; they had, Oliver reflected, in point of fact done quite enough already.

Nothing snarled, nothing hissed, nothing leaped at them from the well; indeed, once the noise of the crash had died away there was no sort of noise whatsoever. Cautiously they peered over the rim into the abyss. Beneath them stretched a spiral chasm of stone, down and down, darker and darker, growing black as coal as it fell beyond reach of the lantern-light. Gazing into it they could discern no activity of any kind, despite Mark's claim to have detected movement within the stonework. They watched and waited for some minutes, but all was quiet as a churchyard.

"Well?" Oliver asked.

"Just so — a well it is, I warrant."

"Pray be serious now, Mark."

"My dear Noll, I am simply being forthright. I believe it must descend to lake level at the very least, just as you supposed. This is where the friars will have drawn their water, so as to avoid lengthy and repeated forays to the village and back."

"But where is the raising apparatus — the stanchion and winch, the rope, the bucket? I see no provision for any such mechanism here, no fittings in the stone. How could they have managed it?"

"Perhaps the bucket was lowered directly from the edge."

"The topmost stones ought to show evidence of repeated wear from the bucket-rope, but they do not."

"Likely the evidence has been erased by time."

"I am doubtful of that," said Oliver, wrinkling his brow. "And they will have had to carry the water along that dizzying trail to the summit. Or did they perhaps hoist it from the ledge? Still, it is strange. What other purpose might there be for a hole such as this?"

The squire caught up a bit of flint and dropped it over the side, just as earlier he'd dropped some stones upon the body of Splayfoot to test for the presence of life. Nothing was heard from the flint in response; no sound of its striking anything, nothing but a noiseless vanishing into the darkness. Another flint was dropped, same result. And so a third.

"Jolly like old Lonewater," smiled Mark, wryly. "No bottom hereabouts either. Nothing but the inky void."

"It must be very deep," Oliver agreed. "Which puts me in mind how difficult it must have been to — "

"*Hush!*" said the squire, abruptly clapping a finger to his lips. "There is something there."

They listened, Oliver not knowing for what. The squire craned out a little over the edge, his face frozen in concentrated attention.

"What did you hear?" Oliver whispered.

The squire raised a hand and shook his head, enjoining his friend to silence. So Oliver obediently held his tongue, just as Jolly-boy had held his — or tried to — so that Mark might complete his examination undisturbed.

"Whispers," said the squire, after a time. "I am sure there are whispers."

A creeping chill gripped the neck and scalp of Oliver, a veritable hoar-frost at high midsummer. He glanced uncomfortably round the cave chamber, at its scowling walls and darkened recesses eerily astir in the chiaroscuro of the wax-lights. "If it's your intention to unsettle me, you're managing a decent job of it," said he.

The squire shut his eyes and leaned out over the well, one ear down, trying with all his might and main to draw in the faintest of sounds.

"Whispers, beyond doubt," he reported. "Whispers, here and there, and something like a rustling of garments. I'm jolly certain of it!"

"I hear nothing," Oliver said.

"What! Nothing?"

"Not a murmur."

"But, Noll — surely you must hear it! Listen more closely, then. It's plain as a pikestaff."

"Really, Mark, there's nothing there."

The squire cast about in frustration and puzzlement for some moments. He scratched his side-whiskers, smoothed his mustaches, lifted the oil-skin cap and rubbed his bald head — at which time a new resource struck him with not inconsiderable force. "Grab up the line there, Noll," he directed, with a brisk snap of his fingers.

"Whatever for?"

"I'm going down."

"Stuff and nonsense, Mark — say you're not!" exclaimed Oliver, quite aghast at this proposition, and with a face that showed it. Nonetheless he gathered up the line as instructed.

"We'll make fast one end of it to this iron ring in the stonework — it appears sturdy enough, if rusted. Good. And we'll run the line through this second ring as well, to be on the safe side, and twist it about the ring a couple of times. Stout fellow! Now insert the crowbar through the ring, just so — and begin to coil the line about it — excellent — now grasp the bar firmly — you see how the stepwise rotation of the bar will release the line. Now I'll secure the tail-end round myself. Here it is our yachtsmen's training at knots will greatly profit us."

"But there is hardly enough line," Oliver protested.

"Not to worry — it need not be so long."

"Why not?"

Mark swung the lantern out over the abyss and pointed. "Look there. Look directly below us, Noll, straight down the side of the shaft. What do you see there, projecting from the stones a distance below?"

Oliver peeped over the edge, and his eyes grew wide as he spotted them — a series of small metal bars or rungs perhaps forty feet below, rising like a ladder out of the darkness.

"Good God, Mark," said Oliver. "You simply cannot go pottering about in there. Surely those bars will not hold after so long a time."

"Their condition, my dear Mr. Langley, I shall of course ascertain before risking a single jolly ounce of my life. Have you forgotten already, Noll? We must learn what the secrets are," returned the squire, effectively quelling all opposition. After binding a short, flat candle to his cap with a circlet of wire — a not particularly sage expedient, Oliver remarked, considering the cap was of oil-skin, and the flame was of fire — the squire lowered himself into the well, planting his boots against its inner curved surface as Oliver paid out the line. By slow, backward steps he contrived to walk his way down the shaft, the candle in his cap providing illumination as the lantern-light receded.

When he came to the bars he examined them closely, to be sure they would not crack or break away from the stones. He tested them, set his weight upon them, kicked at them with his boot; though rusted like the iron rings, they appeared sound. Satisfied, he began his descent. Though he encountered some degree of laxity in the rungs as he proceeded, it was not sufficient to give him pause. The line grew taut as he came to the end of it, at which point he loosed the tie from his waist, trusting his safety now wholly to the ladder in the stone.

As he proceeded his ears caught a suggestion of whispers, but he determined after a moment it was nothing more than his own breathing. There was a glistening dankness to the well here, as revealed by the candle, though it did not seem to affect his hold upon the bars. There was a closeness too, an oppressive sense of confinement, of moist, chilly walls closing in, that he had not expected to affect him. Never, not even in childhood, had he had a dread of such things as closets or coffins, and so hadn't thought to encounter it here in this chimney within the earth. He had little fear of heights, what fear should he have of depths? What fear of the inky void, as black as Erebus?

He stopped to listen; there was nothing but the noise of his own lungs, and so he began to suspect he had indeed imagined it all — the indistinct, furtive movement behind the stonework, the whispers, the rustle of garments. Below him there was nothing but the spiral chasm, leading ever farther down. He felt a sting as a drop of wax from the candle fell upon his whiskered cheek. The exertion of clinging to the bars was starting to tell; a hot sweat had formed on his brow, despite the cold all about him.

He had come far but accomplished little, had gained no further insight into the mystery. Another drop of wax stung him. As he lowered his foot he felt the new rung beneath it giving under his weight. It was at this point he made the decision to return to the cave. Climbing to the top of the ladder he caught the line, knotted it about his waist, and set to hauling himself the remaining distance up the side. He soon started to flag; it was more exertion than he had bargained for. He saw the silhouette of the well-opening overhead, saw the lantern perched upon the rim, saw the face of Oliver glowing orange and yellow in the light. In a burst of activity he scrambled up and over the edge, and with a heavy sigh dropped to the ground.

"A jolly waste of twenty minutes," he admitted, gingerly extracting the taper from his cap. "So there it is, then, Noll — a bootless errand."

"A wasted hour, more like," said Oliver. "Whatever did you find down there, to so occupy your time?"

"Not a thing apart from the rising damp. But surely, it was no more than twenty minutes," returned the squire, with an eye to the dial-plate of his gold pocket-watch.

"I must disagree with you," said Oliver, plucking his own silver ditto from its fob. They compared timepieces; that of Oliver was running fifty minutes and more ahead of Mark's.

"Jolly odd," frowned the squire.

"Did you by chance neglect to wind it?"

"Hardly. I was sure, Noll, it was no more than twenty minutes I was down. And yet, perhaps it *was* longer, indeed — "

"Rather longer! I might have brought the dusty Silla and slogged away at him while you were about your researches. I had whole yards of time."

The squire looked very hard at Oliver but saw no hint of joking there. He frowned again, at a loss to explain the discrepancy in the timepieces.

"I assure you, there's no design on my part," said Oliver, to avert any possible misunderstanding. "Perhaps there is an irregularity of the works, of the hairspring or escapement. That might account for the difference despite your attention to the winding."

"I've had no trouble with it at all. What of yours?"

"None with my piece. It has kept perfect time."

"Then we must assume both are in fine condition."

Five, ten, fifteen minutes passed. Again they compared watches; the result — no difference.

"Look here," said Mark, with a doubtful rub of his chin. "Let us see if the effect can be reproduced just as before. First, we shall both of us set our watches to the identical time — let it be on the hour — so to be sure of our starting-point. Now, you shall wind yours and I shall wind mine, so we've no question on that score. Good. We're both agreed that the times are corresponding?"

"They both are reading the same," nodded Oliver.

The squire fastened the line again to his waist, and a fresh candle to his cap. "I shall descend for another twenty minutes, by my watch's reckoning, and when I return we shall make comparison once more. Agreed?"

Down he went. From above, all Oliver could see of him, after a while, was the faint light of the candle growing fainter as he descended. More familiar with the way now, the squire moved at a confident pace, down and down, venturing some distance beyond the loosened rung. At length he halted and peeped at his watch. Unaccountably, there were nearly fifteen minutes remaining yet before he was to begin the ascent. As he waited there in the dampness of the shaft, clinging to the bars, he berated himself for finding it necessary to pursue this exercise — for surely, was it not Oliver's watch that was in error? And yet...

The appointed time arrived at last. Relieved, he started up the rungs. As he did so he thought he heard the sound of whispering, and paused to listen. This time he was sure it was *not* of his own making, for the whispers continued even after he held a breath. Many whispers from many voices, coming first from below, then from above, then from all around — a faint, urgent, incomprehensible sort of chatter swirling about him, as if there were company there of some kind — a sense of things in constant motion, but motion where nothing whatever was seen to move, where nothing was disturbed, not even the candle-flame.

Without another thought he hurried up the ladder.

Oliver, pacing and pacing beside the well, hands clasped at his back, heard at last the sound of his friend's approach. Looking down he saw the line had grown taut — rather frantically taut, so he fancied — saw that the squire was clambering up the side of the well, without having paused to secure the rope to his waist — was clambering up at rather a brisk pace — rather a heady pace — was charging upward, in point of fact — and so was quite dead-beat by the time he lowered himself to the floor of the cave.

Oliver peered into his face, not a little alarmed by what he saw there.

"What result?" asked Mark, when he had regained enough breath to speak.

There was no response at first.

"What result?" he repeated, swallowing hard.

Oliver fumbled for his watch. "Above two hours," he replied, presenting the dial-plate to view. "Mark, are you ill? You look dreadful."

The squire shook his brains to clear them.

"Twenty minutes, Noll, twenty minutes! Two hours, perhaps, but no more than twenty jolly minutes — *here!*" he said, tapping at his own watch.

To Oliver the squire seemed fretful, agitated, confused even, on account of the disproportion between the times — or was there something more behind it than that?

The disparity was too flagrant now to dismiss. Twenty minutes had lapsed, so far as Mark was concerned, during the long two hours Oliver had waited for him in the cave. In proof of this Oliver offered the wax-lights and the lantern, showing how far they had burned in the interim, as compared to the taper in his cap. It seemed irrefutable; there could be little doubt whose watch was correct. What was more the squire found himself in agreement, knowing from his own perception — from the ticking of his own internal timepiece — that he'd been gone for something longer than the twenty minutes registered on his watch-dial.

It was a truth that could not easily be explained away, and one that brought with it a tremor of apprehension. The squire looked round at the dark prison of the cave, and the guttering wax-lights, and the spiral chasm of the well, and felt that apprehension grow by swift degrees. It chilled him to the heart. The utter silence of the place acted only to magnify it, and magnify his fear that at any moment the whispers might return.

"As so many minutes seem to have passed, by your timepiece there, I expect then it will have gotten late," he said, with something of his usual manner. "Supper and Smithers will be waiting."

Oliver could not agree hastily enough that they should depart, and so they did, but not before the squire took one final action.

"We must lash it down again," he said, with a nod towards the fractured capstone. "And tightly, Noll, tightly."

By dint of struggling they managed to raise the main body of the stone to the rim of the well, and pushed it across. They slid the broken fragment in place beside it, thereby restoring the cover to a degree of wholeness. As they had severed the cords that had held it fast, they were obliged to use the line from the sloop, draping it across the stone and through the rings, several times over, and knotting it tight, as per the squire's direction. Oliver noted how insistent his friend was that the stone be fastened securely, and wondered if Mark was not still convinced in his mind he had heard something there. Yet there had been nothing, as the squire himself admitted.

After supper they retired to the library and there subjected their watches to one last examination, synchronizing them with the shelf-clock upon the mantel and observing all three for the evening. The hands advanced with equal speed; no difference in time was noted among the three pieces, which wellnigh set the question at rest. It was quite simply the final evidence, if perhaps superfluous evidence; for upon returning to Dalroyd from the high wood they had found it was Oliver's watch, not Mark's, which coincided with the clocks in the house.

"So you see, Noll, the farther I ventured into the well, the more slowly did my watch advance," said the squire, throwing himself down in one of the cushioned chairs upon the hearth-rug, cigar in hand.

"Or the faster did mine, and these others here at Dalroyd," said Oliver, standing with his back to the fire.

"Which is jolly unlikely. Look here — I descend into the well for twenty minutes, your watch records one hour; I descend for twenty minutes again, while venturing farther down, your watch records two hours. A humbug? Evidently not, for we have the proof of our own senses. I saw this very watch of mine crawl its way towards twenty minutes, could feel the aching slowness of it in my arms as I hung upon the bars. No, there is no getting round it, Noll. The farther one descends into that cavity in the earth, the slower the time passes there."

Oliver wrung his head and looked down at his shoes, thinking perhaps to read there some solution to the mystery other than the one proposed. It was so clearly preposterous!

"So we may extend our observation to its logical finish," the squire continued. "One might speculate that as one sinks deeper and deeper into that cavity, the hands of time will move ever more slowly, ever more sluggishly, until, at some point, when one has descended far enough, that movement will become wellnigh imperceptible..."

Oliver's eyes expressed the astonishment his lips could not utter.

"Is it not a thought to conjure with?" exclaimed the squire, blowing whole rafts of smoke from his cigar.

"And rank speculation, as you yourself have said. Gracious, Mark — surely one could not descend so far as that?"

"So far as what, then, Noll?"

"So far as — so far as — "

"There must come that point where time ceases to pass entirely, where the hands of a watch will record no movement. A staggering prospect, is it not?"

"A monstrous one, which hardly bears thinking of," Oliver declared. "The very idea of it makes my skin crawl. How is it possible?" He worked away at his own cigar for several moments, while looking thoughtfully again at his shoes. "Who else knows of this, do you suppose?"

"It's jolly plain the friars of the abbey knew of it. And I'll lay you fifty guineas there is at least one fellow dwelling today in Shilston Upcot who knows of it."

"Who?"

"Do you recollect old Bottom's response when you spoke to him of Splayfoot and the caves?"

"Hmmm. To be sure, he seemed genuinely frightened. Do you think this is one of his secrets?"

"We must have ourselves the pleasure of another chat with Mr. Bottom," smiled Mark. "For a stone-cutter and sexton deals in stone, Noll, in mortar and ashlar, and in holes in the earth. Who better to aid us in the present circumstance?"

After Oliver had retired for the evening, the squire remained in the library for some time, watching the fire in silence and smoking, for there was more yet for him to think on — more, indeed, than he had confided to his guest. What he had seen fit to pass over were those final minutes in the well, at the top of the rungs, as he reached for the dangling line. The sense of sound and motion all about him, of being enveloped by things where no things were — ah, that could very well have been imagined, for had he not at least once mistaken his own breathing for such phenomena? As squire of Dalroyd he was not exempt from troublesome fancies. What he could not have imagined, however — and what could most definitely *not* be explained away by any means — was the feel of the hand that had curled itself round his boot, to pull him down, the instant he reached out for the line; a firm, inviting hand, which held for just a moment or two before releasing him.

But a moment was quite long enough, thank you.

On this the squire brooded well into the night, long after his cigars had been smoked out. What it meant he dared not think; what it implied he dared not believe.

Part Two

L I G H T

I'll shape myself a way to higher things,
And who will say 'tis wrong?

JOANNA BAILLIE

CHAPTER I

DISSECTING THE WINTERMARCHES

MARKET day in Shilston Upcot!

From before first light the vendors and their helpers begin gathering in the Low Street and Town End and on the village green. Market stalls are quickly assembled, and quickly occupied. By degrees the village grows bustling and animated, brightening up in the brisk morning flush of the mountain sun. Barrows from village shops are trundled out into the road, and take up their positions; the butcher's boy with his shiny head of hair, the fishmongers and fruit-shop women, the tansy-cake seller, the chandler's man, the confectioner and tobacconist, all find their place. As farmers from the surrounding district begin arriving, the way becomes thronged with carts of every size, sort, and description — pony-carts laden with vegetables, chaise-carts bursting with livestock, milk carts weighted down with heavy churns — while the ground becomes strewn with cabbage-leaves and cobs of corn and pea-pods and celery-stalks, and other like evidence of market day in the mountains.

The dour Mr. Jinkins and Miss Cherry Ives head a local contingent from the Village Arms, dispensing cider and spruce from a portable beer-engine, and seltzer water with mint and cherry for the children. Miss Violet Crimp is there as well, posted beside a supply of her well-regarded waffle-cakes. Miss Margaret Mowbray and Mrs. Fielding are there too, offering for sale fresh flowers from their garden and honey from the busy hives at Gray Lodge.

Sheep, pigs, and cattle from the surrounding estates are brought up for auction. One fat hog of twenty stone, a regular slush bucket, is sold off with no little fanfare, for his boarship is truly the fattest hog ever seen in the county. Pigeons, rabbits, trouts, lampreys, fowls, collars of brawn, neats' tongues, goose tarts, venison pasties, country potatoes, larchberry muffins, all are there for the buying. What price, you ask? Country prices for country products. Barley at four shillings a bushel, oats at two; geese and roasting pigs at three to four shillings apiece; woodcocks, five shillings sixpence a brace; potatoes at seven pence a peck; new-laid eggs, a shilling a dozen.

There is the miller with his white hat, retailing flour and loaves of bread prepared by his beaming wife. There is his compatriot Mr. Lincote, the sugar-baker, drawing a batch of rolls and pouring out steaming cups of black coffee. All about, amateur pastry-cooks and pie-makers, some of them the wives and daughters of prominent members of the community, stand smiling and blushing behind their wares, market day being that day of days on which any and all in the neighborhood might exhibit their culinary talents. "Pies all 'ot, gen'lm'n 'n' ladies, pies all 'ot!" cry the more exuberant of the sellers, expatiating upon the excellence of their goods. Cigars, sandwiches, mountain larchberries, marchpane, gilt gingerbread, raisin wine, wax tapers, soap, treacle — all for purchase at the market, gen'lm'n 'n' ladies, all for purchase!

Roving among the throng are hosts of amateur musicians, drawn largely from the village and from Tarnley, Jay, and Cedar Crag. There is one grizzled old fellow especially who plays upon the bagpipes with the most extraordinary gusto, and can whistle like a bird exceedingly fine. His efforts are met with enthusiastic applause from all present. Fiddlers too are in great request. It seems that nearly everyone in town is there; while one-half of Shilston Upcot is about the day's business, the other half turns out to see what the rest are up to. Twice a month, on the second Friday of the fortnight, the village is jolted out of its usual state of monotonous tranquillity and for a day becomes a veritable Crow's-end in the country. Well, perhaps I exaggerate; but at the very least the village of Shilston Upcot on market Friday is a very lively place indeed.

The hours speed by in haste. The sun climbs high above the lake and darts his bright rays here and there about the valley, in and among the glades and hollows and high-country meadows, and into all the nooks and corners of the town, bathing the bluish-purple stone of the cottages and their russet-colored roof-tiles in a lustrous midsummer glow. Summer in the mountains is fleeting, and such days as this are to be cherished. This particular market Friday is given further note by the attendance of the two ladies Wintermarch of Skylingden Hall, arrived by carriage from the mansion-house with a pair of female servants in tow. All eyes light upon them. Though mother and daughter are not loath to mingle with the townsfolk they are nonetheless reserved in their mingling, as is their wont and reputation. Mrs. Wintermarch looks rather plain and somber, like her clothes; her young daughter, while noticeably prettier, is a little somber too. They seem pleasant enough, though, and courteous, their reticence arising not so much from pride as from a deep inner restraint, the token perhaps of some shared affliction. There is nothing in their manner that can in the least be mistaken for airs, which the village as a whole finds commendable. Mrs. Wintermarch is seen to engage certain of the vendors in the garnering of provisions, which are gathered up by the female servants, who are both as plain and somber as their mistress. It is noted by all that Mr. Bede Wintermarch is not among the party. In point of fact Mr. Bede Wintermarch is never among the party; his austere figure and handsome, hawkish face are but rarely seen in the village.

"And where is he today?" inquire such citizens as feel it is their right to know.

"My husband is unwell, owing to a naturally weak constitution," is the customary response of Mrs. Wintermarch. "Please accept his regrets."

Which reply only compounds the suspicion of the citizens that Mr. Bede Wintermarch is indeed Charles Campleman, reluctant to venture into town for fear of being generally recognized. Besides, it is rumored that the gentleman dyes his hair — if indeed it is his own hair at all — and affects odd elements of dress like spotted neckties, and is widely believed to be someone in disguise. None of the villagers actually admits any such suspicion to Mrs. Wintermarch, of course; rather they express their confidence that Mr. Wintermarch will be materially better in a week or two, and so may accompany his wife and daughter upon the succeeding market Friday. The unpretentiousness of their turn-out is quietly commented upon, as is the nature and quantity of the provisions garnered, and the small prices paid for them. Wesley the joiner's lad, chief informant to the vicar's household as to everything Wintermarch, confides to his youthful associates that there is little going on now at the mansion-house in the way of renovation, suggesting that the rich reserves of cash thought to reside there have all but drained away — if they ever were there at all. Mr. Nim Ives up at the Arms, had he heard this remark, would have wagged his head in endorsement of it, for it remained his belief that the chief affliction of the family Wintermarch was poverty; that Mr. Bede Wintermarch was being tight with his money, was pinching his pence because he had so few pence left to pinch.

Marvel of marvels! There is Captain Hoey, raw-boned and tall, striding through the Low Street. Well, perhaps *striding* is too fine a term for it, for there is a decided hitch in his gait, and he employs a walking-stick — a huge, gnarled, knotted, club-like monster of a thing fully as large as a beadle's staff, and quite as ominous to behold. The Captain is on the mend after his scullioning at the hands of the philosophical Slack, his convalescence having progressed sufficiently for the boldest rider in Talbotshire to have mounted horse and galloped into the village, and to be foraging now among the stalls and barrows of the market. He cuts a whimsical figure in green and red plaid trouserings with braces, a capacious black riding-cloak, high-lows, and his colossal walking-stick in hand; with his tiny eyes like buttons behind his horn-rims, his waxed mustaches, and his nose like a strawberry, the whole of him surmounted by a floppy hat oversized even for his bold cranium, the brim of it riding low upon his spectacles as though he had no forehead. There is too that abiding feature of the Captain's wardrobe, a bandage, wrapped round one of his fingers, the result of a new injury suffered since the scullioning (the Captain, despite his strong denials, being ever prone to such mischiefs.) Even from a distance his voice like a bass viol can be heard above the general clamor of the market, as he haggles over prices.

There is Mr. Arkwright, the veterinary, with his helmet of short dark hair — no need of headgear had he — and his long bushy eyebrows like a caterpillar, and his agile optics, inspecting the conformation of a farmer's mare. Not far off are the vicar and his pretty red-haired wife, the reverend gentleman in gaiters and slightly shovel hat, gazing benignly upon the passers-by through his plated spectacles, and Dinah in a stone-colored habit, doeskin gloves, and a bonnet of powder-blue satin, which sets off her fiery locks quite wondrously. The vicar murmurs privately to his helpmate, how unfortunate it is that Mr. Bede Wintermarch is never at service on a Sunday morning. The good Dinah nods, and freely offers her own opinion in the matter, as they pause for a time to view the ladies Wintermarch over the way.

"Ah, but it behoves us always to be charitable, my love," the vicar reminds his wife, tactfully.

"They *are* a puzzlesome pair," murmurs Dinah, keeping a close watch on them while trying not to spy. "See how even here, in the midst of the market, there is nothing the least grand about them. So plain, so unaffected! And so serious, too. Such pallid faces. It is not so much reserve as *care*, I think, that afflicts them. There is distress of some kind behind those faces. Oh, yes. They seem to me greatly troubled." She wrinkles up her brow in an attitude of cogitation. "Do you think she knows? Oh, but surely she must."

"Knows what, my love?"

"Do you think Mrs. Wintermarch knows the true identity of her husband? His history? Perhaps he has kept it from her for some purpose."

"His true identity?"

"As Charles Campleman, of course."

"Ah, but can we be certain sure of that detail, my love? It remains little more than gossip, you know, despite Mr. Dogger's assertions. And gossip is — "

"Is accurate more often than not," returns Dinah, stealing another glance. "Perhaps the idle talk that's gotten abroad troubles them. Perhaps they are uncomfortable knowing how many here in the village feel about Mr. Campleman. That fellow certainly keeps them on a string! By all accounts they are never long from the mansion-house; their few visits to town are unfailingly abbreviated and purposeful. There's hardly a spare moment for chat. It's as if they are captives of some matter that weighs heavily upon their minds. I sense it particularly in the wife, some concern of long standing. Do you suppose he beats them?"

The reverend gentleman expresses horror at the very thought.

"The little daughter for one seems normal enough, if something timid," pursues Dinah. "You'll note how she never strays from her mother. And those servants! A drearier pair I've never seen."

The vicar can do nothing but shake his head at his wife's train of fanciful conjectures. "My love, the family still are little more than strangers. They are from far away — from the city — from Crow's-end! Whatever can you expect? It will require time for them to find a home here. They'll not be accepted in an instant, not in such a sheltered place as this. We've had experience of that ourselves, you remember, but two years past."

Mrs. Scattergood finds she must agree with her husband in this.

"Nonetheless, I do hold out some hope of seeing Mr. Campleman in church on Sunday," says the vicar, clearing his voice.

His wife turns and fixes her sharp blue eyes upon him.

"My dear vicar," says she, smiling tolerantly, "what a dichotomy you are!"

They continue following the progress of the little group over the way. Mrs. Wintermarch takes an opportunity to look in at a few of the village shops, obtaining there some books and writing-paper from the stationer, Mr. Fussey, some tapers from the chandler, Mr. Tudway, and some few medicinal items from Mr. Nicodemus Binks, otherwise "Coddy," the village chemist. The ladies then wend their way through the market, passing *en route* the grammar school, the guildhall, and the waffle-house of Miss Crimp, to which establishment Miss Violet has lately been recalled at the insistence of her mother's crutch-handled cane. The group pauses for a moment at the table of Mags Mowbray and Mrs. Fielding, where a purchase is made of some few jars of honey from Aunt Jane, attended by a brief exchange of pleasantries; and so they move on.

Not far away, likewise examining the visitors, is a tall, spare, sober fellow with coarse yellow hair hanging from his head like a mop, a high, dry brow, solemn eyes, and a pinched mouth. A cocked hat with a feather in it adorns his head, breeches and bright cotton stockings his legs. It is Larcom, servant-cum-steward of Prospect Cottage, released from the prison of his employment for a time to view the scenes of market Friday. Recognizing now a youthful figure from the Village Arms, one Miss Betty Breakwindow, who like himself has been eyeing the group from the mansion-house, he approaches her and ventures some few scraps of talk upon the subject. But Larcom is no conversationalist; he knows little of words, aside from the musings of his own prideful brain upon the daily injustices of life at Prospect Cottage; he hardly can string more than one or two sentences together at a time, and hope they signify something to somebody. Conversation is not his strong suit. Nonetheless he attempts it now, but failing as regards the Wintermarches, falls back upon gloating, informing Miss Breakwindow how he has of late managed to evade a host of duties decreed by his employer, Mr. Thomas Dogger, on account of certain differences of temperament between himself and that gentleman, and the latter's insupportable treatment of him; that owing to the efforts of Mrs. Dogger, his friend and protector, who understood how he languished under her husband's impertinences, his situation at Prospect Cottage, whether he wanted it or no, should always be secure; upon which point he congratulates himself rather smugly.

Miss Breakwindow in turn gives voice to the inequities attendant upon her own position, and to the insufferability of her own employer, Miss Cherry Ives; how very earnest, how very industrious, how very efficient was Miss Cherry in all matters professional, as concerned the Village Arms; how said efficiency was likewise expected of all others at the Arms, regardless of their station; and how such efficiency as she, Miss Breakwindow, might exhibit, at present or in future, even were it the finest and most apple-pie efficiency ever seen in the world, would never be of sufficient quality to merit approval from Miss Ives.

Larcom nods glumly — he knows no other method of nodding — and contributes some three or four words of condolence, for the plaint of Miss Breakwindow was very similar to his own. His glance strays to her general good features, which albeit are less than perfect, he concedes, but nonetheless admirable. He tosses his cocked hat onto the side of his head, very rakishly so he thinks, and folds his long arms upon his chest, and crosses one leg before the other, exposing a stockinged calf to the general view of Miss Breakwindow; then brings up the subject of the pretty Miss Breakwindow herself and her present state of attachment. Whereupon he is greeted with an astonished snort, a disbelieving laugh, and a toss of the chin, followed by an icy glare as pitiless as a winter moon. These clearly constitute a rebuke for his presumption, for Miss Breakwindow can no more imagine herself enamored of a great solemn scarecrow of a coxcomb, a social pest in knee-breeches, bright cotton stockings, and cocked hat with a feather in it, than she can a howling inmate of a lunatic hospital.

At which juncture a bob of his yellow head by Larcom abruptly concludes the interview, and he takes himself off, to make it clear it was he who had severed the conversation, such as it was. Poor scarecrow! Another abortive skirmish with mysterious womankind for Mr. Larcom, who is outwardly his pinched and solemn self, but inwardly is smarting, affronted by the rejection of his person by so low a thing as a chambermaid. Perhaps he had not understood her aright? No, no, he understood her well enough; he must take the high track.

The insolence of the wench! But insolence such as he had been obliged to endure every day of his life. The insolence of chambermaids, the insolence of masters, the insolence of villagers snickering at his back. Only in the placid, unassuming shadow of Mrs. Dogger had he found respect. But who, he asks himself now, is Mrs. Dogger? A little squab figure of a woman, very drab as to face and dress, kept ever on the trot at home by an overbearing husband. Of what good was such as she to Larcom, in the final analysis? True, her influence might render his situation in the household secure; but for how much longer could he hold out against the tyranny of her husband? How much longer must he be ground daily beneath that respectable gentleman's very sizable thumb? How ever could one such as Mrs. Dogger better his fortunes?

"Today is Friday. Never begin anything on a Friday, it will not prosper," had been the final words of Miss Breakwindow, delivered with some pique, in response to Larcom's luckless attempt at wooing.

"If a black cat enters the house it must not be turned away, for it brings good luck," is a further country maxim that leaps into the head of Larcom, just as a cat of that description comes bouncing out of a shop-door.

"Of course, the bees will remain at home when it is likely to be wet," remarks a voice at his side.

Glancing round he sees he has come to the table in the road where Miss Mowbray and Mrs. Fielding are ensconced, and that it is the kindly Mrs. Fielding who has spoken, in pursuit of a discussion with other ladies of like vintage, together with Mr. Arkwright, on the quality of Gray Lodge honey and its honeymakers.

"That is very true," nods one of the ladies, as Miss Mowbray too concurs.

"This Mrs. Wintermarch seems so very respectful — yet so guarded — so retiring — and her daughter as well," comments another of the women, a stern old lady with a formidable prow, who like so many at the market has been observing the progress of the Wintermarches in the Low Street. "These are, of course, good things; but very much of a good thing is not always, in and of itself, a good thing."

"Mrs. Sepulchra Wintermarch is, in my view, a young woman of the most charming — er — sepulchritude," notes Mr. Arkwright. "Which is ever a good thing, o' course."

"They do not mix much."

"She is a woman much devoted to her husband," says Aunt Jane, in her kindly way. "That is what we have heard, at Gray Lodge, and that is how it would seem. She speaks fondly and highly of him, I am told."

"When she speaks at all," frowns the stern lady with the formidable prow. The little daughter, Miss Rowena, is a pretty child, the lady admits, which is no more than the rest of the village already has acknowledged; she was, perhaps, what her mother might have been had she been handsome. Was that by chance the father's imprint? What there is of her father in her is difficult to ascertain, however, as so very few have laid eyes upon that gentleman since the family's arrival.

Standing in the lee of a cottage hard by is that respectable ornament of his profession, Mr. Thomas Dogger, perpendicular as to carriage and substantial as to chin, watching the tenants of Skylingden Hall through his shiny eyes. A look of thoughtful scrutiny has crept into his inquisitive features. Is there not something about them, mother and daughter there, Wintermarch *uxor et filia* — some hazy, indefinable *something* he cannot put a lawyerly finger on, now that he has seen them detached as it were from the master of the house, apart, on their own, removed from the glare of that gentleman's presence, which had so outshone and obscured them in the drawing-room of Skylingden? So much attention had Mr. Dogger heaped upon that gentleman, so much concentration of lawyerly mind, deriving from the remarks of Dr. Hall in the Skylingden road, that he had taken little note of *uxor et filia*. He had not seen them since, their paths had not crossed since that day; what is it about them that draws his interest now? There is too the lingering matter of Mr. Bede Wintermarch himself, who had as yet failed to undertake the looked-for pilgrimage to Prospect Cottage, to receive advice from the very respectable solicitor there — something which puzzles plain country Tom Dogger even more.

There is something in the countenance of this Mrs. Wintermarch, and to a lesser extent her daughter's, which interests him, and holds him there in the lee of the cottage, as the lady moves about the market, with the young Rowena at her side and her two servants at her right hand. Something in her countenance there most certainly is, in her eyes, in the long sharpness of her nose, in the roundness of her pale brow. Perhaps she reminds him in some way of Mrs. Dogger, for was not Mrs. Dogger renowned for being plain? At which thought the attorney endeavors to suppress a shiver. He notes that Mrs. Wintermarch, plain and pallid though she might be, is in possession of the trimmest of figures, while Mrs. Dogger has no figure, none, none at all; in point of fact has never had one, nor had the least particle of personality to recommend her. Aside from the green tea she had regularly prepared for him every day of his recollection, and her range of domestic talents — which could be found as easily in any competent maidservant — there was little usefulness in her, and even less that was pleasing to a gentleman's eye. Their blessed union was of such antiquity he scarce could remember now why he'd married her. True, she had been of value of late in sampling the concoctions of that larcenous *chef de cuisine*, Mrs. Simpkins; but this was a not unreasonable request, in light of the personal history of Mrs. Simpkins, and well within the metes and bounds of Mrs. Dogger's register of wifely duties.

The attorney knits his brow and resolves to set off at once for the Arms and *aqua vitae*, so to avoid any further contemplation of his domestic arrangements. His shiny eyes light for a moment upon the prim, prideful figure of Larcom a short distance off. His vassal has not seen him, and for just an instant, as if by reflex, the attorney means to accost him with a needed reprimand concerning the state of the silver standish, and the hand-bell at his bedside, and the broken step in the back-passage; then thinks the better of it, recalling how his wife had that morning given leave for their servant-cum-sluggard to attend the market, to acquire certain items for the larder of Prospect Cottage. At which point Mr. Dogger pauses in his thoughts to stare, grimly, with parted lips — a lawyerly posture, though normally it is his lawyer's golden tones that come flowing from those lips, rather than silence — for there, over the way, moving among the vendors and other townspeople, is the little squab figure of Mrs. Dogger herself. Unable to resist the draw of the market, his dutiful wife has herself ventured forth from Prospect Cottage to aid Larcom in the gathering of the comestibles.

Mr. Dogger observes her with that same imperious curiosity as if he were examining an opposition witness's affidavit, or some poor client's scribbled draft of a will. Inevitably he makes comparison between his wife and the slim, womanly form of Mrs. Wintermarch, and his stare grows very grim indeed. Prospect Cottage, he muses, as nice a house as any gentleman could wish to hang up his hat in, could have done so very wonderfully for a bachelor's quarters. Whatever had driven him to that fatal error of matrimony, so many years past? Perhaps the fact that Mr. Parker Pring, his late benefactor, had actively promoted the match, had had something to do with it. ("You must be married, Dogger, you must be married, if you are to be a respectable man," had been that learned solicitor's repeated injunction to him.) Meditating upon the depths of his misfortune, Mr. Dogger takes solace in the contemplation of his personal broad-mindedness and generosity of spirit. Tom Dogger was not one to parade his worth before lesser folk, but certain facts were palpably clear. In the matter now of his wife, had he not always acquitted himself with honor? Had he never failed to point up her virtues, such as they were, to all in the village? Had he not been a fine and exemplary husband in extolling his wife to the skies, whether she deserved it or no? A wife whom he scarcely knew, and who scarcely knew him, though they had dwelt beneath the same russet-colored roof for all these many years? Did he not squire her to church several times each year, so she might hear him read the lesson? Certainly his friend and confidant the vicar would agree he was an excellent spouse, a worthy spouse!

Having glimpsed his wife at large in the market, however, Mr. Dogger finds it expedient now to repair to that genial harborage, the Arms, as had been his plan, and refresh the idlers there with his presence. Drawing up his good nut-brown coat about him, and drawing down the brim of his hat, the humble practitioner betakes himself to Town End, and there ascends the line of stone steps to landlord Nim's establishment on the hillside above.

Let us follow him thither.

CHAPTER II

MR. DOGGER FINDS A CLIENT

"A fine day, Mr. Dogger, sir, a fine day! A *e*-normous fine day, sir, is market day!"

So thundered Mr. Alfred Snorem, the long-serving boots of the Village Arms, upon seeing the brisk, perpendicular figure of the attorney glide in at the door. The worthy establishment was something short of patrons this afternoon, with few loiterers in sight for Mr. Dogger to refresh. Nearly everyone was at the market, or going to the market, or coming from the market, aside from the handful of road travelers who were hanging about the lodge-room waiting on the coach-and-four.

As per custom Mr. Dogger ignored the burly, wild-eyed boots, he of the deaf ear, iron jowls, and untidy haircut. Mr. Dogger had no need for a boots, he was no lodger at the inn; so Mr. Snorem was of little use to him. And as it appeared unlikely that one such as Mr. Snorem ever should be in need of Mr. Dogger's professional advice — or more importantly, be able to pay for it — Mr. Dogger had even less use for him. So he ignored him, and passed on through the entrance-hall. The courteous regard of Mr. Dogger for his fellow villagers did not extend, evidently, to those who were of little service to his pocket-book.

Mr. Snorem for his part hardly noticed the snub, for he was no stranger to the attorney's ways. Nonetheless his wild eyes lingered upon the brisk, perpendicular figure as it strode by. There was little that eluded Mr. Snorem in his informal role as gatekeeper of the Arms, a position over and above his official role as Boots, past master of the polishing of shoes, the brushing of coats, and the lugging of luggage. Like many at the Arms, he was a person of divers talents and abilities.

Mr. Dogger got himself a pint of sixpenny spruce from the bar, which was tended now by none other than the landlord himself, who, though he delighted in the atmosphere of market day, delighted in the atmosphere of his inn even more, and had dispatched his daughter and long Jinkins to represent him. He and the attorney exchanged an abundance of civilities, a respectful smile upon the professional face of Mr. Dogger, a lively and forthright expression upon the rather more jovial ditto of Mr. Ives.

Drifting into the lodge-room, Mr. Dogger observed that the billiard-table was bereft of votaries, unless one reckoned in the very short, very small, very round gentleman in the striped waistcoat, his face red, his hair white, his coat single-breasted and blue, who was walking round and round the table admiringly, with a plump hand trailing upon the cushion. A low-crowned, broad-brimmed hat hung idly by on a peg, and Mr. Dogger supposed it was the gentleman's. He had every appearance of a coach-passenger or other sort of traveler, killing time. The little round gentlemen seemed fascinated by all he saw — by the long racks of cues, by the sundry bills and placards hung upon the walls there, by the mounted trophy-heads, all of which he was looking over — or more often than not looking up at, as he was so very short — with a friendly interest. Having completed his perusal of the billiard-table, he gathered both plump hands to his back and with sparkling eyes commenced a further examination of the items on the walls, glancing from placard to placard, and from bill to bill, stopping now and again to peer at the mounted trophy-heads, which returned his gaze with frozen stares. At one such head he made a little face, which he capped off with a tremendous wink, as though daring the creature to return *that*.

Mr. Dogger was on the look-out for a fit opponent, someone whom he might challenge to a leisurely match and who stood little chance of besting him, and the little round gentleman in blue appeared to him just such an easy mark. So the attorney straightened himself, inhaled a long swallow of spruce, and squaring his shoulders made his very brisk and very perpendicular approach.

The little round gentleman, as it turned out, was indeed a coach-passenger, and as well a physician, one Dr. Tweed by name, with a practice at Crow's-end. After his stop at the inn he was going on to the county town of Malbury, where he had business. Mr. Dogger inquired whether or no he was a player, indicating the billiard-table; whereupon the doctor made a little embarrassed shrug, and explained how he had been admiring the fineness of the construction, though his skills as to the game itself were suspect; but that if Mr. Dogger had a desire to play, the doctor had some time and would be pleased to oblige him. He had naught to do till the coach went out, which wasn't for another hour at the earliest. After acquiring for himself a glass of cider from Mr. Ives, he removed a cue from the rack. The opponents then strung for order of play, the doctor earning first break.

The little old gentleman was so very short, and so very round, he was hard-pressed to position himself for a shot; moreover, the gold watch-chain at his waist kept getting in the way. The rules of the contest prescribed that players must have at least one foot upon the floor while striking. For the little doctor having but one foot upon the floor was very nearly a necessity, in order to reach the ball with his cue, as both shortness and roundness conspired against him. Mr. Dogger, awash in magnanimity, agreed to a temporary easing of the rules to accomodate a person of the doctor's stature, by granting him the use of a small step-stool. The doctor twinklingly offered his thanks, and stepping up, bent (so far as his paunch allowed him) over the rail, and promptly executed a magnificent cannon — his cue-ball striking first the white ball, then the red, before plunging into a side pocket.

Mr. Dogger was momentarily startled; Mr. Snorem, who had delivered the step-stool, loudly exclaimed; the little doctor smiled in his friendly way, apologizing that it surely was chance and nothing more. The attorney sipped his spruce thoughtfully, and narrowed his eyes.

Leaning forward again the doctor made his second shot — another cannon, equally dextrous, striking this time the red ball, then the white, and again pocketing his cue-ball.

Another swallow of spruce by Mr. Dogger, an even wilder shout from the boots, another apology from the little round gentleman.

"Mere fortune," he declared. "Nothing more."

But as fortune quickly piled upon fortune, and chance upon chance, the exclamations of Mr. Snorem grew ever more vociferous, and the polished eyes of Mr. Dogger narrower and narrower. Tap, click, click. The little doctor seemed to be a specialist of sorts at cannons, hitting the balls with wonderful accuracy, and often pocketing his cue-ball for additional points, but neither was he inexpert at hazards. At length, however, as luck would have it, he faltered in his run; and so Mr. Dogger had his first opportunity to join the game. The attorney already had been to the bar and back to recharge his glass, so long had the little doctor been about his work. In the interval a small band of spectators had begun gathering round the table — an audience comprised of nearly everyone else in the house at present — as word of the doctor's astonishing play spread, thanks in no small measure to the thunderous cries of Mr. Snorem.

"I'll 'go bail' you are no hobbyist, sir," remarked Mr. Dogger, keeping his professional face on, to hide his displeasure, while holing the red ball for a winning hazard and his first points.

"By jingo, no hobbyist thar, no, sir!" exclaimed Boots, his amazed eyes fully as white and round as the cue-ball flying about the table.

"I'll admit, I have some little experience of the game," confessed Dr. Tweed with a shy grin, retiring a few paces to observe the other's play. "I did not intend to deceive you, but could not resist a bit of sport. But I do assure you, sir, it *is* only a hobby of mine, a minor avocation, though a pleasureful one. Truly, it is so; I play only occasionally. My medical practice in the city keeps me quite busily afoot to all hours, with but scant opportunity for dabbling in the game."

"It is the same in my profession," said Mr. Dogger, scoring another hazard.

"You are an attorney, I believe you mentioned?"

"Indeed. The practice of law commands nearly the whole of my day, for I am the only professional man in the district, you see, and so all the business roundabout must flow through Prospect Cottage. The laity are altogether dependent upon the Cottage for the furtherance of their causes, a situation which I fear leaves me little time for sport such as this. Even so, country law remains a poor provider. But someone must do the work, sir; someone must attend to the interests of clients and see they are not neglected, and better that someone were Tom Dogger than a hundred others I could think on. And there you have the state of the case, sir, *in extenso.*"

"You kept terms at Clive's Inn, Fishmouth, I believe, sir?"

"Yes."

"A famed institution, well-regarded in circles I know something of."

Mr. Dogger swelled with a little conscious pride, which he was not averse to showing in his professional face, and whisked his long curling locks from his collar. Plain country Tom Dogger notwithstanding, the attorney had steadfastly resisted cropping his hair in the country fashion, preferring to wear it long about the nape and ears, in the city style — or more particularly the Fishmouth style, which he had adopted years ago while a student at Clive's Inn. It was a small thing, true, but secretly it was a big thing to Mr. Dogger; it was one thing more to set him apart from others, one thing more to distinguish him from the common throng, those unschooled in the quips and cranks of the law. Plain country Tom Dogger might eschew city airs, or claim he did, but city hair was another matter. Mr. Dogger was never one to trumpet his merits or his exclusive education; he didn't need to. He could afford to be humble.

"I shall very probably require the services of counsel, here in Shilston Upcot, once all is in order at Malbury," said Dr. Tweed.

"Indeed?" The attorney looked at him in some surprise. Though trolling for clients had not been his aim in calling at the inn, the idea that a client might simply come tumbling into his lap, all unlooked-for — and likely a substantial client at that — was not unpleasing to him. Immediately he assumed an attitude of respectful attention, which in Mr. Dogger was something like the posture a hound takes when catching sight of a juicy fat partridge. Had Mr. Dogger been possessed of a tail, he would have swished it at sight of the juicy fat doctor.

The little gentleman mounted the step-stool and began another glorious run, with caroms of astonishing beauty, which drew rapturous applause from the lookers-on. While executing these maneuvers he described for Mr. Dogger how he had taken leave from his practice to make the journey to Malbury, that the matter there involved some deeds of land owned by a patient of long standing, whose health was most tragically impaired.

"Be assured, sir, that like myself, Prospect Cottage is ever at your service," said the lawyer, swishing again. "Not to worry as regards the character of our representation or the fidelity of our commitment. In attending to the interests of clients we are ever diligent, ever persevering; we are steady, orderly, and regular. We may be in the country here, sir, but that does not mean we have untidy ways." As he said this he glanced briefly at Mr. Snorem, but that untidy gentleman saw nor heard him not, for like most of the audience he was absorbed in the play of Dr. Tweed. "At such time as you are prepared to receive professional advice, Tom Dogger will be more than happy to supply it."

"As you are the sole attorney hereabouts, that may be an inevitable circumstance," said the little doctor, momentarily putting aside his cue, as something like a shadow crept into his genial features. He looked very hard at Mr. Dogger. "I shall be direct with you, sir. I do not deal much with gentlemen of your profession; in point of fact I do not much like them. They are slippery, miry, fishy things, in my experience. They are low opportunists, like serpents lurking in the muck, preying upon the hardships and misfortunes of others, from which action they derive an exorbitant profit."

"Aye, that's true thar, doctor, sir, *e*-normous true!" averred Mr. Snorem, with a mighty nod.

"The lawyers like always a bit of a tussle," said another of the lookers-on. "They seldom cry 'kiss and be friends' till their palms be greased."

"Ooh, aye!" exclaimed several more, coach-passengers all of them, for most in the village were not so public in their views as regards Mr. Dogger and his brethren.

The attorney chuckled softly and wagged his head, something amused by these childish imaginings of the laity.

"Idle fictions, regrettably all too common in certain quarters," he replied, hooking his thumbs in the pockets of his waistcoat, by way of dismissing such fancies out of hand. "An attorney is a respectable gentleman, sirs, a member of an Honorable Society, and an advocate at the high courts of Chancery and Common Law. As a practitioner it is his duty to pursue the cause in which he is engaged, wherever it may lead, at whatever expense, with a zealous and an active regard. It is his duty to be attending to the interests of clients. It is his duty to see that the interests of clients are never neglected. It is his duty to preserve the laws of his jurisdiction. What use is there to laws if they be not preserved, no matter the effort, no matter the cost? *Fiat justitia ruat coelum* — let justice be done though the sky falls. But if I may be so bold," he added, with an eye to the little doctor, "I submit there does exist in this land a class of practitioners, respectable gentlemen every one, I'm sure, who derive the greater portion of their profit — and a handsome profit it is, too, as the doctor here knows full well — by attending to the bodily hardships and misfortunes of their patients, otherwise their clients."

There was a dead pause in the room after this speech, as the audience waited to hear what the little round gentleman might offer in response.

"You are remarkably frank, sir," said Dr. Tweed, after some few moments of thoughtful contemplation. The shadow passed from his red face; his eyes sparkled again, his lips smiled again. "Remarkably frank!"

Mr. Dogger dipped his head and returned the doctor's smile, in sign he accepted the other's appreciation of his candor. "I am quite at your service, sir."

"I'll tell you now, a lawyer who would make excessive costs of me will not be countenanced, though naturally I'll not begrudge him his six and eightpence," said the doctor, with reference to the attorneys' minimum fee that had been prevalent in the realm for some time. "The patient at Crow's-end of whom I have spoken has been under my care for a great many years. He has no discoverable relation, and the superintendence of his affairs has lately devolved upon me. I have of course engaged a solicitor at Crow's-end, a member of an eminent firm, for city business; but tending to matters here in Talbotshire, in such an out-of-the-way corner, will be most inconvenient for him. Local counsel would be very useful."

Mr. Dogger expressed his complete agreement, and so play commenced again.

"Ah — begging pardon, Mr. Dogger, sir, but I reckon you pooshed the ball thar," came the voice of Mr. Snorem, from out of the audience.

Mr. Dogger straightened, serenity on his professional face, irritation on his private one. "Pay no heed to that fellow," he instructed the doctor, with a lazy sigh. "His optics are not what they were in times past. You may examine them yourself, every day for a month of Sundays, and find no disagreement on that score."

Mr. Snorem laughed hugely at this, closing the eyes in question and shaking his untidy hair, as though savoring a jest he alone appreciated. As usual he was too much diverted by the attorney's barbs to take offense, and so was immunized to their sting.

"An amusing sort," remarked the little doctor, applying some chalk to his cue.

Another few breaks were exchanged. Again it was the lawyer's turn; as he was about to strike the ball, a glance across his shoulder revealed the wild staring eyes of Mr. Snorem no more than a foot away, anxiously anticipating the shot.

"Sirrah," said Mr. Dogger, arresting his stroke, "might you see your way clear to remove yourself some few paces behind? A few paces more, if you please. Still a few more. Perhaps you might remove yourself clear to the stables — that is where most jackasses are found."

Another hearty roar from the boots, a round of laughs from the lookers-on. Once the noise had died away Mr. Dogger made his shot, holing his cue-ball after its collision with the red. Another loud objection from Mr. Snorem quickly followed.

"Ah — begging pardon, Mr. Dogger, sir, but I reckon you tapped the ball thar more than once, sir."

The attorney looked to his opponent in the striped waistcoat, and found him nodding sympathetically. "I am forced to admit — I believe you did, sir," said the doctor.

The attorney lifted his nose and eyebrows.

"Am I to be charged with a foul?" he demanded, raising himself to the maximum extent of his perpendicular, an elevation at least six inches above Mr. Snorem and some miles above the little doctor. "Do I hear you aright? You charge Tom Dogger with unfair play? Such an attitude is disappointing, very disappointing. I wonder at it."

Here Mr. Snorem laughed again, and waved off the attorney's poor attempt at a defense with a brawny hand. Chuckling to himself and rocking his head from side to side, as though he scarcely could believe all he'd seen and heard there, he trotted out of the lodge-room to resume his station opposite the booking-desk.

"A reflection of the low state of morality in this county," said Mr. Dogger, with a sweep of his shiny eyes round the audience. "Servants these days are very forward. It is an unfortunate case, one aided and abetted by an indulgent clergy, who increasingly turn away from our time-honored moral and religious precepts — a point which I have made to our own reverend vicar a score of times. So very little respect is shown to professional gentlemen by the lower orders, who seem no longer to know their position. It is most provoking, but that is how the world now goes. The impertinence of some people is past belief. That fellow's bound to come a cropper, for you know, there's no making a whistle of a pig's tail. Far be it from Tom Dogger to find fault with another human being on this earth, but we are in a bad state, sirs, a bad state."

The little doctor agreed with Mr. Dogger, if only to humor him. Yes, servants were grown very cavalier of late. The doctor himself had had difficulty securing a trustworthy man at Crow's-end, once; fortunately he lived now in a small castle of a flat, its portcullis guarded by a fierce Scots landlady who did the cooking and whose daughters did the cleaning and washing, and so he had little call for servants.

"We have a fellow at Prospect Cottage, a monstrous fine sluggard," said the attorney. "My wife is unaccountably tolerant of him, however, and so we keep him on. Though he does little he protests much, laying claim to be the finest serving-man in the village, indefatigable in his exertions. For myself I trust him not, but assign him such trifling tasks as I feel he may be capable of. He is ostensibly a kind of steward at the Cottage, but in title only, for he does nothing to warrant such responsibility. He is largely in the employ of Mrs. Dogger; I have not much to do with him now. I have instead engaged a young clerk from the village, our stationer's man, to assist me in chambers with the copying of documents."

"Your wife, then, directs the household?" inquired Dr. Tweed, innocently.

The attorney stiffened. His nose and brows lifted again. He cleared his voice, and begged to inform the doctor that Prospect Cottage was directed by none but its master, none; that it always had been that way, and always would be that way; that it was exclusively through the efforts of Tom Dogger, in the selection of a wife and such servants as they had endured over the years, that Prospect Cottage was all it was today.

"As nice a house," said the attorney, with a certain dignity of diction, "as any gentleman could wish to hang up his hat in."

The little doctor smiled, and coughed behind his hand, and expressed his pleasure at the attorney's good fortune. The two sportsmen then racked their cues, to the considerable sorrow of the lookers-on, who shortly dispersed.

Mr. Dogger calculated it was time now to reel in his client, and so bent to it.

"Perhaps you would care to visit Prospect Cottage?" he suggested, preparing to escort the little doctor from the lodge-room. "It is not far, if we make haste. We may there enjoy the privacy of chambers. My wife and the aforementioned sluggard are at the market this afternoon."

"I should enjoy that very much," replied Dr. Tweed, plucking his hat from its peg, "but I fear I have not the time. The coach will be going out directly. However, upon my return from Malbury I shall stop here again, and perhaps then we may have our chat."

Mr. Dogger expressed his disappointment, which was very real.

"You have a most delightful situation here," said the doctor, steering himself towards the yard, where the voice of the coachman could be heard calling for the passengers. "Most delightful. Such pretty skies! Such noble and fragrant timber! Such lofty mountains! It will be a joy to return, and resume our discussion in a businesslike fashion. I look forward to it."

Mr. Dogger expressed his own particular joy at this, and so the two gentlemen clasped hands — the one gentleman so sharp and straight, with eyes so polished, the other so short and round, with eyes so sparkling. The doctor mounted the steps and joined the other passengers. The door clanged shut, the key-bugle sounded; the whip cracked, the horses snorted; the coach rumbled out of the yard, gained speed and was gone.

Inhaling deep thoughts and forest air, the attorney retreated to the comfort of the lodge-room proper and another pint of spruce. He threw himself down in one of the easy-chairs by the fire, beneath the stuffed head of the saber-cat, and started in to examine one of the papers there. Almost at once he found himself growing drowsy, which for Mr. Dogger was most unusual. Perhaps it was the influence of the beer; more than likely, though, it was the dreams.

They had troubled him now several nights this week — mad, phosphoric visions full of fury and menace, so disturbing they caused him to start up in his bed in the midst of them. On every occasion, however, his memory of the dream had faded almost at once, leaving him restless and irritable. Hateful nightmares, the substance of which could not be recalled upon awakening — I suppose such things at times must disturb any man, no matter how respectable. If the squire of Dalroyd himself could be visited by such things, why not the respectable solicitor and master of Prospect Cottage? As a legal gentleman Mr. Dogger was used to dealing with facts. Having no memory of these visions meant having no facts, which annoyed him no end. He had a sense, however, that each of the dreams started off in similar fashion — with a feathery rustling at the open casement of his bedchamber, and the sight of a birdlike something crouching there, looking in.

This night Mr. Thomas Dogger will have another dream or two, but unlike the others these dreams will stay with him. He will see himself in the lodge-room of the Arms, at the billiard-table, no longer an attorney but a round, fat cue-ball lying upon the felted cloth. An owl is perched upon the cushion; or rather, a creature he takes for an owl, for there is something distinctly un-owl-like about it, chiefly in the eyes, which are green and glare out from beneath heavy pale brows; in the ghostly white face, in the draggled dark hair sprouting from its head, and in what Mr. Dogger imagines is a most disagreeable disposition. With its talons upraised and a shrill cry in its throat, the creature lunges for the fat cue-ball. At that instant Mr. Dogger will cry out in his sleep, will rise up in his bed and look about him. He will feel his heart fluttering inside his chest, like wing-beats. He will take stock of the situation. He will assure himself that the bars and shutters at his casement-window are secure. He will pour himself some water from the ewer at his bedside. He will drink it, and fall back upon his pillow.

In a while he will dream again, but this time he will dream of a little cue-ball-shaped man, a little doctor with a white head and a red face, rolling about on the cloth. He will see himself, plain country Tom Dogger, striking at the little cue-ball-shaped client with his stick. This dream he will find more to his fancy, and very conducive to slumber; and so the dream will fade and the attorney will sleep, and rise the next morning with recovered spirits.

CHAPTER III

UNDER THE DRIPPING PINES

THE pretty skies of Dr. Tweed had given way to skies of another sort, with huge tiers of dark, heavy clouds like galleons invading the blue expanse, when, some few days after the market, a string of riders was observed spurring their horses along the wooded hill-tops, high above lake and village. A fresh, crisp morning it was, and a fine one for riding, despite the promise of wet weather. The shadows thrown down by the galleons were strewn far and wide across the valley of the Talbots, forming a quilt of moving light and shade upon the landscape. Fresh, crisp mornings like this one, with its great soaring walls of cloud and sky, were made for horses, and horsemen, and horsewomen too — for there appeared to be at least one representative of the fair sex in the mounted string.

At the head of the riders, on a sturdy black gelding, was a youngish, thickish gentleman with a tiny face buried under a helmet of hair — Mr. Tony Arkwright, the veterinary of Shilston Upcot, who, having paraded before them his new foal, a trim fellow named Junius, had invited his companions out for a morning's dash round the countryside. Being the enthusiasts they were, lovers of the spur and saddle, his friends required little urging to accept. Although several dogs could be seen there beside the horses, scampering and yelping with delight — included among them one tiny white-and-liver-colored bundle of energy, Mr. Jolly-boy of Dalroyd — there would be no pursuit of old Reynard today, no hunt, just an invigorating ride to take the air and absorb the magnificence of the mountain vistas.

Among the enthusiasts were the squire of Dalroyd, in command of Tinker, and beside him Mr. Oliver Langley on the chestnut mare. Behind them, on a blooded hunter, was Captain Hoey, bouncing along in his black riding-cloak, with his horn spectacles and his great floppy hat. His scullioned foot had far enough improved that he was able to rise in the stirrups, though it still pained him, and his gallop had not its usual slap and dash; if not today the boldest rider in Talbotshire, he was then perhaps the bravest. In the rear came Dr. Hall, and with him Mr. Tudway, the village chandler, and Mr. Coddy Binks, the little hunting chemist. And threading her way among them, in perfect harmony with Delilah's elastic stride, so free and easy, was the single lady member of the group, Miss Margaret Mowbray, in her brightly colored riding-habit, with her laughing eyes, her ready smile, and all the happy ardor of youth.

Mr. Arkwright had with him today his bow and quiver, for he was an acknowledged master of the bowhunt and the birdbolt. This particular skill he illustrated now by drawing his bow and knocking down a rook in full flight, which one of the dogs happily retrieved. His talents in this line were considerable; he could aim and shoot while astride the saddle, as he had done now, with wonderful accuracy, a natural aptitude to which his companions could well attest, as all had been witness to it on numerous occasions.

They took the cleaner mountain trails and bridle-roads at an easy, bounding gait, up and over the ridges and down through the glens, with tall stands of pine and fir and spreading oaks flashing by on either hand, and the dogs darting and diving in joyous spirit through the underwood. Flowers and flowering shrubs of great beauty and variety, pleasures to the eye every one, lay scattered about the passing uplands. A steady breath of delicious cool air blew across the faces of the riders, and with it a bracing nip of moisture, which caused Miss Mowbray to observe that the rain would be upon them before long. As they rambled on past bosky thickets and groves of pines, past wild nooks and hollows, through open glades and along windy heights, the track growing now more undulating, now level, now sinuous, now direct, the riders strove to keep Lonewater or the Talbots in at least partial view at all times — a useful measure to avoid straying from the safer avenues into the back country, and a possible confrontation with one of the more unamiable denizens of the forest.

At one point, however, for the benefit of the visitor from Crow's-end, they rode off towards a line of meadows that lay concealed behind a screen of timber, a little above them and to the right. In one of these meadows they came upon an interesting tableau — a megathere group, comprised of three full-grown adults, quietly feeding upon the grasses, leaves, and roots that abounded there. Though he had seen ground sloths before, at the zoological gardens in the city, Oliver was nonetheless awed by this sight of the creatures in their primal habitat. He found himself marveling again at the sheer, immense size of them — each was nearly as large as a crofter's cottage — at the power of the musculature lying beneath the coat of dense, wiry hair, at the grandeur of their bearing and their serene disregard of their human observers. Their faces were long and heavy, with massive jowls and squared-off nostrils, sleepy eyes, and tiny ears planted far back on the head. They moved slowly, ponderously, showing little interest in anything but their quest for food. With their lips and snout constantly working they scoured the soil and ground cover for tubers and other choice items, which they dug out with their claws. And what claws they were, too, so long, so smooth, so sharp; and what enormous, paddle-like limbs, with their queer inward curvature. Oliver blinked several times in admiration of the spectacle before him. Much of the hide of these megatheres, the Captain explained, was embedded with scores of minute bony nodules, or *ossicles*, which acted as a discouragement to predators, and together with the creatures' vast size and strength allowed them to pursue their activities in leisurely fashion. Oliver blinked again, and found himself admiring all the more.

While returning to the bridle-road they came across the tracks of wild boar, tapir, pronghorn, and dire wolf, but no sign, thankfully, of short-faced bears. The forest canopy was alive with the chatter of jays, the cawing of rooks, the barking of squirrels, the chiseling of woodpeckers, and the occasional wild roar from some invisible prowler of the higher slopes. Oliver expressed concern lest they happen upon a saber-cat, for he knew that the dreaded monsters often haunted meadows such as these; their fame, or infamy, was far-spread. More than a few times he wondered aloud if a saber-cat might not be stalking them, all unseen. He remarked that as a city man he was particularly fearful of the brutes, and of teratorns too, despite his recent introduction to Mr. Shakes. The Captain and the others sought to ease these worries of his, pointing to the calmness of their mounts as proof no fanged monster was in range of the horses' delicate senses.

During his holiday in the village, Oliver had come to understand a little better perhaps what it meant to be a mountain-dweller. It was nothing like living in the city, nothing at all. Living in the mountains meant taking such things as megatheres, short-faced bears, saber-cats, teratorns, and wild roars in the forest as part and parcel of everyday existence. It meant living with iron bars upon the windows of one's lodgings. It meant being habitually wary during the quieter hours, ever on the *qui vive* for any indication of danger. It meant accepting dawn and dusk as times of particular hazard. It meant riding forth upon one's horse well-provided, and at times going armed afoot as well, such that a rapier, dagger, cutlass, or small-sword was never far from one's hand; and it meant being skilled in the use of each. To mountain people a horse represented more than simply a means of transport; a horse could mean the difference between living and dying, for few things in the valley could outpace a speedy gray like Miss Mowbray's Delilah. (Oliver was never half so glad of his old nag in the city as he was now of the good chestnut mare under him, here on the trail in the mountain forest.) And it meant accepting all of this with a coolness no more remarkable than that of a hackney-coachman negotiating the busy maze of city traffic.

So Oliver was coming to understand what life in the mountains truly was like. He was coming to understand that as wondrous, as splendid, as beautiful as the scenery roundabout might be — as it had appeared to him the day he arrived, and as it appeared to him still — there was a certain risk and danger lurking behind it, as invisible to the untutored eye as that roaring prowler of the higher slopes. Perhaps, Oliver thought to himself, danger was the price one paid for such beauty.

Onwards they jogged along one of the ancient mastodon trails, through Grim Forest and round towards Cranberry Chase, till they came to a rise of ground overlooking the pretty town of Jay. In the distance lay Shilston Upcot, and beyond it the point, with the mansion-house and its great round eye gazing on them from afar. It was on the rise of ground that they heard the first sounds of the rain, in the trees and on the trail, and felt the cold of it upon them as the limpid droplets came sliding off their hats. The Captain informed them that his weather-glass at the Peaks had foretokened a summer shower, that it should not last long, and that his trusted pluviometer was even now taking accurate measure of its intensity.

The riders gathered beneath a tall stand of pines to wait it out. Little Jolly-boy, who was not very fond of rain, came hurrying to the feet of Tinker, where he was scooped up by Mark and placed in the leather pouch hanging from Tinker's saddle. There he remained for the duration, looking as snug as a plum in a plumskin while spying upon the cold, wet world from beneath the flap.

The gentlemen and Miss Mowbray had occasion now to hear something more from Captain Hoey as regards his geological and mineralogical hypotheses. The Captain as a stout Plutonist considered the entire valley, from the Talbot Peaks in the west to the line of distant woods in the east, beyond Lonewater, to have been created by volcanic action. As partial proof of this he offered the nearby deposit of black basalt, a kind of rock that could be found throughout the valley in mixture with the characteristic bluish-purple, granitic stone of Talbotshire. By examining such deposits and their associated loose material, the Captain said, the careful observer could gain a tolerably clear idea of the nature of the processes underlying their formation. Ah, quite, yes, much of it remained hypothesis, of course, and much of that hypothesis was his very own; but beshrew him, there were others, too, men of like kidney, who shared his views. Whereupon he proceeded to cite a host of scholarly tomes, whole passages which nobody understood apart from the Captain himself, and perhaps little Jolly-boy, who was entranced by the Captain's resonant voice like a bass viol and seemed to be hanging on his every word.

The Captain pointed out how very similar was that deposit of black basalt to many of the rocks one might find at the lakeshore, or in the caverns dotting the south face of Skylingden point. Even more striking, he declared, were the syrupy black waters of Lonewater itself, a phenomenon resulting from the coloration and great depth of the volcanic crater in which those waters lay, and from the dissolved impurities and suspended matter therein. Considered together, the presence of basalt, pitchstone, and cindery *scoriae* and other such deposits in the valley was an indication of past volcanic action, when clots of lava had been exploded from the volcano and tossed upon the countryside for miles around. The central portion of the cone had then collapsed; underground seepage and untold seasons of rain and snow had formed the lake, the fractured walls of the great volcano surviving in the hill-tops and mountain promontories that ringed the valley. Gradually the verdure had returned, with such success that thick growths of fir and pine now covered much of the volcanic cone, hiding the scars of the eruption.

"How long has it been, do you think, Captain, since this dreadful event?" asked Oliver. The squire and others already had told him of Captain Hoey's hypothesis, of course, and so he was something familiar with it; here now was an opportunity to question the Captain himself as to its particular details and ramifications.

"Agh, damned hard to know, Langley — ages, eons, I'll be sworn," the Captain replied, managing to look profound with the brim of his great floppy hat resting upon his spectacles, obliterating his forehead. "It would be a stopper indeed if it were not."

"There is some reassurance in that, which I am heartily glad of."

"It was a ghastly affair, I'm sure; I'd not care to have been in Talbotshire at the time. The volcano was pretty large, and pretty broad — in point of fact it was colossal! When it exploded it likely sent the topmost half of the mountain packing, leaving not a baw-cock behind to tell the tale. Fragments of volcanic matter can be found far to the west of the Talbots, and as far east as Ayleshire. What remains — what it is we see here on all sides of us, in the shape of the valley — and this really is quite remarkable — is the stump of the former mountain, its inner surface, with Lonewater there occupying much of the central crater. Bolts and shackles, man," exclaimed the Captain, his tone rising, "we're all of us living inside a damned volcano!"

"A deceased volcano, I should hope," said Oliver, optimistically.

The Captain paused to stroke his mustaches, his tiny eyes like buttons peering thoughtfully from under his floppy hat. "As to ages and eons," he said, "there is abundant evidence of erosion of the geological formations in these peaks and crags. It is a further corollary of my hypothesis. The erosion of a geological formation is a process requiring water, wind, and time — entire ages, eons of time."

"The eruption must have dealt a heavy blow," said Mags.

"By my soul, my dear young madam, it was trouble in the tilt-yard! Speaking as a pupil of the natural sciences, I believe it was one of the great natural calamities ever visited upon the world — though not so great a calamity as the sundering, of course, which was of another sort utterly. But as to how many years, precisely, since this volcano beneath us last vented a sulfurous breath, who can say? Not I. Not anyone. You see, we have not the means to analyze them properly — that is, the rock masses and geological formations — no formula, no system for deducing their age. There's the predicament, and a pox of a predicament it is, too, one I myself have been contending with for more than a few years. By this hand, it's like wringing water from a flint! There are times it puts me quite out of countenance, like this damned foot of mine. All that may be said is this: that the deeper a layer or stratum of rock lies within the earth, the older it must be; for layer forms upon layer, stratum upon stratum, and so it follows from logic that the older strata must underlie the younger."

"A logical deduction, and a brainy one, too, in my view," opined Mr. Arkwright, whose fund of knowledge encompassed nearly everything touching horses and hounds, but nothing whatsoever as regards strata and rock masses and geological formations.

"Might it happen again?" inquired Coddy Binks, the hunting chemist. He was a little, stale, dried-up man, from long contact with the materials in his shop, and smelled of them, too. In his workaday life he was the soberest of tradesmen, scrupulous, cautious, exacting to the point of being finical, deliberate in his every action. Once his workaday life was cast aside, however, and Mr. Binks mounted in the saddle, reins in hand and feet in stirrup-iron, he became transformed into a shrewd and daring horseman, a hard-riding follower of the hounds, fearless, adventurous, as one with his horse as a centaur, and — dare I breathe word of it — in all likelihood the second-boldest rider in Talbotshire. "What I mean to ask is, are we in any danger from it?"

The boldest of riders shook his long bald head with the floppy hat on it. "Who can say? It's received opinion that volcanic action often is preceded by earth tremors and landslips, the venting of reechy air and sulfurous fumes. We have not, to the best of my memory, witnessed the latter phenomenon in these altitudes, and the former only occasionally."

"We have not witnessed them," agreed Mr. Binks.

"That is true," said Mags, "although I admit I have not passed my entire life here."

"Earth tremors only rarely," volunteered Dr. Hall.

"Never reechy air, or sulfurous fumes," chimed in Mr. Tudway.

"Surely that's a good thing?" inquired Mr. Arkwright, knitting his bushy brow.

"More than likely," returned the Captain, with a scholarly clearing of his voice, which sound drew the attention again of Jolly-boy. "It's my belief we are safe for the duration, but bodikins! with such phenomena we can never rest safely on our haunches. For this reason we at the Peaks remain diligent in our efforts to gather intelligence as regards all natural phenomena in the vicinity. The extremities of depth of Lonewater tell us that the underlying store of lava has retreated considerably. The waters remain frigid; there is no evidence for a resurgence of heat in the throat of the volcano. That's a good thing, Arkwright. And there are no active hot springs in the area, none. That's good, too. By this hand, I believe we are pretty safe. And so we are left with a weathered crater of prodigious dimension, a vast natural hollow in the earth whose depths have yet to be sounded. Who can say what may be down there? In the cold black waters, in the caverns and lava tunnels below ground, in the very earth here beneath our boots, who can tell what mysteries lie hid? Bolts and shackles, men — not I!"

"Nor I," smiled Miss Mowbray.

With the rain continuing to fall, the current of conversation drifted to other matters various and sundry, from Mr. Shakes and the Skylingden owl to the sad demise of Splayfoot. No mention was made, however, by either Oliver or the squire, of the two gentlemen's late adventure in the cave, of their discovery of the well or the even stranger discovery they'd made inside it. Though someone did at one point raise the topic of Skylingden — for the great eye *would* persist in staring at them from across the inlet — which prompted Mr. Arkwright to launch into a discussion of the vanished abbey, of the sly monastic gents who had dwelt there and their resort to the practice of wicked and secret arts, a subject upon which he was more than liberally informed. But there was little in his speech that had not been retailed previously at the Arms; and for the present at least, neither Mark nor Oliver had a mind to disclose what they had found in the cave, or its relation to the Lake Friars, till they could understand it better themselves.

In time the shower abated — the precipitation and related meteorological phenomena having eased, as the Captain put it — though the trees continued to shed droplets of rain from their furry branches even as the clouds fled. With the skies clearing the riders exhorted their mounts and moved on for home, the hour having advanced considerably. Their return took them along the winding coach-road from Jay to the Arms, at which worthy establishment the day's excursion was commemorated with cider and spruce and much jovial conversation. At length the riders dispersed to their respective abodes, which for Mark and Oliver meant a leisurely trot back up the road to Dalroyd, while seeing Miss Mowbray safely ensconced at Gray Lodge along the way.

A quiet supper and a game of billiards followed, after which the gentlemen retired as usual to the library, where they smoked out their cigars and talked over a great many matters. It was clear what their next action must be if they were to make progress in the mystery — they must spend a further few hours in the company of the parish sexton, a gentleman who had accumulated stores of information in a great many areas, and was a stone-cutter to boot. Having resolved themselves upon it they sent for the indispensable Smithers to draft the invitation, as a consequence of which Mr. Shank Bottom would find himself the very next afternoon calling at Dalroyd.

A trifle wearied the squire left early for his bed, and like plain country Tom Dogger he had himself that night a dream, which slowly wound its way into his sleeping mind and disturbed its rest. Stretching before him, in this dream of his, was a long, narrow passage without a single door, and at the distant end of it a turning, with a small round window in the turning. There was a pale light like moonlight pouring through the window; and framed in the window-space, in bold relief against the light, was a thing like a human face. It was so far from him the squire could discern little of its features, apart from two glowing green eyes — green eyes deathly still, watching him, examining him.

Though he should like to have kept clear of it, the squire found he could not; he was too curious. He crept forward along the passage towards the window and the face and the honey-pale light, nearer and nearer to the still, silent form with the glowing eyes and the head of draggled dark hair.

And so he came to the round window, and for the first time the thing in it stirred.

"Do I know you, friend?" said a dulcet voice.

The squire drew himself closer to the window, the better to examine the questioner. As he did so the thing leaned in towards him, until thing and squire were very nearly nose to nose at the glass — until the squire realized that the window had no glass, no separation, no defense. All in a moment he saw the thing for what it was, a corpse, which promptly started in to rot before his astonished optics, whole masses of flesh and hair dripping from its skull like raindrops from pine-branches. In silent horror he watched it dissolve; as it did so it growled at him, and bared its teeth, and uttered a wild, unearthly cry full of fury and menace. Then came a sudden noise of wings, and the thing was gone in a rush of wind.

The squire woke with a start and a cry of his own, shivering there in the chilly darkness of his bedchamber. His craggy brow, his arms, his chest all were bathed in moisture. Momentarily confused he caught up his sword and waved it about a couple of times, but there was nothing there for him to slaughter. Even as he did so his memory of the dream began to fade.

"Devil take them!" he reproached himself, for being hoaxed again. "Devil take these blasted dreams!"

Mr. Thomas Dogger, Mr. Oliver Langley, the squire of Dalroyd — the roster of those upon whom such sobering nightmares had been visited stood at three. Or did it? They were but three, true, but might there not be others in the village of Shilston Upcot who had encountered similar phantoms of indigestion, a similar deep troubling of the spirit, in the midst of sleep? Might there not be others who had felt the same sinister presence at the window, glimpsed the same glowing eyes and awful countenance in the night, heard the same flutter of moth-like wings, experienced the same dread premonition of doom rushing on, inexorably — and yet not spoken of it from fear, bafflement, or something else?

How many more than three there were I do not know — but many.

CHAPTER IV

THIRTY YEARS SINCE

BY and by the squire managed to sleep again, though it was anything but a restful sleep, one into which some few more unpleasant visions may have penetrated. As was the usual case now, the more conscious he became the less substantial the nightmares seemed, his recollection of their particulars gradually dissolving with the dawn. He cared not for these meddlesome apparitions that visited him in the night; he knew not their cause, their origin, their purpose in plaguing him. Worse still was this inability to bring them to mind once they had gone, even as their forceful impression lingered. They taunted him with their very illusiveness, defied him to understand them, drove him to scour the corridors of his brain for clues to their identity — which of course made them all the more disturbing.

It was at the breakfast-table that Oliver was heard to relate how he himself had endured another of his own dreams that night — another visitation from the thing like a large bird with green glowing eyes, squatting there at his casement-window. Again he had felt an intellect probing him, interrogating him, challenging him; again he had felt a chill that froze him to the marrow. Oliver was sure now it was no teratorn but an owl in these dreams of his, which had broken his sleep many times now — a horned owl, with a pale, ghostly face, very like the creature he and Mark had glimpsed that day at Skylingden. This was all he could recollect of it, he said, though he was sure there must be more, for on each occasion he had awakened to find himself in a monstrous sweat, mortally afraid and gasping for breath. The squire kept silent as he listened, his body sitting there in its chair in moody rumination, his eyes upon his half-empty plate, his teeth crunching his toast.

Mr. Smithers, who had been standing a little distance behind in attendance upon the breakfast, now approached the table. He made mention to the gentlemen how certain relations of his in the village had of late remarked, in like terms and with reluctance, upon the evil dreams that were coming to them in the night-time — and how he, Smithers himself, had been subject to them too. The butler was much struck by the resemblance of these nightmares to one another, and to those of Mr. Langley; it was, he declared, as if similar images were being impressed upon the minds of many in the village, all at one time. And always, too, the result was the same — the dreamers starting up in a lather of sweat and confusion, only to forget what it was had hurled them from their beds.

"Gracious, Mark, it has all the appearance of a contagion," said Oliver.

"A jolly uncomfortable one," grumbled the squire, wresting himself from his brown study and as well his breakfast. "Uncomfortable to be gammoned so, night after night, but unable to recollect the gammon, to be plagued with vague, persistent feelings of unease that don't signify straw. I tell you, Noll, the not remembering is jolly worse than remembering."

"Perhaps it is something in the water," Oliver suggested. "Some noxious principle, perhaps. What else could cause such delusions of mind? How else could so many be affected at once?"

"We have some of the finest wells in the valley here, sir, indeed in all of Talbotshire, with the sweetest, clearest water," said Mr. Smithers. "I should hate to think there was anything the least harmful to health in their regard. All in Shilston Upcot rely on them, for the lake water is quite unpalatable."

On hearing the word *wells* Mark and Oliver looked at one another, but volunteered nothing in front of the butler.

Pushing on to another topic, Oliver described for the squire his struggles with his latest and longest epigram of the dusty Gaius Pomponius Silla. He was rapidly coming round to a belief that certain of the Latin expressions could not be fully translated into English, with suitable force or effect, by anyone living, as there seemed to be no equivalent modern phrases; as well he was having trouble finding rhymes — in short, he was up a stump. The dusty Silla was causing him as much discomfort as the owl-like intruder of his dreams, to which complaint the lounging squire responded with a crooked smile and his heartfelt regrets.

The breakfast concluded, the gentlemen spent the remainder of the morning at their separate endeavors — Mark at his accounts in the study, with Jolly-boy at his feet, and Oliver laboring over the ancient Roman Spaniard. By mid-afternoon they had accomplished about as much as they were going to accomplish that day, and had reunited in the library — their favorite haunt apart from the billiard-room — when Mr. Smithers entered, ushering in an ancient object that had not the least to do with Silla.

"Come in, sexton!" greeted the squire, affably. "Come, join us."

It was indeed Mr. Bottom, in his suit of rusty black sable, very much patched, with his worn scratch-wig on his head. His shabby mustache was there too, and the sea of stubble roving about his double chins, and the gray smudges about his cheeks, and his close suspicious eyes — a grimy, moldy figure was old Bottom's, and a thick one, moving with a stiff, inelegant motion, as though the grime had infiltrated his sinews, and the mold his bones.

"Thankee, sir," said Mr. Bottom, stepping forward. The squire waved him to the empty chair standing between his own and Oliver's, where the sexton took his place, albeit with some hesitation. He had been to Dalroyd many times in his long life, true, and so the environs were familiar to him; but the present squire's name was Mark, not Ralph, and there was a wiliness attaching to that moody and skeptical young gentleman, in Mr. Bottom's view, which the former squire had been a stranger to.

A decanter of wine and a glass appeared, which the sexton obligingly accepted, along with a tobacco-box to fill his pipe; and so the visitor began to feel something at his ease, even as his eyes kept darting from one to another of the gentlemen, as if he were not wholly trustful of their motives.

As nothing further was required at the moment, the indispensable Smithers bowed himself out at the door.

"And how are you today, Mr. Bottom?" inquired Mark. He was unusually cordial this afternoon, his crooked smile replaced by one of welcome. "Do you have there everything you could wish for?"

"Indeed, I've nowt to complain of, Mr. Trench, sir," replied the sexton, having loaded his pipe and lighted it, and started in to smoking. "Though I remain hard put, sir, to understand the why an' wherefore of my being called here this day."

Cigars in hand, the squire and Oliver traded glances round the thick figure of Mr. Bottom posted between them.

"You may be able to help us — that is, Mr. Langley and myself — as regards a matter of some interest and importance," Mark explained.

"I help thee?" returned Mr. Bottom, with surprise gnarling his rough features. "Is't possible, sir?"

"Truly, it is. Why not take some wine there? Jolly good, is it not? Though not so strident as your own nectar, I warrant."

"A proud wine it is, sir."

"I must tell you, Mr. Bottom," said Oliver, leaning across his chair, "that Mr. Trench and I have made a rather singular discovery."

"A discovery, sir?"

Oliver nodded. "You are familiar with the caves? The caves in the south face of Skylingden point?"

The face of Mr. Bottom — south, north, east, and west of it — immediately clouded. His glass was stayed in mid-course on its journey to his lips; his close, suspicious eyes froze upon the good-natured visitor from Crow's-end.

"Caves, sir?"

"Yes. And one cave in particular, which old Splayfoot likely frequented. We believe it was one of his favored lairs — the very cave, in fact, near whose entrance his body was discovered by Mr. Trench and myself."

The sexton was temporarily relieved; the glass found his lips, the proud wine his gullet.

"This then is thy singular discovery, is it, sir? But surely all in the village know of the short-face by now. And as to singularity, I tell thee true, sir, anything smelling of matter is liable to dissolution."

"Our discovery, Mr. Bottom, has less to do with what was found outside the cave, than what was found inside it."

Mr. Bottom's relief gone, replaced by old friends suspicion and concern.

"Inside it, sir?"

"We discovered there, in a rear chamber of the cave, a most interesting piece of construction — a well for drawing water," Oliver replied. "It was sealed with a heavy capstone, held down by cords running through iron rings in the masonry."

The squire moved to recharge the sexton's glass.

"Have a further taste of the wine, like a stout fellow," he invited. "Jolly delightful, is it not?"

The sexton looked at the wine as it was poured into his glass; he looked at the glass, with the wine sitting in it; he looked from Mark to Oliver, and so to Mark again, as though he half-suspected the gentlemen were intent upon intoxicating him. Not that Mr. Bottom minded being intoxicated; it was simply that he preferred the contents of his old wicker bottle.

"You needn't be concerned as to the pedigree," the squire assured him. "It's an Ayleshire wine, one of the finest in our cellars."

"It is a very nice wine," Oliver agreed.

"Mellifluous. It will do you a power of good."

Mr. Bottom worked to straighten himself in his chair without splashing the wine from his glass, or dislodging the pipe from his hand.

"Which is to say, as to what does trouble me, sirs," said he — turning his head repeatedly from side to side, as though unsure which gentleman to address — "which is why it is thou'st called me to Dalroyd? What help can one such as I be to thee?"

"We should like to know something more about the well in the cave," answered Mark, "and we are of one mind in believing you have some knowledge of it."

"I, sir?"

"I suppose I needn't point out that you are by trade a stone-cutter. The well there was sealed with a lid of clean-hewn stone, sculpted to fit. The entire structure was itself hidden beneath a pile of debris, waste fragments of stone, mortar and the like, much of it drawn no doubt from the rubble of the abbey foundations. Some person who knows something of the stony craft did a jolly good job of closing that well and obscuring its presence. Though it lies at the hinder end of a dank, dark cavern, which was until recently the lair of old Splayfoot, in the south face of the point, out of sight and mind, something nonetheless led that person to bury the well-head under a mountain of rubble, to deter others from getting at it. I am inclined to believe that you were that person. Am I not correct in this?"

The sexton tossed up his shoulders to express his ignorance of the matter. Another bumper of wine was prepared; Mr. Bottom promptly quaffed it off, half from thirst, half to nerve himself. Both the squire and Oliver knew how powerful was the sexton's own grog, and how immune to it he had become; perhaps this fine smooth wine, which he did not often have the pleasure of imbibing, might work upon him unawares and enable them to achieve their end.

"I have nowt to say," declared Mr. Bottom, taking some more wine. He had found it very much to his liking, and a change from the briskness of his usual decoction. "*Nowt!*"

"I suspect the capstone and the rubble pile are your doing. We found there too an object amid the debris, something left behind, perhaps, or overlooked in haste — an antique crucifix on a string of rosary beads. What say you to that, sir? What have *you* to do with the Lake Friars?"

"Nowt!" exclaimed Mr. Bottom, with a tremor of anxiety and a long shake of his head. "Nowt to do with Lake Friars — no — sir!"

"What then do you know of the well? Was it sunk by the friars?"

The orbs of Mr. Bottom screwed themselves down into their sockets. He drew a hand across his cheek, his mouth, his shabby mustache, his glance roving this way and that in anxious calculation.

"I warrant it was young Campleman's discovery at the outset, was it not?" said Mark, lazily inspecting his cigar.

"It was Charley Campleman what found it," confessed Mr. Bottom, with a heavy sigh. "But I had nowt to do with it, sir; I had nowt to do with *him*, in such regard — and nowt to do with Lake Friars! The finding of it is the thing what changed him, sir, in many a divers way. In the days afore it he was an honorable, even-handed, upstanding young gentleman, bright with promise, and the apple of his ancient father's eye. All at Skylingden, all in the village held him in lofty esteem. But after it, sir — after it — and so I've said enough then. Damn and blast, I'll not be courting retribution after near these thirty year!"

"Retribution?" said Oliver. "Retribution from whom, Mr. Bottom? From Mr. Wintermarch?"

The sexton responded with a puzzled frown.   "I don't know nowt about that," said he.

"Do you know something of Miss Marchant, then, perhaps?"

Mr. Bottom put aside his glass — it was empty again — and waved his hand in denial. "I'll not be speaking o' such things," he replied, with fear in his voice. "I'll not be speaking o' such things. For sirs, I tell thee true — there is spirit all about thee!"

"We are given to understand it was you who found the empty boat upon the lake," said Oliver, after a short pause.

"I'll not be speaking o' such things," reiterated Mr. Bottom; whereupon he poured himself another bumper, without the squire's aid, and gulped it down quickly. "I'll not be speaking o' the skiff, sirs, though it were I what did find it. But that were all I found."

"Hardly," said Mark, watching him closely and smoking. "It's clear from your manner that was not all you found, sir, not by a long chalk."

Silence from Mr. Bottom, who had closed his eyes and was shaking his head repeatedly, to fortify his resolve.

"Sexton," smiled Mark, moving his chair a trifle closer to Mr. Bottom's. The squire of Dalroyd, lounging loner though he was, could be a highly persuasive fellow when he wished. "Sexton, there is something jolly odd afoot round here, in the village and at Skylingden, and I am convinced you know what it is. I can assure you, I've no wish to see you put in any sort of danger, if there is any sort of danger to be put in. For myself I care not a fig for danger, but look here — I'll be hanged if you'll be keeping valuable intelligence from me behind that stony countenance of yours. I must remind you that you've a duty and an obligation to the patron of the benefice. Perhaps you'll take some more wine?"

He charged the sexton's glass — once, twice, three times over. The attention of Mr. Bottom soon started to wander; his pipe no longer found its way to his lips, his body sagged, his eyelids began to droop. The vigor of his resistance was diminishing apace. They had only a little time now, the squire recognized, before the sexton slid from their grasp into the welcoming arms of Morpheus.

"Mr. Bottom," said Mark, touching him upon a rusty shoulder to rouse him. "What did you find in the skiff?"

Mr. Bottom peered dimly into the squire's face. He seemed torn now between his fear, and the desire to rid himself of that fear by telling someone of it. Perhaps, he thought, it was the wine that accounted for this growing insufficiency of will. Indeed, it was; and in the minutes before he lapsed into a groggy haze, he gave utterance to words of remarkable import.

"Suicide," said Mr. Bottom, hoarsely. "She what put a period to her existence — Mr. Marchant's daughter — Miss Edith — she it was what took the skiff. He was very kind to me, was Mr. Marchant. That girl — that damned well — devils — poor young Charley!"

"What of Mr. Marchant's daughter?" asked Oliver. "It's said she was in love with Mr. Campleman, but he rebuffed her and she killed herself over it. Tell us then, why it is — "

Here the sexton did a rather unexpected thing — he burst into a watery laugh, which quickly perished in a fit of coughing.

"Thou'rt dead sure, sir, but it ain't it," he said, after he had recovered himself. "It ain't it, I tell thee true. She killed herself, sirs — on account o' the child."

"Hallo! A child? What child?"

"Her own child. What! Dost not believe what I tell thee?"

"He is telling us, Noll, that the daughter of the old vicar was discovered with child, without prior benefit of a husband," said the squire.

Mr. Bottom murmured his drowsy agreement.

"What happened to this child?"

"Bundled off by coach one morning — Miss Edith, that is — what with the earthly shame of it. Sent far away west, over the mountains, to the great city — to Crow's-end — to hospital. And when it was she returned, months after, there weren't no offspring in evidence. Ah, it was a brimful, mighty secret! None knew of it at first but the vicar and his wife, and thy father, sir, Mr. Ralph Trench — he what was very kind to me, and such a good friend to Mr. Marchant — and that old custard of a maidservant, and myself o' course, what lived there behind the vicarage."

"And?"

The eyes of Mr. Bottom turned sad, as if they were observing again the light of days gone and past. "It were a sore trial for Mr. Marchant and his wife, sirs, I tell thee true. They were very kind to me. When that mad girl run a skiff from the beach out upon Lonewater, one cold night, and murdered herself there, she likely murdered her poor father and mother, too — died they both did, of broken hearts, not six months after!"

"What then of the child's father?" asked Oliver. "What of Charles Campleman? Surely this would account for his — "

Another laugh from Mr. Bottom, one which he did not trouble himself to explain; he was too much absorbed in the wine to care. He was heard murmuring to himself some few broken fragments of song, another of those melancholy plaints of grief and loss so favored by him, and by mountain people

generally. For caution's sake Oliver removed the lighted pipe from the
sexton's hand and laid it aside.

"Charley Campleman," said Mr. Bottom, suddenly reviving, "was a
prodigious smart young gentleman — a studious young gentleman — an
antiquarian, keen to spy out all manner of deep and secret histories — all unlike
his old parent, what had little learning and less interest in thinking on such
things, and anyrood was nigh-blinded in his sights. Poor Charley! He was
very kind to me, in his way. Mr. Ralph Trench was very kind to me. Mr.
Marchant too was very kind to me. Have I mentioned, sirs, as I've served five
vicars in my time?"

"Indeed you have, Mr. Bottom," smiled Oliver.

"And what of the boat, sexton?" asked the squire, with pressing urgency.
"Look here — there is more to the skiff than you have told us, sir."

"Skiff," murmured Mr. Bottom, his eyes rolling round in his head like
seasick marbles.

"The skiff, sir, the skiff. What found you there?"

"Owl," groaned Mr. Bottom, rubbing a grimy cheek.

"A horned owl with a white face?" asked Oliver, with a look to Mark.

"With horns," said Mr. Bottom, "and a white face."

"And green eyes that glowed?"

"And glowing eyes of green!"

"And what of this owl?"

"What of this owl?" repeated Mr. Bottom, in singsong.

"What does it signify?" demanded Mark, clutching again at the sexton's
shoulder. "What of the owl?"

"Owl," said Mr. Bottom, staring straight before him at the fire, as if the
events he described were unfolding there in the chimney. "It were afloat in the
air, at daybreak, hard by the skiff — then come fluttering down upon the
starboard side of it, and perched itself there, and set to watching me as I rowed
up to it — this I tell thee true."

"But why should you fear such a creature?" asked Oliver. "Why should
anyone fear it?"

"Green-eyed owl — green-eyed devil!" cried Mr. Bottom. "Such an evil
glare in its sights — such wrathful thoughts in its heart, as don't bear thinking
of — and all the doing of *her!* Come back now it has. I knew not what it were
then, but later — later — "

"What was it, Mr. Bottom?"

"Affrighted the short-face down from the caves, I've a mind it did!"

Another laugh, and another spate of coughing from Mr. Bottom, followed
by a snort; he blinked several times in succession, his limbs relaxed, his mouth

sagged, his head fell back upon the antimacassar — and there he lay, peacefully a-snore.

"I warrant that's the lot of it for now," said the squire, gliding from his seat.

"Frankly, Mark, it confounds me," said Oliver. "Miss Marchant, having found herself with child, is spirited away to the city to keep the matter dark. Some time after her return she takes a boat out upon the lake and there commits her immortal soul to the inky void, in an act of self-destruction. Going in search of her, Mr. Bottom discovers the boat *sans* Miss Marchant, and in her place a creature very like the Skylingden owl, of which he appears mortally afraid. I don't follow it. Perhaps it was not suicide after all? Perhaps it was the owl that destroyed her?"

The squire stood plunged in thought, with his face turned to the window.

"Splayfoot had been warden of the caves and Skylingden Wood for a host of years," said he. "What old Bottom has surmised could jolly well be true. Perhaps Splayfoot was driven from his lair — was in point of fact killed — for the purpose of luring someone to the cave, and thence to the rubble pile, and thence to the well."

Confirmation from Mr. Bottom, in the shape of a snore; at the same moment Oliver exclaimed —

"Hallo! The marks upon Splayfoot's corpse, as though he'd been attacked from on high — from the air — not by Mr. Shakes, but by this owl?"

"It makes simple sense. And as you know I am jolly keen on simplicity."

"If such was the aim it most certainly has been achieved, thanks to us. Likely it was part of a plan contrived by Mr. Wintermarch. It was he who brought the creature here. It was he who allowed it freedom at night to hunt. You see then, Mark, how it follows that Mr. Bede Wintermarch *must* be Charles Campleman. How else should he know of the well? What can be his purpose in wanting it discovered, unless it has some connection to his revenge against the village? Perhaps he set the owl upon Miss Marchant those years ago, on purpose to destroy her? But what sort of owl can outmatch a short-faced bear?"

The squire shrugged, and threw the stub of his cigar into the grate. "As regards any further particulars, my dear Noll, I am not of a mind now to make conjecture."

Mr. Smithers happening to look in at that moment, he observed the sexton dozing in the chair, head and scratch-wig upon the antimacassar, and at once gauged the situation. A soft clearing of his voice announced his presence.

"Ha! Smithers. See that Mr. Bottom here is provided with a jolly fine supper, once he returns to us," the squire instructed. "Give him whatever he

likes, and have a room prepared for him in the terrace wing. And send round
to the vicar that the sexton will be lodging with us tonight as our guest."

"Very good, sir."

"And inform the reverend gentleman there is a task I should like Mr.
Bottom to assist me in tomorrow, and that as patron of the benefice and in
pursuance of the privileges accorded thereto, *et cetera*, *et cetera*, I have made
bold to enlist the good sexton in that endeavor."

"Very good, sir. Will you and Mr. Langley be having your own supper
now, sir?"

"Indeed, Smithers. Lead on!"

Summers are short in the mountains, like men's lives; so observed the
squire at table, once the dishes had been removed and a bottle of Nantle port
retrieved from the cellaret. As for Oliver, he professed to feeling a hint of
autumn in the air, a touch of Michaelmas at midsummer, brought on no doubt
by the previous day's rain. And though summers might be short in the
mountains, he declared, in the fogs of Crow's-end they were wellnigh
nonexistent. Mention of Crow's-end inevitably brought the conversation round
again to the fate of Miss Marchant, and of the child who had been so
mysteriously disposed of in the city.

"Mr. Bottom is of the opinion that the owl of nearly thirty years ago and the
Skylingden owl are one and the same creature, that during the intervening span
it has been absent from the valley, and has now returned in the possession of
the family Wintermarch," said Oliver.

"I cannot disagree with you," returned the squire, who had taken again to
his brooding.

"But to what end? And why should this creature be appearing in our
dreams? It has been alleged that Mr. Campleman is intent upon vengeance of
some kind, for the treatment once accorded him and his family. If Mr.
Campleman were the father of Miss Marchant's child, it will have added to the
enmity of the villagers, if indeed they knew of it, particularly after the young
woman lost her life. That would have placed him rather deep in their bad
books, I should think. She was the daughter and only child of their vicar."

"It's jolly odd," grumbled Mark, who remained unsatisfied. "You see,
Noll, I am convinced there is more yet to be learned. There is more yet that
old Bottom has not told us. There is more, I warrant, that others in this village
have not told *me*. Oh, I'll lay you fifty golden guineas it is so. I am not a man
of many friends, I'm not the sort for it."

"What is this task you have tomorrow for Mr. Bottom?"

The squire broke out his crooked smile. "I suppose I should enlighten you.
You and I will be paying another visit to the cave, and the sexton like a stout

fellow will accompany us. We must grasp our opportunities, Noll, while we may."

For his part Oliver had no real desire to return to Skylingden point; but as Mark seemed to know what he was about, he chose to postpone judgment for now — for the die had been cast, and the sexton sloshed.

"What then of Mr. Marchant and his wife?" he asked. "What to make of them? Of what we witnessed at Dalroyd dock? Perhaps the unhappy couple are seeking vengeance of their own, now that Mr. Campleman has come back to Shilston Upcot?"

"Look here, Noll — you'll recollect old Bottom's response when it was suggested that young Campleman had fathered the child," said Mark, wrinkling his craggy brow. "And his evident sympathy for 'poor Charley' is jolly much more than ought to be accorded the knave in question, don't you agree?"

Oliver admitted that it was so.

"What say you," pursued the squire, after a few moments more of careful thought, of sipping port and smoking, with the crooked smile straying across his features — "what say you to a thesis I have formulated? For in his bibulous way, old Bottom may have provided us with the why and wherefore as regards the disappearance of the former master of this house."

"How do you mean?" asked Oliver, with rising excitement.

"You've heard from his own lips how my revered father was intimately concerned in all that went on at the vicarage in those days. Mr. Ralph Trench was jolly kind to everyone. Perhaps he was jolly kind to Miss Marchant, too."

Oliver stared past the bottle of port at his friend and host, whom he seemed to be seeing clearly for the first time.

"Well, whyever not?" retorted Mark, in self-excuse. "Perhaps it was the squire of Dalroyd who fathered this girl's child. Oh, jolly good Lord, Noll, do not gawk at me so! Do you think it so preposterous? My father put to the blush — she the daughter of the vicar, he the vicar's good friend, the husband of my mother and the father of me! Perhaps it was the enormity of his disgrace that tore him from us. Perhaps my mother discovered the truth. Perhaps he himself conveyed the girl to Crow's-end! At any rate something chased him from Dalroyd, and this is as jolly good an explanation as any I have heard."

"Gracious, Mark, surely not!" cried Oliver, in horrified amazement. "How can you for an instant suspect such a thing of your own father? It's unthinkable. It's too fantastic. It staggers belief, to be sure — and I never knew the man! Though I do know his son, and frankly, there are times I simply cannot make him out. No, no, it cannot be. If your father was guilty of even the slenderest breach of honor in this matter, I'll eat this coat of mine."

The squire responded with a listless shrug, as though he cared little what article of clothing Oliver might choose to ingest. He smiled with half-closed eyes at the cigar in his hand, rolling it gently between a thumb and forefinger.

"Perhaps I do merit condemnation, for wishing to know what the secrets are," he mused. "I suppose my former self, like Captain Hoey, would have cared nothing for such gossip as we have winkled out of old Bottom today. Gossip. Hearsay. Tattle. So you see now where tattle has gotten us!"

CHAPTER V

THERE MADNESS LIES

THERE it was again — in the spaces between the trees, the yawning, vertiginous gulf of sky and black water, against which Oliver had steeled himself on two prior occasions; there again, under his boots, was the trail running across the south face of Skylingden point. Again there were three making the journey — Mark at the head as before, Oliver in the rear, also as before; and between them, taking the place of little Jolly-boy, the short, thick figure of Mr. Bottom.

No jolly boy was Mr. Bottom today. The wine had by now been wrung out of him, through the pleasing mangle of sleep. He had received a fine supper, a fine bed, and a fine breakfast. All indeed at Dalroyd had been very fine, until the master of the house had revealed to him the nature of the morning's business. The objections of Mr. Bottom attendant thereon were numerous, and pointed; ultimately, however, there was no evading the reasoned persuasion of Mr. Mark Trench, no justifying Mr. Bottom's denial of his duties to the patron of the benefice and chief lay benefactor of the parish, duties which Mr. Bottom himself knew to be wellnigh inescapable. Even the vicar could not have helped him now, if the vicar had known what the morning's task entailed, for the needs of the squire must take precedence. In the end Mr. Bottom had little choice but to submit; although he did manage to extract from Mark, in exchange for his compliance, the promise of a gift in the shape of a bottle of Ayleshire wine.

On the whole Oliver was surprised how well the sexton maneuvered his ungainly form along the trail. Like Oliver himself he avoided looking off to his right-hand side, into the vertiginous gulf, taking comfort in the clumps of timber that skirted the trail every now and again, blotting out the view. The squire as usual found the adventure exhilarating, and at intervals took to trotting along with both hands in his coat-pockets, as easily as if he were roaming the terrace-walk at Dalroyd.

In due course they arrived at the rocky shelf. With some hesitancy on the part of both Oliver and Mr. Bottom, but perhaps a certain fascination on the part of all, they edged their way past the body of Splayfoot, which, having advanced beyond the fouler stages of decomposition, was in the process now of withering, and eroding, and shrinking, and crumbling, and collapsing upon itself, as the scavengers of death reaped their grim harvest.

At the cave-entrance the explorers stopped to prepare the usual wax-lights in candlesticks. Mr. Bottom several times expressed his enthusiasm for returning to the horses on the summit above — horses representing a speedy means of placing distance between himself and the cave — but the squire put him in mind again of his duties and obligations, insinuating that if he harbored the least regard for the memory of the old vicar, Mr. Marchant, and for Mrs. Marchant, who had been so very kind to him, he should gladly cooperate in the present endeavor. Whereupon Mr. Bottom muttered something again about persons walking who should not be walking, before retorting that he knew not what the object of the present endeavor was, sir, for the squire had yet to inform him of it. Oliver was himself in some agreement with Mr. Bottom in this, for he too was unsure what it was the squire hoped to achieve here. To Mark, however, there was little mystery to it. It was clear there was more yet to be gleaned from Mr. Bottom; given this, it was reasonable to suppose that the sexton might be more forthcoming if brought face to face with the particular object of their curiosity.

Into the cave they went, past the walls of bare black earth, the somber nooks and frowning masses of rock, and patches of ice glistening in the corners. It had occurred to Oliver, not a little uncomfortably, that some creature of the wood might have taken up residence in the cavern now that Splayfoot had surrendered the lease; but no unusual scent reached their nostrils, no growl of warning their ears, no charging form their eyes, nothing indeed to betoken the presence there of anything but a deathly hush. Not a bat rustled, not a rat scurried, not a cricket chirped in its dark embrace.

In no long time they came to the farther chamber, and approached the well. Seeing it there filled Mr. Bottom with an awful presentiment; the eerie play of light and shadow skulking about its exterior filled him with even worse. How many years had loitered their way into the past since his last glimpse of that odious monument? Not nearly enough!

It was clear to the squire and Oliver that Mr. Bottom was very much afraid of the well, for he gave it a wide berth. Nonetheless Mark invited him to look it over, so that he might assure himself that all was quite secure — which Mr. Bottom shortly did, taking a few cautious steps towards it, and peeping round its outlines with his close, suspicious eyes. He remarked to the gentlemen as he examined it — a timid, hasty, fitful sort of examination at best, as though he feared the capstone might at any moment spring up like a jack-in-the-box — how glad he was to find it corked tight, after these many years, though seeing the fragments of masonry cleared from it did unnerve him some; that it was fortunate the gentlemen had not been tempted to release the ties he'd placed there, as it had been Mr. Bottom's devoutest wish that the loathsome pit should remain forever sealed. At this Oliver and Mark traded glances, for here was the first admission from Mr. Bottom that the closure of the well had indeed been his doing.

Some few minutes more did the sexton expend upon his examination; and a somewhat bolder, more attentive examination it was now, in the course of which his eyes went wide, his jaw dropped, and his hands began to tremble. He cast a dark look round his shoulder towards the gentlemen standing behind. It was now Mr. Bottom's turn to question whether he'd been told the entire truth, for he saw that the capstone was cracked, and that the lines holding it down were comparatively new — lines which, unbeknownst to him, had come from the squire's sloop at Dalroyd dock.

"Someone has been at work here," he murmured, hoarsely. "Someone has been at work here, sirs, I tell thee true — and it's bad work!"

Of this the squire claimed to have no knowledge. Though Oliver would have liked to confess whose work it was, he was overruled by a sharp glance from Mark. Mr. Bottom, however, was not about to be gulled. The sexton may not have been a learned man, a scholar, a graduate of the great university at Salthead, but he was by no means an unintelligent man; he saw how the land lay, but said no more about it.

Oliver found himself questioning again the wisdom of sinking a well here, in this so very inconvenient spot inside the earth, accessible only by means of the dizzying trail across the promontory slopes.

"It weren't always inconvenient," said Mr. Bottom, with a grunt.

"How do you mean?"

At once regretting having spoken, Mr. Bottom mastered his reluctance sufficiently to lead the others a little deeper into the cave, to the hinder end of the chamber, to a dark corner indistinguishable from the many such dark corners the taper-light had failed to illumine. There was, Oliver assumed at first, nothing to be seen there but a dead wall; but it was not so. To both his and Mark's considerable surprise, they found instead a heavy oak door built into the rock. It was studded with nails and so situated as to be imperceivable by anyone making less than a thorough inspection of the cave-chamber.

"Hallo!" Oliver exclaimed, recognizing at once what it signified. "Likely there are several flights of stairs behind this door here, descending from the vaults and undercrofts of the abbey ruins."

"And buried tight," declared Mr. Bottom, "with stones and mortar piled up behind the door — which thou'llst see cannot be opened, sir, for it turns only outwards — and at the crypt entrance atop. And so nowt can be seen of the staircase, at either end."

"A staircase constructed by the Lake Friars, who thus would have had no need of taking the path from the summit."

Mr. Bottom responded with a brusque nod, and a shiver. "Wellnigh thirty year ago it were now, sirs, when the well was corked and the stairs buried tight."

"More likely some eight-and-twenty years, sexton, I should think," reckoned the squire.

"It were indeed after the dread events, sirs," said Mr. Bottom, peering mistrustfully round him, as though he feared being overheard. "After the suicide, sirs, and the demise of Mr. Marchant and his wife, and after the family Campleman had removed themselves from the mansion-house, on account o' the madness of poor Charley and the prodigious ill feeling of many in the village. It were after it all when I corked the well, sirs, and blocked up the stairs — and damn and blast, it's nowt but good riddance to 'em!"

"Surely you had some assistance, Mr. Bottom," said Oliver. "You could not have accomplished this wholly on your own."

"There was some what helped," admitted Mr. Bottom, grudgingly.

"Who?"

"The best I recollect it, there was Mr. Wardrop — he what was the brand-new vicar after Mr. Marchant went off the hooks, and what was uncommon keen to see measures taken — and Tommy Tudway, what is chandler now, and Hugh Lincote the sugar-baker, and some three or four other lads from the village, what had the courage o' lions in their young hearts, in those days, and were not afraid to venture here — for the well, sirs, was all uncorked, o' course — and too there was young Nim Ives, of the Arms, and his brother what lives now at Cedar Crag."

"Landlord Ives?" smiled Mark, with a sidelong glance at Oliver. "Well, there it is, then. I suppose I should not be too startled, for it wholly accords with my view. You'll recollect my wager of fifty golden guineas, Noll. I warrant I've won it hollow."

"I recollect too the landlord's response on hearing of our encounter at Dalroyd dock — how he turned white as paper in the face, and left us rather hastily, to the mystification of his daughter — and as well his reaction to learning that Miss Cherry herself was familiar with certain particulars of the death of Miss Marchant," said Oliver.

Since the time of Charles Campleman there had been little mention of the dread events, Mr. Bottom explained. It was not the manner of thing that ought to be spoken of, most felt, though Mr. Ives and certain of the regulars at the Arms were known to discuss it among themselves, on occasion. It had been hoped that with the departure of the Camplemans and the closing of the well, the dread events would come to a merciful end, and so they had. All had lain quiet these thirty years — or more rightly these eight-and-twenty, as the squire reminded him — until the arrival of the family Wintermarch at Skylingden.

"You've told us that Mr. Campleman was not the same man after he'd found the well," said Oliver. "What happened to him? In what way did he change?"

Mr. Bottom drew a long breath, his eyes roving uneasily about the cave-chamber, his ears alert for the faintest hint of uninvited company.

"Madness, Mr. Langley, sir," he whispered, with a nudge of his head and scratch-wig towards the well. "Madness it is what lies there, I tell thee true. Many what have come under its spell have gone off the latch, one way or t'other; so it is said by others, and so it's been my experience. It set poor Charley Campleman to raving, as it had certain of the ancient friars, some of what in their daft state 'scaped loose from the abbey and come down into the village, all lunatic'd and mad-eyed. Speaking words what had no meaning, swearing and cursing for no earthly reason, with oaths enough to blow the roof off a house, taking violent action where no cause was, as though they'd had a glimpse of the unholy — such as these, sirs, and more! Sitting silent for an hour and more, then on a sudden breaking into unholy laughter, and heaving and puking, and striking out at the air. Things they'd seen there, or heard there, at the well, was what drove 'em to it. It were the antiquarian in him, sirs, what led Charley Campleman here, for he'd been keen on the Lake Friars and their history — what with the ruin of the abbey lying there aside Skylingden Hall — and on the fate o' the friars themselves. First it were the line of steps leading from the crypt what he found, and tracing 'em down into the earth, to this very door, he run upon the cavern. It were one what had been inhabited, now and again, by the short-faces, but it were abandoned at the time. Would to God it had not been so, sirs, would to God!"

"What did Mr. Campleman find in the well?" Oliver asked, with some trepidation.

"Nowt as can be much expounded upon, sir, by one such as I, anyrood. One time it was the young heir came rushing up from the depths of it, on a halter-rope what he'd tied fast to the iron rings there. He was a-peeping at his watch, I recollect, and inquired of me as to the hour o' the day. More than a few times he repeated the same, climbing into the well and climbing out of it again, and a-peeping at his watch, and as lively as a badger he was, to be sure; but never did he share a confidence with me, sirs, as to the nature of his excitement, and so I've nowt to say of it. More than a few times it was I helped him in getting down the well, and long were the hours he passed in those grim depths afore returning, each time livelier than afore. It was one day

then he told me, sirs, something o' the chatter he'd heard there in the well —
a 'cloud of voices,' he called it, all swarming round his head, all jabbering at
him — which is what it was convinced him, sirs, as there were folk alive in
there."

A creeping chill gripped the flesh of Oliver, unsettling him, and causing him
to put off his next question — though it mattered not, for the squire promptly
asked it for him.

"And were there people there, sexton? People in the well?"

"I'd know nowt about it myself, sir, whether they be people or no, for never
once did I venture past the lip of the well, and never would, not in a thousand
lifetimes, and not for the world's sake — of that thou canst be dead sure!"
declared Mr. Bottom, fervently. "Whatever it is it's an evil thing what dwells
there, lying at catch, and can turn a fine, upstanding young gentleman like
Charley Campleman to its damnable ways."

"And you believe it was these repeated journeys inside the well that drove
Mr. Campleman to madness?" asked Oliver.

The sexton nodded. "And not only poor Charley, sir, but she too what
came later to accompany him."

"She? Surely you don't mean Miss Marchant?"

"The suicide, indeed, sir. It were some months after the matter of the child,
some six or seven months, as I recollect it, after she'd been restored to the
village. It were an awful moment when I discovered it, that steely cold
afternoon I spied 'em taking the stairs from the crypt. There was nowt for a
Christian man to do but follow after 'em, sirs, and follow after 'em I did. It
were here, in this very chamber, where I begged Charley Campleman to send
her away, to safekeep her from the devils in the pit. But he would not listen
to one such as I, for he already was under the spell of it; and she herself
seemed not unwilling to bear him company. And so it was, sirs, over time the
girl too came under the spell of it — bewitched her, it did — turned her, sirs,
as it turned the bookish young heir."

"This surely must have played some role in Miss Marchant's death," said
Oliver. "For I have read on more than one occasion, in the city papers, true
accounts of persons of unsound mind who have been moved to destroy
themselves."

"As on the night she took the skiff from the beach, sir — it were little
Coddy Binks what saw her take it — and rowed out upon Lonewater, in the
moonlight, never again to be spied in earthly shape. Or so 'twas claimed!"

"How do you mean, Mr. Bottom?"

There followed a restless pause.

"I don't know nowt about it, sir," replied the sexton, irritably, like a man disturbed by the direction of his thoughts — "and don't care to know nowt about it, and neither should thee, not for the world's sake!"

While speaking Mr. Bottom had grown visibly more nervous, more uneasy, and ever more eager to depart; and so in truth had Oliver, whose own antiquarian zeal was not nearly so persevering as young Mr. Campleman's evidently had been. The squire appeared ready to oblige them, asking Oliver to return with Mr. Bottom to the horses, while he himself would be along directly. The lines anchoring the capstone to the well, he had observed, had now some slight laxity in them, a matter he offered to address while his companions repaired to the summit. Oliver quickly volunteered to assist him, but the sexton did not. As he did not like for Mr. Bottom to undertake the climb unattended, Oliver was forced to reverse himself; and so the two set off together, as per Mark's suggestion, leaving the squire to his solitary task.

As the stillness of the cave-chamber closed in about him, the master of Dalroyd stepped to the well and with his light inspected the fastenings. All were taut, all were secure; all was, in fact, just as he and Oliver had left it. So much for laxity in the lines! Putting the taper aside he began to release certain of the ties from the iron rings. He worked quickly, efficiently. He knew he could not remove the capstone without assistance, but the broken fragment of it was a different matter. Having undone its attachments he eased it off, and so created for himself an opening onto the pitchy dark chasm beneath.

Holding his taper aloft he peered into the abyss. The feel of the hand closing upon his ankle, to pull him down, was still fresh in his mind. He had said nothing of the incident to Oliver, not a word; indeed, he knew not what to say to Oliver about it. What he did know was that he must puzzle it out for himself.

In the makeshift window there was no sound, no sense of swirling movement, no devils, nothing but the pitchy dark chasm. For some minutes he waited for this to change, but no change came. *Time passeth like a shadow*, or so the sundial says; and so time did pass and still no change. He delayed some little bit more, until he knew he could delay no longer. As he was about to replace the capstone fragment, in preparation for going, his senses detected a slight noise — the faintest, softest something of a noise, rising from below. At once he bent his ear to the opening, straining to listen, as he had on that earlier occasion in the company of Oliver. Slowly the faintest, softest something began to grow, began to swell, began to take on power and strength, becoming louder and more pronounced, and more nearly intelligible, and so by gradual degrees resolved itself into a single quiet voice, speaking to him from the darkness.

His pulse racing, his craggy brow thrown into folds, the squire listened to what the well said. More than once he stared very hard into the opening, so shocked was he by what he heard, to see what there was to see there — to see if there were aught to confirm what the voice was saying. He saw nothing, but heard more. The words hit him with the stun of a thunderbolt and left him breathless.

It was only with the greatest effort that he managed to shake himself free of their influence. Tremblingly he restored the capstone fragment and secured the ties, his brow gleaming with moisture in the taper-light, his gray, drab, lumpish face twisted into an expression of disbelief; while in his eyes reposed a wonder and an astonishment that never before had been seen there.

CHAPTER VI

SOMETHING IN THE CHURCHYARD

A waffle-cake is a funny thing. A humble concoction of flour, eggs, and cow's milk, pressed and baked between the studded plates of a griddle, a fair amount of its resulting substance is air. One may be satisfied with its flavor during the eating of it — a flavor much improved by sweet dark syrup from a pitcher, and fresh butter from a butter-boat — and yet so much of a waffle-cake is, in the end, simply air. It is too light in and of itself to be of lasting sustenance, because indeed so much of it is air; and so it must be helped along by the syrup and the butter, and by more — by walnuts, or pecans, or almonds, or larchberries, piled atop the waffle-cake, or by a rasher of ham or cup of plum porridge at the side of it. That is, unless one takes it upon one's self to devour a whole mountain of dry, ungarnished waffle-cake, and in the process ingest an entire atmosphere of air. In this respect eating a waffle-cake was very much like sitting at worship of a Sunday morning, in the church of St. Lucy of the Lake, and ingesting a sermon cooked up by the bespectacled young vicar of Shilston Upcot.

So ran the thoughts of Mrs. Dinah Scattergood, the pretty red-haired wife of the vicar, as she sat contemplating her breakfast in the waffle-house of Miss Crimp, a few days after such a Sunday morning. Why eating a waffle-cake should have put her in mind of her husband's recent sermon — a particularly dry and insubstantial work, offering little sustenance apart from the garnish of an anecdote or three, tossed in to improve the flavor, and to rouse members of the flock slumbering in the pews — she cared not to think. Nonetheless it did, and so she resolved to speak with her dichotomy of a reverend husband about it that very day, and urge him to strive for improvement in his concoction for the Sunday to come.

She chose not to introduce the vicar's sermon as a topic now for conversation, for she knew only too well it would occasion a like judgment from others at table, notably Miss Margaret Mowbray and Miss Cherry Ives. Though Dinah felt it her wifely obligation to correct her husband whenever he veered from the path of tolerableness and good sense — which unfortunately was often, nearly every day — she preferred not to hear of his veering from others' lips, or of the implied criticism therein. In a sense it betrayed her own failure to guide him on the proper course, to address his ministerial imperfections and his lack of backbone and his other manly foibles, which were varied and numerous. *Of what use is a shepherd who does not lead?* was Dinah's oft-posed question to herself, and to her friends; for certainly in the matter of sermonizing her husband was no leader. Any clergyman who can bore himself silly with doctrine and preaching cannot do else but bore others as well, as might be observed in the pews of St. Lucy on any Sunday morning. If the Reverend Mr. Scattergood would expend upon his sermons a fraction of the energy he expended upon his violoncello and his Raviola, Dinah told herself, there should be no cause for her to suffer pangs of conscience while dissecting her waffle-cake at Miss Crimp's. To cheer herself she poured some more syrup into the crevices of the cake, and applied another pat of butter, and volunteered not a word about the good vicar of Shilston Upcot.

On this particular morning, however, she would have no need to concern herself with her husband and his reputation in the parish, for matters of a more lurid and dramatic character already had set the minds of certain of her table-companions astir.

"And so, as I have told you all before, I think it most shameful for Miss Marchant to have put an end to herself," said Cherry Ives, with a nod and a bounce of her shiny dark curls. "Shameful for all of us, for you know it sets a very poor example. There's no need making a ruin of one's life over a gentleman who won't have you. It's not the sort of thing I should have done, were I in her place, nor should any self-respecting woman. Pray, do not mistake me — I have the utmost sympathy for her plight, and how it must have sorely preyed upon her mind. Indeed, I can hardly believe she had her full wits about her at the time."

"She must have been quite mad with love for him," said Miss Mowbray.

"Or just simply mad, to have parted with her life on account of Mr. Charles Campleman. True, he was the heir to Skylingden; but there are other, equally satisfying paths to happiness on this earth than young heirs and mansion-houses."

"Oh, rank heresy!" cried Mags, with mock indignation. "How very provoking."

"I find I agree with you, Cherry, but only after a fashion," said Miss Crimp. "For you know, dear, despite everything, money and position do matter. They are often the most important considerations in affairs of the heart. You yourself are fortunate, for you have your father's inn to manage. You, like myself, have had opportunity; most young women are not so blessed, and must rely upon a husband for their livelihood."

"No one, not even Mr. Dogger, knows the extent of the Skylingden fortune," said Cherry. "Oh, it's quite true, it was Charles Campleman's to inherit, but it doesn't necessarily follow that there was any money left. The old gentleman, his father, could very well have squandered the chief of it, in Malbury, or Crow's-end, or elsewhere. There could have been debts, and where there are debts there must be creditors. Who can say what Charles Campleman's expectations may have been at the time?"

"I do not think that can have been the case at all," said Mrs. Fielding, with the kindliest of frowns. (It was only dear, sweet, unassuming Aunt Jane who could raise a frown one might describe as *kindly*.) The widow knew that everyone else at table knew that she knew things about the history of the drowned girl. She was in hopes she would not be pressed too far today — would not be squeezed and heated between the studded plates of the griddle, like a waffle-cake, as Dinah might have imagined it — but certain remarks had to be responded to.

"I've no wonder the affair was scandalous," said her niece. "It puts me rather in mind of Skylingden itself, its record of ill fortune and unexplained loss, its hushed secrets. I can well understand how a young girl of untested mettle, even a vicar's daughter, being deprived of the gentleman of her choosing, might have viewed her life as without purpose, and without a proper future, and been unable to see a way forward beyond her disappointment. It is not an uncommon malady, I suppose, though most do not drown themselves over it."

"Perhaps you offer yourself and Mr. Mark Trench as an example of the latter?" smiled Cherry, fixing Mags with her bold, bright gaze. "Speaking of which, how goes it with the two of you? We've heard something of the squire's inviting you to the gallop with Tony Arkwright and Dr. Hall and Captain Hoey the other morning. How did it turn out?"

"We all of us turned out, and Mark did not invite me," returned Miss Mowbray. "It was entirely Mr. Arkwright's doing. He asked us round to Timber Hill Farm to show us his new foal. And a very chipper young gentlemen he is, too."

"Mr. Arkwright?"

"The foal, whose name is Junius. A gallop round the countryside was then proposed — *by* Mr. Arkwright — and agreed to by all."

"Very well, then, the squire allowed you to accompany him."

"You're very impertinent, Cherry Ives," retorted Mags, matching her friend's banter point for point. "You know nothing of what transpired that day. Unlike my cousin you are quite enamored of tattle; I've a notion it's a habit common to innkeepers. The gallop of which you speak had not the faintest connection to the matter of Mark and myself, none whatever. It was a pleasant jog to take in the air and the natural wonders of the valley, during which the

Captain found time to expound upon his hypothesis regarding the geological history of Lonewater and the Talbots."

"We are all living in a volcano!" exclaimed Miss Crimp, with an odd mix of alarm and hilarity upon her dainty face of china. "So Captain Hoey informed us during one of his visits. I'm afraid he terrified poor Molly and the girls with his theories. It's fortunate my mother did not hear him — the Captain's voice is quite arresting, you know — though I suppose she would have understood little of it if she had."

"On the contrary, it was likely his voice rather than his theories that frightened the girls," laughed Miss Mowbray. "There is something in it that keeps little Jolly-boy positively in thrall."

"Had the Captain done himself any recent mischief?" Cherry inquired.

"His scullioned foot was on the mend, as was his ailing finger. However I believe I detected evidence of a fresh bruise upon his temple, though he kept it mostly hidden beneath his riding-hat."

"He is forever damaging himself in some region or other of his anatomy, and charging it to poor Slack."

"The Captain has changed not a whit since I have known him," said Miss Violet, as she dabbed some comb honey upon a wedge of toast. "He occupies himself with so many interests, so many learned disquisitions, such a crowd of ideas of such variety and complexity, for so much of the day, as to be little conscious of his actions at any given moment."

"Hence his mischiefs," said Cherry. "His mind is continually racing about him to all corners of the compass, like a rush of startled birds."

"He is a monstrous fine scholar, though he never went up to university. He is an inveterate studier of things."

"And as well an accomplished architect, for it was he who designed his cottage in the tree-tops, his villa in the pines there at the Peaks," added Miss Mowbray. "Though it was largely his tenants and crofters who built it."

"Very sensible of them," observed Cherry, with another bounce of her curls, "for you'd not want a carpenter's hammer or a wood saw within reach of his hands. Who can tell what new mischiefs he might do himself?"

Everyone laughed very heartily at this, and very much at the Captain's expense; after which a little break in the conversation ensued, during which the ladies busied themselves with their waffle-cakes and muffins, and fortifying doses of thick black coffee, while being attended to by one of Miss Crimp's serving-girls, and with Miss Crimp herself always on the alert for the pound of a crutch-handled cane overhead.

"I should like to have known Miss Edith Marchant," said Cherry, taking now what appeared to be a more serious line. "I should like to have engaged her in private and shared her thoughts, to have bolstered her spirits, to have impressed upon her the value of trusting to one's resources. She must have known very little of life to have robbed herself of it, and of all her prospects for the future."

Her companions murmured their agreement, particularly Miss Crimp, who understood only too well the truth of Cherry's words. Her glance strayed to her mother's prized rosewood furniture that stood about the public room — the chiffonier, the old-fashioned cupboard, the tall cabinet — and to the line of ceramic plates ranged along the high shelf like observing faces, collected in distant parts of the realm by her grandfather the crockery merchant. Miss Crimp had had her opportunities to leave Shilston Upcot, to mix with the wider world beyond the mountains, but they had come to naught, partly through her own timidity and inaction, partly through the actions of others. Once too often in her life she had surrendered herself to the forces of circumstance. Would that someone like Cherry Ives had been there in the springtime of her youth, to have shared her thoughts and bolstered her spirits!

"Perhaps then she would not have put a period to her existence," Cherry continued, with reference of course to the late vicar's daughter. "A way perhaps might have been found to prevent it, a means by which her eyes might have been opened. Oh, I've no doubt I could have opened them for her, if given time, through kindness, reason, and friendly encouragement."

"That would have been a fine and admirable thing, Miss Cherry," spoke up Mrs. Fielding. "But I'm afraid the poor young woman would have been in no state to attend to either reason or encouragement."

"How do you mean, Aunt?" asked Mags, growing curious. "Do you suppose indeed she *was* mad?"

"It was thought at the time that her mind was unbalanced," replied Aunt Jane, quietly. She always had disliked this subject — this accursed subject! — and cared little more for it now. The very thought of it chilled her to the marrow. But there was no going back; she had popped it out, and as a result was forced to make a little inward call on her own courage. "The young woman's appearances in the village became gradually less frequent. In time her father saw fit to keep her in at the vicarage, under the care of a maidservant. Sadly, one night she made good her escape, and so you are familiar with the outcome of it. She must have suffered fearful torments in her wild state; though I never myself inquired further into the particulars, from respect for her family and the young woman's poor departed soul."

"And what put her into this wild state?" asked Cherry, rhetorically. "It was love for the young heir of Skylingden, and her refusal to go forward in life without him. She had aspired to live one day at the mansion-house as his wife, as the mistress of Skylingden; which was a day that never would be. Perhaps he humiliated her — the village girl and vicar's daughter who dared to love a Campleman! Perhaps she flew into a rage; perhaps that is what unbalanced her and led her to suicide. Perhaps if I had been there I might have done some good, and averted a catastrophe. As my father has always told me, there are two important things in life: work, and good works. And I for one second him in this."

"You are very sure of yourself, dear," marveled Miss Violet. "You speak as if you had indeed known vicar Marchant's daughter."

"I believe I understand what sort of girl she was," Cherry declared, not with any loftiness or feeling of superiority, but rather more matter-of-factly, and with the best of intentions. "I still am very sorry for her, but really — one sees these sorts of young women round these mountains every day. In Tarnley, Jay, even at Cedar Crag where my uncle lives, it's catch that catch can. These are girls with no further object in life than the snaring of a husband; girls with no thought as to the value of work, or good works; no thought of doing for themselves, no sense of pride in their own resources, no thought of any achievement beyond the capture of a marriage-vow. I am thankful my father raised me differently. And I am sure my mother, had we not lost her when I was but six years of age, would have backed him to the hilt."

"Marriage is a sacred union, a heavenly joining, and as such a worthy goal for any man or woman," said Dinah, who, being a vicar's wife, could hardly have held any other opinion on the subject. "There is nothing amiss in seeking out a marriage partner, or in raising a family, and seeing the love one has for another mirrored in the faces of one's children. Your own parents quite plainly did so themselves."

"No, there is nothing amiss in it," returned Cherry, spiritedly. "But it should not become a ruling passion, as it does with some. On the contrary, a young woman should be urged to develop her talents and interests."

"Which she then will use to attract a husband," smiled Miss Crimp.

"And which is not so very wrongheaded," Dinah added. "It is but the natural condition of women in society."

"Nonetheless, I do wish I could have known Miss Marchant," said Cherry, growing a little uncomfortable perhaps with the response her opinions had elicited. "I should have convinced her of the wrongness of her thinking. I should have persuaded her that her feelings for young Mr. Campleman, however strong, ought not overweigh her feelings for herself. I should have prevailed upon her not to jeopardize her prospects on account of a gentleman who did not care for her. We must be happy with what we have, and shed no tears for what we have not, or cannot have. Yes, I do know what sort of girl Miss Marchant was very well."

"Indeed, we must enjoy life while the opportunity is given us," sighed Miss Crimp, with one or two plump little noddles of her head. "Time passes so very quickly the older one gets. The more precious the days become, the more speedily they depart. I recollect as a child having no consciousness of time whatsoever, no awareness of the passage of the hours."

"Unfortunately time does not defer to the children, nor to any of us," said Aunt Jane, glancing for a moment at her withered hands, which, like her face, had once been smooth and beautiful. "Time cannot be stopped like a chime-clock, though it would be delightful if it could. It runs on of its own accord and for its own purposes."

"Time goes hurtling by us like a river. The days rush relentlessly forward and there's no help for it. Why was it set to running this way? Why are the days *allowed* to rush forward, do you think?" asked Miss Violet, with Slack-like concern.

"Wouldn't it be fine," smiled Mags, "if there were no such beastly thing as Time, and we all could live from hour to hour, and from day to day, without the least change, always to remain as we are now?"

"You are describing God's promised eternity," said Dinah, ever the vicar's wife.

"Yes, I suppose I am."

Eternity, Dinah found herself musing, was a thing the parishioners of Shilston Upcot already had some experience of, for her husband was forever inflicting it upon them from his pulpit on a Sunday morning. Almost at once she felt guilty for thinking this, and crunched the air out of her last morsel of waffle-cake.

Miss Mowbray and Mrs. Fielding spent the remainder of the day with others of their friends and acquaintances in the village, in the cottages and shops in the Low Street and Town End, before at last bending their steps towards Gray Lodge and home. Along the way they passed the venerable market cross with its pillar and steps of good Talbotshire stone, and hard by it the village green and the public well, where they stopped to drink. At length they came to the church of St. Lucy and the vicarage, and to the bridle-path that wound past the churchyard and up through the hollow to the coach-road, emerging there very near the entrance to Gray Lodge. The day was now far advanced, and the early dusk of the mountains was drawing in, after the disappearance of the sun behind the tall curtain of the Talbots.

Walking up the bridle-path, the ladies became aware of the presence of someone in the churchyard. In the loom of the ancient trees, among the crazy tilted tombstones like ships afloat on a rolling sea of ground, a lonely figure with bowed head and folded arms could be seen standing at a grave — it was one of the larger of the monuments in the yard, with a carven angel perched upon it — as if contemplating the memory of the person whose dust lay moldering there. This was not so very remarkable in itself, of course, for mourners are no strangers to churchyards. It was what this particular mourner did next, however, that drew the attention of Mags and Mrs. Fielding; for the mourner proceeded to turn himself about, and with arms outspread began to walk backwards at a slow, deliberate pace, describing a circle round the grave. Once, twice, three times and more the figure marched itself round the monument, as the ladies looked on in some consternation, and in some frustration, too, for the light in the churchyard was very poor and the identity of the mourner could not be made out, even at this short distance.

"Who is that?" Mags asked her aunt. "And whatever is he doing?"

CHAPTER VII

"OH, we must stop him!"

It was Aunt Jane, reaching for her niece's arm in a tremor of anxiety.

"What is it he's doing there?" said Mags, as mystified by her aunt's sudden exclamation as by the odd goings-on at the grave. "And why must it be stopped?"

At the widow's insistence they broke from the path and set off across the burying-grounds towards the lonely figure, who was in the midst of yet another circuit round the tomb. In urgent haste Mrs. Fielding explained how it was a popular belief among some that walking in such a manner round a grave, twelve times in succession, would call forth the spirit of the one buried there and give it voice again in the world.

The lonely figure had now completed its fifth orbit of the monument, and was starting into its sixth.

"Do you suppose it is the tomb of the Marchants — the old vicar and his wife?" asked Mags, rather thrilled to have had another secret from the lips of her aunt. "The apparitions Mark and Mr. Langley claim to have seen at Dalroyd dock. Do you suppose this is the means by which — ?"

Mrs. Fielding said nothing in reply, for she was already quite out of breath from hurrying her steps. As they drew near, however, they realized that the tomb could not be that of the unfortunate Marchants, both dead of broken hearts, for theirs was nothing so grand and moreover was situated closer to the church. The lonely figure, still marching backwards, resolved itself into that of a gentleman in a dark cutaway coat, with a sportish turf hat on his head; a gentleman with a gray, lumpish face, mustaches and side-whiskers, and small narrow eyes, rather closely planted. They saw it was one of the stony memorials to the Talbotshire Trenches round which the figure was circling, and that the figure itself was no other than the present squire of Dalroyd.

It was about this time that the squire became aware of his cousins' approach. At first he was resolved to go on with his marching and ignore them in regular Mark Trench-like fashion, which he did, but for only another orbit or two. He found feminine eyes staring upon him from the perimeter to be a huge distraction; already they had caused him to stumble once in his course. (It is no easy matter to propel one's self backwards round a gravestone on a rolling piece of turf, arms outstretched at one's sides, in the failing light of a churchyard; if you do not believe me give it a try yourself some day, at dusk, and at your own peril.) As a result the squire was forced to bring his odd exercise to a halt, at least for a time. Mags thought he must be inebriated, but quickly realized this could not be, otherwise he should have been unable to perform his acrobatics round the tomb while preserving his perpendicular. More than likely he was chagrined at having been discovered there, and by whom, not to mention a trifle dizzy from his revolving.

They made for an interesting tableau, the three of them there in the loom of the churchyard trees — the squire returned to contemplating the gravestone, his arms folded upon his chest, his head bowed and his back to the ladies, both of whom stood quietly awaiting an explanation. While they waited it continued to grow darker in the burying-grounds, and sadder, as the daylight fled behind the Talbot Peaks.

When minutes had passed and still the squire had offered not a word — which was rather unlike that sardonic gentleman, with an audience of ladies at hand — and just as it seemed he was about to stride off and leave her and Aunt Jane there in those gloomy precincts, his young cousin thought it time to speak out.

"This is your mother's grave," she observed, quietly.

The squire lifted his head a little, and glanced round at her from the corners of his eyes.

"It is," he replied, with something like a hitch in his chin. "I never pass this way without paying due reverence to her memory."

"I've an idea you were doing more than paying reverence."

"If so it is my own affair."

"In a place so public as a parish churchyard, anybody's affair may be everybody's business," noted Miss Mowbray.

"Might I ask then what jolly business my business is of yours, cousin?" demanded Mark, pivoting on his heel to face her.

"Perhaps no jolly business whatever," she answered, with one of her ready smiles. "But in point of fact I am a curious sort, as you know very well, cousin, and when I spy a thing so very mysterious in a churchyard I simply must look into it."

"And so you've drawn Auntie into it as well?"

"You may suppose what you like, Mark. I believe you'd managed about ten spins round your mother's stone there before we broke in upon you. I do apologize for that. We thought at the outset it was the tomb of the Reverend and Mrs. Marchant, and that someone was busy raising their ghosts. Is that not what you and Mr. Langley encountered at Dalroyd dock? The old clergyman and his wife, whom none in the village had any knowledge of?"

"We were witness to something," the squire replied, "but as yet have no proof as to its nature. And there's an end to it for today."

"Where is Mr. Langley, by the by? You and he have been wellnigh inseparable ever since his arrival in the village. It would appear you've quite succeeded in monopolizing his time."

"Mr. Langley will be at Dalroyd at this hour, I should think, wrestling like the stout fellow he is with the dusty Silla. Though naturally I could be mistaken; I am not Mr. Langley's guardian. He attained his majority some few years back, I understand."

"Now you're trying to be clever, and paraphrasing Scripture to boot. Whatever may we expect next? The squire of Dalroyd reading the lesson at service on a Sunday morning?"

"You're too jolly clever yourself for your own good, my girl," Mark retorted, crisply. "Take care it does not lead you into trouble. Perhaps you can see your way clear to leave me for now — my genuine regrets, Auntie, I'll make it up to you — as I should prefer to be alone for a bit longer."

Miss Mowbray had a crisp rejoinder of her own at the ready — she was in fine trim today, from sparring with young Cherry Ives at breakfast — but then thought the better of it, after noting the look of caution in the eyes of her aunt and the serious tenor of her cousin's request. Consequently the rejoinder died on her lips, and instead she heard herself ask —

"What is it you're looking for here, Mark?"

"Answers," was his reply; after which he offered nothing more on the subject. He touched his hat to them, and assured them he would refrain from any further machinations at the gravestone, this day at least.

Mags looked at her aunt, whose anxiety had evidently subsided, and who now was eyeing the bridle-path and its winding ascent through the hollow. Silently she relented; and so they left the squire of Dalroyd to his filial duties, there in the gathering darkness under the close overhanging trees. For her part Miss Mowbray left with more than a shadow of concern upon her ordinarily sunny features. The squire in the churchyard had seemed rather like the grumpy squire she and her aunt both knew; and yet, in some ways he had of late been growing more and more unlike his lounging self.

When Mark returned to Dalroyd he went at once to his study and threw himself into an armchair, where for half an hour he cast brooding glances upon the leafy pattern in the floor-cloth, and the shiny dark wainscot oak, and the oil portraits leering from the walls, and the damask curtains at the window, and the ledgers and accounts spread across his desk, while neglecting every plea of Jolly-boy to be sported with. When the terrier saw that his master was in no mood to respond he voiced a little dejected sigh, and with ears and tail a-droop settled himself down in his rush-basket, until such time as the squire should see fit to play with him.

The half-hour passed. The cloud of self-absorption floated out of the squire's head and was lost to the atmosphere. His brain cleared; he rose from his chair and called to Jolly-boy, and so they had themselves a little romp round the apartment, the squire feinting and teasing, and skulking and taunting, the terrier snorting and scampering; so much of a romp in fact that both participants retired exhausted upon the sofa at the conclusion of it.

A brisk rap at the door announced Mr. Smithers, whose agreeable office it was to inform the squire that the evening meal had been laid on. As the butler's dignified countenance vanished from the doorway it was replaced by the smiling face of Oliver, himself exhausted from his own romp with the dusty Silla and eager now for nourishment and pleasant company. Straightway the squire clapped hands and stood up, bringing Jolly-boy to attention at his feet.

"Look here, then," he said, addressing the dog, "if you're a good fellow we'll see you're rewarded at table. Like all of us you must grasp your opportunities while you may, young man. *Ha!*"

As usual Oliver was much struck by the degree of understanding that existed between Jolly-boy and the squire. The terrier fairly vibrated with excitement upon hearing his master's words, as though he had indeed understood he was about to be fed, and was exhibiting all the proper tokens of same — throwing his tongue with delight and prancing upon the floor-cloth, and whipping up his tail, and discharging little yelps of approval from his lungs. Of course, the explanation was rather more pedestrian: it was an hour now when Jolly-boy normally received his rations — the other hour being at dawn — and the enthusiasm of the squire merely pointed up the fact.

Having emerged from his brooding the squire shortly drifted back into it at table, and so the meal turned out to be a rather dull affair indeed. Oliver took it upon himself to get up a little conversation, by describing his travails with the dusty Roman Spaniard, his struggles to turn the English language inside out, and outside in, and downside-up, to accommodate the Latin. The squire exhibited no material interest in any of this. He plied his knife and fork like a man in a dream, chewing his food mechanically, drinking his wine without satisfaction, his eyes reposing in a vacant stare upon the table-cloth. The only breaks in his trance came with regard to Jolly-boy, whom he now and again allowed a morsel of meat from his plate; aside from this small kindness his thoughts remained elsewhere.

After the cloth had been removed, the squire set about preparing a couple of cigars, in the whimsical manner Oliver had observed some few times before. He lighted the first of the cigars, and calling to Jolly-boy, brought the dog to attention before him. Up onto his hindlegs went the terrier, perfectly rigid save for his nostrils and tail, which were quivering a little in anticipation. The squire placed the lighted cigar in the dog's teeth, put the second cigar into his own mouth, and touching its tip to that of Jolly-boy's, ignited it. He inhaled the smoke for a minute or two, deeply and contentedly, before extracting the first cigar from the terrier's mouth and offering it to Oliver. The visitor from Crow's-end graciously declined, saying he would prepare his own, thank you. The squire shrugged his indifference and pitched the cigar into the grate. Even he, it seemed, was not so fond of Jolly-boy as that!

The gentlemen retired for a time to the library, where Mark's *sombre rêverie* persisted, despite Oliver's best attempts to break it, and so few words were exchanged between them. To pass the time Oliver took down an old octavo from the shelves, a decorative volume in morocco leather with woodcut illustrations, and started in to perusing it, turning over its leaves slowly one by one, but found the subject matter of insufficient appeal to his interest. Another volume being retrieved, it soon was rejected for like reason. And so with another, and another, and still another, and so forth. It rapidly became a futile exercise, this striding back and forth repeatedly between bookshelves and chair like a shuttle-cock. Oliver could not have concentrated on anything that evening, so distracted was he by his friend's behavior; and so he abandoned all thought of books and reading and instead proposed a contest at billiards, which he hoped might wrest the squire from his dark mood. Happily it did the trick, for the proposal was agreed to with alacrity; and a delightful match they had there in the billiard-room, with the players making some splendid runs that would have been the envy of anyone at the Village Arms.

When the contest was over they repaired to the balcony to examine the night, looking out across the back lawn towards Cranberry Chase and Grim Forest stretching beyond. The moon was up and silvering the trees. It was a cool evening, not so cool as to be uncomfortable in a suit, gloves, and hat, though it would be so before long. The nights were noticeably brisker now, as the short mountain summer began its drift towards autumn.

To Oliver's relief it was the squire who broke this latest silence.

"Do you think it reasonable to suppose, Noll," he inquired, with his eyes upon the scenery rather than Oliver, "that Mr. Bede Wintermarch, the austere gentleman whom we met there in the drawing-room at Skylingden, some little time ago, can be a raving lunatic?"

"You ask how it is possible that he can be Charles Campleman, if Charles Campleman had been driven mad? How it is possible he can be that same man, if we are to believe what Mr. Bottom told us?"

"Just so. Would you characterize Mr. Bede Wintermarch as a right jolly crack-brain, from our brief experience of him?"

"I would not. A gentleman of respectable exterior, and so far as I could make out, of an altogether sensible disposition. Sensible, but reserved, and rather too formal for my taste — not someone I should care to knock about with, frankly."

"Not a raving bone in his cranium?"

"None."

"Not a single raving ossicle?"

"No."

"And so how do you propose to explain this?"

Oliver considered a moment. "Perhaps he has been cured?" he suggested, half hopeful, half quizzical. "We have many fine doctors in the city."

"Do you think that possible?" asked Mark, eyeing him doubtfully.

"Possible to have fine doctors in the city?"

"Possible that Charles Campleman has been cured of his illness."

"I suppose it could happen," Oliver replied, stroking his chin. "I am certainly in hopes it could happen. But as I am not a physician myself it is difficult to render a verdict."

"Do you believe old Bottom's story? The whole of it?"

"I've no cause to disbelieve it. Why do you ask? Is he given to dissembling?"

"He has lived in this village since the year dot," said the squire, "and has been known to play at tipcat with the truth, on occasion — for exaggerative purposes."

Oliver considered again.

"I think it likely that certain details may have been afforded a degree of magnification," he answered, slowly and carefully.

"Granted."

"As to the underlying factuality of the events themselves — whether they in truth happened as he described — well, you will know more of that than I, to be sure. I am the stranger here."

"Nonetheless, your disinterested opinion is jolly valuable. You're from the city and have only recently made the acquaintance of old Bottom. How does he strike you? Do you find him credible?"

"In the main, yes. I do not think he lied, in the sense of having concocted the entire business; I do not think it mere stuff and nonsense deriving from the Ayleshire wine. What point would he have had in view? What advantage to be gained? To what end should he lie?"

The squire looked out again upon the back lawn and Cranberry Chase, upon the crowding underwood and the giant firs and pines rising like castles in the moonlight.

"My thoughts run to similar lines," he admitted.

After another interval of reflection he ventured upon a topic, the substance of which would directly send shivers through the flesh of Oliver. In calm, methodical fashion he recounted his late adventure at the well, explaining to Oliver how he had undone the ties from the capstone fragment and removed it, how he had gazed again upon the inky void inside the well and heard a voice there speak to him. Oliver listened in rapt suspense, growing by turns surprised, disturbed, alarmed, fascinated, fearful, horrified. He had found their last excursion to the cave not at all to his liking; the thought now of Mark's having deceived him, his having remained behind ostensibly to secure the fastenings, but instead releasing them and uncorking the well — and hearing again sounds and voices from it — good God, it was simply too much!

"What if I were to tell you, Noll," said the squire, gazing off into the night and smoking — "what if I were to tell you it was my revered father's voice I heard there?"

This statement Oliver found more indigestible than any of the notions of Mr. Shank Bottom.

"How can you be certain it was your father?" he asked, visibly shocked.

"Oh, indeed, I've no doubt in my mind it was he. At first I did not recognize his voice, true, for I was but a child and my mother still alive when last I heard it; when last I heard it ring out here within these very walls of Dalroyd. It sounded jolly familiar, and after listening closely for a time it struck home who it was — Mr. Ralph Trench, ninth squire of Dalroyd and illustrious scion of the Talbotshire Trenches! Certain particulars which the voice then communicated to me, recollections of my boyhood and matters known only to our family, served to convince me of the fact."

"Was it truly the voice of your father, or merely how you recollect your father's voice to have sounded? It is quite a far-off remembrance; so many years have passed since you last heard him speak. Perhaps it was a hoax. Perhaps you've been gammoned by them. What was it Mr. Bottom called them? Devils in the pit?"

"It was my father's voice," the squire persisted. "And it had my father's memories. It told me of things, from days long gone by, which I myself had quite forgotten in my own mind. Scenes and forms of my earliest recollection, fond remembrances of my father and myself, passing once more before my eyes. How can this be gammon? Who else could know of such things? Only my mother, and some even she knew nothing of."

"I was of the impression you bitterly resented your father," said Oliver. "Resented him, in point of fact, for most of your life."

"That is of no consequence now," said the squire, drawing fiercely on his cigar. "It does not signify. How little you understand me, Noll. We are as chalk to cheese, you and I."

"Hallo! You are far from the easiest gentleman in the neighborhood to make out," returned Oliver, a little exasperated. "I recall plainly your insistence that you never could forgive your father for abandoning his wife and child, and that you jolly well hoped he was dead, and how you wished I'd not plague you with this same tired theme in bringing up the name of Ralph Trench. You've scarcely exerted yourself to keep his memory green these nearly thirty years. And what of these latest beliefs of yours regarding your father and Miss Marchant, and his supposed connection to her mysterious child? How he made a shipwreck of his honor and so found it necessary to desert you and your mother? To be sure, you confound me no end!"

"Well, thank you very much, Mr. Langley. Perhaps you'd prefer it if the ninth squire of Dalroyd were one of old Bottom's devils in the pit? Well, perhaps he is — who can say? For myself I don't care a jolly fig; whether he be a devil or the prisoner of devils, after these many years I simply *must* know the truth behind my father's disappearance."

Oliver threw up his hands. "Gracious, Mark, I cannot believe we are talking of such mad, impossible things! Devils in the pit? A cloud of voices? Your father doling out secrets from the well? It is sheer lunacy, creeping upon us now just as Mr. Bottom described. Just as it crept upon Charles Campleman, and upon Miss Marchant, following their visits to the well. Upon your word of honor as a gentleman, Mark," he implored, gripping his friend by the shoulder and looking him earnestly in the face — "upon your word of honor you must swear never to return to the cave at Skylingden point, and never again to open the well. You must keep clear of it; there is a mortal poison there. Will you swear?"

"I can promise nothing," the squire replied, obstinately. "I must learn what happened to my father now that the opportunity affords. Can you not appreciate the significance of it, Noll? The whole puzzle turns on it. Perhaps my father never abandoned his family and his estate, never took fright and cut his lucky over the hills and far away. Perhaps he never left Shilston Upcot of his own volition. Perhaps he never left Shilston Upcot at all."

"And instead has been making his home inside the well? That is rather preposterous, I think!"

"No more preposterous than your devils in the pit. You saw the effect the well had upon our timepieces. You know yourself what abides in those inky depths — a vast endless ocean of existence, an eternity upon earth. Do you deny it? Consider the implications of it, Noll! My father alive there, unaltered in form and appearance for these eight-and-twenty years, and a prisoner perhaps, willing or unwilling."

"And consider too the equal likelihood it is a hoax," Oliver countered. "Suppose this poison in the well can simulate your father's voice and memories. Suppose it meant to lure you there, just as years ago it lured Charles Campleman and Miss Marchant with temptations of their own. Good God, are you so keen to lose your mind? You have heard the testimony of Mr. Bottom; you know the fate that befell Mr. Campleman and Miss Marchant. That is why you simply must promise, Mark, here and now, never, never to return to Skylingden point. You must leave the well as it is, for all time, just as Mr. Bottom wished, or I fear some dreadful catastrophe must strike us down — how or when I cannot tell, but I feel it!"

"I can promise nothing," the squire said again, ruffling his brow. "I can promise nothing so long as my father lives. It's in for a penny, in for a pound. Where is Smithers, then? Come, Noll — we must hunt up Smithers, double-quick!"

CHAPTER VIII

BLOOD ON THE GROUND

THEY found the indispensable Smithers in his small apartment below stairs, enjoying a pipe and a book now that his day's many tasks had been completed. Unlike Oliver, the old retainer was evidently of sufficient ease in mind and spirit as to allow him to concentrate upon his reading. He glanced up with a dignified but friendly curiosity as the visitors arrived at his door. When he saw who they were he hurriedly shut the book, laid aside his pipe, and rose with a courteous air. A smile broke from his frosty beard and whiskers and smooth upper lip, as he straightened his shirt and waistcoat — he had put off his coat, believing his work was done — so as to present a seemly appearance to the master of the house. Smithers the indispensable had served the family Trench and Dalroyd nearly his entire life; indeed, he knew no other life. To him life and Dalroyd were one. Whatever private opinion he may have held as regards the moody and difficult tenth squire was just that — private, known to none but Mr. Smithers himself, for in matters concerning the family he was the soul of discretion. His allegiance to Dalroyd and what remained of the Talbotshire Trenches was as firm and unyielding as good Talbotshire stone.

"Is there something you require, gentlemen?" he asked, in his finest manservant's accents.

"There is, Smithers," said Mark, stepping forward. "May we intrude upon the comfort of your snuggery here for a brief space?"

"Of course, by all means, sir," the butler replied. He offered the squire his easy chair where he had been reading, beside the lampstand with the rush-light and shade on it, but Mark hastily declined, inviting the butler instead to resume his seat while he and Oliver arranged themselves on the pinewood divan.

"Ah! Scott, I see," said Oliver, admiringly, as his glance fell upon the closed book.

"Oh, indeed, yes, sir," replied Mr. Smithers, with an appreciative regard for the other's discernment. "*Woodstock*, yes — a particular favorite of mine, sir, as to both period and character. The time of the Great Civil War has ever been of interest to me."

Mr. Smithers being of wholesome Scotch extraction, chiefly on his mother's side, his taste in authors was perhaps not surprising. If not Scott upon an evening, then Smollett; if not Smollett, then Burns, or Thomson; such were some of the names — Scottish names nearly every one — writ upon the volumes jostling one another there in the bookcase of the butler's snuggery of an apartment below stairs. Mr. Smithers often wondered what had become of that wild land of heather and crag, of green valley and sandy coast, of firth and loch, Highland and Lowland — none of which he had ever seen — since the sundering; indeed, like many he wondered what had become of all the lands of their forbears since darkness and cold had been visited upon the world.

"*Woodstock*. There are not many who would call it their favorite among the Waverleys," Oliver remarked. "They would not place it even in the first rank, perhaps. It is moreover an English novel, without a Scotch setting."

"Yes, it's true, sir," agreed Mr. Smithers. "But still it remains a favorite of mine. I have read it a score of times now, and am ever cheered by the doings of Colonel Everard, and Roger Wildrake, and Sir Henry Lee, and Trusty Tomkins — and of course, Mr. Louis Kerneguy."

"They are marvelous inventions, I agree. First-rate."

"And there is too the ghost and his merry pranks, sir, the so-called 'good devil of Woodstock.' A marvelous invention in its own right, founded of course upon authentic historical evidence. Such matter always makes for effective reading in a quiet country house like Dalroyd, late at night. I'll confess, sir, to liking a wee bit of a chill, now and again, in my books; though of course the invisible agent in question was of human devising, intended to drive the Rumpish Commissioners from the noble seat of Woodstock. There is as well the fine scene in which the young Cavalier Wildrake gains an interview with the Lord Protector. It is a delightful book, sir; I never tire of it."

Oliver voiced his concurrence, and acknowledged a fondness himself for *Redgauntlet* — another volume not in the forefront of the Waverleys, but immensely enjoyable nonetheless, with the region of the Solway Firth for background and an atmosphere of Jacobite nostalgia, fine characterization, especially as regards the aged and unhappy Prince Charles Edward Stewart and his blighted cause, and a degree of autobiographical interest. Mr. Smithers smiled in recollection of certain of the scenes from that Scotch piece, and began to remark upon them, one by one; then growing suddenly mindful of himself and his station relative to the visitors, his features acquired a more sober and deferential cast.

"I've rambled on long enough, I believe, sirs, about my books and such. How then may I be of service to you? Is there something you require in the library? More brandy, perhaps?"

"Nothing of a material nature, Smithers, not to worry," Mark replied, keen now to be about the matter that had sent him and Oliver to the butler's apartment. "It is something rather more in the line of intelligence — some information that likely you alone, of all of us here at Dalroyd, may be in a position to provide."

"I, sir?"

"I have had another of those troubling dreams of late," the squire explained, with a side-glance to Oliver — "a dream of an incident from my childhood, one which I had not given the least thought to in many a twelvemonth. A jolly odd sort of dream it was, Smithers, and not a little dramatic. It has been plaguing me no end. No doubt you have some knowledge of the incident, seeing as you were present that morning, if I recollect aright."

"Which morning was that, sir?"

"The morning my father returned to Dalroyd after sustaining a bloody injury to his arm. I remember Dr. Hall was there as well, and I thought it curious at the time that my father should have arrived injured *and* with a doctor in tow. It was a horrid, unsightly thing for my young eyes to have beheld, as I recollect it, what with the gore from my father's wound upon the ground and the back-stairs, and staining the floor there in the kitchen, and my mother sobbing frantically, and you yourself in attendance upon our village physician and his ministrations. Do you recall the incident, Smithers?"

While Mark spoke the butler shifted uncomfortably in his chair. He blinked his eyes, he bit his lip, and set one corner of his mouth a-twitching. He swallowed hard a time or two, and drew a hand across the thin gray hair of his head, across his frosty beard and ruddy cheeks, as his gaze strayed from point to point about the room. It was all too clear he remembered the incident.

"Ah," he said in answer. "Yes, sir — an event of the most unfortunate kind, which I do remember. There was indeed a good deal of your father's blood shed that brisk cold morning, sir, until the doctor managed to restrain the flow of it. It was no easy miracle, you know, for an artery had been severed clean. I've no doubt it was the doctor's swift action that preserved your father's life."

"I see."

"Though he recovered from his wound he remained in poor health. It was a most trying period, sir, for all involved — not simply for your father, but for all at Dalroyd who revered him for a just and honorable man."

"Indeed," said Mark, frowning with what might have been a twinge of conscience. "Sadly, it affected my poor mother most. I remember her clinging to me and weeping, the sight of her face discolored by tears. The event made a powerful impression upon me at the time, but I venture my brain must have taken steps to expunge my recollection of it. It was only recently that that memory was restored by the voice of my — that is to say, by this jolly odd dream of mine."

The squire and Oliver traded hasty glances, as they waited for the butler's reply.

"Sir?" asked Mr. Smithers, not certain what it was the squire desired of him, and trying as nicely as he could to find it out.

"Look here, Smithers — perhaps you'll tell us something more about the business," Mark answered. "How came my father by his injury that morning? Who inflicted it upon him? Why was our village physician in his company when he arrived at Dalroyd? What did my mother know of it all? Did the incident have any connection to my father's disappearance?"

The butler looked more uncomfortable yet, not so much from a dislike of the squire's inquiries or the general topic, Oliver felt, but from some deep inner conflict. His subsequent answer bore out that suspicion.

"I know something of the events of that morning, yes, sir," he replied, with a dignified clearing of his voice. "It was your father, however, sir, who directed me and the others to say nothing of the matter to anyone. He wanted none to know of it. He was most firm in that regard."

The squire was brought up short by this answer. Here was a pretty kettle of fish, and an unexpected one! Here was the loyal family retainer adhering to his duty, striving to comply with the wishes of a revered former master, the ninth squire of Dalroyd — and here now was the son and rather less venerated tenth squire, asking that he renounce that allegiance in favor of the son's own particular wishes. A bit of a rub there was, and the squire well knew it.

"It would seem I've placed you in an awkward position, Smithers," he admitted.

"Yes, sir."

"However," Mark ran on at once, "I can assure you that with the loss of my father and the devolution of his title and estates by due succession upon myself, I am fully empowered to release you from any and all obligations attendant upon your service to him, with the hope of course that you might see your way clear to assist me. At all events I remain respectful of your bounden duty to my father, and commend you for your long service to our family. You are a stout fellow, absolutely, Smithers, and the heart and spirit of this household. But I warrant that my father, were he here today and informed of the present circumstances, would gladly release you from your bond. Well, there it is, then."

"The present circumstances, sir?"

"By which I mean these hateful nightmares that have afflicted many of us in the village, yourself included — the jolly odd demise of Splayfoot, the short-face — the two figures Mr. Langley and I encountered at Dalroyd dock — Mr. Wintermarch of Skylingden Hall and his family's singular taste in pets. It is my belief, mine and Mr. Langley's here, that these things have much in common. Oh, I'll lay you fifty guineas it is so. And I am convinced my father's disappearance is related to them as well."

Mr. Smithers declared how he had been suspicious of some connection in that regard, but did not elaborate further.

"So that is why you must tell us, Smithers, all you know of that morning's events at Dalroyd, the cause of the trouble, as it may afford us grounds to explain why my father took himself away."

The butler by now seemed resigned to the fact that to please the son he must displease the father. But the father, however revered, was long dead, and matters were pressing; and so the son, moody and difficult though he might be, won out.

"It was, as I have stated, sir, a brisk cold morning," the butler began, gathering himself for the task as best he could. "It needed some time for the fire in the kitchen to chase the frost from the window-panes. When I arose I saw that your father already had left the house, having taken nothing whatever for his breakfast, which was most unlike him, for he was ever partial to his early toast and coffee. As I was working there at my duties, a while later, there came a shout from outside. Staggering up the back-stairs and into the kitchen, with the aid of Dr. Hall, was your father, ghastly white in the face and with the blood pouring from him just as you describe. The doctor gave me instructions that I might assist him in binding up your father's wound, which as I have said was of a right grievous sort. What little I learned as regards the cause of the trouble, sir, came solely from your father and the doctor on that morning — some of it I overheard, some of it was told me directly — on that morning and only that morning, sir, for they never spoke of it afterward. It was on that morning too that your father, hardly able to form the words from pain and weakness, entreated us never to reveal that there had been an affair of honor in the Chase, and that he had gotten the worst of it."

"Hallo! A duel?" exclaimed Oliver, with a glance in Mark's direction.

The butler nodded solemnly. "The only ones privy to it were the two gentlemen themselves and their designated seconds. They had met early that morning in Cranberry Chase, and there the duellists had it out with their small-swords. Evidently it was all very quick. Your father was wounded and escaped to Dalroyd with Dr. Hall, who had acted as his second. The other gentleman was not so much as pinked."

"Who was he?" Mark demanded, with a grim forceful expression. "And what was the affair concerning? Whose honor was defended?"

"I've no idea, sir," the butler apologized. "I never was told, and never discovered afterwards, for the affair was kept wholly dark. Perhaps your mother learned the finer details of it, but I never did. Everything I know I have told you, sir — that the squire your father fought a duel of honor that morning, and was bested, and might have perished but for Dr. Hall."

Mark stared hard and long into the air after hearing this. The pieces of that dark forgotten memory, stirred to life not by any dream but by the voice from the well, tantalized him with their incompleteness. Through his child's eyes and ears he recalled again the scene there in the kitchen — the horrid groans from his father, the flowing eyes of his mother, the terrified countenance of the housekeeper, Dr. Hall's steady attendance on his patient, the reassuring presence of Smithers. How his parents must have suffered that morning, in their separate ways — what agonies they must have endured! He remembered too the large hot tears that had burst from his own eyes, and stolen down his cheeks to mingle with the blood of his father on the stone flagging.

Why? What was the offense that had precipitated the combat? Whom had his father challenged, or been challenged by?

Mr. Smithers had not considered it his place to find out such things, particularly after Ralph Trench himself had enjoined him to secrecy. It had all been kept dark, as he said, since that brisk cold morning, and seemed in danger of remaining dark this moonlit night, for there was little more the butler could tell them, aside from the fact that it was some few months after the incident that the ninth squire of Dalroyd had vanished.

With this knowledge in hand the gentlemen left the indispensable Smithers to his pipe, his Roundheads, and his Cavaliers, and returned to the library.

"Look here, Noll — did I not tell you once how jolly like old Bottom our village physician is, how there was a world of secrets lurking behind that placid countenance? You see now I was right in that."

Oliver was forced to agree. "To be sure, he will have had many confidences from his patients; it is part and parcel of his vocation. Pray tell me now — what it is you suspect as regards your father and the affair of honor?"

"Though some points still elude me, beyond doubt it is jolly close to the truth," answered the squire; whereupon he described for Oliver his belief that Mr. Ralph Trench, being the father of Miss Marchant's child — who would then have been Mark's own half-sibling — had been challenged by one who had ferreted out the secret, the combat being undertaken in defense of the girl's honor, or the squire's, such as it was. "Perhaps that is why my father ordered that it not be spoken of. He had been called out over it and lost, and been disgraced. More than likely he told my mother something of it before he vanished. If only *she* could speak to me! What keen, sharp pain the revelation must have caused her," he lamented, "and I knew nothing of it."

"Who do you suspect challenged him?"

"Ha! There is a fine question, Noll. Likely it was someone who knew the girl and felt duty-bound to defend her."

"Not her own father?"

"Hardly. He certainly could not have bested a Trench of Dalroyd, not by a long chalk. Besides, your reverend gentlemen are not much given to duelling; they're too jolly comfortable in their livings for that. And if memory serves it runs counter to their preaching and dogma, which credulous sorts round this parish set store by. No, I'll warrant it was someone other than the lambish vicar. It would have been a gentleman in fighting trim, for my father was ever a sturdy man — until that morning."

"What of Charles Campleman?" Oliver suggested.

"Perhaps," returned the squire, with some enthusiasm. "Perhaps he regretted his treatment of the girl, and learning of her condition and its attendant circumstances, upon her return from the city, issued a challenge to my father. She may jolly well have confided in him and given him the necessary particulars."

"You'll recall however that Mr. Bottom referred to him as the 'bookish' young heir, a studious young man given to antiquarian pursuits. Could such a person have drawn his sword upon your father in fair duel and bested him?"

"A gentleman in fighting trim, Mr. Langley, need not lack for catholic tastes," observed Mark, "as you yourself may attest."

"I thank you for the compliment, wholly unwarranted as it is," Oliver replied. "Though I suppose in the main you are more right than not concerning the challenger."

The squire shrugged. "Likely Mr. Charles Campleman was half-crazed at the time; his growing madness will have furnished him with vigor and energy he may not ordinarily have possessed. It may even have incited him to the challenge."

His guest expressed some doubt at this, however. And why should the voice of Ralph Trench there in the well have reawakened this particular memory, among others, in his son? Why speak to him of dishonor and defeat?

"He was simply being forthright," Mark replied. "He understood I was seeking the truth as to the motive for his disappearance."

Still, it did not sit well with Oliver; there were missing elements of the puzzle that it seemed only Dr. William Hall could provide. But the physician with the face of pale calfskin was a circumspect man, one not known for his liberality with words. And he was not a servant beholden to the master of Dalroyd. Would he tell them what they wanted to know?

"Absolutely he will," the squire declared, confidently. "I shall appeal to him in the name of charity and for the sake of my poor mother, should he balk."

"He still may tell you nothing."

"Then I shall dig into him a little with my spurs. My mother, Noll! She married my father when she was little more than a girl, loved him wholly, and died too soon because of it. She was one of those women who have but a single object in life, marriage; but a single great love in life, her husband; but a single great passion in life, her family. When one element is lost it shatters all sense of balance. She never recovered from the loss of my father; it drained her will and extinguished her spirit. She was still a young woman, Noll, and I myself scarcely eighteen, on the black day she died."

"I recollect the moment in our chambers there at the college, in Salthead, when the news reached you," said Oliver, deeply moved. "Nearly a week it took for the message to arrive through the heavy winter snows."

"And so I was there, and she was here," said Mark, staring vacantly into the fire. "Her eyes closed for the last time — the change of death came — her soul fled this sorry world into the great darkness — and I was not with her! Her body already in its winding-sheet and screwed up in the ground before I knew anything of it. The seasons of the year would return, and so the next year, and so the next, but my mother would never come again."

"It was no fault of yours, Mark."

"I knew nothing of the true state of her health, how swiftly she was failing. My mother's letters to me were happy ones; they never spoke of *her*. I knew nothing of her last illness until she was dead and gathered into the churchyard mold. In life she gave herself completely to her husband, and he left her for good; so she gave herself to her son, and he left her to die."

"You are charging yourself with an offense you did not commit, assigning blame where no blame belongs," Oliver protested. "You could not know how low she had sunk while we were at terms there in Salthead. It was her prerogative; she did not wish to worry you and distract you from your studies. Do not berate yourself."

"Until the last time I saw her," murmured the squire, standing with his fists clenched beside him, "and I believe until the day she passed from this life, she expected at any moment to hear my father's steps again in the gravel drive. And what do you think? She would have taken him back in an instant. In an instant, Noll! Well, neither he nor I warranted such devotion as that."

So saying he abruptly quitted the room, leaving Oliver to his own devices — leaving him free to ponder again the view from the balcony, and the melancholy expanse of Cranberry Chase, upon which the moon seemed to be shining now with a different light.

CHAPTER IX

PORTRAIT OF CHERRY

DASHING here, dashing there, approving this measure, denying that, aiding a kitchen-maid one moment, exhorting a waiter the next, checking this detail, checking that detail, then checking them both again, issuing instructions and cross-instructions and countermanding others — such was the cloud of stir and bustle through which Miss Cherry Ives of the Arms sailed nearly every day of her life. Taller than her father the landlord she was, and slim, and not to mention a good deal prettier, what with her bold forehead (a gift from her late mother), and her gaze lively, bright, and unflinchingly direct (that from her father.) An open, honest, undesigning face it was, for an open, honest, undesigning young woman. Her quick, purposeful stride bespoke earnestness and competence, and a keen attachment to her duties, her enthusiasm bubbling up in her like soda-water in a bottle. She saw herself as a picture of efficiency, a quality whose absence she could not abide in others. She was, at heart, a perfectionist, upright and firm of purpose in all her dealings, who could not accept the least weakness of will in those under her. She was ever pushing, ever urging, ever striving for improvement in herself and others. She was the mainspring of the Village Arms, and her subordinates the little wheels going round and round. She was, in the opinion of those who were in a position to offer such opinions, a most estimable young person for a woman.

To superintend the chambermaids in the cleaning and airing of the rooms was the chief joy among her various priorities: seeing that the rooms were scrubbed, and washed, and furnished with white linen and lavender, and ewers of clear fresh well-water, and warming-pans, and plenty of candles, and turf for the fireside — pleasant, clean, light, flower-pot-decorated rooms overlooking the lake and Town End, sporting every comfort that a traveler, dusty and seedy from the road, might desire and indeed had come to expect from such a well-regarded establishment as the Village Arms.

"Have your senses about you, girls, and see that you use them," was the daily injunction of Cherry to her staff, in the carrying-out of their duties. "Always have our guests' needs uppermost in mind at every turn. Now, then, settle your cap-strings, and remember, girls — we are the Arms."

Overseeing the activities in the kitchen was another of her pleasures. "Fetch this, fetch that," was her refrain to the lesser folk who dwelt there, and

"Prepare this, prepare that," to the higher orders, after holding grave council with that highest order of all, the cook, on a host of matters culinary, as for example the nature of the evening's fish-sauce, or the consistency of the marchpane, or the planning of the next day's breakfast. The rapid whirl of voices and the rattle of dishes were like a symphony to her; the spectacle of servants to-ing-and fro-ing with well-ordered precision, all the day long, a delight to her eyes. Even as she loved to see the chambermaids bustling about the corridors, distributing towels and soap to weary newcomers, and scampering for warm water for them to wash in, and rushing up and down staircases upon this errand or that, so too the lowest scullery-maid in the kitchen, scrubbing her pots and saucepans, was to Cherry a joy to behold.

In glancing about the daily company in the lodge-room, she was ever on the alert for persons in want of something. If a particular guest desired pen, ink, and paper, to dispatch some letters by post, she saw to it that the materials were quickly obtained. "What is there to read in the house?" another might inquire, and so she would guide him to the county newspapers (hopelessly obsolete but in fine shape to be read), or to the cupboard of musty volumes, which numbered among its treasures a dog's-eared copy of the *Book of Verses*, and a little song-book for the musically gifted (or not), and a little jest-book for those in need of spiriting up, and a psalter for the irretrievably devout, and more than a few of that species of sensational volume, illustrative of the rigors of country life, with titles like *Bone Cruncher of the Mountains*, *In the Shadow of Short-face*, and *Saber-cats I Have Known*. City persons of quiet mind invariably were appalled by the contents of these latter tomes, just as they were appalled by the mounted trophy-heads ranged about the walls, high and low; heads looking so lifelike in death that the more gullible accepted Mr. Snorem's assurances that the beasts had perished while in the act of ramming themselves through the woodwork. More often, however, the mission of Cherry in the lodge-room was of a less dramatic character, as asking one of her subordinates to repair the curtain-pegs at the French windows, round the billiard-table where the devotees of the game had assembled.

Though the female domestics comprised her domain of particular interest, she found employment too in the supervision of Mr. Jinkins and the pot-boy at the beer-engine, whenever her father was absent from the tap. She went so far sometimes even to take charge of the ostler and stable-hands when a long-stage coach came rolling into the yard, watching as the horses, hot and weary, were liberated from the traces, while a fresh team from the stable had their cloths removed and were put to. The result was, that a better-kept house was not to be found anywhere in those altitudes; so that the establishment of Mr. Nim

Ives, widely known for its genial, square, and above-board treatment of travelers, had become a prime halting-place for conveyances running upon the road between Crow's-end and Malbury, Hoole, and beyond.

As might be imagined there was little in the way of rest for Cherry, during her hours of labor, aside of course from her weekly breakfasts at the waffle-house of Miss Crimp, when she and her party of friends held forth with agreeable frankness upon matters arising in the neighborhood. Each day, at the Arms, during the slack hours when the servants were at their *table-d'hôte* in the kitchen, Cherry herself would take on certain of their duties so that no lull intruded upon the smooth running of the household. Rest, it seemed, was not for her; she must be involved in everything, whether it be as simple as putting on a kettle, or conducting arriving guests to their apartments, with Mr. Snorem, that most stentorian of boots in his close-fitting waistcoat and black calamanco sleeves, hauling up the luggage. Though Cherry herself held the keys of the establishment during its open hours, upon the clock's striking midnight — the last of the regulars having gone out and the last of the inmates gone back in, and she having shut and barred the house door, and held a ceremony of review and dismissal of the servants, all of them wishing her a good-night, and she in her turn wishing a good-night to all — upon the clock's striking midnight, then, she would dutifully return the keys to her father, who hung them on a little board beside his bed, next to his cutlass, poniard, and small-sword, in the event he were roused from his sleep on some errand of necessity. His daughter ran the Arms for him all day, he said, and so it was only proper he should take command of any and all circumstances arising in the night. Even so, to her father Miss Cherry Ives was nothing less than the final authority on all matters of concern in his house.

"Halloa there! Coach in the yard!"

Such was the call, whose sound would draw Cherry, and her father, and Mr. Snorem, and several of the porters, and sometimes Mr. Jinkins, from the bustle of the inn to the bustle of the yard. She loved the excitement of it — the jolting and swaying of the four-wheeler as it rumbled to a halt — the snorting of the horses, the jingling of harness and the clatter of iron shoes — the weary faces of the travelers, both the outsides and the in, peering down with that kind of exhausted joy travelers exhibit at the end of a long, dusty ride — that yearning for the heavenly comfort of food and drink, and delivery from the hazards of the road — and the realization they had at last reached that heaven, and here it was in the shape of the Village Arms, in wildest Talbotshire — well, perhaps not heaven, but a *haven* at any rate, and a place of refreshment for both man and horse.

"Welcome, ladies! Very welcome, sirs! Please to alight, ma'am. This way, this way," her father would sing out, as the steps were flung down and the door opened, and the insides climbed out of the box, and the outsides climbed down from it. Straightway the guests would be ushered through the entrance-hall to the desk, where the assigning of apartments or private sitting-rooms was superintended by Cherry (of course), and the transport of the luggage for those staying on effected by Mr. Snorem and the assistant porters, with the dusty coats and hats of the travelers immediately given out to brush (another of Mr. Snorem's areas of expertise), and the special requirements of every person attended to, in such a flurry of activity, with Miss Cherry Ives at the center of it, as was a marvel to see.

The trust of everyone was in Cherry. She was unswervingly conscientious, a trait both her father Nim, and her godfather, Mr. Coddy Binks, the little hunting chemist, especially admired; so that travelers bearing valuables were given over to her special care.

"Lay by this box, please, my dear, for the couple in number twenty-three," she might be told, confidentially, by an older gentleman — one mightily impressed by the lively eyes and pretty smile of the daughter of the landlord, so agreeable after the dust and tedium of the road — "for it is full of money."

"Ah, merely a small charge of money," the gentleman's wife then would interpose, nicely but firmly leading the poor sot away — "but like a husband it must be guarded nonetheless. Come, *my dear*."

So Cherry would superintend its safe disposition for the night, until the gentleman — or more likely the wife — should call for it in the morning prior to boarding the coach.

As a result of his daughter's youthful energy and industry, Mr. Nim Ives was largely free most of the time to roam about the house, in furtherance of those convivial impulses for which he was renowned: his jesting, his laughing and sporting with the assembled company, regulars as well as visitors, his jovial supervision of proceedings at the oak bar; now and again roving through the lodge-room, or closeting himself with members of his personal circle — secure in the knowledge that the real work of running the establishment was in the capable hands of his daughter, the mainspring, and her minions the wheels.

Thus the hour might find him communing with a bottle-nosed gentleman from Crow's-end, as regards the foggy weather in that metropolis; or in high chat with a sober parson from Malbury, on the relative merits of levying a rate or raising a subscription for repairs to the steeple of St. Lucy's; or boasting to a portly fellow with gingery whiskers, how he had in his cellar at that moment twenty hogsheads of the finest spruce-beer in Talbotshire, all of it as clear and smooth as honey, as delectable as cream, and as potent as larchberry brandy. So did his daughter free Ives of the Arms to be at his best, which only served to further the house's reputation, the hospitality and good cheer of the landlord being acknowledged up and down the coach-road — and all of it because it was his daughter, the lively picture of bustle and efficiency, who ran the show.

There were some young gentlemen in the village who fancied that this same daughter of the landlord had a pretty eye (which she did), and that it was reserved for them (which it was not.) They were hopelessly at sea, these young bucks, so far as their perception of Cherry was concerned. There was no earthly cause for fretting, was Cherry's thought, because she had no beau, no match, no dichotomy. She was one of the handsomest girls in the village by far, and one of the most earnest and industrious, and wholly loyal to her father and her father's house (these latter quirks being sufficient to chill the ardor of the most persevering of suitors.) It was not that Cherry disliked their attentions, or their sundry impertinences, or even their persons; it was simply that she found these young gentlemen, in the main, uninteresting — decidedly less interesting, in point of fact, than superintending the regular operation of the Arms. She was, as Mr. Tony Arkwright might have phrased it, a high-spirited filly with an aversion to double harness. She did not require either the attentions or the impertinences of young gentlemen, for Miss Cherry was fortunate enough to have a brain behind her lively gray eyes, and with it she comprehended things that few of her peers perceived. In this she was blessed; and in this, too, she was cursed.

She was known to take pleasure in scuttling such little encounters as came across her bow, now and then, in the course of her daily patrols: as for example the *tête-à-tête* upon the landing one day, third floor back, between Miss Eliza Stroughill, an upstairs chambermaid, and the risible figure of Larcom, servant-cum-steward of Prospect Cottage. The garish Larcom, having failed in his pursuit of Miss Betty Breakwindow and others of her stamp, in descending order of desirability, had settled at last upon poor Eliza, who, despite having some sense to recommend her, had inexplicably grown enamored of the attentions of the solicitor's man. Larcom had just apprized Miss Stroughill, for perhaps the dozenth time, of the unjust treatment accorded him by his master, Mr. Thomas Dogger — "It's more than my job is worth," he was heard to grumble, stringing together there more words into a single sentence than ever he had at Prospect Cottage — and Miss Stroughill, suitably aghast, was on the point of complaining in kind about her own tormentor, Miss Cherry Ives, when that lively and efficient ogress happened to appear at the stairhead above.

"Eliza Stroughill," said Cherry, folding her arms.

Which was all she needed to say, whereupon the *tête-à-tête* broke down, from being broken up. Miss Stroughill ascended with dismal eyes and a heavy tread towards her mistress, while the prideful Larcom, with a bob of his yellow hair and his cocked-hat with the feather in it, took leave on his long bony legs in breeches and bright cotton stockings.

On this same day there transpired several additional incidents of note, which warranted the attention of Miss Ives.

"Cherry, m'dear," her father often would say upon such occasions. "Look to it."

And so she did. There was for example the windy kind of blustery sort of little gentleman, in coat and trousers as rumpled as his hair — as though his own bluster had blown through them — who had been listing to starboard at the oak bar for above half an hour, and for whom the dour Mr. Jinkins had refused to draw any more liquor.

"You're a dirty skunk," drawls the customer, meaning Jinkins.

"Sir?" returns the long-faced drawer.

"And a white-livered hound. Do you understand me, sir?"

"Sir?"

"And a rat-catcher. A cad, a scoundrel. A mutton kidney. Haw-haw!"

"And you're another," retorts Jinkins, crisply.

"And a puling — and a puling — "

Here the gentleman calls again for grog, having taken such umbrage at the drawer's refusal that he can think of no more insults, and moreover has begun weaving dangerously on his feet; at which point the comely features of Miss Cherry act as a kind of substitute tonic upon him. At her urging he totters off in the direction of the lodge-room, where he is last seen lying extended upon one of the rustic but comfortable sofas round the hearth, in a dead sleep, under the watchful gaze of the saber-cat on the chimney-piece.

Later that day, following the arrival of the coach from Crow's-end, a lady of mature years is carried from the vehicle in a waning state (this without prior benefit of the beer-engine at the inn.) On their ramble through the Talbots the lady, being prone to alarms, had looked out at her window and taken for a charging short-face what the coachman and the other passengers had identified as a frolicking pronghorn; and as no one, not even the lady's crow-trodden, henpecked husband, could convince her of her error, it is left to Cherry, assisted by a pair of chambermaids, to escort the lady to a room, there to vinegar her forehead, and rub her hands, and tickle her nostrils with sal volatile, and administer other such remedies as might return the poor city creature to a semblance of herself. In the evening this same lady, recovering, claims to have seen a ghost in her room; but it is only Betty Breakwindow in a white smock and cap, pouring fresh water into the lady's wash-hand basin and seeing that her dressing-table is properly appointed. The lady having risen in her bed — and inquiring, feebly, "Could someone please bring me a biffin?" — takes one look at Betty there in the glow of the wax-lights, utters a shriek and collapses onto her pillow; this to the great consternation of her husband, who, when he is informed of it at the billiard-table, where he is in the midst of a run, chuckles to himself in his beard and promptly executes a splendid carom, to the general applause of the lookers-on.

At the end of this same busy day, at dusk, while her father is entertaining members of his circle at the oak bar, the capable Cherry strolls outside into the yard to catch her breath and enjoy the drowsy faded light of a summer's eve.

Mr. Snorem at his station in the entrance-hall nods and smiles to her as she passes. "A fine evening, Miss Cherry, e-normous fine it is, by jingo!" cries that gentleman of the wild eyes and iron jowls, in tones that might have brought down a mountain.

She looks up at the rising moon, and at the stars that were coming out, and in particular at one glittering red jewel she remembers Captain Hoey had told her was the warlike face of Mars. Perhaps it was just such a jewel as that, or a comet glowing in the firmament, or a shooting star, that had crashed to earth and brought about the great sundering; or so she had heard. The thought of it gives her some discomfort, however, whereupon she quickly brushes it from her mind.

The last of the day's coaches is expected directly — it is overdue — and she decides to remain a bit longer in the yard, to be on hand to greet the passengers. She exchanges some few words with the ostler and one of the helpers, and visits the horses in the stable, before settling down on an ancient stone seat, under the fir tree that stands just inside gates at the entrance of the yard.

It is a fine night indeed, after a fine day, and very quiet under the tree. The noise and bustle of the inn hardly reach her here. The air all round is sweet and still. Her eyes drift across the road, to the darksome underwood and the solemn files of timber cloaking the hillside. Abruptly her brow contracts, as she realizes that there is something or someone there, watching her — a crouching form, buried in the shadowy nests of branches of a nearby clumber pine.

She starts up, and walks out through the gates.

"Who is it?" she calls aloud. "Who is there?"

No reply. She ventures farther into the road. Despite the moonlight it is hard to see clearly into the tree; beyond doubt, however, there is a figure of some kind there, only dimly perceivable, squatting among its lower branches. A figure, but whether of an animal or human variety she cannot tell.

She steps closer, nearly to the opposite verge, and peers up into the tree. She sees there is a face there, too — a scowling countenance framed by draggled dark hair, with fearsome eyes glaring from under heavy pale brows like two green lights in the darkness, like twin stars in the firmament of foliage.

Of the human variety the creature must be, for it promptly speaks to her.

"Do you know me, friend?" says a dulcet voice, as unlike the face as a dock to a daisy.

"How can I know you if I can't see you?" returns Cherry, boldly. "Climb down from your perch there, and show yourself."

Her command is coolly disregarded.

"You presume to know me," says the other.

"What have I said? When have I presumed? When have I said I know you?"

Cherry is of the opinion now it is a waggish prank, the work perhaps of one of her more troublesome subordinates at the inn.

"You say you know me," replies the dulcet voice — "but you know nothing, friend."

She steps closer still, to the foot of the clumber pine.

"You are a pretty one," says the prankster in the tree.

Cherry concedes there may be some truth in this statement.

"And a lucky one," adds the voice. "Perhaps if I had been a lucky one matters would be otherwise now. But they turned their backs on me, the lot of them. So none will be spared."

"Who turned their backs on you? Who are you?"

"Ask rather who I was."

"Very well. Who were you, then?"

"Ah! I need not tell *you*, friend. You ought to know, for you say you know me."

Cherry claps hands to her hips, with a view to bringing the mischief to an end. Before she can effect her own resolution, however, the figure of the prankster draws back into the bristly shadows of the pine needles; there is a hooting cry, a flutter of wings, a rush of wind, and something goes flying off into the night in the general direction of Grim Forest. Startled, Cherry runs into the road but can see nothing more of it from there.

Prank or no prank, she finds herself a little troubled by whatever it is she has confronted, and perhaps a bit less self-confident. The thought is unsettling to her, and the youthful Cherry is one not easily unsettled. She takes courage by issuing herself a muttered reprimand for her faintheartedness, however temporary, following which a new object gains her attention — the distant rumble of an approaching coach-and-four.

Hurriedly she returns to the yard and calls for the ostler and Mr. Snorem, to make preparation to receive the latecomers.

CHAPTER X

THE DOCTOR'S VERDICT

WHEN Dr. William Hall answered the knock at his door, in his stone-built cottage there in the little curly lane off the Low Street, he expected to find on the step some anonymous serving-man come seeking the physician's aid on behalf of his master or a member of his master's household. What he did not expect to find was the moody and difficult squire of Dalroyd, and with him the squire's rather more good-natured friend from the city. The doctor may have been surprised at this, but he hardly showed it. His smooth, featureless face recorded no change, apart from the subtle lift of one eyebrow, and perhaps a flicker in his eyes of palest blue. After a moment he invited the gentlemen in, with the makings of a smile as thin and placid as the wispy scattered strands of hair that adorned his head.

The visitors had seen the doctor's trap in the yard and hoped to find him at home. They hoped too he was not preparing to leave upon his rounds directly, in which case they would come back at a more auspicious time; whereupon the doctor assured them he had an hour at least to spare. He offered them chairs round the inglenook in his drawing-room, a bright, cozy chamber with pleasant views of the village green and market cross and the adjacent cottages.

The doctor's own cottage was a modest one — the entry, the paneled drawing-room, small dining-room, and dispensary on the ground floor; the doctor's bedchamber, study, and tiring-room on the first floor, under the russet-colored roof-tiles; kitchen and comfortable quarters for his housekeeper and her son at the rear, next to the wash-house and stable. At present both the housekeeper and her son — the latter employed as groom and gardener — were in the shops purchasing needed goods, and so the doctor had been obliged to answer his own door; which was not so very unusual for him, for his was anyway an informal household. He was a gentleman not given to ostentation or pretense. He could easily have afforded a grander style of life, a grander house in the upper village, a grander carriage than his humble trap; but he chose to forgo such trifles. The doctor preferred his more modest dwelling off the green, in the little curly lane in the heart of the village. It made it easy for those of his patients who could to pop in at a moment's notice and see him for this complaint or that, whenever, like the squire and Oliver, they saw his trap was in the yard. He was one of that radical breed of medical men, fast disappearing from the cities, who look upon their profession as a kind of sacred office. Because the doctor was not a man to wear his heart on his sleeve did not mean he had no heart to wear, not in the least. He was and had been for years one of the most respected figures in the community. If he was to some a sphinx — seeing much, hearing much, saying little — he was by no means an unfeeling one.

Some thoughts of a like nature may have crossed the mind of Mark Trench as he and Oliver took their seats round the hearth, where a low fire was burning in the dog-grate. The doctor's role in the still mysterious affair of honor in Cranberry Chase, so long ago, in which the ninth squire of Dalroyd had been wounded, had given the present squire some pause in his thinking on it; and had given him too a new appreciation of the doctor himself.

Which supposed, of course, that all Mark had received from Smithers and the voice in the well had been the truth. The notion that Smithers might not be trusted quite staggered belief, as if the sun one morning had risen wearing spectacles and a sugar-loaf hat, and so he quickly dismissed it; however, the voice in the well was another thing entirely, as Oliver had not ceased reminding him.

As the doctor already had some tea drawing it was a simple matter for his guests to partake. He apologized for being able to offer them nothing more robust than an infusion of peppermint (very good for the digestion), but he feared his household cupboard was mostly unacquainted with the stronger waters. The doctor preferred to take his daily draught in the convivial atmosphere of the Village Arms, where, he said, the pleasures of observing the assembled company added spice to the ale.

So they settled in, the doctor waiting with silent attention to hear what had brought the squire and Oliver to his drawing-room, the squire and Oliver for their part wondering how and when to bring the subject up. The squire made some commonplace remarks concerning the recent jog round the valley with Tony Arkwright, in which the doctor had been a participant; which elicited some few like words from the doctor in response, but otherwise served little to advance the discussion.

The preliminaries exhausted, there was nothing left but to plunge into it.

So the squire explained how he had had another of those disquieting dreams of his — the same convenient fiction he had palmed off on Smithers — in which a forgotten memory of his childhood had been resurrected, and how its chief outlines had been confirmed by his butler, who related something of the events of that brisk cold morning of yore when the doctor had acted as his father's second, and later had saved his father's life there in the kitchen at Dalroyd. These matters he related crisply and succinctly; following which a rather substantial pause ensued, while the doctor glanced from the squire to Oliver, to his folded hands, to the floor, to the window, to his tea-cup, and so back to the squire again, and so forth, with the same placid smile on his face of pale calfskin, and the same glassy calmness in his blue eyes, as he debated in his mind how best to respond.

Ultimately it was Oliver who stepped into the breach, for he could bear the suspense no longer.

"And so we've come, Dr. Hall, in hopes you might tell us what you recollect of the incident," he explained. "The recovery of this memory has been particularly troubling to Mark. There is only so much Mr. Smithers knows of the events that led to the late squire's injury. It became quite clear, during our interview with him, that you, as the squire's second, were the gentleman we should consult, as it were."

"I see," returned the doctor, still glancing from his visitors to his hands to his cup, and still smiling.

"It would be of terribly great help to Mark if you could see your way clear to — to — "

"To betray a confidence?" the doctor finished, with another lift of his eyebrow.

Oliver nodded weakly. A further pause intervened.

"Look here, now," said Mark, growing impatient. "Whatever it is my revered father may have done, whatever transgression he may have committed, surely after these many years there's no harm in informing his son and heir of it? I should advise you that Mr. Langley and I know a jolly good deal about it already. What we lack are certain of the particulars as regards the affair in the Chase, as for example — who was it who challenged my father, and what were the terms of the challenge? Whose honor was being defended? I'll admit, doctor, that I'm not a man of many friends; I'm not the sort for it. But I do consider ourselves to be friends. So look here — you've kept the matter dark these eight-and-twenty years, in accord with my father's wishes, like the stout fellow you are. Surely it's time to relax this little vow of yours? As his son and the heir to his estate I can and shall exert my rights."

The doctor was observing Mark through his pale eyes, observing him more intently perhaps that his general composure might have suggested. He crossed his legs, and patted the corners of his suit of navy-colored cloth, here and there, and cleared his voice, taking advantage of the interval to collect his thoughts.

"I expect I do owe you something of the kind, Mark," he said, quietly. "Something of an explanation. On whole it shouldn't cause any present harm, I don't believe — so long as I have your assurance you'll not take it beyond the bounds of this cottage."

"You have it," Oliver volunteered.

For a brief instant the doctor's calm features reflected annoyance. Likely he disapproved of the newcomer's intruding upon such a private and delicate matter; but as it was clearly the squire's choice that Oliver be present he withheld his objection.

"There is a price to be exacted for keeping silence," he began, after a warm swallow of his tea. "I must confess, over the years it has occasioned more than its share of injustice and regret. As Smithers told you, all those of us there in the kitchen that morning were bound over to secrecy by your father. It was not, however, for his sake that he sought our vows, but for that of another who is long since dead — in consideration of which I expect it will break no bones to tell you, in confidence, what little more I know of it."

"What little more?" returned Mark, in some surprise.

"Yes, for it is not so very much more than your butler already has related. You seem to be laboring under a misapprehension that your father was the gentleman challenged. That was not the case; rather it was he, the squire of Dalroyd, who sent his cartel on behalf of another."

The squire received this second surprise with a ruffling of his craggy brow. "It was my father who issued the challenge?"

"Yes."

"By God! To whom was it sent?"

"It was sent," replied Dr. Hall, brushing a particle of dust from his trouser-leg, "to our humble and respectable village solicitor there at Prospect Cottage."

"Rather not!" Oliver said in astonishment. "Mr. Dogger? Why, we took it to be Charles Campleman, surely — and that it was *he* who had challenged Mark's father, not the other way round."

"Never in my life would I have imagined it," said Mark, his face slowly relaxing into a crooked smile. "Our sanctimonious Tom Dogger."

"A younger and trimmer Tom Dogger, in those years, and one well-practiced with his cutlass and small-sword. It was swords he chose — for it is the offender's prerogative to select the weapons — and with his blade inflicted an injury, dreadful in the extreme, which opened up a vessel in your father's arm. The resulting hemorrhage was most extensive. But as for saving your father's life, Mark, I can accept little of the credit; it was only through the kindness of Providence that he survived. By any reasonable measure he should have died that morning from the loss of blood."

"You jolly well underrate yourself, sir."

The doctor shook his head gently.

"And what was the offense that precipitated the challenge? What was the nature of the dishonor?" pursued Mark.

"Mr. Dogger, you see, in the course of private conversation, had apparently taken the side of the rich young heir of Skylingden, who was not so well thought of then, by voicing one or two ill-mannered remarks concerning the daughter of our vicar — by that I mean our vicar of those years, of course, old Edwin Marchant. Even then our local solicitor was a meddlesome character, and a rising pharisee, quick to denounce what he viewed as the 'low state of morality' in the parish. He had only just been named junior partner in the firm of his benefactor, Mr. Parker Pring. It was this same Mr. Pring who acted as his second in the Chase, just as I acted for your father."

"What was the nature of these remarks?"

"They had to do," said the doctor, hesitating a little, "with suspicions of an impropriety involving Miss Marchant and Mr. Campleman."

"Referring no doubt to young Campleman as a 'gentleman of discerning tastes,' and to the vicar's daughter as a 'silly chit of a girl,' or a 'bad lot, wholly bad,' or something like?"

"I expect there were words to that effect, yes — among others."

"And this was sufficient for Mark's father to call him out?" Oliver asked.

"Well, yes. You see, the squire — that is, Ralph Trench — was not only the patron of the benefice but also a close friend of the Reverend Marchant and his wife. It was he who recommended Mr. Marchant for the living after the death of old Scroop. The squire always was vigorous in his support of the parish and its incumbent and active in parochial concerns. He had a particular fondness for the Marchants — he and the vicar oft were seen of an evening in the card-room of the Arms, playing at piquet — and accordingly felt an obligation towards their daughter and only child, in whom he took a benevolent interest."

"Ha!" Mark muttered, darkly.

"I beg you pardon?"

As the squire did not deign to answer — he was leaning back on the sofa with his arms crossed and a glint in his eye — the doctor proceeded with his narrative.

"As squire and patron, and the dear friend of the Marchants, your father felt a particular responsibility towards their daughter; he was, in point of fact, her godfather. When the indelicate remarks of Mr. Dogger were brought to his attention, he sent the gentleman his cartel, and they agreed to meet secretly in the Chase at daybreak. The result of that meeting you already know."

"My father was knocked to smash, while Tom Dogger came off without a mark."

"Yes."

"Was it conducted fairly?"

"To the smallest point. It was all because of your father's boot, you see: he slipped on the meadow-grass — from the freshness of the dew, and perhaps from overeagerness — which created an opening for the near-fatal thrust. It was not a lengthy combat."

"So Smithers informed us."

They drank their tea in silence for a time. Here then, Mark reflected, was the source of that polite but very tangible coolness of long standing, which existed between the village physician and plain country Tom Dogger. Here was what had set them at variance. Here was the explanation for the attorney's frequent mocking references to the doctor as "Aesculapius," "Squire Bone-setter," "Hippocrates," and the like. It was no wonder the physician held himself consciously aloof in the other's presence — and all on account of past friendship and regard for Mark's vanished father! In consequence of which the present squire found his own regard for the doctor strengthening even more.

Oliver meanwhile had cast an eye round the drawing-room, noting the old-fashioned furniture, the paneled oak walls, the wide comfortable hearth with its hanging kettle and firedogs, the casement windows with their old diamond-pane lattices, the geraniums in bow-pots, the ornamental knick-knacks — observing how tidy and precise it all was, as tidy and precise as the doctor himself in his suit of navy-colored cloth, his usual professional attire. The feeling grew upon Oliver that he and Mark had intruded upon the doctor's time for perhaps long enough, that the village physician needed to be about his rounds. The squire did not share this opinion, however, for there was still some ground to get over.

"Look here, doctor," said Mark, again with some impatience, "can you tell us something of the fate of that girl's child?"

For once the doctor's features underwent a significant reordering of expression.

"Ah — so you know of it," he said, drawing a long breath. "From Mr. Bottom, perhaps?"

"Yes."

"Of course it must be Mr. Bottom," the doctor murmured, as much to himself as to his visitors. "Mr. Bottom, residing there at the vicarage, catching stray scraps of conversation — "

"How many in the village knew of it?"

"Scarcely anybody at first, apart from your father and those at the vicarage. But truth will out, as the common phrase is. The notion began to gain some currency in the public mind, becoming the object of much sly gossip and conjecture. Many must have guessed the nature of her indisposition after the girl was sent to Crow's-end. Perhaps they did not express it so very openly, for they had no proof, but it was in their minds and eyes. Their demeanor towards her was much altered upon her return, as you may easily imagine. Many were infected by their example, such as our very respectable Mr. Dogger. As for Mr. Campleman of Skylingden Hall, he was held in particularly low esteem as a result; his rumored fascination with wicked and secret arts, and the growing oddness of his behavior, did little to help his case. But enough — one should not speak ill of him now, or of Miss Marchant; it would not be charitable, as our present vicar is fond of saying. The poor young gentleman became quite insane, and the girl of course took her own life. Her parents were inconsolable."

"Most in the village were convinced that Charles Campleman was the father of her child?" Oliver asked.

"It was common report that the girl was enamored of him, and that there had been trysts in the high wood and at the abbey ruins. Evidently the young gentleman grew weary of her attentions after a time. It is not so very unusual."

"And Mr. Dogger knew of this when challenged by Mark's father?"

"His remarks concerning the impropriety between Miss Marchant and Mr. Campleman bespoke as much. Though voiced in private they came to the notice of the squire, through the agency of one who had overheard them."

"Mr. Bottom again, I suppose?"

"I can't say. Possibly."

"Well, doctor, I suppose you can appreciate the hypocrisy of the situation," Mark smiled, grimly. "A fine lot of forbears, these Talbotshire Trenches!"

"The hypocrisy of it? How do you mean?"

"That my revered father should challenge a man for calling the honor of the Marchant girl into question, when it was my father himself who was the cause of her dishonor."

"I don't believe I follow you," returned the doctor, looking genuinely puzzled.

"Truly, doctor, so long as confidences are being broken here, there's no further need to protect the reputation of my father by shifting blame to young Campleman. Eight-and-twenty years is jolly long enough to be propagating a humbug round this parish."

"Protect your father's reputation? Propagating a humbug? I don't understand you, Mark."

"I refer to my father Ralph, the ninth squire of Dalroyd and so-styled dear friend and sponsor of the vicar Marchant and his wife — and a considerably dearer friend of the vicar's young daughter."

It took some moments for the import of the squire's words to register with the doctor. When it did his face assumed its second notable alteration of expression, reflecting equal parts disbelief and indignation.

"Surely you examined the girl before they bundled her off," said Mark. "You must have been consulted before she was removed to Crow's-end, to be delivered of the child in a more private circumstance. Surely, too, you must have been suspicious of the true role of my father in the business. I merely point up the hypocrisy of his challenge to Tom Dogger, when it was my father himself who was to blame for the girl's predicament."

Dr. Hall shook his head. His eyes of palest blue fixed themselves on Mark with a muscularity that was unusual for them. "You could not be more wrong, or more misguided — more unjust — or more discourteous of your father's memory. Your suggestion is perfectly shocking to me! As a gentleman and a physician I can assure you, your father had not the least connection with Miss Marchant's predicament, as you term it, and certainly not in the fashion you propose. It is quite beyond the reach of question. Gracious God, Mark — your father was an upstanding, virtuous, noble-hearted gentleman, one of the finest I have known. He played hazard with his own life to defend a young woman's honor."

"What there remained of it," laughed the squire. Though inwardly troubled by the doctor's response, and with some slight distrust of his own thesis creeping into his head, he nonetheless held to his position. "It was a lie and he jolly well knew it. I suppose you'll next be denying it was my father who arranged for the girl to be packed off to Crow's-end?"

"I'll not deny it, for it was he indeed. He took charge of the particulars himself, owing to his acquaintance with certain charitable institutions in that city. It relieved the vicar of a ghastly burden, at a time of trial for his household, and was accomplished with all speed and discretion."

"What became of Miss Marchant's child?" asked Oliver, breaking in, for he was rather curious as to this point.

"I cannot tell you, for neither Ralph Trench nor the vicar saw fit to disclose anything more to those outside the family. What I can tell you is that the girl was confined at the lying-in hospital in Ripplegate — I expect you know the place, Mr. Langley, being yourself a resident of the city — an institution whose chief governor I had some knowledge of when I was a medical student. It was there the child was born. In due course it was given over to a childless couple, I believe, to be raised as their own, through the good offices of one of the benevolent societies."

"And so it lived?"

"It was received into a respectable household, I believe, though how far beyond infancy it progressed I can't say. The measles, scarlatina, whooping cough — these are no respecters of respectable households, Mr. Langley, and cause the deaths of many children each year."

"Was it a little girl, or a little boy?" Oliver asked.

The doctor did not know. The late squire had confided in him but little as to the disposition of the infant; indeed, it had been the squire's belief that the fewer who knew the circumstances the better. He had made assurances to the vicar that all would be kept as quiet as possible, and that a genteel Christian home should be found for the child to be brought up in. It was doubly painful for the Marchants — not to have seen their grandchild at its birth, and never to see it during the short remainder of their lives — and to endure the attendant suspicion that fell upon their daughter. It was a tragedy, the doctor declared, that the girl had in the end resorted to suicide; it must have been altogether dreadful for her, knowing in her heart the cruel thoughts that every day were passing behind the eyes of the villagers, her erstwhile friends and acquaintances, when they looked on her.

"But I repeat — you are mistaken, Mark, if you suppose your father had the slightest dishonorable part in it," the doctor said. "How came you to think such a thing? I scarcely can believe it of you."

"A point upon which we heartily agree, doctor," said Oliver. "I have several times remonstrated with him on the implausibility of it, but he's as obstinate as a turnip."

"What more can you tell us of this vicar's daughter?" asked the squire, attempting to divert the current of conversation. His thesis was not nearly so tenable in his mind now as before, and was growing less so by the moment. "Is it your opinion she jolly well took her own life, and that it was not taken from her?"

"I have no reason to doubt it," the doctor replied, rubbing his chin in thought. "Of course, because her body was never found and properly examined, one cannot really say."

"What of old Bottom's story? His claim to have seen an owl roving about the area where the girl's skiff was found? Don't you think it odd that a creature of similar description should be in the hands of Mr. Bede Wintermarch of Skylingden? Don't you think it more than mere coincidence? For I'll lay you fifty guineas it *is* more!"

"I once heard that tale of Mr. Bottom's," nodded the doctor. "It was related to me in confidence over a cup of the sexton's grog. I've never known how much store to set by it; though I fail to see it how it can be of more than passing significance. Really, Mark, you are making matters more complex than they need be — and you yourself such an advocate of simplicity in all things."

"Have you had no ill dreams of it?" the squire asked, leaning forward in his chair, his elbows on his knees, his craggy brow thrown into folds.

"How do you mean?"

"Nearly everyone we've questioned has owned to having these nightmares, as Mark and I have," Oliver explained, with no cheerful expression. "Dark visions of a malignant, vengeful presence watching and waiting, in some cases offering veiled threats, and taking the form of a thing like a huge bird — like an owl — with green staring eyes, tufted horns, and the rudiments of a human countenance. The remainder of the dream largely vanishes from memory soon after, though the sense of dread, as of some impending calamity, lingers on. To be sure they are vile, noxious, hateful things."

"I have had some experience of that which you describe," the doctor admitted, after a little uneasy reflection. "As have certain of my patients of late, who have complained to me of an inability to sleep owing to the effects of these nightmares. Neither valerian nor mandragorn has any power against them. But surely, Mark, they cannot be anything more than coincidence?"

"You have heard my wager," the squire replied, smoothing his mustaches. "But look here — what you've told us today, doctor, is jolly useful, and has cast new light upon these mysteries. Never, for example, would I have guessed it was Tom Dogger whom my father met in the Chase."

"Do you suppose Mr. Dogger has had ill dreams of late?" Oliver asked.

"I shouldn't expect so," opined Dr. Hall, folding his hands and abandoning all circumspection for once. "More usually it is others who have ill dreams of *him*."

CHAPTER XI

FATHER AND SON

MORNING in the mountains, one summer's day.

The wide flat sheet of water that is the lake lies glistening in the early sun. A faint mist like steam rises from its surface, obscuring the distant range of hills on the opposite shore. The sun itself is climbing slowly out of the east; its light shines down upon the gently rippling waters, flashing and sparkling there like a Milky Way on earth. The slopes hard by and their great curtained rows of pines are suffused with a rosy glow. The air is thin, fresh, and cool — it is, after all, mountain morning air — though there will steal upon it a warmth as the day progresses, an all-too-brief period of extravagance in the brief summertime of the mountains.

There is the plash and chuckle of wavelets lapping against the rocks, and against the creaking timbers of the pier. A line of demarcation between two colors, black and green, marks the point where the deeper body of the lake joins the shallower waters round the pebbly beach. In the green haze vague dark forms are seen to glide, the refracted images of smallmouthed bass and lake trout, and fishes of the humbler varieties, drifting over the pitchy silt and ooze of the lake bottom; while numbers of energetic and noisy ducks roam the surface above, beating their bright orange feet like oars to propel them along.

A small boy sits observing from the planks of the pier. He is attired in the finest of small-boy mountain-summer clothes — a morning coat, and a loose shirt with a frill round the neck, and trousers and waistcoat all in one, and high-lows. He is an altogether fit and out-of-doors-looking sort of small boy, with an abundance of soft brown hair beneath his cloth cap. More than once he is seen to glance round his shoulder towards the pebbled slopes, where the footpath leads down from the road, as though waiting for someone to join him. On a sudden there is an outburst of barking, and a gentleman in a ditto suit of brown fustian and an old slouch hat comes striding along the path with a couple of dogs at his heels. He is a tall, limber, light-hearted man, with a spring in his step and a merry whistle on his lips. In his hands he carries a pair of slender trout-rods with whalebone tips, a basket and tackle-box, some bait, and other like materials for angling.

When the boy sees him and the gamboling dogs he jumps to his feet with a shout. The dogs, a retriever and a hound, rush out upon the pier of planks to greet him, the both of them scampering and yelping, while the tall gentleman follows at a leisurely pace. Upon reaching the boy the gentleman pats him affectionately on one tiny shoulder, and offers him one of the rods; then both sit down upon the planks, throw their legs over the side, and busy themselves with assembling their gear.

The face of the tall gentleman is gray, drab, and lumpish; his eyes are small, narrow, and rather too closely placed, with one lying slightly above its partner. Under his slouch hat he is perfectly bald, save for the few scanty tufts of hair round his ears, and the fringe encircling the back of his head like a second collar. The mustaches above his full lips are elaborately curled and waxed, but the remainder of his face is clean-shaven. He is not a handsome man, not a fashionable man, and never has been; but to the small boy in the cloth cap he is the finest man in Talbotshire.

Together they prepare their lines and lures, their bobbers and sinkers, the gentleman whistling softly to himself over his work. When all is ready they shift their rods and bait to the pier-head, where a fine small sloop is moored, and there cast their hooks to the waters. Throughout the morning the gentleman in his firm but kindly way instructs the boy in the finer points of casting, striking, and hauling in the catch. The boy hangs on his every word, as though the gentleman were nothing less than the supreme authority on all matters angling on this earth — which, for all the boy knows, he is — and learns quickly. The two dogs, whose names are Saucy and Blue-bell, post themselves behind the fishermen, their ears and eyes alert, their tongues poking out of their mouths, their noses sniffing the air and the growing catch in the basket (these same noses having occasionally to be batted away by the gentleman when they have sniffed too closely.) To indulge them the gentleman tosses the dogs such occasional smaller fry as come within reach of the hooks. The dogs bark at the fish, and at the jays chattering in the trees, and at the ducks on the water, while the ducks squawk at the dogs; with the result that everyone has a jolly good time there at Dalroyd dock, on a summer morning in the mountains, one day.

At intervals, when the lines are slack, the boy glances up into the face of the gentleman beside him — the gray, drab, lumpish face smiling beneath the slouch hat, the face with the craggy brow and the waxed mustaches; a face deemed unattractive by the standards of society, but something arresting nonetheless. Though of course the small boy knows nothing of drabness, or lumpishness, or unattractiveness, or society; he is too young for judging. All he sees is the joyous, kind, open, light-hearted, generous, strong, confident, invincible countenance of his father.

At which point the morning sun begins to fade, and the features of the gentleman in the slouch hat grow dark. The boy thinks perhaps a stray cloud has come between the sun and earth, but it is not so. When he turns back he sees that the gentleman is no longer beside him there on the pier, but has moved off, and is moving off farther still, like a shadow across the landscape, growing smaller and fainter with each passing second. The boy stretches out a hand, pleading tearfully for his father to return. Then a monstrous black veil of gloom inserts itself between the boy and the bygone time, and drives it all from sight.

The squire of Dalroyd wakes with a jolt. It is morning, it is summer, the sun is up; but it is as far from that bright summer's morning of his childhood as the moon is from marzipan. It is the first dream he has had in a long while that does not seem like a nightmare. There was no angry, vengeful presence watching from the round window, no fierce green eyes, no draggled dark hair; nothing but an innocent small boy at the lakeshore on a day long past, enjoying life with his father and dear old Saucy and Blue-bell at Dalroyd dock.

And yet, on further thinking of it, was it not a kind of nightmare too?

So long, long ago! Such bright days and so many bright years stretching before him then, before the coming of the darkness.

How could he have forgotten the Long Ago? Why had this so very pleasant scene, and countless others like it, been selectively expunged from his memory? Who could have done it? Who could have wiped clean his mental slate, except the squire of Dalroyd himself?

"You jolly fool," he is heard to mutter into his pillow, in self-reproach. "You jolly, jolly fool, you!"

What perverse instinct was it, what monstrous, misguided element of his own nature, had brought him to such a pass — had heaped upon the memory of his father such bitterness, such resentment, such exaggeration of each trifling imperfection, so many rank aspersions and distortions of fact, so many outright falsehoods, such injustice upon injustice, unkindness upon unkindness, all undeserved, these eight-and-twenty years? By what self-deluding mechanism had his memories of the bad — of which there were so very few — assumed such creditable dimensions, and supplanted his memories of the good? What absurdity of reasoning had possessed him, to pour out such venom upon his missing father? Why had all his recollections of the kind, generous man who was his father been excised in favor of coarser cloth? How had these abominable beliefs of his arisen, if not at the urging of his own imagination?

His conscience smote him for it. It was only too clear his father had been an honorable man, one who would never voluntarily have left his wife and son.

Something had happened to send him away, Mark was sure of it now, something quite beyond his means to resist. But what?

What was it the doctor had said? The ninth squire had been an upstanding, noble-hearted gentleman, keen to fulfill his responsibilities in the parish and the community. In every way, in every season, his father had performed the duties required of him as master of Dalroyd, no matter how burdensome — which realization prompted the tenth squire to reflect, with growing shame, upon his own meager contributions to parish life. Perhaps his cousin Mags Mowbray had been correct in her assessment of the grumpy squire and his locking himself away in gloomy chambers to mope over the great wrong inflicted upon him and his mother by Ralph Trench. Perhaps Oliver had been correct, too. How truthful were his recollections of his father, and how much were they the product of his own fancy, molded by years of moody rumination?

What cause was there for moody rumination now, for moping about in gloomy chambers, if indeed the ninth squire had not abandoned his family as once thought, but had instead been taken from them?

Hurriedly the squire rose and dressed. At the breakfast-table he made little use of conversation, other than to ascertain that Oliver would be engaged through the early hours of the afternoon, powdering away at the dusty Silla — a design that suited the squire to a T, and accorded well with the plan that was then forming in his mind.

Seeing Oliver safely ensconced with the dusty Roman Spaniard, the squire betook himself to the stables, where he had his groom prepare the black mare for riding. Instructing the man to tell no one he had gone, he gathered up a coil of rope, dropped a handful of tapers into his coat-pocket, and tossed his oil-skin cap on his head. Taking care to avoid that side of the house in which Oliver's chambers were situated, he quietly jogged the mare into the coach-road, *sans* Tinker, *sans* Jolly-boy. It was a simple precaution, leaving his four-legged friends behind — so that Oliver, should he tire of his labors and go off in search of Mark, would find those two members of the trio still at Dalroyd, and thereby conclude that the squire too was still somewhere about the premises.

Once in the road he observed his customary pause of reverence above the hollow, looking down on the place where his mother lay sleeping; then he spurred the mare onwards, through the crossroads and past the grimy milestone and into the narrow winding track that led to Skylingden. In no long time he was in the high wood, on the bridle-path that ran round behind the mansion-house. The house itself with its great circular eye, its lazy wandering roof-line, its walls of old Talbotshire stone streaked and crossed with oak timbers, lay dozing in the sun. There was as usual no sign of activity; though the squire thought he glimpsed a dark figure at one of the windows in the topmost tier, but whether the dark figure saw him he could not tell.

He trotted round towards the southerly precincts of the wood, through the glade and past the abbey ruins, and past the blocked-up entrance to the long stairs, which lay somewhere among the scattered stone blocks and fragments of mortar. At the verge of the summit he drew rein and picketed the mare in the same grove of young trees where he and Oliver had stopped before. Immediately he set off along the trail, down and across the slant face of the promontory, and in due course arrived at the rocky shelf. Stepping nimbly past the withered pile that was Splayfoot's remains, he struck a light and made his way through the outer chamber of the cave, and so found himself once more at the well.

Not a moment did he waste in useless thought. He unfastened the ties and removed the capstone fragment. Securing his coil of rope to the iron rings, he dropped the tail-end of it through the opening into the pitchy dark chasm. He placed his gloved hands upon the well, and bending over the aperture stood and listened for a while in the taper-light.

It was not nearly so long this time before the sounds came to him. Gently, softly, beginning with the stealthy rustle of garments, the voices rose up to him from below. There were more of them now than before, many more. Somewhere among them, he knew, was the one particular voice that had drawn him back to the well, and that mattered to him the most. As he listened he found himself overcome by feelings of unutterable peace and happiness. He heard the voices, heard their promises, and found them radiant, dazzling, joyful. There were promises of rest, promises of relief, reward; heady promises of life never-ending, of universal bliss in the depths of the well, in a vast cavernous realm where no days or nights are and no time passes. As they spoke the voices grew gradually bolder and more insistent, until Mark could feel himself starting to succumb under their influence.

Peering through the opening he saw that the darkness within the chasm had been routed, and replaced by a kind of phosphoric illumination. He saw that the well-shaft was not a bare, black, empty thing, not an inky void, but was instead filled with phantoms — a profusion of hazy, spectral forms, all swimming round and round each other in restless haste, whirling and swirling, wheeling and diving.

Whereupon the chorus of their voices grew bolder still, as they lofted their invitations to him.

"We are the many. We are the way. Come, join us!"

"Leave your false philosophy!"

"Abandon your false God!"

"Abandon His swindling and cruelty!"

"We are your friends!"

"We are the true path — all else is blasphemy!"

"We are the eternals!"

"We are truth and mercy!"

"Save yourself before it is too late!"

"Join us and live forever!"

"Forsake us and die!"

And then, a little above the rest —

"Is it you there, Mark?"

Such words had their due effect. The squire fell back on his heels, momentarily staggered by the force of it. The truth that had flashed upon him earlier was for all intents confirmed — his father had indeed discovered the well, had gone down into it, and never returned. The thought struck him, too, why the villagers of yore who had assailed the abbey had found no one there, despite having seen no one leave. He knew now where the Lake Friars had gone.

He examined the fastening of his rope to the iron rings, to verify it was tight and secure. He would, he decided, make the attempt to go down into the well and bring his father back. It was evident that the ninth squire of Dalroyd was alive somewhere among the swirl of spectral lights; evident too it had been his father's own hand he had felt on that earlier occasion, curling round his boot to stay him.

He understood that in going down the well he himself might not return, just as his father had not. He understood too that in the process he might be driven mad; so that even should he manage to succeed, his condition might in the end be no better than that of one of the crazed friars who had fled the abbey, perhaps no better than that of Mr. Charles Campleman himself. And what of the state of his father's mind now, after eight-and-twenty years in the pit?

Or was it only eight-and-twenty seconds?

Regardless, the tenth squire of Dalroyd and last of the Talbotshire Trenches refused to believe he could not master the situation. He was bent upon his course; he would retain firm command of himself and allow neither the spectral voices nor the contemplation of eternity to sway him. The happy recollection of that bright morning at Dalroyd dock, of the whistling, light-hearted man with the waxed mustaches and the old slouch hat, stole again into his mind and nerved him to his purpose. Was it the secret acknowledgment of his guilt that impelled him? Nostalgic yearning for a father he had so little known? Or simply compassion for a terribly wronged man? Whichever it was that drove the squire, he was resolved he must get to his father now and set all to rights, whatever the cost.

He lowered himself through the aperture and began his descent. The sound of the voices was in his ears and everywhere around. He could see the lighted forms swarming about him in the air, and feel their coldness like a foggy mist against his skin. It was like descending through a cloud. Was that not how Charles Campleman had described it? A cloud of voices?

His foot struck the uppermost of the metal rungs. He shifted his grip from the rope to the ladder of bars, and resumed his descent at a rapid pace. Before long he heard his father's voice, somewhere near at hand. But all was not right; though he could hear the voice of Ralph Trench he could nowhere sense his presence. There was little in the voice or its subtleties of tone to remind him of the light-hearted gentleman of his dream. There was not an ounce of his father's good nature, his warmth of heart, his humor there; there was nothing but the voice — a voice, now that he heard it closely and clearly, that was not so jolly much like the voice of Ralph Trench after all.

Perhaps it *was* a hoax, a mortal poison, as Oliver had termed it — not his father's voice, but simply how he recollected his father's voice to have been. It was just another of the many voices in the cloud of spectral forms that was writhing about him, pressing him, coaxing him, exhorting him, tempting him. How then could they know of privileged matters from his childhood with his father, incidents known only to the family?

He turned cold to the very roots of his vanished hair, as he felt a hand grasp his ankle and wrap itself round his boot, just as before, to pull him down. As it did so another hand seized the opposite ankle, a third hand his leg; and so another his shoulder, another his arm, another the nape of his neck, as he fought to keep hold of the bars in the wild phosporic light.

"We are the many! Join us!"

"Abandon your false doctrine!"

"It is your best hope!"

"It is your *only* hope!"

A salty flood of moisture was leaking from his brow and stinging his eyes. Glancing round he saw that the well-shaft was wider here, that it had in fact been growing progressively wider the farther he descended, as though it were expanding into an entire vast other world below ground. This he saw but little more, for the hands upon his body abruptly tightened their grip. Greater and greater numbers of the phantoms swarmed about him. With a sickening qualm he felt himself being peeled slowly from the bars.

"Hang you!" he cried out defiantly. "Hang the lot of you!"

Somewhere below him, not so very far off, another voice began speaking through the cloud. A much fainter voice this one was, but a most familiar one; for what had caught the squire's attention and held it was the whistle that preceded the words. The sound of it froze him to the bars and for the moment thwarted his opponents. A crooked smile spread across his face and half the distance to Dalroyd. There was no mistaking either the whistle, or the voice; no mistaking the invisible tie that stretched from the speaker to Mark and bound them together. It was beyond the reach of question; it was the voice of his father calling to him from below. That earlier, more insistent voice may have been a hoax, a humbug, but this one most assuredly was not. What it said had a profound effect upon him; it gave him renewed strength, and filled him with confidence — and in the same breath saddened him to the very depths of his being.

Renewed strength and confidence were what he needed in his struggle against the spectral forms. Having resolved to prosecute the search for his father to the fullest extent, the words spoken by the voice caused him now to veer from his purpose. He had no choice; now it was he who must abandon his father. With a heart surely as heavy as any human heart ever could be, so heavy that its weight threatened to stall his escape, he began to work his way up the bars. He felt the hands starting to release, one by one, as he climbed — felt the power of their grip failing — heard the voices growing softer, fainter, their promises less rapturous, less overwhelming, as his courage reasserted itself — felt the swirling cloud of spectral lights dissolving all about him —

And so he found himself again at the top of the rungs. He clutched at the rope, and despite his sadness and utter weariness of spirit, and the tremors racking the muscles of his arms and legs, set about the task of hauling himself the remaining distance up the well.

He had very nearly achieved his goal when the voices rose up in his ears, and the hands again clamped themselves upon him. On the instant he struck out at the cloud with his legs, which action dislodged him from his perch and set him swaying to and fro. He felt his gloves slip along the rope; for one terrifying instant he thought he was going to fall. In desperation he cast about for some small ledge or crevice that might sustain his weight. It was then he saw the black silhouette of a man intrude itself upon the taper-light above; saw the man reach out for him through the opening in the capstone; heard the man call to him — a man he thought looked jolly like Mr. Bede Wintermarch of Skylingden Hall.

The squire was in no position to wonder at it, or to question it. With a mad cry he tore himself free of the spectral forces, scrambling and clawing his way to the rim of the well, where the arms of Mr. Wintermarch helped him through the aperture.

Dazed, exhausted, his body awash in sweat, his energy spent, he collapsed on the ground, his limbs trembling as though in a violent fit of ague. The figure of Mr. Wintermarch was quickly at his side.

"Mark! Mark! Pray God — you are all right?"

Why should Mr. Bede Wintermarch address him with such familiarity? Through the burning in his eyes he strove to make out the features of the tenant of Skylingden. He blinked several times, wiping away the perspiration with a gloved hand. At length it dawned upon his jumbled faculties that the gentleman kneeling beside him, the dark silhouette, his savior, was not Mr. Wintermarch of Skylingden Hall, as he first had thought; it was only Oliver of Bucket's Court, Highmarket, Crow's-end.

"Devils," he whispered, gripping his friend by the shoulder. "Devils in the pit!"

"We must close it, for good and all," Oliver declared. Immediately he rose to his feet, lifted up the heavy capstone fragment and wedged it into place. He then undid Mark's rope from the iron rings and lashed the stone down tight, all the while ignoring the squire's feeble protests.

"When I observed that Tinker was in his stall and Jolly-boy in his basket, and you and one of the other horses nowhere to be found — and your groom remarkably confused as to the whereabouts of that horse — I knew where you had gone," said Oliver, kneeling again. "Thankfully I grew tired of the dusty Silla when I did and sought you out. How long have you been down?"

Mark shook his head. To his surprise he found that his oil-skin cap with the lighted taper was no longer adhered to it, but must have been lost during his flight from the well. Likely it was with his father now.

"What hour is it?" he asked, coughing hoarsely.

"Half-past five o'clock. I suppose you left directly after breakfast?"

The squire nodded.

"You were dead right, old Noll," he said, racked by another fit of trembling. "As regards the voice — cod or genuine — I'd been gammoned — no help for it now — jolly keen of you."

"I can't say the knowledge pleases me."

"Dead right, yes — but only in part."

"How do you mean?"

"My father," Mark replied, coughing again — "my father is indeed inside the well. I felt his presence there. He spoke to me of many things; then he warned me off. The devils may jolly well have gammoned me once — gammoned me twice — but they could not keep him from me. My father — my poor father, whom I have so cruelly maligned," he said, with a dismal groan — "my father is imprisoned there, and we can never get him out."

CHAPTER XII

WHO IS MR. WINTERMARCH?

THE oak bar round the beer-engine of landlord Nim, in the card-room of the Arms, was alive with discussion. Word had gotten round, regarding the late encounter of Miss Cherry Ives with the thing in the clumber pine; and there was no shortage of opinion as to who or what that thing might be. Some thought it almost certainly a teratorn, perhaps Mr. Shakes, that gentleman rover of the celestial sphere; others thought it a vulture, a condor, an eagle, even a stork. No one among the veteran regulars, however, made mention of the Skylingden owl, which struck Cherry as rather odd, for it was from her perspective quite the most likely candidate. Neither could anyone in the teratorn camp, or the condor camp, or any of the other camps, or even Cherry herself, explain how such a creature might have acquired the power of speech.

You say you know me, friend. They turned their backs on me. None will be spared.

Equally odd, in Cherry's view, was the response of these same regulars to the message the thing in the clumber pine had imparted to her. These older men, these veterans of the village — all of them well-schooled in its deeper secrets, like solemn professors of village lore, unwilling to expound upon their hypotheses save in private chat with members of their own fraternity — were observed to mutter and grumble among themselves, and exchange a host of significant glances, conveying to one another their grim notions as to who or what the prankster might be. The normally bright sky of the landlord's countenance, his lively gray eyes and forthright expression, even they were afflicted with an overcast. But no amount of coaxing by Cherry could persuade her father Nim or any of his circle to admit to anything of more than trivial substance; which was perhaps just as well, for in her own mind the landlord's daughter and mainspring of the Village Arms had formed a few substantive notions of her own.

Among the veterans gathered there in the card-room were Mr. Tudway, the chandler, and Mr. Lincote, the sugar-baker, and his friend and compatriot the miller, and the little hunting chemist, Mr. Coddy Binks. There too was Mr. Bottom in his habiliments of rusty black sable, keeping solitary company with his grog in a corner of the room — watching all, hearing all, revolving in his thoughts all manner of suspicions that came his way, and appearing to grow more restless and uncomfortable with every swallow of his nectar.

And there too was Mr. Thomas Dogger, with his chin and his long sharp nose and his eyes shiny and sleek, having left off his labors at Prospect Cottage to make one of his frequent strolls through town, to relieve his brain of its accumulated clutter of the law, and to lubricate his lawyer's golden throat by means of the beer-engine at the Village Arms. No grumbling, muttering, suspicious man was he: he was only a simple country practitioner and professional adviser, one entered upon the honorable roll of solicitors of the Court of Chancery and attorneys at Common Law. What had solid, practical, professional men of the village like himself — and like the miller, the sugar-baker, the chandler, even Mine Host of the Arms — what had such men as these to fear from a mischievous prankster, was Mr. Dogger's rhetorical interrogative to the assembled company. Was it the state of the case that good men of this parish had something to fear from a scoundrel lurking in a tree? Were such men as these now gathered at the oak bar wont to be bullied by shadows? Mr. Dogger found it disappointing, very disappointing; moreover he wondered at it. Inevitably the momentum of his rhetoric got his professional juices flowing, and set him to questioning Cherry, to ascertain whether there might not be grounds for an action at law — with its attendant bill of costs — in regard to the miscreant in the clumber pine.

Most were convinced now — as indeed Mr. Dogger had been for some while — that it was Charles Campleman, recovered from his illness, who had returned to the mansion-house in the guise of Mr. Bede Wintermarch, to pursue his revenge against the good people of Shilston Upcot. The thing in the tree, Mr. Dogger explained, was most likely his doing; trickery of some kind, aimed at plaguing Mr. Ives through the landlord's own valued daughter. It was Mr. Dogger's professional opinion that the prankster was most likely a servant, who had disguised himself there in the clumber pine and warbled his odd remarks to Cherry, before releasing a bird into the air as a sort of *coup de théâtre*. It was not so very mysterious after all, nor so disquieting, smiled the attorney, with a sweep of his shiny eyes round the company, some of whom could be seen nodding their heads in agreement. Yes, yes, it was Charles Campleman's doing, that was abundantly clear, it was *ipso facto*. Why else should Mr. Bede Wintermarch (as he styled himself) have come here, to Talbotshire, and gone to ground in the mansion-house, as plainly *incognito* as a refugee from the Insolvent Debtors Court, if not to carry out his plot? Why else should he dispatch his wife and daughter — if truly they were his wife and daughter — upon periodic errands into the Low Street, unaccompanied by himself, if not to gather intelligence for the effectuation of his mischiefs? Why else should Mr. Charles Campleman have returned after so many years, and in such a fashion, but to avenge himself for the unjust treatment accorded him by not a few persons in this village?

But mind, Mr. Dogger made no accusation! It was merely a matter for speculation, and an issue of some personal and professional curiosity.

The regulars reflected darkly upon their memories of the young heir — upon his bookish, introspective nature, the growing eccentricity of his habits, his antiquarian rambles about the abbey ruins where the dreaded Lake Friars once had reigned, his gradual isolation from the community, his rumored dalliance with vicar Marchant's daughter and its consequences. And was there not in these reflections, perhaps, an unspoken admission on the part of the townspeople of their own culpability in the matter, as recognized by Mr. Dogger? For all recollected how the young heir's increasingly unorthodox behavior had been received in the village — how his delving into black and secret arts had alarmed the citizens — how the rumors of an *amour* with Miss Marchant had shocked and appalled all good Christian souls in the parish — how public sentiment had rapidly turned against him — how the family Campleman, what there was remaining of it, had been obliged to abandon Skylingden Hall for the city, owing to the young gentleman's unsoundness of mind and the ill will accorded him by the villagers.

Yet no one, even while holding Charles Campleman accountable for his transgressions and for Cherry's prankster in the tree, saw fit to mention the parade of hateful nightmares that had of late afflicted many in the village; no one, it seemed, had any answer for *that*.

At which point the company found their thoughts interrupted by a subtle shaking of the house. All conversation was halted; pipes and cigars stopped being smoked; glasses and tankards ceased commuting from hand to lip; eyes looked about in sudden concern and bewilderment.

Came a further shaking of the inn, and another, and another. Rumbling vibrations of the ground, following quickly one upon the other, rattled the house, its contents, its inhabitants. Someone in the lodge-room cried out that it was an earthquake. The guests immediately began making for the house-door, afraid that the rafters and the russet-colored roof-tiles were about to come crashing down upon them; just as Cherry and her father rushed quickly to assure them this would not happen, for the staff of the Arms and the regulars understood well the cause of the disturbance.

Both timely and vociferous was the announcement made then by Mr. Alfred Snorem, from his post opposite the booking-desk —

"*Thunder-beasts in the road, by jingo!*"

No earthquake then, but an earth-shaking spectacle nonetheless. With their fears considerably eased many of the people walked out into the yard, together with Cherry and her father and others of the Arms, to view the arrival of the mastodon train, to see the mastodon men and their shaggy red charges, for there were not so many such creatures — either men or thunder-beasts — in these latitudes now as before.

With their heads nodding and their massive bodies swaying, and their legs like tree-trunks plunging with rhythmic force upon the ground, sending tremors throughout the valley with every step, the mastodons came marching up the road. There were four of them, in single file — magnificent specimens all, each standing nearly fifteen feet at the shoulder, with tusks heaving from side to side, and ears rippling, and large soft eyes vigilant and alert. They were arrayed in full harness, with passenger cabs and freight platforms slung along the back and flanks of each animal. The cabs atop all but the last appeared to be fully laden with passengers.

Like majestic ships of the road the mastodons came to anchor, just beyond the gates at the entrance of the yard. Calls went out from the drivers in the cabs; slowly, gently, with wonderful grace and delicacy, the creatures lowered themselves to their knees until their bellies rested on the ground. Cord-ladders were unfurled from the cab-doors, and the process of setting down the passengers got under way. It was overseen by the chief of the mastodon men, a crisp-haired, stiff-faced, timber-looking man in loud plaid trousers and a pork-pie hat, who had command of the lead bull. The remaining animals in the train were mastered by the three young sons of the leader, crisp-haired, stiff-faced, timber-looking saplings quite clearly derived from the parental oak. It was common for the mastodon trains to be operated as family businesses; indeed, not only the drivers but the thunder-beasts themselves often were family too, as in the present case, with the lead bull and his brother heading the train and two of their cousins bringing up the rear.

"Hallo and how are you, Mr. Jarvey?" said Mr. Ives, grasping the hand of the gentleman in the pork-pie hat.

"Proper fine, Mr. Ives," returned the chief of the mastodon men.

"What news with you? How did you find Malbury and the country roundabout?"

"Proper fine, though there's been saber-cats reported at Wycombe; but it's no impediment to the beasts, Mr. Ives, as you well know. We've nearly a full charge of passengers on this excursion. I've no doubt you've accomodation sufficient in this fine harborage of yours?"

"Cherry, m'dear," smiled Mr. Ives, turning to his daughter, "we have accomodation sufficient?"

"We have, Father," answered the capable Cherry, already about the task of superintending the new arrivals as they descended from the cabs. "Welcome, ladies! Welcome, sirs! This way then, if you would, please..."

"Aye, you're welcome to the Arms, *e*-normous welcome you are, sirs and madams!" boomed Mr. Snorem, as he and the assistant porters began gathering in the luggage as it was handed down from the freight platforms. "Now mind how you go thar!"

One of the persons clambering down — with some difficulty, it must be owned — was a very short, very small, very round gentleman in a blue coat and a striped waistcoat, with a red face and white hair, sparkling eyes, and an easy smile. A low-crowned, broad-brimmed hat adorned his head, a gold watch-chain his paunch. As the gentleman made his way through the entrance-hall he was observed by Mr. Dogger, who, not being disposed to squander his time and energy upon so unprofitable a thing as a mastodon train, had remained in the card-room with his pint of sixpenny spruce. He recognized the newcomer at once as the little doctor from Crow's-end, returning from his important business at Malbury; a gentleman whom Mr. Dogger had reason to believe he could do business with, but to whom he should never again propose a friendly game of billiards. The two men greeted one another, the very brisk and perpendicular Mr. Dogger on one side of the handshake, the very short and rather more globular Dr. Tweed on the other. The doctor had completed his transactions in the county town and was making the return journey to Crow's-end, but would be staying the night at the Arms, so that he and Mr. Dogger might resume their prior discussion in a businesslike manner, as agreed.

"A delightful situation. Such fine waters! Such glorious mountains! Such fragrant timber!" enthused the little doctor, peering out through the long side-row of windows in the card-room. "It will be very useful to have local counsel here, someone upon whom I may rely, and whom I may visit now and again. I have thought it over much in the interval and it will well serve."

"You are unencumbered, then, sir, and at liberty to call upon us in our office and chambers at Prospect Cottage?" inquired Mr. Dogger, putting on his professional face, and smoothing his hands the one over the other as though in a dream of warm water and wash-balls.

"At liberty for the entire evening," replied Dr. Tweed, cheerfully. "But I must go out with the train at first light."

"Of course. Not to worry, we shan't detain you long. It is high time we two put our heads together, high time. You will, I trust, find your call a satisfying one. Though country law is a poor provider and Prospect Cottage is not fashioned of gold, nor even gingerbread, we make do, sir, we make do.

It is, if Tom Dogger may be so bold, as nice a house as any gentleman could wish to hang up his hat in."

Mr. Dogger was pleased; the little doctor was pleased; and so the gentlemen advanced in their good opinion of each other, and betook themselves to the oak bar, where the attorney got himself another pint of spruce-beer, and Dr. Tweed a glass of cider, with which to celebrate the commencement of negotiations.

As the novelty of the train's arrival subsided, and the thunder-beasts were turned out in the glade beside the Arms, and the passengers made comfortable in their quarters by Cherry and her staff, the other guests and the regulars came grouping in to resume their activities. At the oak bar some further mention was made of Mr. Bede Wintermarch and his merry pranks, and as well his motives; at which point the little doctor, imbibing his cider there in the company of Mr. Dogger, put down his glass and looked about him with a measure of surprise on his ruddy features.

"Truly," said he, addressing those who had been speaking, "I do not mean to appear meddlesome, not in the least, but I could not help overhearing. This Mr. Wintermarch to whom you refer — he is a resident of this town?"

The veteran regulars afforded him a few grudging nods but little else, being reluctant to discuss anything of the business with a complete stranger, particularly one from the city. Mr. Dogger, his lawyerly instincts sensing that something of importance was about to be disclosed, exhorted his fellows to relate for the doctor certain of their conjectures as regards the mysterious tenant of Skylingden.

"Ah, I see," the doctor nodded, once a few words of explanation had been delivered up. "Skylingden Hall. Yes, yes, of course, now I understand your confusion."

"What do you mean, our confusion?" demanded Mr. Tudway, a little huffily.

"Ah — pardon me for being so candid, sir, but it's rather clear to me your Mr. Wintermarch simply cannot be this Charles Campleman you speak of, if by this you refer to the Charles Campleman of Skylingden Hall."

Mr. Tudway replied that that was the man.

"Then I fear you conjecture from weak ground on that score, sir, for surely he is the same unfortunate gentleman I have been attending to for some years now."

"Do *you* know Charles Campleman?" asked Mr. Lincote, the sugar-baker, with amazement in his eyes.

"How do you mean, unfortunate?" asked Mr. Tudway.

"Ah, indeed, yes, your Mr. Charles Campleman is alive, but rather hopelessly impaired, and has been for much of his adult existence," returned the little doctor. "As for 'unfortunate,' I meant it simply in a compassionate sense, for as it happens Mr. Campleman is a patient of mine, you see — at the Dudderies, in Crow's-end."

The pork-pie hat of Mr. Jarvey turned round from the bar, and his head and eyes with it.

"The Dudderies!" exclaimed the mastodon man, fixing his gaze on Dr. Tweed. "Why, that there's a mad-house, proper fine. As my boys should well know, for their mother's cousin from her father's side has been gnawing at the roach-bugs in his cell there, whenever the fancy strikes him, and picking at his fleas, and stuffing fish-bones into his ears, and laughing to himself, and rabbiting on in a gibberish all unknown to anybody, for many a twelvemonth now. They pays top shilling for their tickets of admittance to catch him at his antics, they do, such visitors as desire to see the hospital and view the inmates."

"My word — the lunatic asylum," murmured the vicar, pushing back his spectacles.

"Mental hospital," the doctor hastily corrected him. "A place of retreat, sirs, established upon the principles of the former Bethlehem Royal, where distracted patients may be looked after and shielded from the buffetings of society. Madness and melancholy are ills as surely as are the pox and spotted fever, and such institutions perform a valuable service. The resident medical officer as it happens is a member of my club, and quite a good fellow. He does an excellent job."

The veteran regulars, those solemn professors of village lore, found it necessary now to re-examine their hypotheses as regards Mr. Wintermarch and the prankster in the clumber pine, which had been blown to atoms (their hypotheses, not the tree) by the city doctor. If Mr. Wintermarch was not Charles Campleman — who then was he?

"Well, if that don't take the biscuit," declared the sugar-baker.

"Wintermarch not Campleman!" said Mr. Tudway, frowning.

"Perhaps we have naught to fear," suggested Mr. Lash, the schoolmaster, in a hopeful key.

"Fear?" returned the little doctor, with friendly inquisitiveness. "Why should you fear this Mr. Wintermarch?"

Mr. Shank Bottom, having attended to this conversation quite long enough, from his place in the corner, abruptly broke from his chair and stumbled forward with his wicker-bottle of grog in hand. He took a ferocious swallow of his nectar, and put the bottle away in his pocket. He drew his coat-sleeve across his mouth, and wiped the gray smudges of stone-dust from his cheeks, before addressing the assembled company.

"Fear," he growled, screwing up his eyes something awfully. "O' course there's much to fear — this I tell thee true!"

"Then tell us more, sir, if you please," smiled Dr. Tweed, observing the sexton as he might a specimen in a jar, or more likely a lunatic new-arrived at the mad-house, and making a cursory assessment of his afflictions, of which the foremost appeared to be the grog.

"What didst thou think?" cried out Mr. Bottom to everyone present, bringing silence down upon the card-room and the oak bar. "Didst thou think it were Charley Campleman up at the Hall? Didst thou think *I* should not know Charley Campleman, him as was always kind to me? I tell thee, it's true — that man Wintermarch is no more Charley Campleman than is that water-butt in the yard there!"

Mr. Bottom, despite the nature of his occupation and his personal unattractiveness — or perhaps because of them — had an ear like a hare; he knew everything that went round in the village. And so he had been secretly watching and listening for some weeks, nosing here and nosing there, gathering intelligence from every corner, until the full horror of the situation had become clear to him; all the while enduring the preposterous suppositions of others as regards the tenants of Skylingden, and keeping silent.

The sexton shook his fist in warning. "Mr. Bede Wintermarch? Damn and blast, it ain't Mr. Bede Wintermarch as thou shouldst fear there at the mansion-house. Not him, but her! Retribution, after near these thirty year, from the spirit what is all about thee in the night — *that* thou shouldst fear!"

With an explosion like something between a retch and a laugh, which nearly sent his old scratch-wig flying from his head, Mr. Bottom quitted the room — without offering anything more by way of explanation, and having cast a considerable pall over those around him, who were left to puzzle out for themselves the meaning of his outburst. The last they saw of him he was drinking his grog in the yard in the company of Mr. Snorem, both of which gentlemen Mr. Thomas Dogger ordinarily had little use for.

But plain country Tom Dogger was of quite another opinion now, as regards Mr. Bottom and what Mr. Bottom had had to say; for the other's speech had struck him most particularly. First the revelation of the little doctor, then that of the sexton. Perhaps the others in the card-room had not yet grasped the import of Mr. Bottom's words, but Mr. Dogger certainly had. His lawyerly instincts had been too, too correct!

Which meant that Mr. Dogger began to do some very unusual things. He began to grow visibly uneasy; his face paled; his roundish forehead was seen to glisten; his eyes lost their luster — in short, his professional face began to melt, in full view of the laity, and his personal face to show through. He called to mind the images of Mrs. Wintermarch and her daughter in the Low Street, on a certain market Friday not long before, recollecting with a troubled air the features of the young wife that had so interested him — her eyes, the shape of her brow, the lengthy sharpness of her nose. Something like a chill coursed through his lawyerly frame.

And so he did another very unusual thing — he forgot all about the little doctor, and the little doctor's business, and the matter of the costs to be accrued, and walked straight out of the Arms; and not even the trumpeting of the thunder-beasts in the glade adjacent could shake him from his trance.

CHAPTER XIII

SIX OF EIGHT

"HA!"

It was the squire, standing at the desk in his private study with a crowd of papers spread out before him. He had lit upon one particularly interesting item — a piece of correspondence some many years old, which had been the cause of his exclamation, and which he was now busily examining.

"What have you found?" asked Oliver, placing himself at his friend's side.

"When I was in the well, my father told me of some letters he'd given to the old vicar, Edwin Marchant. He said there would be answers in them. It occurred to me that they might be among the letters our own fine vicar saw fit to turn over to me, at his wife's urging, not so long ago. I thought I'd burned them, or tossed them to the mountain winds, or otherwise disposed of them. Well, it's a jolly good job I didn't — for what a letter have I here found!"

"What is the substance of it?"

"Here," said Mark, handing the sheet across. "Peruse it carefully, Noll, like a stout fellow, and give me an opinion."

Oliver ran over the faded lines of the missive. At the end of it he raised his eyes and peered into the face of his companion, in some trouble how to express himself.

"Well, there it is, then. What think you?" asked the squire.

"You might knock me down with a hat-brush," was his friend's astonished reply. "This throws an entirely new light upon the matter, to be sure. But what does it mean — in the larger sense?"

"What it means," said Mark, tapping the paper significantly, "is that Mr. Bede Wintermarch there at Skylingden Hall is perhaps not the hobgoblin he has been made out to be."

Oliver read the letter over a second time. In the space at the top of it was a brief annotation in a separate hand, that of a person calling herself Mrs. Fotheringhay, and which was directed to Mr. Ralph Trench of Dalroyd, informing the ninth squire that the letter had been forwarded to him so that its contents might be made known to "the concerned party."

Both the address and the identity of the letter-writer had been obliterated. The letter itself went as follows —

Monday evening.

MY DEAR MRS. FOTHERINGHAY, — May I take the opportunity to thank you again for your kind and virtuous service in the matter of our little child. She has been, is now, and ever shall be, the ruling light and spirit of our household, since that blessed morning a fortnight past when she first entered our lives. For so many years divine Providence had chosen not to favor our union, that it seemed my husband and I should remain forever childless. For those many years we accepted this stern decree, and bore our disappointment without complaint. Now that our dear little girl has come to us, however, all has changed. The days are brighter now, the nights are never lonely now, and the future stands before us. It is to you, and to your worthy and charitable Society of St. Sepulchre, that we owe our great good fortune, and offer our gratitude for your kindness to us. We shall always thankfully recall your generosity, and shall be ever obliged to you, as we are ever rejoicing in our dear girl.

In remembrance of the good offices of your Society, and in grateful acknowledgment of the debt we owe in respect of the child, we have christened her SEPULCHRA — she is anonymous no longer! — so that in this wise the recollection of your kindness will remain within our hearts, for so long as Providence may grant us these fleeting hours on earth.

Believe me, Mrs. Fotheringhay, I am, &c. &c.,

"You see, Noll, how well it fits together," said the squire, when Oliver had done reading. "I thought it a jolly odd name for a woman, and so it is, too, and there is the tale behind it. Edith Marchant was delivered of a girl child there at Crow's-end, and Mrs. Wintermarch is that child."

"You believe then that she is the cause of the family's settling here?" said Oliver. "That it is she, rather than her husband, who has come seeking vengeance — in her mother's name?"

"Perhaps."

"For the conduct of the villagers towards Miss Marchant, after her return from the city, and for her suicide?"

"You'll remember, Noll, how Mr. Bede Wintermarch told us it was his wife who had prevailed upon him to 'abandon the fatigues of the city for country air.' It was she who had 'heard good reports' of our little community of Shilston Upcot. A tidy arrangement."

"Yes, indeed, I do recollect it."

"Or — perhaps not," said Mark, making an abrupt about-face.

"How do you mean?"

"Did the lady strike you as the deceitful sort? She did not me. I sensed nothing in her but wifely duty, politeness, submission. Moreover the circumstances of her birth were kept dark. You'll note the letter here, which hints strongly that her new family were ignorant of her origins — 'She is anonymous no longer.' How then did she discover her true history?"

Oliver confessed he had no ready answer for this.

"Which leads me to consider a third possibility," said the squire, with his eyes full of thought.

"Mere coincidence?"

"I should be jolly surprised if it were! I take no stock in coincidence."

"Perhaps they are leagued together in this, the husband and the wife? But if the husband is Charles Campleman, and Charles Campleman is as well the father of — "

Oliver shuddered; it was too ghastly an idea for thinking on.

"Then he simply cannot be Campleman," he murmured, in a kind of soliloquy — "or someone else indeed was the father of the child. Or perhaps they are not husband and wife at all?"

The squire himself paused for a time to reason the thing out, looking quietly on the letter and smoothing his side-whiskers.

"We must rid ourselves of this creature, this owl," he said, at length. "To that end we must capture it. It is the key to the entire business. And we must do it straight away, before it is allowed to accomplish whatever it has been brought here to accomplish. Devil take these blasted dreams!"

"And how do we do this?" Oliver inquired, with knitted brow. "Do we make a rush at the mansion-house, as your brave-hearted forbears rushed upon the abbey, and remove the creature by main force? I'll admit my preference runs more to robins and bobolinks, but what is the owl that it represents a danger to us? To be sure, these dreams are irritating, noxious things; but we have yet to demonstrate any causative connection, or plausible means by which this creature might be influencing them. And the idea that it is the same owl that frightened Mr. Bottom thirty years ago is simply conjecture."

"Look here, Noll — again it is too much coincidence for my taste. We can agree there is reason to suspect this bird's involvement in the demise of Splayfoot?"

"We can."

"And in this way it lured us to the cave and caused us to discover the well."

"You are ascribing an intelligence to it, then, as distinct from that of the person or persons who brought it here?"

"This is no ordinary winged creature of the night, Noll. It's jolly likely it murdered Splayfoot, a short-faced bear — a short-face, Noll! — and we the both of us witnessed the trouble it gave Hoey's teratorn. A beast capable of such actions must be possessed of an almost supernatural ferocity."

Oliver looked closely at his friend, a gentleman who no more than a few short weeks past had had nothing but disdain for matters theological and spiritual.

"My father told me of many things in the well, in those minutes that were longer than any I have ever known," the squire went on, with a subtle darkening of his voice. "He told me how he had been set upon by a huge owl with horns and a white face, and green phosphoric eyes. He had trotted up to Skylingden on a horse one afternoon to take some exercise, and to inquire after young Campleman, whose illness had grown particularly severe. It was some months after the affair in the Chase — his injured arm being still nearly useless to him — and shortly after the death of the girl. After paying his respects at the Hall, he was riding out through the gates when an owl flew at him from a tree hard by, screeching violently, with its wings raised and its claws fully spread. It loosed my father from his horse, and drove him towards the abbey ruins and the entrance to the long stairs, which lay open there, for it was before the sexton had blocked it up. The bird forced him down the staircase, down into the inky void, by fiercely and repeatedly striking at him with its claws and beak. Retreating, he eventually found himself in the cave far below. He somehow managed to fire a match, and saw the well crouching there before him. Just as he approached it, however, his light went out. At that instant the green eyes came shooting towards him from the darkness. The force of the collision threw him against the well, and he went tumbling over, unable to stop himself owing to his injured arm. So was he launched into eternity. The next he knew he was in the grasp of the devils in the pit, where he has remained ever since. That was the cause of his vanishing; that is how my father was lost to us. My father, Noll — whom we shall never see the like of again."

Oliver was quite overcome by the power of his friend's narrative, and was rendered silent for some minutes after. He looked again into the squire's face, but saw nothing there except conviction and a grim seriousness of purpose. It was no hoax, no delusion of mind, no residue of the attacks of trembling that had followed Mark's last journey into the well. The events he had described were wholly real to him; or at the very least, he believed them to be real.

"But to what purpose? If this was a deliberate course of action, as you suggest, what offense had your father given to Charles Campleman?" Oliver asked.

"None. You must realize, Noll — it is not Skylingden vengeance, nor even Crow's-end vengeance, that is to be levied against this village."

His words gave Oliver cause for reflection. Abruptly, in one sudden disbelieving flash, the squire's third possibility laid itself before him. It was a notion that froze him to the spot. His eyes grew very wide, his mouth gaped; he ran a hand through his abundant curling hair.

"It is Shilston Upcot vengeance," he said, in barely more than a whisper.

"We must remove this creature from our midst," declared Mark, "so that it cannot succeed in completing what it began one fine night, eight-and-twenty years past. The dreams, Noll, think of the figure in the dreams. Do you not recognize it? *Smithers!*" he called aloud, ringing the bell.

The loyal retainer and his frosty beard promptly materialized at the door.

"Sir?"

"Look here, Smithers, send one of the manservants round to the Peaks, double-quick. Have him advise Captain Hoey that Mr. Langley and I and certain others will be arriving there directly" — he shot a quick glance in Oliver's direction — "for a council of war."

"Very good sir," replied the butler, wholly unruffled by the announcement, and making dignified preparation to withdraw.

"And Smithers!"

"Yes, sir?" (Smithers delaying his exit.)

"Send another fellow round to Dr. Hall's cottage, requesting that the doctor meet us there at the Peaks, if he is not engaged at present, or so soon as he is at liberty to do so. If the doctor is from home have the fellow search out the doctor's trap. Where the trap is, there too will be the physician."

"Very good, sir." (Smithers again preparing to withdraw.)

"And Smithers!"

"Sir?" (Smithers delaying again.)

"Dispatch a third man to Timber Hill Farm, asking Mr. Arkwright to join us at the Peaks as well."

"Yes, sir. Is there anything more, sir?"

"No, there's an end to it for now, Smithers."

"Very good, sir."

"And you'll advise the fellows to jolly well look sharp about it!"

"Yes, sir," replied Smithers, bowing, and so made his respectful exit at last.

"Come along, Noll. We ourselves must call at Gray Lodge before moving on to Hoey's."

They took up their coats and hats and made their way to the stables, where Tinker and the chestnut mare were quickly prepared for riding. Saddles and harness were applied, girths were tightened; the gentlemen stepped into the stirrups, the reins were gathered up, the horses given a touch with the spurs; and away they went. Once in the coach-road they made direct for Gray Lodge, where they informed Miss Mowbray that her presence was requested at the Peaks. Only the sketchiest of explanations was given her by the squire, but the unusual earnestness of his manner, his complete devotion to purpose in the exercise of his request — characteristics so different from those of the careless, lounging squire she had long known — were sufficient to persuade her of the gravity of the circumstances. Unexpectedly her aunt, Mrs. Fielding, asked if she might be permitted to accompany them, which request naturally was granted. A gig was readied with all speed, with Delilah between the shafts, and so the two ladies, with the gentlemen riding before, were soon on the road and making for the Peaks.

They proceeded westward through Grim Forest, that vast ocean of evergreen and oak rolling between Lonewater and the Talbots, and in due course came to the little private lane that led to the Peaks. The ground ascended for a time, the trees fell away, and they emerged onto that spacious upland meadow, so very lush and green, in the midst of which stood the Captain's tall tower of a house, rising from its little island of a hill like another Lindisfarne.

Inside they found the Captain with his nose in a bandage, and the bridge of his horn spectacles similarly adorned, and several bruises upon his temple. It turned out he had been struck face-on by a homicidal tree — one *Pinus contorta*, or lodgepole pine — only the day before, while tramping about the woods in an effort to invigorate his scullioned foot.

"So you'll please to note, Squire Mark," said Slack, the dreamy-eyed philosopher, "how it is not just myself who is the cause of the master's mischiefs, for of this one I am wholly innocent, and he instead the guilty dog."

"But you have devoutly wished for it, chuff," returned the Captain, with a stupendous frown, and a warning wag of his bandaged forefinger, "and that itself speaks to your guilt."

"I suppose *that's* true," admitted Slack, sighing. "And so it's true, too, that matters at the Peaks never change — come summer, come winter, come frost, come sun. Pardon for making so free, sir, but what is the point of it all, I ask?"

This deep-rooted mystery of existence would have to be left unsolved, however, at least for the day, as the remainder of the visitors had begun arriving. They gathered in the Captain's study at one corner of the house — nearly every room at the Peaks was a corner room — where the squire, in precise, unsparing terms, described for them the late discoveries he and Oliver had made: the cave at Skylingden point, the well of the Lake Friars and the devils in the pit, the contents of the letter from the locked press at the vicarage, the dismal fate of the ninth squire of Dalroyd. The wonder with which his words were received manifested itself in the faces of his auditors, in the form of undisguised astonishment. The Captain's tiny eyes like buttons exploded behind his spectacle-lenses; Mr. Arkwright's long bushy brow flew up into his helmet of hair; Miss Mowbray uttered a little gasp, and then another, and touched a hand to her lips, while her kindly aunt turned white as a plate.

All sorts of murmurs ran round the room. Even Dr. Hall was amazed at the revelations, and showed it in his own face of pale calfskin. Now at last he understood the nature of those vague feelings of familiarity in the drawing-room at Skylingden.   He had thought at the time that the source was Mr. Wintermarch; but now he saw it was not, that the source was instead the female side of the family, more particularly Mrs. Wintermarch, and that there was no connection at all to the husband — a gentleman who, though he might bear some faint resemblance to Charles Campleman, was certainly not that man. Suddenly it was so very clear to him: in the looking-glass of Mrs. Wintermarch's countenance were indisputable reflections of vicar Marchant's long-dead daughter, and of the old vicar and his wife too. Why had he not seen it earlier? And was there not even something more in those features of the woman named for St. Sepulchre, another few items of physiognomy he could almost just identify — ?

Captain Hoey, cogitating profusely, began pacing the length of the room, to and fro, with his long bold stride — though with still something of a hitch in it from his damned foot — and with such intense concentration of mind, flinging his raw-boned giant of a body wholeheartedly into the effort, with one hand at his back and the other stroking his mustaches, and his button-eyes thrown upon the floor, that the others thought themselves in some danger of being trodden on.

"As a pupil of the *natural* sciences, I believe this phenomenon has assumed a trajectory wholly outside my field of experience," he declared, his voice like a bass viol oddly muted by the bandage occluding his nose. "Though it is provocative, most provocative, I'll be sworn. A real stopper, in point of fact!" Suiting the action to the word, he pulled up and looked fixedly at the squire. "But as to these devils of yours, Markham — this is more or less superstition, not scientific theory."

"A logical deduction, in my view, but not helpful," said Mr. Arkwright, smiling. As the resident scholar of the late abbey and its friars, he was particularly fascinated by what Mark had told them. "The matter is a deep one, and must be sifted further if we're to get anywhere. For instance, what to make of this creature as has been plaguing our dreams? What of the owl at the mansion-house? And what of this owl as drove your father to his death, Mark,

or whatever existence he has there in the well-shaft of the sly monastic gents?
I wonder, then, what's your view of it?"

"I should perhaps invite Mrs. Fielding to answer for me," said the squire,
with a glance to his distant relation, "for as all of us are aware, she is jolly
knowledgeable on matters of popular belief. Is that not so, Auntie?"

The good widow, though she had been anxious to accompany her niece and
the others to the Peaks, had some trouble now as regards her natural reserve,
which left her hesitant to reply; but noting the looks in the eyes of all around
her, and understanding only too well the grimness of the situation, she
overcame her reluctance, particularly after the squire leaned forward in his
chair and said —

"It's the dead girl, is it not?"

Mrs. Fielding, always so amiable and unaffected, nodded slowly and
cautiously.

"You have suspected for some time?"

"Yes."

"Suspected what?" asked the veterinary, not comprehending.

"Ah, the ineluctable consequence of self-slaughter," said a dreamy voice —
not Mrs. Fielding's, but that of the amateur philosopher.

"How do you mean, Slack? Aunt Jane?" asked a puzzled Mags, looking
from the one to the other. "Is this another of your Talbotshire secrets?"

"There is a belief among some, my dear," said Mrs. Fielding, choosing her
words with care, "that those who have taken their own lives on this earth must
inevitably defer their claim to eternal bliss, and their departed souls be refused
entry into the other world, until proper restitution is made in this one. For
suicide, as you well know, is a practice proscribed by our own blessed faith."

"It is further believed," said Slack, taking it up, "that the immaterial essence
of the self-slaughterer may take refuge in any bodily form as may happen upon
it at the point of death, in which it may survive while its measure of earthly
exile is observed, during which time it will be wholly unable to rest."

"You say that the ghost of this girl is in that bird?" exclaimed Captain Hoey.
"Bolts and shackles, man, that's amazing, utterly amazing!"

"I fear it's true," nodded Slack. "I am sure of it. It is her due reward for
her misdeed. But it is, too, her advantage, for the essence will command great
power while in its bodily host; it is, in point of fact, a liberated spirit trapped
between worlds. Once you are dead, I suppose, all sorts of new avenues are
opened to you. Ah, such mysteries, such mysteries!"

"But she is not dead," said Oliver, "or is she? I must admit, I'm rather
confused on that point."

"She is, and she is not," answered the philosopher. "She may be dead so far as her past human existence is concerned, sir, but nonetheless her essence remains abroad in the world, in the shape of a nocturnal rover of the celestial sphere — and, I fear, a something surly and ferocious one. For after you are dead you are no longer really human, are you?"

"By this hand, it's a staggerer!" cried Captain Hoey, with a tremendous slap of his forehead; which action caused him no end of wincing, for he had struck himself square upon his bruised temple. "The trajectory of it," he said, when he had sufficiently recovered, "lies utterly beyond the realm of any natural science with which I am acquainted. Belly-timber for the mind to think on! Though I have remarked many a time how little is known of the caverns and lava tunnels below ground, in this damned volcano of ours, and of the black waters whose depths have yet to be sounded."

"But why not a fish?" spoke up Miss Mowbray.

"Pardon, Miss Margaret?" said Slack.

"If the young woman perished by drowning — in the water, you know — why should it be an owl? Why not a fish?"

"A fish, I suppose, or some other such denizen of the master's black waters, has not the freedom, nor the capacity for wandering, as a passing rover of the mountain skies," replied the philosopher. "Speaking now as a deceased human person, as an essence in search of a new abode, having put a period to my own existence, I should think a fish altogether too — too cold — too foreign — too very *fishy*, for my liking."

"Dr. Hall, you will recollect old Bottom's story of the owl he encountered at the skiff," said Mark.

The physician replied that he did recollect it.

"Ah, I have heard it, too, sir," said Slack.

"Same here," said Mr. Arkwright.

"Same, utterly," added the Captain.

"So much for old Bottom's confidences," the squire observed. "I'll warrant it was the dead girl herself there in the skiff, new-hatched in the body of this owl, and most vilely altered as to disposition and character. Perhaps she was urged by the devils in the pit to make away with herself; perhaps they planted the notion in her head; perhaps they possessed her; or perhaps it was her own idea, the consequence of grief and madness. I have little doubt it was something of the like. But now we must take steps — we must grasp our opportunity while we may — before her aim in returning has been achieved."

"What of Charles Campleman?" asked Mags.

"I myself am convinced he has jolly little to do with this. In fact, I don't believe Charles Campleman is here in the valley at all."

"That's true, Squire Mark," said Slack, "for I have been to the Arms just this morning, where it's said a fat little doctoring fellow, a city man, has confessed that Charles Campleman is a patient of his in the mad-house. And the grave-digger further has admitted that the man at Skylingden is not Campleman, and never has been. Ah, the mysteries!"

Some few moments passed while these latest tidings were digested. It was Miss Mowbray, a young woman herself, who was the first to recognize the simple truth of the matter.

"It is *her* revenge," she said. "It is Miss Marchant's, for having her child taken from her — for having it torn from her arms, and given over to strangers like any common puppy — and for the cruel disregard accorded her by those in the village, the thousand slights and injuries, which drove her to take her life and so has placed her in her present dire state."

She looked round at the others, who were seen nodding in agreement as the strength of her argument took hold.

"What are we to do?" asked the doctor.

"What of the owl?" asked Mr. Arkwright.

"We must harden our hearts," the squire replied, "and capture it."

"Precisely," said the Captain, with a sort of plunge. "We shall ride at once to Skylingden and take possession of it, so that we may examine this remarkable creature for ourselves, this ghostly hawk of the night air. To danger's gate! Now, where is my hat?"

"On the contrary, sir," said Mark. "I can jolly well assure you, the creature will object most vehemently to any such action, as will its rightful keeper, who it appears is the dead girl's own daughter, whether she knows it or not. Consider that this same animal has likely been responsible for the death of old Splayfoot, a full-grown short-face. I myself should not care to tangle with it. There is, however, a safer and more prudent alternative."

The Captain arrested his going long enough to think the point through, then dropped his huge frame into a chair and stretched his legs out before him. "Proceed, Markham," he acquiesced, with a wave of his hand with the bandaged finger on it, and a few noddles of his long bald head.

"I suggest we engage the services of your teratorn."

"Mr. Shakes?" said Slack. "Our own gentleman rover?"

"He has had the experience already, has he not, and on more than one occasion, of scuffling with this owl?"

Here Oliver recalled the noisy clash of the birds in the night air over Dalroyd, the deadly ferocity of the combat, the furious screeches and weird, evil cries. He recalled too the fact that the owl had acquitted itself rather well that night — rather too well, he thought.

"Of course we shall provide assistance to your fellow," the squire went on. "As you know Arkwright here is a dead shot with his bow and birdbolt. If he can disable the creature by clipping one of its wings — cripple it so as to impair its flight — the teratorn can drive it to ground."

Mr. Arkwright, pleased by the squire's appreciation of his talents, agreed to make the attempt. But how were they to go about it, he wanted to know? How to bring the creature and the teratorn together, and he, the bowhunter, within striking distance?

"Not to worry, my vassal the scullioner there will see to it," the Captain assured him. "He has charge of the gentleman. What say you, chuff?"

"I've the very thing," replied the philosopher, "and we've young Mr. Wesley to thank for it."

"Wesley, the joiner's boy?" said Oliver.

"The same, sir. A courageous lad, game to the backbone."

"And what might the very thing be?" asked Mr. Arkwright, naturally much interested.

The philosopher responded with an oracular smile. "Begging pardon for making so free, sir, but might I leave the matter there for now, and say only that the master's hounds haven't a step on Mr. Shakes? Your servant, sir."

The veterinary stared at Slack, stared at Mark, stared at the Captain; the Captain stared back through his horn rims and shrugged. "My vassal there," he said, "though a damned churl and a varletto, and a malapert, is nonetheless a fellow scholar in his way, and a scholar has his methods. Bodikins, Arkwright, if he tells you he can deliver this remarkable creature, believe it."

Now it was the turn of the only one present to raise an objection to the venture so far, to raise it.

"But is this creature not possessed of an imperishable soul?" asked Aunt Jane. "Dare we strike it down in such a manner? I'm afraid I simply cannot agree with you, Mark. Oh, my heart sinks at the horrid idea of it! Would you treat another human being so — would you hunt it down, wound it, cage it up? Who can know what will happen? What if it does not turn out as you expect? What if the animal dies — would that not be the same as murder? And if it dies, what might be the consequence? Something far worse, perhaps!"

Much affected by gloomy forebodings and ominous fancies, the widow retreated into herself. The many wrinkles time had traced about her kind eyes and face served to heighten the anxiousness of her expression.

"But, Auntie — " Mark began.

"You might just as well save your breath, cousin," said Mags, placing a hand upon her aunt's shoulder. "She is not disposed to second this scheme of yours, and frankly, neither am I."

"Cousin!" exclaimed the squire, taken aback by this further defection.

"My dear young madam!" cried the Captain.

Despite whatever deeper feelings she may still have harbored for her cousin the squire — feelings she knew would only come to naught — Miss Mowbray held her ground and would not be moved. But as neither she nor her aunt had any clear alternative to offer, to prevent Miss Marchant — or whatever remained of a vicar's daughter behind those fiercely glowing eyes — from doing whatever it was she meant to do, their resistance produced no profitable result.

In short, the men were very keen on proceeding, the ladies were not. But as there were six of them (the men) and but two of the other (the ladies), the motion was carried. And so the council of war broke up.

"Though it does hardly seem like sporting odds, in my view, winging the bird that way," said Mr. Arkwright, as he stopped to put out his cigar.

"They are exactly the same odds my father had," said Mark.

CHAPTER XIV

The Battle on the Moon

"By the by, Noll — would you care to hear another thing my father told me?" asked the squire, of his friend from the city.

The two had remained in the Captain's study, while the Captain himself and Slack had gone about certain preparations for the interesting exercise to come. The doctor had rattled off in his trap to one of his patients in the neighborhood, to whom he had pledged a consultation, after which he intended to return, while Mr. Arkwright had struck out for Timber Hill Farm to fetch his bow and bolts. The recalcitrant ladies of Gray Lodge, unable to be persuaded of the folly of their position, had departed for home, but not before lofting one final unsuccessful plea for the gentlemen to come to their senses.

"I don't know if I should," said Oliver — in reply to the squire's inquiry, not the ladies' plea — "for what you have told me already is unsettling enough. This contest we are about to engage in has my nerves in a state, and we have not yet had even a sighting of the creature."

The squire smiled as he relaxed upon the Captain's sofa, his hands clasped behind his head, his eyes floating about the room in a meditative haze.

"What if I were to tell you, Noll," he said, a little mysteriously, "that much of what you and your churchly acquaintances know of heaven and earth, in a philosophical sense, and of mankind's place in the world, is so much humbug? So much jolly stuff and nonsense, as you yourself might term it."

"I should say you were either a prophet, a drunkard, or very much in need of Dr. Hall's assistance," said Oliver, having regained the chair he had occupied during the council of war.

The squire smiled again as his eyes roamed about the walls of the study, and the grave old faces keeping guard in oil and varnish, and the lengthy rows of books and the Captain's weather-glass and his other instruments there, and the tall bright windows.

"The hobgoblins in the pit," he went on, "are only too happy to offer you the things you desire or require, or believe that you desire or require, and will lay them before your astonished optics like so many pretty gifts at Christmas-week, all tied up with promises of joy and life without end. It is a jolly appealing prospect, I can assure you, to have such a treasure freely within your grasp. With this and other like encouragements they will draw you in, just as my father and I used to draw in our catch at Dalroyd dock. Just as they lured the ancient friars and young Campleman and who knows how many more to the brink of madness, and beyond — for madness is the result when a mortal intellect is confronted with the infinite. So would madness have come to me had my father not intervened. The disproportion between the finite and the infinite, you see, is too vast for earthly brains to contemplate; only by joining with it can the infinite be looked in the face. But once one has been inhaled by the pit and united with the inky void, then will one discover that the promised treasures are all so much straw. Oh, it is eternity all right, have no doubt of that — an eternity spent in worshipful servitude to a horde of hobgoblins."

"These ideas of yours, Mark, I admit I find rather disturbing," said Oliver, sure now that he wanted to hear no more about the pit or its inhabitants, but just as sure he would. "I simply cannot accept them. Likely they are the combined product of your nightmares, low spirits, and over-fatigues."

"Suppose, Noll," persisted the squire, musingly, "suppose that so far as the 'other world' is concerned, this promised heaven of yours, this eternal bliss of Auntie's — suppose that it instead is a realm of devils, a vast inky void governed by hobgoblins, and nothing more?"

"I would as lief believe in nothing beyond this present existence — nothing but oblivion, and the fragmentation of consciousness — as I would a dark heaven ruled by devils. But you must concede, Mark, if there are devils then surely there must be an Almighty."

"Ha!" exclaimed the squire, abruptly snapping his fingers and rising. "You must absolutely scrub your mind of all such received opinion. Scrub your mind of your accursed faith! Imagine instead, Noll, that there are *only* hobgoblins. Imagine that this so-styled transcendent 'Almighty' of yours is simply a fabrication of mortal intellect, an abstract ideal created in response to the very real threat of devils? Is it not jolly comforting, to credulous sorts like yourself, to believe that a mighty God of goodness holds sway over fallen angels? For if devils be nothing but fallen angels, it diminishes something of their power, does it not? Fallen angels are much less to be feared than mighty gods. But if, in truth, these hobgoblins *are* mighty gods — and there is no overruling force to restrain them, no just and powerful Almighty — what hope can there be for humankind?"

"It is a quelling thought, and a horrid one, and I can only pray that you are wrong," declared Oliver, wondering now if perhaps the finite and the infinite had indeed come to blows inside the brain of the squire, and if his friend were not in danger of going mad. "It shivers me to the quick to think there may be no goodness in the other world. Eternity in a dark heaven or in the pit is not a happy choice. But aren't you being just a trifle excessive? What have you become, a sort of Albigensian in reverse? When before you were nothing at all, from what I could tell, aside from the lounging master of Dalroyd and a firm non-believer. Sometimes, Mark, I simply cannot make you out."

"You must admit, Noll, that it goes jolly far towards explaining this sorry world of ours. It can for instance explain such a despicable business as the coach upset at Crow's-end, on the cliff road, and the passengers flung to their deaths in the icy water below, among their number the pair of children, brother and sister, not yet five years of age. An act of God, is that not the term for it? Why not an act of hobgoblins? This world of ours is simply made for them. Would a God of goodness allow the pit to exist? Would a God of goodness have condemned this girl, this suicide, to the lot she has drawn? Has it not occurred to you, Noll, that your vaunted Almighty might be a jolly fine monster in private life? Or belike He's an entire troop of them!"

The eyes of Oliver expressed the objections his lips had not the chance to utter.

"I did not think you would hear me, any more than our fine vicar has," the squire ran on, folding his arms and settling himself again on the cushioned sofa. "He's too jolly comfortable there with his living, and his tithes, and his rates, and his wife, and his parsonage-house, and his garden, and his violoncello. Well, I don't care a fig. And look here, I'll tell you another thing, Noll" — (Oliver inwardly steeling himself against a further revelation) — "I was forewarned of this. Oh, I see the doubt and mistrust in your face there. I was forewarned, Noll — we were forewarned, in point of fact — and we did not heed the warning."

"When were we warned, and by whom?" asked Oliver.

"By the old clergyman that morning at Dalroyd dock. By the vicar Marchant himself! Surely you recollect the questions the fellow put to us, when he and his yokemate came stealing out of the mist? 'Have you seen our Edith? Have you seen our girl?'"

"It seems to be well established that the old couple roamed the lakeshore for some time after their daughter's disappearance, searching for her body, and never found it, and that they died of broken hearts. Hence the vicar's inquiry."

"Only partly true, Noll, for it was not an inquiry at all but a warning, intended for me, to beware their daughter. Have you not grasped the significance of it? 'Have you seen our girl? Have you seen our Edith? *SHE IS HERE!*'"

Oliver drew a heavy breath. He had not before considered the old clergyman's words in such a light; but neither, he knew, had the squire, until now.

"They understood jolly well that I, as the son and heir of their nearest friend, the ninth squire, should be an object of her wrath, and so came to warn me," said Mark. "My father was her first victim, for the part he had played in having her removed to Crow's-end, and her child given over to the worthy Society of St. Sepulchre for the dispersal of inconvenient offspring. My father was the architect of the plan, taking it all upon himself in order to spare his friend the vicar the trial of it, and as a result suffered the consequences. Why, I should not be surprised if the vicar Marchant and his wife themselves did not perish from something more tangible than 'broken hearts.' Perhaps they were affrighted by something that came to them in the night? Do not gawk at me so, Noll, for I understand perfectly what I am saying. You must remember, we are not dealing here with anything *human*, as Slack so rightly pointed out to us. And if you should care to know another thing — "

"I should rather not," Oliver replied, steeling himself again. "All you say makes my flesh creep."

"Look here, where do you suppose she has been for most of these eight-and-twenty years? With her child, naturally! I'll lay you fifty guineas — no, make that an even hundred guineas — that this creature has been at the child's side from her early infancy. Now the child is grown and has a child of her own. Do you recollect the wife's response there in the drawing-room at Skylingden, when asked by you, Noll, how she had fixed upon our little hamlet to settle in? 'I don't quite know why I chose it, a kind of feeling, I suppose, which told me we belonged here.' I'll lay you another golden guinea this 'feeling' came to her in the shape of a dream, and we both of us know something of dreams, don't we? It was that creature that induced her and her family to settle here, so that *it* might settle its score with the rest of us."

"I have had dreams similar to yours and those of others in the village. But what have I had to do with Miss Marchant's reversals in life?" Oliver countered.

"Not a jolly thing," replied Mark, with a little shake of his head. "Absolutely nothing. But you are here, Noll, you are simply *here*, in Shilston Upcot, in Talbotshire, in the summertime — and you are in her way."

This unpleasant discussion Oliver was only too glad to see terminated by the reappearance of Slack, who informed them that matters now were nearly in readiness.

Together the three climbed the several flights of stairs to the landing with the French windows in it, and issued forth onto the parapet. There, one by one, they bounded across the swaying plank-bridge to the villa in the clumber pine. As before Oliver was more than a trifle anxious as regards his leap over the unsteady boards, sure that he would be dashed to ruin upon the ground so far below. But the cords and cross-ties of the suspension held, for the few seconds that were required for him to scamper across; and so he found himself once more aboard the Captain's ingenious cottage in the tree-tops. There the three of them were reunited with the Captain, who was busy about his spyglass. The servant went at once to the chest of drawers, and removed from it some few items of a slender and delicate appearance, wrapped up in cloth.

"What have you got there, Slack?" Oliver asked. "Is this part of your secret armamentarium?"

"It is, Mr. Oliver, sir," replied the philosopher, with a sigh. "It is, in point of fact, the whole of it. Apart from the gentleman rover, of course."

The servant extended a gloved hand. Resting in the hollow of it were three golden brown flight-feathers.

"I acquired them from young Wesley," he explained. "He offered them to me, not long ago, in exchange for a goose-pie and some larchberry pudding with which to surprise his old grandmother. It is plumage from the owl, sirs! Yes, yes, please to examine the feathers — there is one for each of you. They are so very light and soft, are they not? Such pliancy makes for noiseless flight, I am told. It occurred to me that they might some day be of use to someone."

The Captain too was enormously interested, for he had not laid his button-eyes upon them before.

"I'll be sworn, I'd no idea my vassal the scullioner had possession of such rarities, elsewise I should have appropriated them," he rumbled, and proceeded to make a close inspection of the feather at hand, by holding it up to his bandaged spectacles and running his tiny eyes over every detail of it. "Precisely — it is owly plumage indeed — genus *Strix* of the Accipitres of Linnaeus — hawks of the night air — note the absence of the aftershaft — and at the base of the quill there the *inferior umbilicus*, which once opened into the follicle and through which the blood of this remarkable creature once flowed — utterly amazing!"

"However did the boy obtain them?" Oliver asked.

"It was during one of his visits to the mansion-house with his master, to make some small improvements about the property," replied Slack. "As they were departing, very late in the day, he saw a lady in a top-floor room off the gallery release the creature from a window. The lady, he claimed, was none other than the mistress of the house. He stayed behind, and when she had gone snatched up some feathers he saw lying about the floor. Very game of the lad, sir, very game!"

"And what are we to do with them?"

"Begging pardon, sir," said the little servant, "but it is not a question of what *we* are to do with them, but what our gentleman rover is to do with them."

The sun had by now slipped behind the long curtain of the Talbots; already that very bright, very clear, very cold piece of celestial stoneware known as the moon, painted over with markings like a human face, was rising to supplant it. It looked to be a very full face that would be shining in the sky this night.

The gentlemen were soon joined in the villa by Dr. Hall. Not long after, a shout from below announced the arrival of Tony Arkwright, and with him his own armamentarium of quite another sort. The Captain, turning from his spyglass, called down to the veterinary to maintain his post there; after which he nodded to Mark and the others to indicate that he and the glass were prepared.

"Our Mr. Shakes already has paid his call for the day, here at the sky-house, and received his ration of fish and saveloys," said Slack, with a glance at the chime-clock. "But since he was a tiny lad — since he was Tiny Osbert, in fact — he has become practiced in responding to the call of a wood whistle. At such time of day he often is in the vicinity, behind us there, in the depths of Grim Forest, and within range of hearing. If he so chooses he may come to us. Of course, he has been much distracted of late; perhaps he will not answer."

The Captain had another look through the glass. Slowly he swung the tube to the southeast, towards the distant inlet and Skylingden above it. He located the topmost tier of windows of the mansion-house, and the one window in particular that he knew very well by now — the window at which he had on several occasions observed the release of the huge owl, by the woman with the odd mixture of resentment, resignation, and fear in her eyes. She was no servant, he knew, but apart from that he had known little else, until the recent market Friday, when he had for the first time glimpsed the Wintermarch ladies there in the Low Street.

"That is how *I* identified her," he said, squinting through the eyepiece, "as the wifely Wintermarch. I hadn't the benefit of the joiner's boy's intelligence, for it seems my vassal the scullioner there neglected to inform me of it. So there's a pinch for stale news. And bodikins," he exclaimed — "there *is* the lady!"

He surrendered the glass to Mark, who in his turn surrendered it to Oliver, who then surrendered it to Dr. Hall. They saw that the curtains had been drawn aside and the sash raised, and that Mrs. Sepulchra Wintermarch was standing at the window. Just as the glass was returned to the Captain the woman's somber figure vanished from sight; after another moment or two the owl appeared and launched itself from the window-ledge.

"Bird's away, chuff!" cried the Captain.

Hearing this, Slack removed a tiny carved whistle from his waistcoat-pocket, and going to one of the open windows of the villa, placed the instrument to his lips, inhaled deeply, and blew. The result was an extraordinarily high-pitched and strident blast of sound, so piercing that the visitors immediately clapped hands to ears to shield themselves from the force of it. The servant hastily apologized for not apprising them beforehand of the impending discomfort, then promptly released two blasts more.

"A wood whistle," said the Captain, commiserating, "can be a damned noisome business. And a real stopper!"

As the daylight continued to fade and the moon continued to rise, the gentlemen waited for some response to the call. When none came they waited some more, hoping for an answer before the light dimmed too far for Mr. Arkwright to employ his armamentarium.

Fortunately the response was not much longer in coming. A harsh, eerie cry, wilder and more unearthly even than that of the wood whistle, split the air, and split the tree too it seemed, for it was followed at once by a severe jolting and jarring of the villa. The drowsy light was blotted out of the east window; huge talons like razors gripped the sill as an immense vulture-like form thrust itself into the window-space.

For the second time Oliver was forced to rein in his alarm at sight of the crimson head and pitchy dark body of the teratorn. It was so very difficult for him, a city man, to conquer his natural disaffinity for this evil winged omen of the skies. A teratorn was, no matter how strongly Slack or the Captain or even Mark might beg to differ, an ill-looking bird. With its sharp cold eyes it was examining the inhabitants of the villa, especially Dr. Hall and the stranger from Crow's-end, with similar thoughts perhaps as to the ill-lookingness of human beings. Yet seeing the body of the monster jammed into the window-space there, with its crimson head so grim and forbidding, and its folded black wings so sedate, and its stance so clerical, Oliver could not help but be reminded of a reverend archdeacon of the Church in a party-hat.

The philosopher stepped to the window and delivered up a stream of those kindly words and phrases, which were intended to comfort the evil winged omen and assure it that all was right. The bird responded at once — there was no question of its and the little servant's being on anything but the best of terms — another sight that filled the city man Oliver with perfect wonder. Even the Captain joined in with his voice like a bass viol, still muted somewhat by the bandage on his nose.

When they had done placating the bird, Slack held out before it the three feathers, which the teratorn's cold gaze immediately fixed upon. The monster extended its head downwards and forwards until the fearsome beak lay just alongside them. The head was then gently turned, first the one way and then the another, and the nostrils on either side of it drawn slowly past the feathers

— for like certain of the vultures and as well the Captain's hounds, teratorns are a species capable of tracking by scent.

Another few murmured words of comfort from Slack, and what sounded like an instruction, and the crimson head and hat of the archdeacon abruptly reared up. It seemed to Oliver that the bird must have recognized the odor; and as well perhaps it should, for was it not the odor of an enemy the monster had engaged on more than a few occasions before?

Without further notice the teratorn leaned out from the sill and flung itself off, leaving the clumber pine and the villa quivering in its wake.

"He's making straight for the mansion-house," reported the Captain, peering through his glass.

"Good old fellow!" said Slack.

"What was that last command you gave him?" Oliver inquired.

"Asking pardon for making so free, Mr. Oliver, sir, but it was not a command," replied the servant, hastily. "One does not command Mr. Shakes. I merely *requested* that he fetch." At which point the dreamy-eyed Slack, reverting to his philosophical and rather more Mrs. Fielding-like state, turned away and murmured to himself, in a kind of aside, "And what the result of it will be now I know not, though I fear it could be very bad!"

The Captain craned out from the south window and called to the veterinary below —

"We're down directly!"

In quick order they abandoned the villa, making their way back across the plank-bridge and down the several flights of stairs to the foot of the Peaks, where the horses had been assembled by the Captain's superannuated stable-hand. The doctor's horse had been taken out of the shafts and a saddle fastened on, the better for the doctor to ride him by, and a gamebag for the capturing of the quarry buckled to the saddle of the Captain's own tall mount. A number of the hounds had been released from the kennel and were playing round the feet of the horses. The scent of the quarry was given them now by Slack, while the Captain and the others mounted into the stirrups and joined Mr. Arkwright in riding forth upon the meadow.

"Good luck to you, gentlemen!" the philosopher called aloud; then, with one or two dismal turns of his head, began muttering again to himself as he watched from the steps. "What is the point of it all, I ask? What will it get us? I fear I've grown rather hippish of late. Shall we live to see another Michaelmas, I wonder? Oh, why did I keep these feathers? I should have refused them. But I fear we must now stand the hazard of the die. Life's an odd sort of play — how very inconsequential, how very transient, how very parlous is our time upon the boards — and the playwright a lunatic, one with oysters for brains, and vinegar in his belly, and blood of marigold tea. Write me no words, mad sir, and sing me no songs, for likely we're doomed, however things turn out today — ah, the mysteries!"

Already the noises of battle were in the air. The teratorn had been swift about its purpose; it had flown in a direct line towards the promontory and there engaged the owl in the quiet of Skylingden Wood. By means of various clever dodges and maneuvers it had succeeded in driving its opponent out of the forest and across the inlet, where it altered its strategy and instead allowed itself to be pursued in the direction of the Peaks. No sooner had the riders gathered together in the midst of the meadow than the winged combatants came streaking overhead, filling the air with their wild screeches and weird evil cries.

Whirling and diving they fell to there in the sky, as the giant moon rose up behind them. Its placement in the heavens was such that the greater part of the battle was observed in a kind of silhouette, as the darting forms of the contenders beat and slashed their way across its cold bright face. Time and again the two of them met there on the moon, the owl warring and thrusting in a show of frenzied violence against the larger teratorn. More often than not it was the owl that plunged and struck, more often than not the teratorn that parried. After a while there could be little doubt of it — the owl was surely, gradually overwhelming its opponent, crashing and colliding with the reverend archdeacon in what Mark could only describe as a tempest of supernatural fury. Both the squire and Oliver understood now why there had been no gatekeeper at Skylingden, and no need of one, and why the birds in the high wood had gone silent since the arrival of Mr. Bede Wintermarch and his *ménage*.

While the others were observing the progress of the combat, Mr. Arkwright dismounted and made ready his armamentarium. He donned his bracer and glove and threw his quiver across his shoulder. Stepping forward he drew his bow, aimed, and loosed the first of his arrows at the target. It was a dicey business, for the target was uncommonly agile, and he dared not by accident harm the teratorn; he could let fly only when the birds for brief moments had drawn apart in preparation for a fresh assault. Even so most of his bolts went wide, missing the target by a considerable margin. A more difficult task the veterinary had not encountered for quite some while, in the exercise of his special talent; but he was resolved he would not be beaten.

Again the contenders engaged, again they separated. The teratorn, visibly tiring of the combat, dropped down and away and flattened its wings as it described a broad circle around the meadow. The owl glared at it from on high, and rather than giving chase remained suspended in the air with its tail-feathers spread. Mr. Arkwright immediately saw his opportunity. He nocked another arrow and raised his bow, with his arms at nearly full stretch; he anchored, aimed, released; the string *thupped* and the arrow went flying in a swish of wind.

The owl spun about with a bone-chilling cry of pain and surprise. The arrow had pierced it cleanly. Even from a distance Mr. Arkwright could see the green phosphoric eyes glowing in the creature's head, the fierce and startled look as it searched the ground for a new enemy. One of its wings was clearly damaged; it was having trouble raising it sufficiently to maintain altitude. At that moment Mr. Shakes came gliding round in his orbit of the meadow, and noting the owl's predicament launched an attack. Despite its injury the bird was still able to navigate, however unsteadily, forcing Mr. Arkwright to prepare another arrow. Before he could loose it, however, the owl, having evaded the plunging teratorn, went flirting and fluttering across the meadow and over the trees, in the direction of the village.

"By this hand, it's cut its lucky!" cried the Captain, spurring his horse into a canter. "Forward, hounds, forward!"

With the dogs yelping round him the boldest rider in Talbotshire led the charge into the twilight of the forest. Closest on his heels came the squire and Oliver, followed by the doctor, then Mr. Arkwright with his bow and bolts. They turned from the little private lane into the coach-road and made direct for Shilston Upcot, the Captain in his enormous black riding-cloak and floppy hat sounding a kind of vocal hunt's-up at the head of them. Then the boldest rider in Talbotshire really crammed away, breaking out into a gallop and putting considerable ground between himself and the others, and was quickly lost to the bends in the road and the gathering dusk. The hounds too seemed to melt away, though their voices could be heard ringing like a ghostly chorus through the vast lonely wood.

The squire and Oliver had given the spurs to their own nags, but Tinker and the chestnut were not blooded hunters and so no match for the Captain's mount. Mr. Arkwright had been slowed by the need to regain his saddle, and the doctor by the age of his old trap-horse. There was some delay then before they bounded through the crossroads and gained the top of the Low Street, which at that hour was largely void of activity. What activity there was in the village at such an hour was pretty much confined to the Arms, which could be seen glowing like a lantern in the trees above Town End. They searched the immediate area but found only a couple of tradesmen shutting up their shops. There was no sign of Captain Hoey and the hounds nor of Mr. Shakes. More than likely the teratorn had wearied of the combat and flown off to seek easier prey; as for the Captain, who could tell?

The squire was plainly disappointed. Ordinarily he was a fine huntsman and Tinker a serviceable horse in the field, but this was no occasion for hunting-pink and no common hunt. He and the others would have to trust that the boldest rider in Talbotshire was even now closing in on the quarry.

In speaking to the tradesmen they learned that the Captain and some hounds had passed by at a lively clip ("Slap dash," as one fellow termed it, "and not so long ago, neither.") So they pressed on, knowing now that the trail led into the village, and were exploring round the purlieus of St. Lucy's when they heard again the voices of the dogs, though very much subdued; then the Captain himself came riding out of a by-lane with his cutlass drawn. Behind him rode Mr. Coddy Binks, the little hunting chemist, who had heard the baying of hounds and automatically sprung upon a horse to join the field. The hounds, however, appeared to have lost interest in the chase and were milling about in confusion, with much whining and fretting, and tails a-droop, and anxiety staining their furry countenances. It was as if they had caught a glimpse of the quarry and found it not at all to their liking.

The Captain's frustration showed on his own face, as he drew bridle and paused to straighten his hat in the liquid glare of the moon.

"The remarkable creature has eluded us," he announced.

CHAPTER XV

PURSUIT BY OWL-LIGHT

MR. Shank Bottom, abiding there in his small hut of a workshop behind church and vicarage, in the loom of the ancient churchyard trees, had heard the noises of the chase and was immediately concerned. It was a reflex on the part of Mr. Bottom; he could not help himself, for there were spirits all about him, as he himself would have told thee true. He laid aside his pipe and his wicker-bottle of grog — which vessel harbored an altogether different kind of spirit — and glanced round him with a searching distrust into the remoter corners of his workshop. With fear and suspicion his eyes glided about those places where the light of the turf-fire did not reach, as though he half-expected to find something monstrous there in the shadows. When he found nothing of the sort his hard features relaxed a little; his eyes returned to his pleasant bit of fire, his pipe to his mouth, and his bottle to his lips.

After a time, once the noises had died away and he had imbibed a sufficient quantity of his nectar to sustain him, he rose and went to the window. Peering out he thought for a moment he saw something dart across the sky overhead, and light upon one of the fir-trees in the churchyard; but he could not be sure. He returned to his bottle for another nip of grog, to cheer himself, and gnawed upon some cheese, and warmed his hands at the fire, before resuming his post. As he watched he saw a heavy form drop to the ground, from the branches of the fir-tree, and begin advancing with a stiff, birdlike gait, straight through the church-garden and towards his own door, with what seemed to Mr. Bottom like no very pleasant intent. It was, he saw, an owl of quite extraordinary dimensions, with two green phosphoric eyes and a white face, and two tufts of feathers or "horns" projecting from its head. One of its wings was being carried at an odd angle, as though it had been injured. The mind of the sexton flew back to a certain dread morning on the water, many years past, and to the unholy evil sort of thing that had confronted him in the abandoned skiff. The very hairs of his old scratch-wig seemed to rise up on his head; his collar started to wilt; in a qualm of panic he rubbed the gray stone-dust from his brow and began making preparation to flee.

It was then he heard sounds in the road that betokened the approach of riders. The unholy evil sort of thing heard them too, and crept silently off. Shortly after there came a brisk rap at the door. The sexton looked out to behold the master of Dalroyd and his visitor from the city there on the step, with neither an injured wing nor wild phosphoric eye between them. Still, he could not be too careful.

He pried open the door a few scant inches, and inquired in gruff tones into the nature of the gentlemen's business. The squire answered with a question of his own, as to whether or no the sexton had seen the Skylingden owl of late? Mr. Bottom said he had not, that he knew nowt about the Skylingden owl, and that he didn't care to know nowt about it and neither should thee. The gentlemen advised him to keep a sharp look-out, as the creature had been wounded and was loose somewhere in the neighborhood, and very likely much perturbed.

Footsteps were heard behind them in the gravel walk. It was the vicar, who had been dispatched by his wife to learn something of the recent commotion in the Low Street — which, what with his violoncello and the maestro Raviola's daunting exercises, had largely escaped his notice. Mark and Oliver were undecided how far to trust the reverend clergyman, for they knew he would be both skeptical and appalled; so they merely reiterated what they had told Mr. Bottom, that the owl from Skylingden had been injured and was in a right state and jolly dangerous, and that any sighting of it should be reported to neighbors. The vicar adjusted his spectacles and thanked the gentlemen for the warning, and returned to the parsonage-house — glancing uneasily to all sides of him as he stepped along the walk — there to mollify his pretty red-haired wife and resume his communion with his musical muse.

Both the squire and Oliver were of a mind now that they should divide their forces, as the other members of the party already had done, so that they might search the village streets and the neighboring district to greater effect. Suiting the action to the word, then, they separated, each going his own way with his cutlass at the ready.

Mrs. Dinah Scattergood, having been briefed by her husband as regards the matter pertaining — and having made an appropriate face at mention of the name of Mark Trench — duly released her helpmate from his obligation, with a slim murmur of thanks; whereupon the reverend gentleman took up his 'cello and his Raviola, while Dinah returned to her boudoir and her knitting.

Now in this boudoir of hers was a fair-sized window, of clumsy sashes and square latticed panes, a window that, sitting two flights above ground with nothing but dead wall around it, was consequently without bars, as they had been deemed superfluous. This same window of clumsy sashes being now open a little to the air, Dinah became conscious, by gradual degrees, of a subtle noise like scratching from just outside it. Having relegated what the squire of Dalroyd had told her husband to her mind's drawer labeled "Ridiculous in the Extreme," she boldly went to the window to see what the cause of the noise was. She raised the glass a little and looked out into the dusky moonlight, through the aperture between the sash and the sill, but saw nothing; nothing below her, nothing to the right of her, nothing to the left of her. Drawing in her head she resumed her wifely employment, only to hear again, very soon after, the subtle noise like scratching, followed by a moan.

She returned to the window and lifting the heavy sash opened it the wider. Again she found nothing; again she resumed her knitting. Some moments more of pleasant employment followed, before the air was torn by an almighty crash, as a huge bird came flying out of the night. It had thrown itself against the window and was making every effort to squeeze through into the room. It was a horrible, ghastly thing, with a scowling face and fierce green eyes, and blood strewn everywhere about its plumage. At sight of it Dinah cried out and tossed up her needles and knitting. Her husband's 'cello in the adjacent room instantly went silent, as the good vicar himself came dashing in with bow in hand. Taking quick stock of the situation he leaped valorously to his wife's defense.

The creature was struggling to force itself through the opening, and so the vicar did the only thing left to him to do — he lunged at it with the point of his bow, like a duellist wielding his small-sword, to drive the intruder back out into the night. His wife took up a position safely behind him, urging him on with an excited rush of warning cries and frenzied commands. The vicar lunged and leaped, pressed and jabbed, engaged and disengaged, landing hit upon hit; though his weapon was of but a slim and fragile construction, as compared to the owl's vicious claws and snapping beak, which responded furiously to his every thrust. In the end, however, he managed to ward the creature off, though not before causing considerable harm to the fabric of his small-sword.

After closing the window and drawing the shutters, the vicar raced down the staircase and out the door. Despite his apprehension as regards his own safety, he was determined to warn his neighbors as the squire and Oliver had advised him; it was, after all, the charitable thing to do. At that moment he heard a rider coming along the street, and recognized him as none other than Mr. Langley himself. The visitor from Crow's-end had just completed a search of the lanes nearby, without result. The vicar quickly described what had happened and pointed him in a new direction, to the southwest, up and away from the Low Street towards that part of the village lying by the foot of the Skylingden road.

Oliver hurried off at a brisk trot, his eyes and ears very much on the alert. He caught glimpses of a birdlike shape fluttering in the beams of moonlight, first over here, then over there, as it hopped from one tall castle of a tree to another. His suspicions were further raised by his mare, who had begun to snort and shake her head, and voice little anxious cries of protest, in sign of a growing restiveness. He patted her neck to reassure her as best he could, while spurring her on in the indicated direction.

By now he had passed a number of cottages, the inhabitants of which could be seen gazing curiously through the bars of lighted windows, or standing at open doors or on household steps, in some puzzlement as to the significance of the riders heard galloping about in the streets, and the baying of the hounds, which had attracted notice over the last hour. But as it was far too complicated a matter to explain in a few words, Oliver, as he ambled past, merely touched his hat-brim and trotted on.

The way led upward over some loose ground to the brow of a hill, where a line of cozy villas commanded broad views of the lakeshore from the foot of the Skylingden road, before that avenue commenced its climb towards the promontory and the mansion-house. Oliver spotted a green light flitting about the timber at the back of the villas, and made for it apace. After searching the woods for a time it seemed he must have lost the track, for he had no further sighting of it; nonetheless the chestnut was behaving as though something in the vicinity was very much amiss. Oliver exercised his eyes as keenly as possible, to identify anything suspicious in the cathedral of trees looming about him, but without success.

Debating how next to proceed, he drew bridle beneath a shaggy drooping pine; but as the chestnut seemed even more restless there, he made almost at once to go on, when something like a drop of rain splashed from the brim of his hat. Oliver wondered how a drop of rain could possibly have gotten there, for it was a cloudless sky in which the full moon was shining; and yet there it was, a drop of dark liquid; and there was another, falling upon his coat-sleeve. As he bent to examine it a third drop landed on his riding-glove. He looked at it disbelievingly, for it was a *very* dark drop, not at all like rain. He raised his eyes — another drop, a hot, steamy one, fell on his cheek, and rolled part-way down it — and found his gaze returned by two eyes of a wholly different sort, no more than a few feet off: two huge, green, phosphoric orbs, staring fixedly at him from an overhanging branch.

A predatory hiss, a snapping and clattering of the beak, attended the stare; the body of the owl swayed to and fro on the branch with a slow, hypnotic motion. For the briefest instant the head of the creature winked from sight, its place taken by a woman's head with draggled dark hair, and teeth bared in a fearsome rage, and the fierce green light shining through the two pits in her skull where her eyeballs once sat; then in the next moment it was an owlish face again. The next Oliver knew there was a wild cry, a rush of wind, a storm of feathers, and the vile thing was upon him.

The weight of his assailant rolled him from the saddle. He fell to the ground, lightly stunned, and clutching his shoulder, which he thought surely must have been broken for it was hurting him enough. The drops of rain from a cloudless sky had been drops of blood, from the creature's damaged wing and other injuries; though the loss of this vital fluid appeared to have little effect upon the savagery of its attack. Its claws and beak tore at his thick riding-coat and underjacket as they would have torn at his mortal flesh. His cutlass was all but useless to him, for it had gone sailing into the underwood as he fell; likewise his horse, who had fled in terror at sight of the owl. And his shoulder pained him so.

He tried to protect himself by rolling up into a ball and covering his head with his wide-awake. He lashed out with his available arm, in hopes of keeping the creature at bay, but it was an unnaturally large and heavy owl and not about to be dissuaded. He knew he could not endure many seconds before the bird's fearful weaponry cut a path through his clothing. He shouted for assistance, praying that someone at the villas might hear him; but as he was a little apart from them there, in the lonely wood, there was not so much chance of a rescue as he might have supposed.

Then it was he heard another sound, the most welcome of sounds he could have imagined, coming not from the villas but from the forest demesne itself — the clattering sound of shoe-iron bounding over turf, and the jingle of bridle-bits — the sound of a rider approaching at a good lick; then the sound of a horse squealing, and the noise of boots and spurs striking the earth as the rider dismounted. Lifting his hat and peering across his good shoulder, Oliver beheld there the tall, horsy shape of Tinker — great, ugly, barrel-chested, sixteen-hands, incomparable, majestic, magnificent, fiddle-faced Tinker, panting and snorting — and beside him the squire of Dalroyd with his cutlass raised.

"Cover your face, Noll, cover your face!" commanded Mark.

Oliver instantly obeyed. He heard the deadly swish of steel through air, the wild screeches of the owl, the cries of Tinker, the groaning and grunting of the squire as he wielded his blade. He peered again from under his hat; what he saw both fascinated and horrified him. It was Mark — his eyes ablaze with a fearsome rage, like the mad, blazing fury of revenge — both hands gripping his sword and heaving it viciously from side to side — this way, that way, this way, that way, in great, furious lunges — as though he meant to erase from the sight of mankind every last minute particle of the creature, which so far however had managed to evade his every thrust.

"No, Mark, no! It is she! It is the poor drowned girl! Gracious God, you must not destroy her!" cried Oliver.

Too late. The bird faltered for just an instant, long enough for the squire to deal it a tremendous blow, a towering blow. The creature howled, crumpled, started up, staggered, escaped another swing of the blade, then leaped into the air and flew off toward the line of villas.

"How are you, old Noll?" gasped Mark, panting and snorting not a little like Tinker, as he knelt beside his friend. "Are you injured? Anything damaged?"

"My shoulder," Oliver complained, raising himself to a sitting posture and grimacing. "I have broken something in it, I fear. It pains me terribly."

"We must find the doctor at once," said the squire, with the utmost concern.

"No! No — most likely I shall recover, to be sure," said Oliver, looking pale and weak. "You must go after her before she assaults another. She already has attacked the vicar's wife. But you must capture her, you must not further harm her. It was *she* — Miss Marchant — I saw her face, Mark! Where has Captain Hoey gotten to?"

"The boldest rider in Talbotshire appears to have ridden straight out of the county. By the by, Noll, where is your mare? Where is the chestnut?"

"Took fright and bolted."

"Ha! And what shall we do with you now?"

"Leave me," said Oliver. "There is blessed little you can do for me. Allow me to rest here. It will give my nerves time to settle themselves. I shall wait for you."

The squire paused, uncertain how to proceed. Then he smiled one of his crooked smiles, grasped his friend's arm — his good arm, that is — and exclaimed, "Stout fellow, Noll, upon my life!" Then he was in the stirrups and away.

The owl's track was simpler to follow now, for the creature was making a considerable disturbance as it went bouncing from tree to tree. If the hounds had been in the field they would have quickly trailed it down. Bolts and shackles, Mark thought, where was Hoey and his gamebag for the capturing of it?

He emerged from the woods onto the brow of the hill. Before him lay the dark flat expanse of the lake, with the moonlight reflected in its gently rippling waters; to his right lay the villas, very prettily situated at the foot of the Skylingden road. One of these houses, a spacious stone-built cottage that sat atop a little rise of ground, proudly overlooking its lesser brethren, now caught his eye; for it was towards this particular cottage that the owl was dipping and lurching in its crazy line of flight. The squire spurred Tinker into a gallop and followed on.

Once arrived at the villa the owl proceeded to hurl itself with considerable force against the door. Amazingly the creature turned round at once, fluttered a little in the air, and repeated the maneuver. A third time it struck the door, and a fourth time, before flying off. In answer to this curious summons the door opened, just as the squire was drawing rein.

A tall, spare, sober figure with solemn eyes, a pinched mouth, and yellow hair like yarn hanging from his head, appeared on the threshhold. He glanced round him on the step a time or two, when he did not at first see anyone, before spotting Mark and Tinker. A slightly baffled expression took hold of his prideful countenance, when he realized that neither squire nor quadruped could have been the cause of the raps at the door.

"Larcom!" exclaimed Mark. "Shut your door, double-quick!"

"What is it, then?" inquired the servant-cum-steward of Prospect Cottage, raising his nose.

At that moment his very perpendicular and very respectable employer, Mr. Thomas Dogger, materialized in the doorway behind him.

"Who is it, Larcom?" demanded the humble practitioner, in his lawyer's golden tones. "Is it a client? If so, you may inform him as to the customary hours of attendance at our office and chambers. He's not to expect a professional man and gentleman of the law to be — "

"Larcom! Shut your door!" cried Mark.

Both master and servant appeared in some confusion; at which juncture the owl with its bloodied plumage and shining eyes came wheeling round from an adjacent villa, and drove straight at the open door of Prospect Cottage.

Larcom saw it and uttered a shriek, and was on the verge of obeying Mark's command when he found himself thrust out onto the step, courtesy of a hard shove from his employer. The owl, diverted from its course by this obstacle, and showing perhaps the effects of its injuries, misjudged its trajectory and went crashing against the doorpost. This caused it to whip violently about, its momentum shooting it past the startled attorney and into the cottage, where it came to rest at the feet of Mrs. Dogger, who was reading peaceably in the drawing-room. Whereupon her husband effected a hasty exit, shutting the door behind him and fleeing with his servant in the direction of the Low Street.

The squire leaped from the stirrups and ran into the house, in time to see the little squab figure of Mrs. Dogger retreat in terror through the door opposite. As she was turning to close it, to put a shield of good sturdy oak between herself and the creature, the owl scuttled past her; the door swung shut, a bolt was heard to drop; and so Mark found himself face to face with the shield of oak and no means to pierce it.

He threw his fist against it, calling for Mrs. Dogger to unfasten the latch. His efforts were met by sounds of a most fearful to-do from within the locked chamber, as if some heavy object or other were being flung, repeatedly and violently, against the walls. There were bumps, thumps, crashes, smashes; the brittle shattering of glass, the upsetting of furniture, the thud of collision upon collision; sounds as if some dreadful tempest of nature — or was it supernature? — had taken possession of the room.

Another horse galloped up to the villa, and then another, depositing Mr. Arkwright and Dr. Hall on the scene. The gentlemen quickly joined the squire inside, explaining how they had come across Oliver in the wood and recovered the owl's track. The doctor had wanted to remain with the injured man and attend to his shoulder, but Oliver would have none of it, insisting rather that the physician accompany Mr. Arkwright to the villas to lend assistance.

"What's going on in there?" asked the veterinary, confronting the shield of oak with his bristly caterpillar of a brow. "It sounds like a catastrophe, in my view."

"It is as if the creature were deliberately throwing itself about, flinging itself against the walls and furniture," said Mark.

"To what purpose?" wondered Dr. Hall.

The squire was about to offer a response when the dreadful tempest of nature abruptly quieted itself. It was eerie, the blank empty atmosphere of silence after the rather extraordinary uproar. Mark cupped his ear to the shield of oak, listening, but could detect no sound from within. Again he beat his fist upon the boards, calling out the name of Mrs. Dogger, and again there was no reply.

"Look there!" exclaimed the veterinary, pointing.

Round the four sturdy edges of the door — top, bottom, and sides — a mysterious green radiance was spilling out from the locked chamber. Of only a modest intensity at first, it flared rapidly into a show of color and light so brilliant that the gentlemen were obliged to turn away their eyes. It lasted for no more than a few seconds, perhaps, then went out like the snuffing of a candle.

Shortly after the latch was lifted; the door turned slowly on its hinges, to reveal a gasping and coughing Mrs. Dogger, her drab, unattractive face and drab, unattractive clothes spattered with fine droplets of blood. When she saw the three gentlemen she whimpered a little and fell down in a swoon. She was promptly evacuated to the drawing-room and placed upon the sofa, to be looked after by Dr. Hall.

"Lor!" exclaimed Mrs. Simpkins, the larcenous cook, who had emerged from the kitchen in a panic and was gazing open-mouthed at her stricken mistress.

Smoke was pouring from the adjoining chamber, which was a kind of back sitting-room, for the lamps and wax-lights had been overturned during the *mêlée* and several small fires were burning in the corners. Together the squire and Mr. Arkwright grabbed up what they could in the form of rugs and mats and quantities of water, to smother the flames, which if not extinguished would have threatened Prospect Cottage with a sizable conflagration.

That accomplished, they were faced then with the full spectacle of the devastation — the shards of glass from mirrors and latticed panes, the tumbled furniture, the paintings and draperies hanging crazily or torn from their moorings, the scattered china-bowls, copper plates, and other knick-knacks; not to mention the innumerable spots of blood that were everywhere present, on the floor, on the wainscot, on the ceiling, on the furnishings and books and shattered panes of the casement-windows, and on the ironwork that guarded those windows.

Upon the floor at the hinder end of the room, beside the cobbled stone chimney-piece, was the creature itself, lying motionless on its breast with its head turned a little to one side and its wings extended. The spread of those wings was altogether enormous; from tip to tip it accounted for nearly three-quarters of the breadth of the sitting-room. The Skylingden owl was a very large owl indeed.

Mr. Arkwright approached it with all due caution and respect. As a veterinary surgeon and the bowhunter who had nearly brought it down, he naturally was keen to inspect its bloodied externals, but even keener to know first whether it were alive or dead. After a few moments of careful examination he glanced round to Mark to assure him that the spark of life was quite extinct, that the remarkable creature had indeed expired.

"It was a hard tussle for this night-bird, and ultimately to no purpose," he said, a little regretfully.

The squire looked down at it sprawled on the floor with its head aside and its eye half-open, staring at nothing. No wild phosphoric light showed in that empty orb now, nothing but the awesome frozen stillness of death. Ah, the mystery! Here it was at long last, the creature that had been responsible for his father's disappearance so many years before, and the very last thing his father had seen before being plunged into the pit. Yet, strangely, it gave him no pleasure now to view its mangled corpse, but instead left him chilled to the heart and all the more uneasy.

It is she. It is the poor drowned girl. Gracious God, you must not destroy her.

There arose now a fresh commotion, as through the entrance-door strode Mr. Thomas Dogger, with his military perpendicularity, his servant, and the vicar in tow — the vicar being the very respectable attorney's own confidential friend, or so the lawyer imagined, whom he had gone off to pluck from the parsonage-house. Visibly shocked by all he saw about him, the reverend gentleman turned immediately to Dr. Hall, to ascertain how he might be of service to him and the patient, who had yet to respond to the hartshorn or other restoratives fetched by Mrs. Simpkins from the medicine-chest.

The master of Prospect Cottage squared his shoulders, cleared his voice, and with his eyes shiny and sleek proceeded to an inspection of the State of Things at the Cottage, a place which, until this evening at least, had been quite as nice a house as any gentleman could wish to hang up his hat in.

"See here!" he cried. A livid frown contracted his forehead as he viewed the disorder in his *sanctum sanctorum* of a sitting-room. "See here! Where is the miscreant responsible for this? It's a sad selfish dog who would burn a man's house to frighten his wife. We may be poor as to chattels here but we are not without resource. This is very provoking. It shall cost a pretty sum to effect these repairs. Well, I'm very much deceived if there be not cause here for a suit at the county assizes — "

"For pity's sake, lay aside your suits for a time, Dogger, your wife is all insensible here," said Dr. Hall, with a surprising ring of anger in his voice.

"As you will, Aesculapius," sniffed the attorney, with an unfeeling glance at the doctor, as if to say, "When doors are open, dogs will enter." After a *pro forma* peep or two at the recumbent image of his squab little figure of a wife, he returned to his sitting-room to contemplate the dishevelment of it. A spectator, marking the scene, might have observed that Mr. Dogger did not actually enter the room, but took care to maintain a respectful distance between himself and the monstrous bloody something lying dead beside the chimney-piece.

"Larcom," intoned the lord and master of Prospect Cottage, "I shall look after Mrs. Dogger myself, as soon as she is restored to consciousness through the aid of our learned vicar there. You will look to the sitting-room and see that it is tidied up, and you will be diligent about it. You will put some steam on. You will wash away this blood, and restore the furniture and carpets, and see that the looking-glass and the casements are mended. And you will remove that — that — that whatever it is there."

The yellow head of Larcom bobbed in sign of attention, his eyes as large as saucers with taking in all he saw there. Once the magnitude of the task at hand became clear to him, however, his expression quickly soured, his pinched mouth forming the silent words that he, Mr. Larcom, was nobody's char.

The reverend Mr. Scattergood himself was still a trifle dazed by the recent events. He had taken a quick look in the sitting-room and seen the owl there on the floor, and known at once from its markings it was indeed the same creature that had threatened his wife at the window of her boudoir.

"And so you see, if you had dealt with it effectually here at the vicarage, you should not have been called from home, and Mrs. Dogger should not have been so ill-used," said the pretty Dinah, when her husband returned to her later that evening. "Your faintness of heart has failed you again. How you have survived in this world for so long without a backbone is quite an enigma to me. At times it is more than my job as your wife is worth to endure it."

"Yes, my love," sighed the vicar, drawing on his nightcap.

CHAPTER XVI

AN END — AND A BEGINNING

MRS. Thomas Dogger had at last regained her wits — what there was of them, as her husband was known to remark — and was convalescing in the pristine seclusion of her bedchamber, a few days after the late disturbance. Though she was materially better and had taken some food, she still had nothing to say to Mr. Dogger, having made no response to his inquiries — there had been two of them, both concerning the whereabouts of his green tea, that favored staple of the attorney's diet which she customarily prepared for him, and which he had not tasted since the incident — her refusal having something to do perhaps with the fact that her respectable gentleman of a husband had run out at the door in her moment of peril; had left her in her time of need; had forsaken her, and taken their man Larcom with him.

Perhaps.

After those few days had idled their drowsy way into the past, Mrs. Dogger got up one morning at her usual hour, in an effort it seemed to recover her normal habits, and spent some time privately with Larcom on matters as regards the house and grounds, and some time too in the kitchen, where she finally set about the job of preparing her husband's tea. It was evident to Mrs. Simpkins that the roster of ingredients of this tea had grown a fair bit, beyond the simple combination of herbs, leaves, and spices which till now had served as the basis of the infusion — a roster that included a host of unusual items which her mistress had had Larcom fetch from the chemist's shop of Mr. Binks, and as well certain roots and flowers from the spacious garden of Prospect Cottage, items which Mrs. Simpkins (striving to be discreet, though that is hard to do in a small kitchen) did not recognize as constituents of any variety of tea with which she was familiar. As she worked Mrs. Dogger took pains to assure both her servant-cum-steward and her cook that the added seasoning would improve the quality of the tea enormously. The inspiration for it had come to her in a dream, or so she said. Mrs. Simpkins, being of a naturally larcenous turn of mind, had her doubts as to the veracity of this statement; however, she was in no position to overrule her mistress on this or any other matter, and neither was Larcom.

Later in the afternoon Mrs. Dogger, claiming fatigue, returned to the solitude of her bedchamber, taking with her the fresh tea she had made and her tea-things. It should be noted that she did not herself partake of the concoction, there in her bedchamber, but laid the pot of it aside and settled down to wait, composing herself very comfortably in her four-poster with several pillows at her back, the better to admire the very pleasant view of lake and woodland in her casement-windows.

In no long time — for it *was* tea-time — a low knock was heard at the room-door, and Mr. Dogger, being announced by Larcom, came in.

The attorney approached his wife's bed, and rubbed his hands together, and smoothed the gray curling waves of hair that splashed about his neck and collar, and asked Mrs. Dogger how she was getting on. She had not been disposed to see him during her illness, he said, had not spoken even once to him, or of him, and this he found most disappointing. It was high time, he said, high time that this enforced silence was lifted; for a gentleman in his position, a gentleman of consequence and property, one who was after all lord and master of Prospect Cottage, it was unseemly that the mistress of the house should be avoiding him so. And what was more, he wanted his tea.

He asked her again how she was faring, in that tone of voice he assumed whenever he expected the reply to be delivered up promptly and succinctly. It was the same tone of voice he used for clients who were reluctant to part with needed intelligence, or who offered too much information of a useless character, or who were simply too dull-witted for him to waste valuable time on. He would have an answer, he said, or would know the reason why.

"But do you know *me*, friend?" smiled his drab little wife, watching him from her pillows.

The question was quite unanticipated, and caught him by surprise; too, there was something in Mrs. Dogger's own particular tone of voice that seemed strangely altered. In short, the attorney was as much perplexed by the manner of the question's asking as by the question itself. He knew not what it signified, he knew not the point of it, and this troubled him.

"Of course I know you. You are my wife. You are Mrs. Thomas Dogger. You are the mistress of Prospect Cottage. You are a fortunate woman."

"Never, never, did you want it thus; never, never, though a child there was," returned Mrs. Dogger, in a weird kind of singsong.

Again Mr. Dogger found himself in some confusion. Again he did not understand the point of it.

"We have got no children, and cannot have," said he, ruffling his brow. "But I suppose it is not sufficient for you to be the wife of Thomas Dogger, a respectable member of the legal profession, and to abide in such a nice house as this, and to be thought of so well by all and sundry. It is not enough, I suppose. I wonder at it — ah, but then women, priests and poultry have never enough."

Whereupon his wife in the bed did another strange thing: she threw back her head and burst into an hysteric laugh.

"Fie, Thomas, fie!" she exclaimed. "Though it rain hazel-nuts you will never be aught but what you are. But help for spilled milk there isn't any."

"You're making no sense," declared Mr. Dogger, growing concerned that there was something profoundly amiss with his wife's mental faculties. "You are not in your right head. Your brain is disordered. It is the shock, the injury you received. You do not know what you are saying. Your thoughts are all in a muddle."

"Yes, it is the injury, the great injury and injustice you did me, Thomas, some thirty years since. Even the tamest animal will turn when driven too hard. Do you know me now, friend?" said Mrs. Dogger, smiling again.

A spark of recognition flickered in the attorney's eyes. He stood very straight and threw back his shoulders, and stared down his long sharp nose at his wife. As he did so a vision of another face, that of Mrs. Sepulchra Wintermarch, crossed the retina of his memory; a face, he now realized, whose general outlines he had glimpsed countless times before — in his own looking-glass.

"You know me, then, don't you, friend Thomas?" said Mrs. Dogger, pouring out some tea. "Forgive my negligence in not making this for you sooner, but as you know I have been unwell. Drink up — it will do you a power of good."

She handed the cup and saucer across, the cup loaded with the green elixir he so cherished, and its expanded roster of ingredients. He accepted it mechanically, his eyes round and wide and fastened on her.

"You — you — !" he gaped.

"So you do know me, Thomas? Though I am no longer as you recollect, in outward form and feature."

He drank his tea in several quick nervous draughts, out of distraction, disconcertion, apprehension. Larcom and Mrs. Simpkins, who had been quietly eavesdropping in the passage, out of sight, were peering in now at the door in helpless fascination.

"What are you playing at?" demanded the attorney, something more like his lawyerly self. "Despite your appearance you are certainly not my wife; that is *ipso facto*. Where is she? Where is Mrs. Dogger? What have you done with Mrs. Dogger?"

"Not to worry, Thomas, she is here with me, though there is precious little she can do about it. Fie, Thomas, fie! What care should you have of her? Little enough care you had for me or our child. For these many years have I watched over her, our little girl. I have been with her always; she has never left my guiding protection. I attached myself to her and her so-styled relations in the only way possible, in the only form possible. Having been released now from that form I have acquired another. Is there not some justice in it, Thomas?"

"Justice?"

"You were a bold young solicitor then, new-returned to the village; you are an old solicitor now, a practiced artist in the quips and cranks of the law. You know something of justice, I think, or ought to, though you value it not an atom. What think you of *my* justice, friend?"

As he drank his tea, which he thought had a rather peculiar flavor, Mr. Dogger began to imagine some very peculiar things. He began to imagine that a mysterious green radiance had taken command of his wife's eyes, and was shining forth in two fearsome beams of light; that there were draggled dark locks of hair dripping from her head; that the face of a young woman long forgotten had supplanted the drab familiar countenance of Mrs. Dogger. The sight of it rendered him — a member of the honorable roll of solicitors of the Court of Chancery and attorneys at Common Law — oddly speechless. And what was more, his own body was beginning to feel very peculiar now. He looked with rising alarm at the tea in his cup, realizing he already had drunk the chief of it.

"What knavery is this?" he cried out.

"You used me very badly, Thomas," said Mrs. Dogger. "The years can provide no escape for you. Mr. Campleman may have had his failings but he was ever a gentleman, a most honorable young man. Never would he have used me thus, as you did, for so shallow a purpose. Never would he have offered me his false sympathies, as you did, and most certainly he would never have discarded me — nor made such hypocritical insinuations, to safeguard his own reputation, that he must fight a combat over it! Twice now you have discarded me, Thomas. What should be the price of that? But you will learn soon enough. It was while he was absorbed in his studies that Mr. Campleman showed me the way, when he showed me the well."

Mr. Dogger swallowed very hard and looked again into his cup. The odd, cloying flavor of the tea had gotten in his throat and he couldn't get rid of it; he could feel it spreading like a contagion into his skull.

"And so here we are, married at last — and a nice little dumpling of a wife I am, ain't I, Thomas?" exclaimed Mrs. Dogger, all smiles and self-possession. She took up the hand-mirror from her bedside table and examined herself in it, her fingers gently exploring the unfamiliar features she saw there. "She has not at all a taking style of beauty, has she? But she must do. Oh, whatever happened to my buttermilk cheeks? My pretty chin? My precious blue eyes? Food for fishes long ago, in black Lonewater, I do suppose."

"You devil — you have poisoned me!" groaned the attorney, making as if he had just taken a pill of extraordinary circumference.

"Brazen it out, Thomas — it is far better than you deserve. It is also not at all what you think. Gracious, we are looking very pale today."

"You were always a bad lot — wholly bad — " was the attorney's final utterance. His eyelids fluttered; his tea-cup fell from his hand with a crash; his body sank into the chair beside his wife's bed in a not-so-very-respectable heap.

Larcom and the cook had witnessed it all from the passage. The high, dry brow of the servant-cum-steward was damp with drops of fear. He was aghast; but shortly, realizing that his troubles would be significantly reduced by the departure of his bitter lord and master, a ray of comfort darted across his prideful visage.

"None will be spared, Thomas," said Mrs. Dogger, with a wag of her finger towards her crumpled pile of a husband. "There is justice in *that*, I think. Off you go, then."

"Lor!" cried Mrs. Simpkins. "Look there, Mr. Larcom, sir!"

How speedily circumstances may change! The smile was struck from Larcom's mouth, as he watched the body of Mr. Thomas Dogger rise soundlessly from the chair. There it stood, perfectly still, very straight as to back and square as to shoulders, with its arms hanging at its sides and its eyes pointed forward in an empty stare, as though awaiting some instruction. Consequently Mrs. Dogger informed the body that it was to remove itself to the drawing-room, and remain there for the time present.

"Off you go, Thomas," said she, with an impatient whisk of her hand.

And so — horror of horrors! — off the body went, marching stiffly through the door, all unmindful of a disbelieving Larcom and a terrified Mrs. Simpkins, whom it passed on the way, and betook itself to its destination, something awkward as to gait, but otherwise very submissive and *piano* about circumstances generally.

"Lor!" whispered the cook, clutching at her apron-strings. "God-a-mercy, Mr. Larcom, sir, God-a-mercy!"

"The pretty part of it is, he is not dead, but perfectly aware; conscious of all that surrounds him but incapable of commanding himself. I'm sure it must be quite distressing for him," smiled Mrs. Dogger. "Passed you no sheep that way, you sheepish maids?" (This in a louder key, making it plainer still she was cognizant of the two spies on the threshhold.)

Seeing they had been discovered, both steward and cook stepped gingerly forward, prepared to accept whatever fate might await them.

"Madness comes only to those who resist, who choose to contemplate the spectacle of the infinite through the lens of a mortal mind. Do they not understand it is immortality that is on offer? Deathlessness, imperishability, freedom from corruption. And what is required in return? So very little. But of course, my thoughts tended in the same direction when it was first presented to me; I, too, resisted. His obstinacy landed Mr. Campleman in the madhouse, for as a scholar he could never fully relinquish himself — he wanted to study it all, to master it. Over the years, however, I have grown to appreciate the beauty and the rightness of it. Worshipful servitude! It is better than they deserve. It is not so very much to ask, don't you think, Larcom, for the gift of time without end?"

Larcom nodded his yellow head in solemn agreement, though he had not the vaguest notion what his mistress was rattling on about. His single thought was that she herself must have gone completely mad, as a result of her fright; that her brain was diseased, as his lord and master had suspected; that she was quite daft; to which effect he traded glances with Mrs. Simpkins.

Then again, there was the awful thing waiting in the drawing-room.

Mrs. Dogger proceeded to inform her cook and steward that others would be arriving at Prospect Cottage, later that day and the next, at selected intervals, to receive their cups of tea; for she already had sent the notices of invitation ("At the particular request of Mrs. Thomas Dogger, to celebrate her recovery from her late illness.") First would be young Mr. Arkwright, of course, he of the bow and birdbolt; then Dr. William Hall, who had spared the life of that accursed Ralph Trench, the chief cause of her troubles; then Mr. Ives of the Arms, for shunning her as had so many others in the village, and of course that insolent daughter of his — "She presumes to know me, Larcom, better than I know myself!" — and the vicar Scattergood, poor trusting dupe, so enamored of his childish notions of faith, and his spiteful little wife — "Though she is pretty enough to be sure, and I should have liked her lineaments better in my glass; but her husband intervened, and so he will have cause to regret it." And there were more — the two women from Gray Lodge, both relations of the house of Trench; and that man Hoey, the disagreeable giant with the cavernous voice and the hungry hounds; and not least that odious scion of the house of Trench himself, there at Dalroyd, and his lap-dog of a friend from the city; and others, too, over the next few days, who would find themselves called to Prospect Cottage, and not one of whom would be spared.

"And Larcom," Mrs. Dogger went on, with a significant inclination of her head, "know too that there will be further reprisals. Tomorrow we shall prepare a good deal more of my green tea — a gracious good deal more — and your services will be engaged in the distributing of it. You will take it and pour it into the public wells, and into as many of the private wells as can be managed, until the entirety of the drinking-water in the village has been fortified with its contents. Once the inhabitants of Shilston Upcot have had their dose of physic, they will find themselves drawn inexplicably to the grounds of the mansion-house, and the ancient foundations of the abbey, where there is work to be done and something for all to see.

"When that has been achieved, we ourselves shall be moving house. We shall be departing Prospect Cottage for Skylingden, there to join my daughter, over whom I have maintained a mother's careful vigil all this long time. Though that Mr. Edgar to whom she is yoked has proved something of a disappointment, albeit a useful one, particularly after he found himself in arrears from the gaming-tables, and so was obliged to look out for a new name and a new abode. Debts and quarrels lay heavy on him; the poor gentleman was very much dipped, and had little choice but to flee his creditors. That is how my daughter and her household found their way to Talbotshire, with what remained of her small inheritance. Should Mr. George Edgar choose not to abide with us there in our new *ménage* at Skylingden, he will receive his cup of tea and give us no further trouble. Mark me, Larcom," cautioned Mrs. Dogger, sitting up very tall in her bed, not at all like her old squab little self, "see that you tread the path of compliance, for if you stray from it you yourself will join the others at the well."

Larcom nodded; and though he did not know yet what well it was she meant, he knew somehow it was not a place he should care to visit.

"And what of me, ma'am?" asked the cook, peering with goggle eyes at this new and frightening mistress of hers.

"You will accompany us, of course, Simpkins."

"Yes, ma'am," said Mrs. Simpkins, not at all sure whether to be thankful or not.

"And then we shall have quince-cakes and marmalade. Oh, it has been so very long since I have tasted quince-cakes and marmalade! And we shall have madeleines, too, and larchberry pudding, and blancmange, and warden pies, and panadas, and syllabubs, and brandy-snaps, and other suchlike delights. You will lay them on for us, Simpkins, once we are settled at Skylingden."

"Yes, ma'am."

"And then we shall go a-blackberrying," Mrs. Dogger went on, with evident pleasure. "And we shall make jams and cider, and oat-bread, and black rabbit pie, and drink morning draughts of sweet milk-and-water, and steaming tumblers of flip in the evenings. But mark me, we shall partake of no fowls, hot or cold! We shall play at ombre, and quadrille, and old piquet, and have *Sellenger's Round* on the pianoforte. We shall make of Skylingden what we will, and take the air round the valley, but we shall take no boats out upon Lonewater."

"Skylingden!" murmured Larcom, his breast swelling with pride (a commodity of which he had so much, he was forever having to discharge a quantity of it to ease the pressure.) Wheels within wheels were whirling round inside his yellow head. His solemn eyes moved to the casement-windows, and to the mansion-house and its own great round window of an eye, which was looking down on them all from the high wood — no longer an ogre's eye, thought he, but a warm and welcoming one. They had scorned him, these townsfolk of Shilston Upcot, and called him a coxcomb; made light of him and his long bony shanks, and his knee-breeches, and his cocked-hat with the feather in it. Oh, the thousand and one slights and impertinences he had been made to endure! Now the world had gone all downside-up, and it was he who would shortly be reigning steward of Skylingden.

"I myself will have charge of the household," said Mrs. Dogger, with such a stern glance of warning as made Larcom wonder if she could not read his very thoughts. "Let that be clear and manifest. The two of you will serve me, and my daughter, and her bankrupt of a husband, Mr. Edgar, and little Rowena. See that neither of you puts on airs." She took up the hand-mirror again for a further view of herself in the glass. "It is so very delightful to be restored to human form, if not the pleasantest one. But let there be an end to self-congratulation for now. We have much on our plate."

Had he been standing a few paces nearer the casement-windows, and looked out, the prideful Larcom might have spied a person crouching there among the shrubberies; a person who had heard the whole of this quite remarkable conversation in the bedchamber of Mrs. Dogger; a short, thick person of sixty odd in a suit of rusty black sable, with an old scratch-wig on his head. But as Larcom was not in a position to observe this person, he did not observe him, and so did not cry out and bring him to the attention of his mighty mistress; as a result of which this person, trembling with fear and panic, was able to steal silently away.

POST SCRIPTUM

MY fellow-traveler broke off his narrative here and looked about him in some distress, with that pale, gloomy, anxious expression of his; for it appeared he was about to enter upon the most ghastly and deplorable aspect of his story. All unthinking I offered him some water from a pitcher on the side-table, but he declined it and instead called out for the landlord of the establishment.

"Yes, sir, Mr. Langley, sir?" responded Mine Host — a sturdy, broad-aproned, bluff-visaged, quintessentially innkeeperish sort of practical, mutton-fisted, pinchbeck-shoe-buckled kind of mountain publican — as he looked in at the door of our private room there at the Waterman, in the pretty town of Jay.

Despite the advanced hour, my companion called for something rather stronger than water in a pitcher.

"I was awakened, late one morning, by a plaintive whine in the corridor outside my bedchamber," he went on, once his pipe had been recharged and his drink brought to him, and he had partaken of the liquor sufficiently to nerve himself. "Lying there abed, I discovered that a most unnatural hush had fallen over the house. Ordinarily there should have been plenty of noise and stir all about me, plenty of to-ing and fro-ing in the passageways, and on the staircases, and in the apartments above and below, as the servants went about their duties; but on that morning there was none of it, only the mournful yowling outside my room-door. I recognized the voice at once as that of Jolly-boy, and it confirmed my suspicion that something must be very much amiss, for he never once in my experience had acted so before."

Again my companion hesitated. He took a long pull at his drink, to steel himself the more, and several whiffs at his pipe, and brushed a hand through his unruly curls shot through with gray, before continuing.

"Sir, I shall never forget the scenes of that terrible day, under a louring sky, as the brief summer of the mountains neared its end; they are forever etched upon my memory. My host had gone off the evening before to Prospect Cottage, in response to an invitation from Mrs. Thomas Dogger. I too had received a card, but as I was still myself mending from the fall off my horse, I chose to remain at Dalroyd, and asked Mark to deliver an apology in my absence. My shoulder still pained me; as it turned out nothing had been broken, but the muscles were bruised and the joint itself grievous sore — the bone having been briefly wedged from its socket, and most competently put right by Dr. Hall. A taut bandage and a sling had then been applied. The doctor had as well given me an embrocation for general stiffness, but it did little aside from impart an unpleasant aroma to the air. The squire before leaving for Prospect Cottage had delivered some first-rate brandy to my room, as he thought it would cheer me. It was just the thing, and did much more good than any embrocation, in consequence of which the water in the ewer at my bedside went all untouched that night. Little did I realize that by this action he had saved my life; and what was more, that it was the last time I should ever gaze upon the face of Mark Trench.

"Dressing as hastily as I might, in consideration of my immobile arm and shoulder, I went out into the passage to see what was the matter. In the course of my investigation I found that the entire house, from cellars to russet-colored roof, from terrace-walk to spacious back lawn, had to all effects been abandoned. It appeared that the servants had broken off in the thick of their labors, for signs of interrupted activity were everywhere present. I looked in the library, in the drawing-room, in the billiard-room, in the squire's bedchamber, his private study, in the kitchens, the servants' hall. I looked in the snuggery of Mr. Smithers and found plenty of Scott but no Smithers there, though he had been very recently. Everywhere I went little Jolly-boy followed behind, sniffing and whimpering. He was searching for his master, but his master like everyone else was nowhere in evidence.

"I left him in the house and betook myself to the stables, where I found Tinker gone; most disturbingly, it appeared from the condition of his stall that he had never returned from Prospect Cottage, and so neither had Mark. As the Dalroyd groom too had gone missing, I was obliged to saddle the chestnut myself — no easy task in light of my condition — and hurried out of the drive to see what could possibly have happened, my initial curiosity having given way rapidly to concern, then to alarm, with each revelation.

"While still on the high ground I happened to glance across at the far-spreading vista, from the Village Arms to the spire of St. Lucy and the roof-tops of the village proper, towards the inlet and Skylingden. It was then I saw them — here and there, from every quarter round the village, from every lane and avenue, from every clump of woodland, numbers of tiny figures were making for and ascending the Skylingden road. Some of the figures were on horseback, but most were marching along on foot. I gave the spurs to the chestnut and soon came upon a group of them trudging along the road. A few I recognized as regulars from the Arms; others I had seen about the village and the Low Street, their genial faces familiar to me but their names unknown. All semblance of geniality had been struck from those faces now, and replaced by a blank and staring expression, by eyes with no more life in them than if they had been painted on their heads; their arms hung loosely at their sides, as though drained of all energy; their footsteps were clumsy, plodding, mechanical. Like a troop of clockwork figures they were, marching relentlessly on despite all obstacles, as if in obedience to some irresistible command. There was, as I would shortly find, no stopping them.

"As I gained the top of the Low Street I spied others of their kind approaching from the lower village, making for the crossroads and Skylingden. Among them I recognized Mr. Tudway, the chandler, and Mr. Lash, the master of the village school, and Mr. Lincote, the sugar-baker, and members of their families. There was no talking with them, no dissuading them. They acted as if they were wholly unaware of my presence; if I drew bridle in the road they simply marched around me. Behind them came others in groups of four or five, some being conveyed in open tumbrel-carts like criminals to the hangman, or French traitors to the guillotine. In one such vehicle I spotted Miss Violet Crimp of the waffle-house — Miss Crimp, who had secretly dreamed of being freed from the dull confines of her life, and who it appeared would soon obtain her wish — she, and her aged mother, and Molly, her mother's maidservant and nurse, the three of them staring vacantly at the world through frozen eyes of glass. Like the others they did not respond to my urgent pleas. I saw women there, and men there, and young children in their company — good gracious God, innocent young children, sir! — their gazes similarly fixed and their ears unheeding. Glancing up I saw that a coach-and-four had climbed into the Skylingden road, with passengers inside and out — a vehicle I identified from its distinctive coloration as a Malbury coach — and both driver and guard bolt upright at their posts, looking straight before them as they rattled on towards the mansion-house. The coach must have halted overnight at the Arms, and with the coming of daylight had resumed its journey, but with a very different destination in view.

"I rode to Prospect Cottage only to find it locked up tight, seemingly empty of life. No one responded to my repeated knocks at the door. As there was no sign of either the squire or Tinker, I spurred the chestnut into the Skylingden road and raced towards the summit. To my surprise I discovered that the sad parade of humanity was making not for the mansion-house, as I had supposed, but for the abbey ruins beyond it. There — calmly, serenely, with an almost lamb-like docility — they were disappearing, one by one, into the earth. I understood then that the staircase leading to the cave had been unblocked, at both the crypt entrance and below, and that the marchers were going to the well.

"It was there too that I came upon Tinker. He was cropping grass beside the abbey ruins, untethered, and still wearing his saddle. Seeing him shivered me to the quick; I cannot describe how my heart sank within me when I realized that his master may indeed have suffered the same fate as the rest. I called out for Mark but there was no answer, of course; nothing but the clockwork figures vanishing down the staircase, souls ripe for capture by the devils in the pit. Dismounting, I plunged through the entrance and down the stone steps into the darkness. The atmosphere within was stifling in the extreme; more than once I was of a mind to turn back, as much from my own faintheartedness as from the close, oppressive conditions; but there were marchers before me and marchers behind me, so I had little choice but to bottle up my fear and cork it down.

"When I arrived at the cave-chamber, I found its interior lit by a number of tallow candles arranged in sconces. The capstone of the well had been removed and a cord-ladder unfurled from the brim. A glowing green vapor like illuminated steam was rising from the shaft. Those before me — the men, the women, the children, with their empty stares — were climbing methodically over the side and descending into the pit. The utter quiet with which the operation proceeded, the perfect indifference exhibited by the villagers as they went to their doom, were awful to behold.

"'Stop! Stop there, all of you! Good God, you must not allow yourselves to be cozened so!' I cried out, but to no purpose. Even as I thrust one person aside, to dissuade him from his course, another took his place; and so the first would resume his path to the well while my attention was trained on the other. They offered no physical resistance whatever to my efforts, and yet those efforts were wholly in vain.

"I had no means to lift the capstone into place — even were my shoulder sound I could not have managed it alone — and so instead I took aim at the cord-ladder with my knife. But the ropes were stout and heavy and my soft blade made little impression on them. I found I could no longer endure the atmosphere in the cave or what was happening there; my head began to spin, my limbs trembled, my body wavered on my feet. The next I knew I was on my knees on the rocky shelf, gulping whole mouthfuls of cool, clean air, for once oblivious of the vertiginous gulf of iron sky and black Lonewater before me.

"I made my way slowly along the trail to the summit. There I climbed upon the mare and galloped through the open gates of Skylingden, past the vacant keeper's lodge and down the avenue of trees, and drew rein square in front of the mansion-house. The odious round eye high up in the great porch, in the flat of the gable-wall, was pouring its sinister gaze upon every living creature, near and wide. No longer merely an elegantly fashioned wheel window, it was, to my mind, an evil thing indeed — so far had my view of it changed in the days since the squire and I had ridden to our interview in the drawing-room. The dismal, weather-beaten frontage of old Talbotshire stone, the dingy oak timbers, the great top-hamper of decoration, the lichen-stained roof, the saw-edge gables, the brooding nests of chimney-stacks, added to the climate of menace. I called aloud for Mark, praying he had not succumbed to the horrid fate of the others; searched all round the outbuildings, back and behind, round the coach-house, the stable-yard, the vinery, without success. Returning to the grounds fronting the house, I mounted the steps and knocked loudly at the entrance-door in the great porch — once, twice, three times — but no one came. Abandoning the effort I was about to spring into the stirrups when I detected movement in one of the windows on the floor above. There was a brief ruffling of the curtains, and the figures of Mrs. Sepulchra Wintermarch and her young daughter, and behind them the handsome and hawkish Mr. Bede Wintermarch, appeared at the glass. Their attention was absorbed in the somber spectacle beyond the perimeter wall, where the townsfolk were proceeding so tamely to their doom. The faces at the window were looking out upon the scene not in triumph, however, as one might have supposed, but with something more akin to fear and wonder. In that single moment I understood that the Wintermarches were themselves little better than prisoners in the mansion-house. I waved an arm — that one linked to my good shoulder — to gain their notice, and called out again the name of my friend; to which Mrs. Wintermarch responded with a slow, sad, hopeless shake of her head.

"There was only one thing to be done. I hastened back to the abbey ruins, drew my cutlass from its sheath, and mustering what remained of my courage ventured once more into the dark suffocating atmosphere of the staircase. On reaching the cave I immediately attacked the stout fabric of the cord-ladder with the greater cutting-power of my steel. With grim satisfaction I watched as the severed ropes disappeared down the steaming throat of the well. More than a little wearied by my exertions I stepped back a pace or two, and found myself abruptly face to face with a pretty young woman whom I recognized as one Miss Betty Breakwindow, a maidservant from the Village Arms. To my complete astonishment she was not the least troubled by the absence of the cord-ladder, but mounted to the brim of the well, placed her hands calmly atop her head, and stepping forward dropped from sight into the pit.

"It was then I knew that all indeed was lost. I fled the awful place and returned to the summit, where I collected Tinker and led him behind the chestnut down the Skylingden road. Casting about what to do next, or where to turn, I went to the vicarage in search of Mr. Scattergood, but as I feared he was gone, as were his wife and their servants. As I was riding past the churchyard, along the bridle-path that led to the coach-road, I heard for the first time that day a human voice other than my own, coming from the sexton's hut. A coarse, gravelly voice it was, and it was singing; or rather it was trying to sing, for there was little or no melody, and the words were indecipherable from constantly jostling one another, as though the singer had been partaking very liberally of his cups. I suspected the minstrel was Mr. Bottom, and upon entering found the gentleman himself slumped in his chair before a dead fire, his eyes glazed and his senses half-awake. His entire person — in point of fact the entire hut — smelled overwhelmingly of grog. It took some time to recover him sufficiently, and to cajole him sufficiently, that he might tell me what he knew of the calamity that had befallen the village. At length, after many Mr. Bottom-like divagations and evasions, and much glancing back and before him to ascertain that no lurking eye discerned him, he related the conversation he had overheard at Prospect Cottage; and so the vast true scope of the horror was laid before me.

"I was nearly as much shocked by his story, as by the knowledge that here was the man who could have warned his fellow villagers of their coming ruin, and yet had not. Here was the man who could have averted a great tragedy, and yet had not. Here was the very man who could have stopped my friend Mark Trench from going down the well, and yet he had not. What he had done was drink himself into a great stinking stupor, after learning of the plot, and kept on drinking, and so never gotten round to warning anyone. Even Mr. Bottom, it seemed, was not immune to the effects of his grog when drunk in such quantity.

"'Have I understood you aright?' I cried — for I could scarcely believe it — 'Have you kept this knowledge entirely to yourself, these past days, and failed to alert a single person? Failed to alert even the vicar, your friend who has been so very kind to you? Good gracious God — such indifference — such disregard for your fellows — it's monstrous!'"

"He broke into a stream of angry mutterings. 'Damn and blast,' he growled, by way of justification, 'there's been bad work in the high wood, I tell thee true, and I don't care to know nowt more about it — and neither should thee!' Whereupon he got himself another bottle of grog and settled back in his chair, loading his pipe and meditating on the empty grate with a doom-laden countenance.

"To reproach him for his grave inaction was pointless; recriminations would not restore those who had been lost. Instead I left him there, to be haunted by his own thoughts. I wondered what would become of him, what he would do with himself, how he would survive. In time he would run short of his grog and need to find an alternative; but there were a host of empty cottages now for him to scrounge in, not to mention the Village Arms. The lake water was unpalatable, from the many dissolved impurities in it, but there were the streams trickling down from the snowy tops of the Talbots; moreover, the autumn rains would soon be arriving. He would manage, if the creature in the mansion-house permitted it. As I stepped to the door I very nearly relented and invited him to take a coach with me — for there was, I knew, a Crow's-end coach due from Malbury in a few days — but in the end decided against it, leaving him instead to shift for himself.

"Dalroyd remained as I had left it, desolate and joyless. The next several nights I spent alone there, hoping for Mark's return — alone save for the company of little Jolly-boy — were among the longest and dreariest of my life. Wakeful nights they were, too, filled with those loud, mysterious cracking noises that oft are heard at night in old houses. Many a time I went off to investigate, thinking that perhaps someone had returned, that Mark had come back at last; but there was never anyone there. Hour after hour I heard the clock strike at the stair-head, while revolving myself endlessly round under the bedclothes like a skewered fowl, from trying to sleep. The days were drearier still. I went nowhere; I ate nothing but brown loaves and larchberries, and a few sweetmeats, and drank only cider and brandy. I inspected for the hundredth time the faded gilded backs of the books in the library; I stood upon the balcony smoking cigars and contemplating the view, as the squire and I so often had done. On the last night I sat for hours composing a heartfelt letter to my friend, which I left upon the desk in his private study, in the event he might some day return to Dalroyd. Whose eyes might next run over its contents, in truth I had no notion; but I prayed they would be Mark's.

"The long night wore itself away and delivered up the morning at last. There was nothing more to do but to effect my escape while I might. The coach for Crow's-end would be passing through that day, and I could not know when some action might be leveled against me by the inmates of Skylingden. As I could take neither Tinker nor the chestnut with me, I turned them both out on the back lawn, in the company of the other horses, and there said my good-byes. To bold and faithful Tinker I whispered, that if by some miracle his master might be restored to the world, it was only right he should be there at Dalroyd to greet him. I believe the good old fellow understood me, for he answered with a whinny and a gentle bob of his head. Tears threatened to flood my eyes; hurriedly I returned to the house, gathered up the single portmanteau into which I had compressed my needful belongings, and with Jolly-boy at my heels departed with a heavy tread. My final good-bye was reserved for old Dalroyd herself — for her graceful gables and soaring roof, her very pleasant shrubberies, her shady eaves, her stretch of garden with its rosy sea of flowers, her welcoming windows like so many smiling eyes, which were the only eyes left in her now to watch me go.

"I saw no tiny figures in the Skylingden road that morning; all must have by now completed the awful journey. Likewise there was no one at the Arms when Jolly-boy and I reached it. The gates were standing open, as was the house-door. As I passed into the entrance-hall, I felt at once the absence of Mr. Snorem and his hearty, booming welcome; no maidservants, waiters, or pot-boys bustled about the place; there was no long Jinkins at the beer-engine behind the great oak bar; no travelers lounged about the lodge-room, no one at the piano, no one at billiards; chief of all there was no Mr. Ives to greet me, and no Miss Cherry to see that matters were in apple-pie order. There was nothing but a vast silence, and doors on the jar, and an occasional breath of wind, and the menagerie of trophy-heads staring from the walls of the lodge-room — and gloating a little, perhaps, now that their own measure of revenge had been exacted. It struck me then, how very much the look in the eyes of the trophy-heads resembled that of the villagers upon their pilgrimage to eternity.

"I met the coach for Crow's-end round noon, and at once endeavored to warn the driver and the guard of the catastrophe that had occurred. They little understood me, thinking perhaps that I was touched in the upper story — I could hardly blame them — for it was their first stop in Shilston Upcot since a week; but once they had tramped about the inn and beheld the extent of the disaster, and found no Ives, and not a living leg in sight in all of Town End and the Low Street, their opinion of me changed remarkably. Their eyes grew wide indeed, once their brains had accepted my argument, and they became suddenly very keen to leave, as did the passengers. The coachman announced they would change horses instead farther on, and mounted to the box. I entrusted my portmanteau to the guard, and took up a disengaged seat with little Jolly-boy in hand. Then away we went, rolling out of the yard and into the road towards Grim Forest and Cedar Crag, and the high mountain passes through the Talbot Peaks, and so on to Crow's-end and the eventual conclusion of our journey."

Here my companion stopped, to catch his mental breath as it were, as if from exhaustion at having relived the events of his tale. He looked askance through the lattice windows at the remnants of moonlight that were stirring in the dark waters of the lake.

"Then Mr. George Edgar — or Mr. Bede Wintermarch, as he called himself in Talbotshire — was in effect little more than an insolvent debtor, a bankrupt," said I, to fill in the pause. "And so your friend the squire was ultimately correct in his surmise."

Mr. Langley nodded absently, taking another swallow of his drink that was stronger than water.

"It was simply his own bad fortune to have married the daughter of Edith Marchant," I went on, half to myself. "The same bad fortune that had plagued him at the gaming-tables. He little realized the nature of the family he had married into. But, surely — Mr. Ralph Trench had shown nothing but kindness to the Marchants. He was a close friend of the vicar's, and Miss Marchant's own godfather."

"I fear it was of no consequence. It was he who had the child taken from her, to shield her parents and her from disgrace. It was vengeance wholesale, without a scrap of mercy and without regard for niceties. It is always so when revenge becomes sweeter than life."

It was long past time to retire for the night. The landlord had been dropping hints on us for the past half-hour, with subtle glances and clearings of his voice, for he had finished shutting up the house and was pining for the comfort of his bed.

"I should have perished but for Mark Trench," said Mr. Langley, with gloom and regret haunting his tired eyes. "He drove off the owl, and later gave me the brandy that kept me from the well-water at my bedside, saving me from a fate he could not save his own self from. All the hurts I have suffered in my life, before or since, are no more than the bites of fleas by comparison. I'd have eaten my coat, sir, if there were something I could have done to preserve him. He was my single true friend. Ah, but at least the poor fellow is with his father now. Whatever can it be like, do you suppose, an eternity of worshipful servitude? To know that it never can, that it never will come to an end? The horror of it — can you imagine the horror of it, sir?"

"And little Jolly-boy?" I inquired, attempting to turn the conversation from this most unpleasant subject. "What became of him?"

"He lived with me for several years after in Bucket's Court. But I don't believe he ever truly accepted me, though of course I cared for him as well as I could; it seemed to me he always was expecting his master to appear directly and rescue him. He often would spend hours sitting at the hall-door, listening for a familiar step that never came. He never grew used to city bustle, I don't think. He died some three years ago now, and lies buried at the foot of the ash tree in my back-garden.

"The Shilston Upcot of my fondest recollection is a golden place, a place of snowy peaks and lofty castles of forest, of stone-built cottages and russet-colored roof-tiles, all bathed in the blue summer sky of the mountains. You see now what it has become, and why it has so troubled me to pass this way again. You see now what a merciless evil roams the corridors of the mansion-house — roams them still! For you yourself today saw the rising smoke in one of the chimneys." He fastened on me his dark, melancholy gaze, which once had been so wide and luminous. "And so I was called to Wycombe, and was obliged to make a journey I have dreaded these eleven years — for there is no other way to Wycombe, sir, than by the coach-road."

"What of the ownership of Skylingden?" I asked him. "Tell me, was it ever settled?"

"As I understand it, the house remained the property of Mr. Charles Campleman until his death in the Dudderies, only some year or two after the events I have described. Since then it has been adrift on an interminable sea of Chancery suits, with claims and counter-claims put forth by dim and questionable relations; with briefs and counter-briefs, and huge volumes of affidavits and other nonsense; with endless motions and referrals, and swearings and interrogatings, the whole of it engineered of course by the learned gentlemen of the law, whose costs it is said have accrued now to the amount of several tens of thousands of pounds. On more than one occasion agents of the Court were sent into Talbotshire, to Shilston Upcot, to extract the Wintermarches — or the Edgars, or the Marchants, or however you choose to call them — for failing to deliver the rent payments; but the men who were dispatched never were seen again, and after a time the Court stopped sending them. And so the Chancery business continues to grind on, with no judgment in sight. Ah, but that is how the learned gentlemen of the law prefer it, is it not?" he smiled, with a faint shred of a laugh.

It had by now grown very late; the landlord looked in on us again, with drowsy eyes, and so we relented at last.

As we went to our rooms an owl hooted in a tree outside. The pale, disquieted look returned at once to my companion's face, adding imaginary weight to his years. I had come to understand that the Oliver Langley of eleven years past and the Oliver Langley of that night were two very different men, as a result of one brief summer sojourn in the mountains. No more did I wonder at his deep troubling of the spirit; rather, I wondered how I myself might have responded had I stood in his shoes eleven years before. The disturbing conjectures of the squire of Dalroyd preyed upon my mind all that night, as they have on many a night since.

Suppose there is no just and powerful Almighty? Suppose there are only devils?

We departed the valley of Lonewater directly after breakfast, consigning its secrets and its secret prisoners to the wake of our flying coach-wheels. As the Talbot Peaks were lost to view behind us, the dismal shadows of the previous night seemed to lift, and it was with a feeling of relief that we bent our course to the east and the newborn sun. My thoughts turned inevitably to my own little Chancery business, that of my uncle's estate, and I wondered what I should find at Hoole; I trusted it would be nothing half so monstrous as Mr. Oliver Langley had run upon in Shilston Upcot.

My fellow-traveler was set down at the Checkers, the principal inn of the post-town of Wycombe, while I continued on into Ayleshire. Before we separated I asked him, seeing how his mood had been improved a little by the bright morning and the miles we had placed between ourselves and the Talbots, if he had ever published his translation of the *epigrammata* of the ancient Roman Spaniard.

"No, sir, I never managed it," he replied, growing suddenly introspective and gloomy again, so much so that I immediately regretted having broached the subject. "I wrote nothing further beyond that which I had composed at Dalroyd. The manuscript of it lies amid the gathered dust and cobwebs in my chamber there; I left it behind when I set off for Crow's-end. For you know, it had lost all importance to me."

And so we parted. The last I saw of him as the coach pulled away, he was standing with bowed head at the door of the inn, immersed in a world of reflection of a type I could myself scarcely imagine, nor cared to.